Fire Horse

Book Two of Circ de Tarot Series

Kimberley D. Tait

This is a work of fiction. Character names and descriptions are the product of the author's imagination. Any resemblance to actual persons, living or dead, is entirely coincidental.

For more information, contact kimberleydtait@gmail.com

Cover by MiblArt

Website; https://kimberleydtait.com/

ISBN 978-1-7380904-5-7

Contents

Acknowledgements

As anyone who writes knows, creating a world out of nothing can be a lonely endeavor. We authors sit at the computer, watching the world go by as we hack out a story from a block of granite, hoping others will love it as much as we do. That said, I have been blessed with many supportive friends and family, and I would like to express my deepest appreciation for each and every one.

First, I must thank my twin sister, Patricia. She asked me to write her a circus story—so I did! If it hadn't been for her, this series would have never gotten onto the page. She is my best and worst critic, and she keeps me from making a fool out of myself. For that I am eternally grateful.

I want to thank my dear friend and fellow writer, L. M. Spilsbury, for asking me the tough questions and holding my hand through the process. I would also like to thank my U.S. editor, Mat Machin, for always being honest with me, and my Canadian editor, Jill Durkin, of Bright Owl Edits, for her kindness and support. Moreover, I want to thank my mother, Jean, for her love and compassion, Barbara Tait, for her love and undying support, and Lisa Tarot, for answering my questions about all things tarot.

Thank you also to the Scottsdale Historical Society, for helping me research railway lines of the 1930s Southwest. If I've made any mistakes with accuracy, the fault is completely my own.

Lastly, I would like to thank Leon Agapi, my Romanian grandfather, for all the inappropriate fairytales he brought with him when he sailed to into Montreal in 1926, on the White Star Line, and for bestowing his gift for storytelling, his *magie*, to me.

Introduction

Fire Horse is *Book Two of Circ de Tarot* series. For the best reading experience, you should read ***Vandemere***, *Book One of Circ de Tarot* first. Even though *Circ de Tarot* series is complete as a duology, I am planning to release a third book in the series in the fall of 2024.

This is a work of fiction. Wherever possible, I have tried to use real places, but I have taken certain liberties with events, institutions, and circus activities. Even though I have researched train schedules and bus routes of the 1930s, it's difficult to know exact times and dates. My knowledge of trains of that era could literally fit on the head of a pin. When I first wrote ***Fire Horse***, I had Vandy arriving in Scottsdale by train. After researching railway lines of Arizona, and conferring with experts, I found out that no trains ever went to Scottsdale. They did, however, stop in Tempe, which is very close by. Subsequent changes were made to the story, as I have strived to be as historically accurate as humanly possible. Many thanks to the Scottsdale Historical Society for setting the record straight.

This book is a gritty depiction of life in the American Southwest during the 1930s. It contains, but is not limited to, graphic violence, coarse language, sexual assault, self-harm, and sexual situations. Some of the book's darker themes may be offensive to sensitive readers. Please use discretion when deciding if this book is for you.

Prologue

I was on my back. Lying somewhere in darkness. A nameless fear filled my mouth with ashes, and I couldn't breathe. Couldn't make my lungs work. I pulled air in through half-parted lips and wheezed past the tightness in my throat. The muscles along my spine contorted into painful spasms as beads of sweat soaked into my hair.

The harsh echoes of my panting bounced off dim walls. I searched the gloom for something familiar I could ground my consciousness to. Something that would chase away the ghosts of my past.

Instinctively, my hand went to my left leg, hidden under the blankets. Dread built itself into certainty, and I prepared myself for the horror of what I might find.

My leg was still there. It was still attached to me. Sure, it was lumpy and scarred. Broken, yes ... but *still there*. I felt the feverish burn of healing tissue through the pad of linen bindings and almost wept. I wasn't stuck down the rabbit hole. Wasn't strapped to an operating table either. No one was holding me down. No one was slicing through my thigh with a bone saw. I was safe in my bed, in California. I was just having a bad dream. A nightmare.

The horror of what I'd seen slowly dissipated.

I never did go back to sleep. Memory had me trapped between sleep and awareness, binding me to that place where the mind deceives and the imagination flirts with insanity.

I sagged against the pillows, letting my eyes adjust to the dark.

Furniture emerged from the shadows. Shapes of things I recognized appeared against the white walls. I focused on the outlines of my own belongings; the chair in the corner, the old oak desk, the tapestries on the wall, and slowly regained a sense of *place*.

Outside my bedroom door, the hall clock chimed the hour. I counted out the tinkling notes as my heartbeat eased back to normal again.

Three o'clock.

I rolled over and fumbled for the blankets, pulling them back over my chilled shoulder. It was far too easy to burrow into that comforting darkness. Too easy to surrender to the silence that pressed against my ears. Easy to give into fear and stay put. I had a job to do. I'd made a promise to a dying woman, and pulling the covers over my head, hoping the world would leave me alone would only prolong the inevitable. Arizona called to me. Like it or not, I would have to go.

I, Vandemere Alexander Petruska, had been commanded to follow the *magie* into the hell my forefathers had bestowed upon me, and I alone would have to answer for their crimes.

Chapter One

My leg wasn't healing any faster than my heart was after losing my mother. October was on its way out and November was coming in fast. If I was going to respect Ma's wishes and take her ashes to Arizona before the weather turned against me, I was going to have to move my ass along.

Lieutenant Clarence Dawson, decorated member of the Oklahoma City Police Department, father to Ellen Lyla Dawson and persistent thorn in my side, sent another telegram a week later, informing Jimmy he was coming to Fresno to get his book back and that he wanted to talk to me.

News of this spurred my anxiety through the roof.

I approached Jimmy Custer, my boss, the next morning, knowing he'd be distracted by a truckload of new hay that had just arrived. The day was cool enough to cloud my breath in front of my face, and the tips of my fingers were already frost-nipped and tingling.

The sun shone down from a bright blue sky, illuminating the trappings of the circus life I'd been born into. Jimmy's property might have been utilitarian, but it was definitely not unkempt. There were storage barns for trucks, and carousel pieces, and some of the midway rides even had their own covered building. Everything had been packed away for the off-season in an organized system only Jimmy could understand, but one only had to ask where something was and he could tell you without even consulting the books. There were pens for the animals, lots of tall fences to keep the big cats from escaping into Fresno and causing a ruckus, and a multitude of outbuildings were cast like dice around the main house.

And horses.

I'd gotten so used to the smell of animal dung; I didn't even notice it anymore. My nose had numbed itself to the stink of camels and lions and Jimmy's Russian bear long ago; it was actually the smell of fresh hay that caught me by surprise that day.

A chilly wind blew in from the mountains, sending a smattering of fallen leaves across my path. I was glad I'd put on my coat. It was a nice day for working in. Not so nice for a laid-up invalid like me.

My trusty pair of crutches were the only means I had of getting around. I hobbled my way over to where my boss was standing next to the flatbed trailer parked in the yard, calling, "Hey, Jimmy? I need to talk to you about something."

He was still wary of my grief. Unsure of what to say. I'm sure he felt one wrong word would open barely healed wounds. I noticed he couldn't quite look me in the eye.

He dropped what was left of his cigarette and ground it out with his foot. "Sure thing, Van. What can I do for you?"

I watched the hay being hoisted up through the loft door. A rope and pulley system hauled the sheaves up through the narrow door above the stables and a few of the guying-out crew took turns pulling them through. It was hand-over-hand as they stacked the hay in the loft.

Jake Topher sneered at me from the door under the gables.

I shot a look right back at him. With Ma gone, I didn't have to put up with his meanness anymore, but it didn't stop him from hating the very sight of me.

Jimmy was still waiting.

I cleared my throat and spoke my mind. "I want to take Dolly with me to Arizona."

To give him credit, my boss took it better than I thought he would. He pushed his flat cap further back on his head and regarded me with those tired blue eyes of his. "How are you going to get a blind mare all the way to Scottsdale, smashed up the way you are?"

I already had an answer for him. "I've decided to take the train. I'll pay to have Dolly loaded onto one of the boxcars they use for shipping cattle overland. She'll have her own stall, and I'll be with her the whole time. It won't be much different than loading her up in the circus trailer."

Jimmy fixed his gaze at something over my left shoulder. "I don't think that's such a good idea, Vandy. What if something happens? What if she spooks and runs away? She won't know where she is. How will you catch her with no one around to help you?"

I bent my head. Every time I thought I was done with grief; it would come out of nowhere and stab its claws into my chest. "Dolly only has a few more months to live. You said so yourself. I can't spend any more time away from her. If I go to Arizona, there's no telling how long it'll be until I can make it back home. She needs me."

"Why don't you take the winter off?" Jimmy suggested. "Your mother never said you had to take her ashes to Arizona right this second. You should be resting. You need to give yourself time to heal. I mean, look at you. You can hardly walk. I don't think this is a wise decision."

No, it probably wasn't.

"If I put this off any longer, I'll lose my nerve." I swallowed around the rock in my throat. "Ma ... she'll know. I don't want to disappoint her again."

Jimmy's own sorrow showed up in his tone. "Your mother was never disappointed in you, Vandy. Wherever she is right now, I'm sure she's very proud of you."

My vision blurred. "I never realized she was that sick."

Jimmy stared at his feet. "Yeah, I know. It's hard."

I rubbed a knuckle under my nose and blinked furiously.

Jimmy pretended not to notice.

I leaned on my crutches, watching the hay going up into the loft until the pain of my mother's passing eased back into something more tolerable.

"How are you going to pay for this crazy scheme anyway?" Jimmy asked, once he was sure I'd gotten my emotions back under control. "It'll be expensive to ship Dolly by train."

"Ma left me a few dollars," I said. "It's not much. My hospital bills pretty much bled her dry, but there's a bit of money left over."

I hadn't known about Ma's rainy-day savings. I don't think Jake did either or he would have raided that too.

Theresa, our farm cook, was the one who had presented me with the small, metal container marked *Ceylon Black Tea*. It was the same day my mother's ashes had been returned to me. I'd been sitting at the breakfast table, digging the heels of my scabby hands into my eyes to stop myself from weeping.

I counted out forty dollars and some change. My mother's nest-egg. After my stint in the hospital had robbed her of everything she'd worked so hard to bank away, there was still just enough left in the tin to get both Dolly and me all the way to Arizona, hand Ma's ashes over to my father, and take the train back home.

"I still don't think it's a very good idea," Jimmy insisted.

I was already tired of haggling with him. "I've made up my mind. There's a train leaving Tulare at the end of the week. It'll take me as far as Tempe. I can walk the rest of the way to Scottsdale. If all goes well, I should be back here by the end of December. Then Dolly can live out the rest of her days in the place she knows best ..." My voice cracked. Sadness got the better of me, and I had to stop again.

Jimmy busied himself by digging his toe through the dirt.

I propped myself up on sheer stubbornness. I wouldn't embarrass myself by breaking down in front of all these men. Especially Jake. After biting my lip hard enough to leave a mark, I was able to continue. "There's something else I need to ask you."

"What is it?"

"I want you to tell me about Vandemere."

"Vandemere, the *horse?*"

I resisted the urge to roll my eyes. "Yes, Vandemere, the *horse*. Sal told me once that you knew the story of how Vandemere died. Seems everyone knows about it except me."

Jimmy fumbled in his breast pocket for his battered pack of cigarettes. He tapped another one out and paused a moment to get it lit. I didn't sense anything nefarious in the way he distanced himself from the question, but he *was* taking a long time to reply. He blew smoke into the crisp fall air. "As far as I know, Vandemere died in a fire."

"I already know *that*."

"Shit, Vandy ... what more can I tell you? Bonnie was the one to ask about this, not me. All I know is there was a fire at some circus long before you were born, and the horse was killed."

I scanned his care-worn expression for hints of deception. For some reason, Lieutenant Dawson came to mind. He'd be the one to get to the bottom of this. Not that I'd ever ask him. That'd be the day.

"I tried talking to Ma about Vandemere but she just kept changing the subject. I mean, what's the big deal? Why all the secrecy? The only reason people lie about a tragedy is because they must have had something to do with it."

"Well, if I knew what it was, I would tell you, and that's the God's-honest truth."

Jimmy smoked his cigarette in silence while I pondered the wreckage of what my life had become. The energy between us was still within the boundaries of agreeable and I figured it was safe to push him a little further.

"One more thing. I'm going to try riding Dolly today."

His reaction was predictable. "Vandy ... no."

I held up one hand. "I'll just walk. And I won't go far. I need to sit on Dolly's back. See how my leg holds up."

He shook his head. "I won't allow it. She's not safe to ride. What if she has another dizzy spell? She could fall on you and then where would you be?"

Probably in a lot worse shape than I was in now.

"She'll be okay," I said. "I'll know when she's had enough."

He looked at me like I was a stranger. "Why are you being like this?"

"Like what?"

"Like your father."

I didn't know whether to be insulted or flattered.

"Jimmy," I said, "I know you're only trying to look out for me, but with Ma gone, I'm on my own now. I need to start making decisions for myself."

He hissed out a thin stream of smoke. "When are you going to realize this isn't a one-man operation?"

I stared at the sheaves of hay going up into the loft, bracing for a lecture.

"We're *family*, Petruska. You need to get that through that thick head of yours." He gestured to the small crowd of men gathered in the doorway of the barn. "These are your people. The people you can rely on. These are the men who've got your back."

"Except Jake," I pointed out.

"Yes, well ..."

"Why'd you even hire him?"

"I did your mother a favor."

"Get rid of him."

"I can't do that. Only if he gives me a reason to."

I spat out a laugh. "He likes to beat people up. Isn't that reason enough?"

Apparently, Jimmy's patience was limitless. "He's an extra pair of hands, and he hasn't caused any more trouble since the day you arrived. Just stay away from him and you'll be fine."

Jake must have heard us talking about him. He stood back from the door in the hayloft while the other men did most of the work and pinned me in his sights.

I glared back.

If I had to be honest, I was scared of Jake Topher. He was mean, and he was slap-happy with his fists. Worse, he'd been instrumental in my mother's addictions. He had never raised a hand to Bonnie Petruska, but he had no problem knocking her son around when she wasn't looking.

The well of my hatred for him ran deep.

I'm ashamed to say it, but I was the one who looked away first. "I appreciate everything you've done for me, Jimmy, but I'm taking Dolly with me to Arizona. It's no use trying to talk me out of it. And hey, maybe the desert will be good for the both of us? I hear the weather's nice this time of year. Maybe I can finally talk Del into that road trip to the Grand Canyon he was always promising me."

The very thought filled me with dread.

Jimmy dragged hard on his cigarette and flicked the butt away. "Nothing good will come of this. You mark my words."

"Dolly will take care of me," I assured him. "I'll be her eyes and she'll be my legs. We'll make a fine team. You'll see."

Despite my determination, there would be no riding for me that day.

Dolly, ever the patient soul, stood quietly as I made various attempts to mount up. I tried standing on overturned buckets. Tried standing on a stack of wooden boxes. Hell, I even had Dodger put his hand on my ass and shove me aboard. Nothing worked. I could only get as far as lying across Dolly's knobby spine while Dodger grabbed fistfuls of my trousers and pushed.

Healing bones and disused joints screeched at me. My face contorted under this new creation of pain, and I had to slide back down to earth again.

"Give it time," Dodger said, with forced cheerfulness. "You'll be back in the spotlight before you know it."

I wasn't so sure anymore.

Chapter Two

I boarded the train in Tulare. Nearly everything I owned was packed into the cloth satchel I borrowed from Jimmy. He'd gifted me the black coat I'd worn at Ma's funeral, plus a pair of loose-fitting trousers that hid my splinted leg from prying eyes. I had one clean shirt, the hand-me-downs given to me by the nurse, back in Oklahoma, and I had shoes too, but I could only wear the right one.

No amount of cursing would see me through the effort of ramming my swollen left foot into the other shoe.

I tied it to the strap of the cloth bag slung over my shoulder and wore a heavy sock instead.

I carried my mother's ashes in a Mason jar. She fit nicely into the satchel, along with her tarot cards and a few stones of turquoise I'd saved after Jake raided most of it.

I made sure no one saw me put Dawson's book, *Liber Mortuorum,* into the satchel as well.

There was no doubt in my mind that the lieutenant would be gunning for me. Some small part of me still held out hope that I had retained a fraction of the circus brat I'd been before my accident had all but destroyed me, but now I had a lawman *and* a monster clawing at my heels, and I wasn't prepared to deal with either one.

As I led Dolly up the ramp and into the boxcar, I threw out a silent prayer that it would be Clarence who got me first and not the monster.

There was hay and feed stacked in the corner of the boxcar for Dolly, and enough water to see her through the next few days. We would have to share the boxcar with a small herd of cattle. I thought they might object when they realized we were going to be neighbors, but they were surprisingly well-behaved and would eventually take to the *clackety clack* of the steel wheels on the tracks like it was a bovine lullaby.

This particular train wasn't set up for horses. I'd paid extra to have a stall added for Dolly and the rail company had obliged. Her pen was constructed out of wooden slats, and a gate that sat crooked on one hinge like a bad tooth. Not exactly The Ritz, but she had a deep bed of straw, some cows for company, and I wouldn't leave her side during the entire trip.

Jimmy studied the accommodations and held nothing back. "Is this a joke?" He gave the side of the makeshift pen a shake and the whole thing threatened to fall apart.

Jimmy's reservations cranked up the pressure on my already stretched reserves. I stood at Dolly's head while she settled in and gritted my way through a smile. "It's only for a few days."

I didn't need the Petruska *magie* to know what he was thinking. Probably the same thing I was. That my mother had put this on me without understanding the full cost of what this was doing to my health.

Jimmy surprised me by stepping forward and pulling me into his arms. He was wearing a peacoat over his usual jeans and flannel shirt, and his embrace was warm as wool. He smelled like hay and camels.

He wasn't used to doing this. Hugging folks. His arms were stiff around me, and I sensed the gesture was more for him than it was for me. Like he'd wanted to do this for a long time and just hadn't worked up the nerve.

I balanced on my good leg and raised one arm up so I could hug him back. "Take care of yourself, Jimmy."

He handed me a paper bag. "Something for the road. Cook packed you some bread-and-butter sandwiches and a few apples. Should be enough to tide you over. Does Del even know you're coming?"

I added the paper bag to the already overloaded satchel and closed the flap. "It's best if he doesn't. Otherwise, he might skip town." I managed to keep the bitterness clear of my expression and tried on a small laugh instead.

"Make sure you send me a wire when you get there," Jimmy insisted.

"Sure thing, Boss."

He hesitated long enough to skim a quiet gaze over my downcast eyes. "Why do I feel like this is the last time I'll see you alive?"

I didn't trust myself to speak.

He gave me a sad smile and a backward wave as he trudged down the ramp.

A couple of railway hands hauled up the wooden ramp and locked us in. The train whistle blew shrill. The engine roared to life. The steel wheels sparked and whined as the boxcar jolted along the tracks.

The cows milling about on the other side of the partition stomped and shit almost in unison.

Dolly rolled her eyes when she heard all the nervous bawling going on next door and tossed her head against the lead line I'd clipped to her halter. A train ride was a new experience for her, but deep down, she was a steady old girl. Once I calmed her down with some easy words and a scratch along her crest, my old gray mare settled in fine. She buried her nose in her hay and left the worrying all to me.

That train ride would haunt me for the rest of my days.

After a couple hours of standing on one leg, my back started complaining. Cramped muscles had me holding my breath and shifting around for a more comfortable position. A few hours more and I had to lean against the slats of Dolly's pen to keep myself upright.

By the time the sun dipped between galleons of cloud and twilight came on, everything hurt. I pressed my knuckles into my teeth as a throbbing pain drilled into my left thigh. I knew from experience that it was only going to get worse.

A distraction was what I needed. I wrenched my mind off the dull agony that never left me alone and thought about Ellen Dawson instead. I thought about her freckled nose and her honey-blonde hair. Her blue eyes danced across my mind, tempting me to forget all about my vow of self-imposed celibacy. My arms ached to hold her again. I pictured her mouth clamped over my own. How her breaths would tangle with mine.

Sadness got in the way of any shred of happiness I might have scraped off the shit-stained floor of my life. Loss and grief; we were old friends now. I sighed on a different kind of pain than the one grinding away in my thigh but there was no one around to hear it.

Ellen probably hated me by now. I made a promise to myself I would go to my grave trying to protect her from the villainy of a hellhound from the Underworld. If I had to break her heart to do this, at least I knew it was for all the right reasons.

I missed having her around. I don't know why. She was as crass as any yard hand. Every other word that came out of her mouth was a lie, and she *lived* to taunt me.

I attributed this sudden longing to grief over my mother's death and Dolly's declining health. Both had left me vulnerable to Ellen's memory. I saw things in our relationship that weren't there. And why would a girl like Ellen fall for a banged-up circus brat like me anyway? I was on the road so much, it's not like I could offer her anything in the way of a settled lifestyle. I had nothing of value to call my own except a few trinkets in a satchel and an old gray mare who was on her last legs. Anyway, she was Clarence Dawson's adopted daughter and that made her off-limits to someone like me. She wasn't related to me the way Clarence was, but it was enough to put the brakes on our budding relationship.

It didn't stop me from imagining a domestic setting where the two of us could be happy, but it was just a made-up version of something I was aching for and just couldn't admit it. I harbored a wistful yearning for a girl—*any* girl—who would accept me for who I was. Who would love me despite all my failings. I wanted to prove that I was worthy of a woman's desire, if only someone would give me the chance.

I didn't understand women at all. I had spent the better part of the past three years pining for Sylvia Rheinhart, a girl who had never once shown me a crumb of affection, only to come to my senses, too late to prevent the right one from hanging herself.

Poor Grace. She deserved better.

I blamed myself for all of it.

I leaned my head back against the rough planking of Dolly's stall and made the mistake of closing my eyes.

My mind conjured up the hunger I'd felt in Ellen's kiss.

A weary smile broke across my face. She couldn't have known the reason I'd spurned her affections and that was how it was going to stay. I would have done anything to protect her from incurring the same fate as Grace. If she despised me for pushing her away, it was for the best. I had a murderous entity dogging my every step, and I'd seen what it could do to the people I loved. I would have sacrificed everything I had left in me to keep Ellen Dawson safe from harm.

Regret looked a lot like shame in the failing light.

Ellen didn't seem the type of girl who would pay me back for breaking her heart by hanging herself in a broom closet like Grace had, but I worried just the same. I couldn't in good conscience put another person in that kind of peril, so it was for her sake that I resigned myself to a life of dreary celibacy. I would likely remain a virgin until the day I died.

The day I died?

I mulled this over while the floor of the boxcar rocked under my feet.

Something was becoming clear to me. Even though the Petruska bloodline had bestowed this gift of *magie* to me, it was selective with the information it revealed. I could see a lot of things, but I couldn't see death. Not in its physical form. Not while it was happening. I think if I could predict where and when death would strike, I might have lost my mind by now.

It was probably a blessing that I never saw my own death looming on the horizon. Ignorance cast me like dice into a future so perilous I would have to look upon my own survival as something of a choice; to accept death as a final solution. Or choose life and suffer the consequences.

Unfortunately, I would have to face that peril a lot sooner than I expected.

Chapter Three

The train rumbled into some nameless station in the middle of the night and shuddered to a noisy halt. We'd already chugged through the mountains a few days ago, and I'd damn near froze to death climbing into some of the higher elevations. Fortunately, the weather remained agreeable, and there was enough body heat coming off the cows to stave off frostbite.

I woke up to find myself half-buried in straw. I was on the floor of the boxcar, and Dolly was a gray shape standing over me. Confusion had me scrambling for a familiar landmark to align my mental compass to. I didn't know where *here* was, only that it was miles away from anywhere safe.

Dolly reached over to ruffle my hair with her whiskery nose. She didn't know where she was either and I was a reassuring presence in her world of shadows.

I got my arms underneath me and sat myself up, groaning. The boxcar stank of cow shit and urine, and the sour air reeked from their belching.

The conductor wandered down the tracks, holding a lantern aloft.

"How is everything in there?" He swung his railway lamp around and shone it through the cracks in the planking, half-blinding me. "You still alive?"

"Yeah, I'm fine." I rubbed my aching thigh. "How soon before we get to Tempe?"

He seemed rather chipper for a man who'd been on a train all day. "It'll be a while yet. Do you need anything?"

Drugs came to mind.

"No."

"I've got a bit of beef stew here." He pushed a battered tin cup between the slats. "I saved you some."

I shielded my eyes against the glare of the lantern. I realized, with a sinking feeling, that if I wanted the stew, I was going to have to stand up to get it. This presented me with a challenge. I'd removed the splint from my leg so I could rest better on the floor of Dolly's stall and I already knew I couldn't stand on my own.

You could always crawl, my mind reasoned.

Bugger that.

"Hang on." I put a hand on Dolly's knee so she would know I was about to move. "I'm coming."

"Why are you even in there?" the conductor asked. "Why don't you sit up front with us?" He checked his pocket watch while I levered my way up the side of Dolly's pen and finally gained my feet.

"I can't." I stared bleakly at the cup the man held through the gap in the boxcar and grabbed my crutches. "My mare's blind. I need to stay with her."

"Blind, you say? She can't see at all?"

"She can see some. Shadows, mostly." I panted this out. All this work for a cup of beef stew? I forced stiff muscles into service and made my way over to the side of the boxcar.

"Thanks." I wrapped cold hands around the mug. I was really hoping the stew would be worth all the effort it took to get it.

It was.

I devoured the stew and considered asking for seconds. "Where are we anyway?"

"We're a few miles outside of Yuma." The conductor took his cup back and lowered the lamp so now he was just a voice in the darkness. "Got a few head of cattle to off-load. If we make good time, we should be in Tempe by dawn."

I expected him to walk away; to go about his conductor business of running the train on schedule and checking for stowaways. This was 1939 after all, and the easiest way for a man to get himself to a better life was to steal a ride on a passing train.

He raised the lamp until he had me in his sights again. "Isn't that kind of dangerous, keeping a blind mare alive like that?"

Something about the way he said this made my stomach lurch. "What do you mean?"

His voice hardened into coldness that seemed terrifyingly familiar. *"I mean, what if she runs off? What if she runs into things? What if something spooks her? What would you do, Vandemere Petruska?"*

My mind froze. The floor beneath my feet seemed to sink away.

"How ..."

"Do I know your name? Oh, Vandemere ... I know everything about you."

The light from the lantern pierced my eyes. I shielded my eyes with a flattened hand. I *tried* to speak, but nothing came out.

The entity mocked my soundless terror. *"You're trapped in here, you know. You and your horse. Shall I burn it down? I could, you know. I have the fuel, and I have the flame. I could set the boxcar on fire, and you would die, right along with your horse."*

An image filled my head.

I see ...

A horse on fire.

It walks slowly through the flames. Fire on its back. A flickering orange is caught in its eyes.

Everything is burning ...

I smell the acrid stench of smoldering hair.

I pressed the heels of my hands against my eyes and choked back a cry.

Dolly was suddenly behind me. I felt her shoulder tense against my hip. She rounded her milky eyes into that shattering light and sniffed the air. She pinned her ears flat to her neck, putting herself in between me and the evil *thing* speaking through the conductor. I was too stunned to understand what she was doing, how she was sacrificing her own safety to protect me. Had I known, I would have stopped her. I would have *died* for her, not the other way around. Instead, I stood paralyzed while Dolly curled her neck around me.

She snapped her teeth at the shadow behind the lamp, snorting violently.

It was enough to send the demon running for cover.

The night became ordinary again. Crickets resumed their chirping in the long grass. The train engine puffed and steamed, breathing quietly like a sleeping dragon.

I came back to the sound of my own ragged panting.

The conductor aimed the lamp at my face. "You're *sure* you're okay in there?" His voice sounded perfectly normal this time.

"I—I ..."

I tried to answer. God knows, I tried ...

"*Won't be long now*," were the conductor's parting words. He swung the lamp as he walked down the length of the track, calling out, "*See you soon, Petruska.*"

***

I pounded on the wooden ramp. I screamed at the top of my lungs, hoping someone would hear me and let me out.

The wind ripped my voice away.

Sleepy towns flashed past. I caught a glimpse of them through the gaps in the sides of the boxcar, too far away for anyone to hear my desperate calls.

It was pointless to call for a rescue. No one would have heard me over the shriek of wind and wheels. I yelled simply to release the soul-shattering panic overtaking my mind.

The cattle, hearing the fear in my voice, bawled out in terror.

Dolly stood stiff-legged in the deep straw and shook.

I gripped the slatted side of the boxcar and felt the old familiar pressure leaning on my chest. I knew in my head that the boxcar wasn't shrinking but it didn't stop hysteria from sucking the wind out of me. I was down the rabbit hole all over again, and now there was a good chance this *thing* stalking me would make good on its word at the next stop, toss a lighted match into the tinder-dry railcar, and fry us all.

I tried yanking one of the wooden planks off the ramp locking us in, but I just ended up hurting my hands on the rough edges.

Eventually, I wore myself out. The futility of trying to break out of here left me aching in every joint, and I couldn't stop shivering. My shirt was soaked through to the lining of the coat Jimmy lent me and my voice was raw from all that shouting.

I wrapped my arms around Dolly's neck and nestled in closer to her. I pressed myself into her warm shoulder. Repeated over and over. "The walls are not caving in. The walls are not going to crush you. It's all in your head ..."

The floor of the railcar shifted under my feet. The steel wheels whined into a clacking roar, competing with the sound of the cattle hollering on the other side of the partition. Whatever had abducted the conductor and taken control of his body had scared them too, and it took forever for them to settle down again.

Dolly blew soft breath against my hip and lipped at my pantleg.

Let her protect you, Vandy ...

I woke up with a start, looking around wildly. "Ma?"

I was sitting on the floor of the boxcar. I must have fallen asleep. My back was against the wooden rails of Dolly's pen and my chin was buried in my chest.

I tucked cold hands into my opposite sleeves and shivered. Muttered, "Jesus Christ ... I'm losing my mind."

Dolly stood over me, quiet as a ghost, her right hip cricked as she rested a toe.

Annie Lee stared back at me.

I wasn't surprised to see her. She'd been following me around for a while now, ever since I'd left the hospital back in Oklahoma.

At first, she'd been a pale outline hovering around me. A wisp lost in twilight. Silent and watchful. But she'd figured out how to make herself more visible to me. It was only a matter of time before she tried to get my attention.

"Hey, little mouse." I breathed this out, hoping I wouldn't scare her away this time. She appeared to me in a child-like shape of transparent mist, dressed in a flour sack dress. Her cotton candy curls floated around her head, and there was nothing but grace in the way she gazed at me. "How long have you been standing there?"

Her voice was hardly a whisper inside my mind.

You use the magic?

"The *magie*?" I corrected. "I will ... for you, darlin'."

She smiled, and it damn near broke my heart.

Everyone sad, she said.

I sighed. "Yes, everyone is very sad. They miss you."

He didn't mean to do it.

I tried to understand. Despite everything I'd been warned *not* to do, I used the *magie* to tap into her energy. I exhaled on a long, deep breath and sent out psychic threads, knitting them into her own memories.

"Who killed you, Annie?"

I not killed.

My mother had told me once; it was hard for them to grasp the meaning of death when everything on the other side was so *alive*.

I tried a different approach.

"Who took you away from the circus?"

The music place?

"Yes, the music place. Can you give me a name?"

I show you instead ...

The train hit a bend in the track and tossed us all against the side of the boxcar. The cows cried out their distress, and Dolly scrambled to regain her footing.

I was wide awake now.

I raised my head, wincing as a new pain went shooting through my skull.

I looked around for Annie, but she wasn't there anymore.

It was still dark out. Frosty tendrils of mist seeped through the slats of the boxcar, but I could make out shapes in a scrubby landscape whipping by.

Everything smelled of damp earth and wet cow.

Had I been dreaming?

I held my hands up to the light coming off a cluster of industrial buildings squatting in the distance. Sure enough, there were a couple of fresh scratches in my palms. One of my fingernails stung. I noticed it was bent and torn. A gleam of blood filled in the half-moon of the nailbed, and I sucked it away.

Nope. Not a dream. I was trapped inside a boxcar, hurtling through the desert with a possessed conductor at the helm. Probably consorting with an insane engineer as well.

If that wasn't bad enough, I'd brought Dolly into this nightmare with me, an innocent soul now at the mercy of a fiend from the Underworld.

All my fault.

Here in the darkness, with only a few cows as my witnesses, I allowed a few tears to slip down my face. It was over quickly. Habit made me stifle the waterworks as soon as they'd bubbled to the surface. I cleared the burn out of my throat with a few sniffs and sighs.

"Sorry, Dolly." I mumbled this out when her hazy eyes searched for me in the gloom. I scrubbed my face with a damp sleeve. "Crying is for babies. Right?"

She didn't judge me. She lowered her head and nuzzled my hands when I cupped them around her mouth.

"Everything's going to be okay," I assured her, as if saying it would somehow make it so. "I don't know how to fight this thing yet, but Ma must have had something up her sleeve when she sent me out here." I stroked Dolly's eyes the way she always liked it. I ran my palms down her broad cheeks, and she sighed in contentment. "I just hope we don't all burn in hell because of it."

Dolly went back to eating her hay.

I hauled the satchel over and got things organized in my lap.

My mother's ashes were still safely tucked inside. Her Mason jar fit nicely into bag, next the extra clothes I'd brought with me, as well as a few rolls of clean linen bandages for my leg and a small bottle of tincture of iodine. A few tumbled turquoise stones from the Sleeping Beauty mine we'd visited as a family all those years ago rattled around in the bottom of the bag; memories of better times.

I had one butter sandwich left, and an apple.

I hesitated to eat them. If I *hadn't* dreamed up that horrific scene back there at the last stop, it meant I'd already chowed down on the conductor's beef stew. My imagination conjured up worst-case scenarios of poisoning, or overdoses of laudanum. Every little twinge in my gut churned up thoughts of an agonizing death, and my heart raced uneasily.

Dolly smelled the apple right away.

I didn't mind sharing it with her.

She repaid me by slobbering all over my pants.

I wiped my hands on the front of my coat and turned back to the satchel resting in my lap. I dug out *Liber Mortuorum* from the satchel and cracked open the pages.

Something fell into my lap.

I picked it up and squinted at it.

It was a tarot card. *Strength*: the same card my mother had pressed into my hand the day she left me in the hospital.

It had been hidden in between the pages of Dawson's book all this time.

I had no idea how *Strength* had gotten there. The last time I'd seen this particular card was when I'd stuffed it into my jacket pocket, right before I ran away from the hospital in Oklahoma.

It had been with me on the bus.

Margaret.

She must have slipped the card into the book while I'd been sleeping beside her on the Greyhound bus, bound for California.

She'd used the tarot card to mark a page near the middle of the book. The idea that a kindly, middle-aged woman had gone rifling through my pockets while I was unconscious put a damper on my already shaky trust issues, but at least she hadn't robbed me!

"Margaret, you old *babushka,*" I murmured wryly. "What are you trying to tell me?"

I scanned the page in Clarence's book she'd marked for me, looking for a clue as to why she would have done this.

One image stood out; a demon, painted in red and black. Terrifyingly familiar.

A man disguised in the shape of a wolf snarled at me from the page of this ancient text. Black eyes burned into mine. His bloodied lips gaped over a mouthful of teeth—teeth that looked like porcupine quills. He stood on thick, muscled legs, and his massive hands ended in claws that could have been knives instead of talons. He was covered in matted fur, and his shoulders were the size of Clyde's, Jimmy's Strong Man.

When I stared into those bestial eyes, it all came tumbling back; the savage attack on me in Dolly's stall the day I first met Annie. My mind conjured up the memory of the creature's hot breath scorching my face, the quilled mouth ripping into my stomach and yanking my intestines out through the meaty wounds. The putrid stench of his breath lingered in the back of my throat, and terror tied my guts into knots.

The author had given him a Romanian name.

Cel Care Ia.

Translated to English, it meant; The One Who Takes.

The wolf-thing had a golden-haired child clasped to his breast. Even I could see the poor kid was petrified.

I scanned unfamiliar scripture, looking for something I could decipher; a Romanian word here or there that would tug at some recall buried deep in my brain. Ma would know how to read it. But me?

From the few words I could pick out of the heavy script, I realized the creature was an Elemental. A faerie, designed to scare little kids into behaving themselves lest they get carried off into the woods, never to be seen again. To my knowledge, Elementals were mostly harmless, relying on trickery and deceit to get what they wanted. I'd never heard of one actually *killing* anyone before. Not even one as horrifying as the one who glared back at me from the pages of this ancient text.

Until now.

It didn't make sense. Why would an Elemental be so attached to the Petruska family? And when had it become so aggressive? What had I done to warrant this kind of attack?

I closed the book on my enemy and stared into the darkness. Thoughts scattered like dead leaves through my consciousness. My mind kept trying to light on something tangible, but all I ended up with was a confusing snarl of questions and the promise of another wicked headache coming on.

I pressed the heel of my hand against my forehead and wondered if I wasn't slowly going insane.

I put the book aside and dug through the satchel until I found my mother's tarot deck. This was my only connection to her magic now, and I'd brought the cards with me to keep her *magie* close. They were a comfort to me. An old friend. I felt Ma's energy infused in the hand-painted images, and all the other Petruskas who had read them before her.

I'd kept the integrity of her *magie* protected by wrapping the cards in one of her silk scarves.

I shuffled the cards in the dark.

Anything to keep the terror at bay.

I held my mother's ashes in my lap and chose random cards from the deck.

Fuck you, *Cel Care Ia* ... or whatever the hell your name is.

I don't know whatever possessed me to taunt this thing ...

I used the *magie* to read the images. I recited the tarot, building my connection to the Petruska legacy. I held a card against my breast. Said aloud, "*Ten of Cups*. A happy house. A declaration of love. Family bonds."

Of course, this card *would* show up. These were the things I yearned for. Things I wanted but kept secret from the world. Treasures I didn't deserve. Little turquoise stones that everyone else got to keep, but always seemed out of reach for a prickly cactus like me.

I turned the card over, but I already knew it was the right one.

I chose another card and hid it against my coat. "*Eight of Swords*."

Figures I would draw this card next. The image showed a woman bound and blindfolded, caged by the eight swords stuck in the ground. That was me in a nutshell. Tied up in my own wretched life, unable to move forward or back. The blindfold told me I was missing something. Something important. Something vital to my survival.

Tell me something I *don't* know, was the thought that stalked through my head.

I pulled *The Magician* next. My shaking hands drew strength from its message and my nerves steadied.

Okay. Finally, a good card.

I recited to the air. "As above, so below."

My voice became nothing more than a feeble whisper in the darkness. "*The Magician* controls the four elements of life: Fire, Water, Earth, and Air. He has all the tools he needs to manifest his desires. He brings unlimited potential to the table before him, and the alchemy he wields is power in its purest form. He is a call to action. He will lead you into battle with an iron truth in your sword."

Fancy words for a broken soul.

The Petruska *magie* had bestowed upon me the ability to act as a conduit between the earthly realm and spiritual planes, and so expected me to shoulder the responsibility of trust without ever questioning its motives. Whatever came out of my mouth was driven by the Divine, and if people didn't like what I saw in the cards, *I'd* be the one they would blame. Shoot the messenger, and all that. It wasn't fair, but what could I do? Was I to bear witness to this Godly will without hesitation? Didn't I have any say in the matter?

On and on, I went through the cards, passing the time. Finding solace in the shadows of my ancestors.

The last card I pulled was *The Tower*. The illustration showed a tall, medieval structure sitting atop a mountain with ancient runes scrolled all around the base of it. A lightning bolt zig-zagged out of the sky, carrying enough power to carve a path right down the middle of the pillar, sending stones flying in every direction. A man and woman had thrown themselves off the parapet, trying to escape the flames licking up the sides of the tower, and I didn't need the *magie* to tell me the end of *that* story.

I never liked this card. Too much destruction in the image. *The Tower* card signified a lot of change, and probably some pain thrown in for good measure. If I was to measure it against my own life, I would have to say I was in for some serious shit. Pulling *The Tower* card could only mean one thing; that pieces of me would have to come apart before I could be made whole again. To me, that sounded a hell of a lot like going to war.

As a new dawn broke over the desert in a wash of fiery crimson, I hugged my mother's ashes to my chest and talked myself out of bolting for home.

We were approaching our destination at last.

In my hand, I clutched a piece of turquoise that had belonged to my mother before she gave it to me. Like her magic—and her love. Things inherited from a family sworn to protect me.

These were the only weapons I had at my disposal. Worthless items to a demon of the Underworld bent on killing me.

A knife would have been better.

I had neither knife, nor the courage to wield it, so the turquoise would have to do.

Chapter Four

By the time the desert landscape brightened through the slats of the boxcar, I had resigned myself to a fight I couldn't win. I fully expected to die that morning, but I wouldn't go down easy.

I prepared myself for battle. If not for my own sake, then at least for Dolly's. And the cows too. They didn't deserve to be lumped in here with the Petruska curse. It wasn't their fault they'd been corralled with a dirty Gypsy being pursued by a Romanian demon.

The air grew warmer even if I didn't. The town of Tempe shimmered and danced on the horizon. The smell of creosote permeated the air. The Arizona desert was rooted in my childhood memories as far back as I could remember, and all it took was one whiff of sagebrush and baked earth to bring it all back to the surface again.

I hadn't slept much since the incident with the conductor last night. Fatigue scratched my eyeballs, and I spent the better part of ten minutes just trying to get to my feet again.

I lowered my pants and had a look at the bandages wrapped around my thigh. Decided they could go another day. Muscles didn't want to work, and exhaustion made my hands shake.

I zipped up my pants, strapped my useless leg back into the splint, and fitted my crutches under my armpits. I made sure my mother's ashes were stowed away safely in the satchel.

The train slowed to cross the trestle bridge over the Salt River. Wheels sparked and screamed.

Sensing something was up, Dolly followed me through the crooked door of her pen. She bumbled her way over to the locked ramp and bumped her nose on the wooden slats.

"No, Dolly." I pushed her back. "You stay here. This is my fight now, not yours."

The train braked roughly into the station. This was no more than a couple of rundown buildings and a platform constructed of wooden boards that buckled in the heat. I didn't know exactly where I was, but wherever *here* was, it was tethered to civilization by a sprawl of human habitats and surrounded by a vast open landscape. I'd never been to Tempe before, or if I had, I'd been too young to remember it.

I peered through the gaps in the side of the boxcar while the train screeched to a halt. Got a glimpse of flour mills and silos; the usual town industries, and one giant butte that looked like something God had dropped out of his pocket and hadn't bothered to come back for it.

I could smell the muddy stink coming off the river.

The cows kicked up a fuss on the other side of the partition. I think they were as fed-up with train travel as I was.

My breath quickened. Fear was a lead weight in my belly.

I had everything ready to go. Coat buttoned up. One shoe on my right foot. The satchel containing all my worldly possessions sat snug across my chest, and Dolly was secured by a lead rope clipped to her halter, waiting patiently behind me.

At my feet was a full bucket of water—the last dregs from the drum that had kept us all alive for the past few days. I also had my crutches.

Nothing like a medical device for fighting off a demon!

I stifled a panicky laugh.

The conductor whistled as he approached. He counted the boxcars until he was right in front of mine. "Hullo? Hey, kid! Are you still alive in there?"

He lowered the ramp with a pulley system, and the Arizona heat hit me like a punch to the face.

I'd forgotten how hot it got in the desert.

I waited. Waited for the match to strike. For the fuel to splash over me, and the flames to roar ...

The conductor, a beefy man with reddish cheeks and wheat-colored hair stood at the bottom of the ramp. When he noticed the bucket in my hands, he tipped his conductor's cap back off his brows to get a better look. "Excuse me. You can't take that. It's railway property ..."

I didn't give him the chance to finish. I heaved the entire contents of the bucket at him.

I soaked him. Got him right in the face!

He reeled back, sputtering, hands flapping. "What in the *Sam Hill* ..."

I shook one of my crutches at him. "You ... you stay back, Monster!" What *did* you call a demon as old as Hell anyway? My voice rasped worse than a creaky wheel, but the circus brat in me came shining through. "Stay back! You think you can burn *me*? Back off, or I'll show *you* a trick or two!"

The conductor was too busy coughing to take any notice of my pathetic threats.

I looked around frantically, taking in details of my surroundings in the span of a blink.

Tempe was a rough-and-tumble puzzle of pale roads and dusty buildings built on land as flat as my palm. Beyond it, nothing but open desert and some humps of hills in the distance.

And one damn butte.

Nowhere to run. Nowhere to hide.

I threw the empty bucket at the conductor just for good measure. My aim was wild, and the bucket clanked away harmlessly.

He ducked purely out of instinct. "Have you gone crazy?!" He mopped his sodden face with a crumpled handkerchief. He looked at me as if *I* was the monster. "Why'd you have to go and do a thing like that for? I was nice to you!"

I wasn't sure, but I think I was talking to the *real* conductor this time; the man who'd shared his supper with me and had checked to make sure I hadn't died in the night. He didn't deserve a bucket of water flung at his head. Still, the other one could show up any time, and I wasn't taking any chances just to save face.

I tightened my fingers around Dolly's lead and threatened the man with the end of my crutch. "Back up. I'm coming down."

A handful of station workers who'd seen everything, came out of the sun-bleached building and rallied around the conductor.

"This kid giving you trouble, John?" one of them asked. His muscles bulged under his cotton shirt and the skin beneath the printed bandana around his neck was as leathery as an old boot. He was about as big as the broad side of a barn. He looked like he could flatten me with one swat of his fist.

The conductor, whose name was John Riker, as I found out later, must have seen the panic behind my defiant eyes and decided he really didn't want *that* kind of trouble on his hands.

"It was an accident," he asserted. His rather damp demeanor got everyone calmed down. "The kid was just emptying a bucket of water out the door and I happened to be in the way. He didn't mean it." He half-smiled at me but his tone was stern. "Young man, it's not like I don't appreciate a cold shower first thing in the morning, seeing as it's so damn hot out here, but maybe next time you could *warn* a man before you douse him."

"Vandy," I said.

"Pardon me?"

"My name. It's Vandy Davidson."

One of the station workers cocked his head. "Of the Davidson Ranch? *That* Davidson?"

"Maybe. Who's asking?" I was still wary of the group at the bottom of the ramp. Escape was within sight, but there was a wall of simmering animosity standing between me and freedom. And I still had to get Dolly safely down the ramp.

Mutterings followed.

Apparently, the circus brat had ruffled a few feathers.

"Listen, son," the conductor said.

"Vandy."

Riker wagged his head at me. "I'm *trying* to be helpful."

I raised my crutch. "All of you, back up! I have to get my mare down this ramp. She can't see, so I need to go slow."

John Riker set his hands on his hips. "Look, kid ..."

"Vandy."

"Good golly, you're trying my patience! Come on down from there. As long as you're on my train, I'm responsible for you. You don't have to be afraid. No one is going to hurt you."

"Yet," one of the station workers added.

The conductor glared. "Shut up. He's scared half to death as it is."

My gaze went to the four men waiting for me to descend. "Which one of you knows Del Davidson?"

A pause followed.

One of them answered for the rest. "Who *doesn't* know Del Davidson?"

"Where's his ranch? How far is it?"

The heat was already getting to me. The sweat spiking the hair over my forehead traced a line from temple to jaw. I was overdressed in the wool coat. My bad leg shook badly when I tried to put some weight on it, and my eyes were gritty from lack of sleep.

"It just this side of Scottsdale," said the one wearing the bandana. "Bit of a hike from here. Cross the river, six miles to the east, then about another five south of town." He pushed a sun-bleached flat cap back off bushy brows. "You're his son, aren't you? The circus rider. Vandemere. He calls you something else though. Not Davidson. Something foreign. He talks about you all the time."

Even my voice paled. "He ... talks about me?"

"Oh, sure. He says you're the best damn circus rider he's ever trained." The man grinned and the guarded expression fell away. "Hey, maybe you could put on a show for us?"

I was having trouble catching my breath. Suddenly, the ripples on the horizon had nothing to do with the morning heat, and I could feel my lips going rubbery.

"Uh oh," John Riker said, "you don't look so good, son."

I didn't feel well either.

"I'm coming down," I said.

John Riker eyed my bum leg and the crutches under my arms. "Do you need assistance?"

I hung my head. "Yeah, I think I do."

The men were all business. They got Dolly down the ramp and on to the platform without any help from me. She had a man on either side of her and another holding her tail. They went slow and easy down the ramp until she finally stood on the platform.

They weren't quite so careful with me. One of the station workers hooked his elbow up under my arm and lugged me down the ramp. He sat me down in the shade of a tattered awning and handed me a baloney sandwich while another man went to get Dolly some fresh water.

After scrutinizing my sickly pallor, the station worker wearing the bandana bought me a bottle of Coca-Cola from the ice machine inside the train depot.

It was the best damn soda I'd ever tasted.

"What happened to your leg?" Bandana-man asked, eyeballing my splint.

I told the story for the umpteenth time. "I broke it falling off this mare here during a performance in Oklahoma. It wasn't her fault."

I didn't tell them *whose* fault it was.

Best not to name names, out here in the vast Arizona desert.

I tipped the bottle of Coca-Cola against my mouth and let the soda wash the dust out of my throat. "I've been in the hospital for months."

"That's rough." Bandana-man stood holding on to Dolly for me. He stroked her crest and studied my flushed face until I squirmed. "Del never said anything about an accident."

I stared at the bottle sweating in my hand. "I doubt he even knows."

"Is he coming to pick you up?"

Another question I didn't feel like answering.

"He doesn't know I'm coming."

"How are you going to get out to the ranch then?"

"Walk, I guess."

This raised some eyebrows.

"Surely, you're joking?" John Riker replied. He was still a bit sodden around the edges, but his mood improved as his clothes slowly dried off in the sun.

"Why don't you just ride the horse?" one of the other men asked.

"I can't." I stood up. I managed not to groan, but it came at a cost. The horizon tilted, and I felt my knees threatening to toss me to the ground. I handed Bandana-man the empty soda bottle. "Thanks for everything. I should get going. Six miles you say to the crossroads?" My heart sank at the very thought of it.

They all looked at me as if I were crazy.

"You'll never make it," Bandana-man said.

I took Dolly's lead from his weathered hands and undid the buttons on my coat. "Then I guess you don't know me very well."

"Hey... wait."

I paused.

Dolly walked straight into me. She looked as embarrassed as a horse could be, but I laid a hand on her broad forehead and silently told her not to worry.

Bandana-man smiled. For some reason, he looked about as embarrassed as Dolly did. "My name's Daniel Bronson. Here. Take this." He untied the sweaty bandana from around his neck and held it out to me.

I gaped at it. I didn't really want it, but he insisted.

"It's a gift," he declared. "So Del knows we were good to you. Word gets around." He met my gaze half-way, and his face turned a deep red. "Ya, I've been known to break a few heads—all in the name of disturbing the peace. But people got the wrong idea about the boys and me. They think we're a bad crowd. I just want someone to know it isn't always like that. We all deserve a chance to make things better, right?" He scuffed his feet in the dust. "It's rough out here, is what

I'm saying. Sometimes a man needs to answer with his fists. Sorry if we scared you. We didn't mean to."

I was suddenly ashamed. Not of Daniel. Of myself. Of my own selfish pride.

Standing before me was a man who could admit he'd made a mistake. Who could own up to it when I could do nothing of the sort.

Daniel flashed me a grin that took years off his face. "If you need anything kid, just holler. We're always nearby. Ask for the Bronson brothers. We'll come running. No questions asked."

Words failed me.

He touched my shoulder with a rough hand. The gesture was too well-practiced to be impulsive, and I wondered if he didn't have children of his own. I sensed that under that tough exterior lived a gentle heart; a secret that needed to be guarded from a world of lawlessness and violence out here in the Arizona wilderness.

I smiled my thanks, praying he wouldn't notice the way I was gulping back traitorous emotions.

I tucked his bandana into my pocket.

He wandered away, heading back to his brothers, who were getting chatty with Riker. They abandoned me on the platform next to the train engine that puffed out steam like some mythical beast.

Apparently, I'd been dismissed.

Dolly pawed the ground beside my foot, anxious to get going.

I put my crutches into motion and led her down the platform.

We headed into a vast wasteland that was as beautiful as it was terrifying.

I walked into the desert—if you could call it *walking*. I couldn't use my left leg at all, so the right one had to do all the work. My armpits were already sore, and the heels of my hands were bruised and hurting.

Things weren't likely to improve much over the hours of gimping past sagebrush and cactus.

I hitched my way along the sandy track that took us out past the town limits.

Dolly's trailing footfalls stirred up little eddies of dust as she plodded along beside me. She followed me into whatever nameless terrors waited for us out here in a desert of thorns without a hint of hesitation.

And wait for us, they did.

Chapter Five

After Dolly and I had walked those grueling six miles to the crossroads, the enormity of the task my mother had set for me became painfully obvious. Sweat poured off me, gluing my shirt to my skin. My mouth had dried up and all I could taste was salt. My body cried out for water. My cheeks were already turning red in the fierce sunshine, and it was only by sheer concentration of will that I kept moving forward at all.

Dolly was coughing; a kind of spasming hack that sent her stumbling forward. I had to stop many times to let her rest. I was growing more alarmed by the minute.

Sweat turned her hide dark. Her sides heaved, and her legs were splayed out when we stopped. I saw for myself what Doc had meant about her bad heart.

The sun beat down from a merciless sky. The town of Tempe and the Bronson brothers were a faded hope behind me.

Ahead of us?

Nothing but scrub and cactus as far as the eye could see.

A few cars had driven by, the last one having rattled past us more than an hour ago. A dark-skinned Mexican in a colorful poncho rode past us on a burro, but he didn't stop or speak to me.

I moved Dolly off the road when two men on horseback drove a small herd of cattle up behind us. I recognized a few of the cows. I think they were the ones that had been on the train with us. They ambled by, tails swinging, kicking up a cloud of dust that sent Dolly into another coughing fit.

My fear gave way to anger. Why the hell was I even out here? To confront my father? Ask him ... what? Why he left us?

Fucking *stupid* ...

Dolly's steps became less steady. She was sick, and panting, and I didn't know what to do. Helpless, and beaten down by this hellish heat, I stared down every memory I had of Del Davidson. All the times he'd hurt me, ridiculed me, or made my mother cry, collided with an overwhelming surge of resentment. Any hint of affection I'd felt for him back at the train station turned to poison. Every step brought me closer to the man who had thrown me away like I was *nothing*. He had lifted me up, had taught me how to be proud of who I was, only to shatter my heart and leave me broken in the dirt.

He'd promised me he'd always be there to catch me when I fell.

All lies.

I limped along this endless road, sweat stinging my eyes, fury stealing the strength from my bones. My stomach soured on a rage that had no outlet, and my heart was pounding fit to burst out of my chest. The crutches hurt my armpits, and my left leg begged me to give up this farce and simply lie down in the dirt and die.

My shadow was a puny thing beside me. It was if my body had melted under the punishing sun, and I felt about as small as that puddle outlined in the dust.

Dolly stayed by my side. I'd taken my coat off—because I was going to pass out from heat stroke if I didn't—and I'd laid it across her neck to shield her eyes from the sun. Her nostrils flared with every breath and her lower lip was slack. Her ears were damp too and drooped at half-mast.

Anger drove me onwards. Anger and stubbornness. Fucking Petruska pride. I was a circus brat, and I was mad at the world, and there was no way in hell I was going to break the vow I'd made to my mother on her deathbed. I would do this for her—only for *her*. I would haul my sorry ass across a million deserts to please her. It was the last kind thing anyone would ever do for her, and I was going to respect her wishes even if it killed me.

God help you, Del Davidson, I thought darkly.

No goodness shone through the stain on my soul. Del had turned me into this callous bastard, so it was only fitting that I show up on his doorstep and give it right back to him. Years of pain had scarred me. Had hardened my heart against the people who actually loved me. I was scared, and I was hurting, and I didn't know how to be anything else but a cold, snarly, son of a bitch.

Another half-mile of walking through this breathless heat left me staggering. All that pointless rage turned on me. It sucked the last vestige of fortitude out of my body, and I finally had to stop.

I swore under my breath. I let loose a stream of foul language that would have earned me another ringing slap from Nurse Steele. What had been an arrogant test of my endurance was fast becoming a real concern. I realized I could actually *die* out here, along with my poor, sick mare.

I leaned against Dolly for support. "This is *insane*, Dolly." Emotion clogged my voice, but I couldn't have cried even if I wanted to. I just didn't have enough moisture left in me to spare a single tear. "We have to go back." I hauled Dolly around, catching her up when she stumbled. "Come on, old girl. Let's go back to town. We'll do this another day."

I was looking down at the ground when a noise seeped into my consciousness.

At first, I thought it was the wind, or thunder. It sounded different from thunder though. Thunder would have ebbed into silence. And the skies were clear, so how could it be?

I looked up into the sky.

Not a cloud in sight.

Dolly must have heard it too because she stopped dead. Her head came up, and she craned her neck around to peer into the desert, ears swiveling.

I tried to see what she was searching for, but nothing seemed out of the ordinary. Just some brittlebush, a clump of yellow cups, and buckhorn cholla growing among the prickly pear.

And thorns. *Everything* out here had thorns. Arizona wanted to either sting you, prick you, bite you, or cook you.

When I ran my hand along Dolly's shoulder, she tried to shudder it away.

"What is it, girl?"

She was nervous. She twisted her body around so she could get a better look at the horizon, dragging me along with her.

I saw it then. A towering cloud of dust, heading right for us. It rolled along like a tidal wave, slow at first, then gathering speed. A wall of brown fog tumbled towards us, as big as a mountain, and roaring like a freight train. It ate up the earth with an insatiable hunger and all the landscape disappeared behind it.

The hair on the back of my neck stood up. My eyes widened at the sight of all that dust, and I knew there was no escape. My only thought was to shield Dolly from the worst of it. I turned her tail to the monster bearing down on us and pulled my coat over her eyes. It was all I had time to do before the dust cloud engulfed us.

Day turned into night.

Wind screamed like a hurricane. I couldn't breathe. Couldn't see. My lungs were filled with dust. There was dirt in my mouth. Sand in my eyes, and my flesh was blasted with a thousand needles.

I felt Dolly's lead rope running through my palm.

I clamped my fingers around it, catching it halfway down. "*Dolly* ... " My cry was feeble. Choking. It was all I could get out.

She nearly yanked me off my feet. Her bellowing whinny carried over the screaming wind. I gripped her lead rope tight in my right hand as she hauled me across the road; a road I couldn't see.

There was sand up my nose. Down my throat. I coughed and swallowed dirt, and couldn't get any air in. The wind shrieked like a wild thing sent from the skies to kill me.

This *thing* ... calling over the blasphemous wind devouring the desert, shrieked, *"I have plans for you, Petruska ..."*

I was inside its belly. Me and Dolly.

The air was charged between the flying grains of sand. Static electricity flashed like bolts of lightning. One of the shocks must have gotten Dolly. I felt her jerk on the end of the line. She was there *somewhere*, in all the dust.

The rope whizzed through my hand. It was like trying to hold on to fire, but I wouldn't let go. Not even when my hand burned white-hot, and my flesh peeled away.

I stumbled forward and my feet lost contact with the earth. I fell against her side, stumbling. I managed to right myself. If there was pain, I never felt it.

"Dolly!" I cried. "Don't run ..."

She must have heard me somehow. She skidded to a halt, and she stayed beside me like the loyal, brave horse she was.

Something came out of the storm; a vague shape that clothed itself in the dust and wind. It spoke to me over the keening in my ears. "*How do you like the storm I made, little Petruska*?"

I coughed violently, inhaling more debris. Thought, *Christ,* it could control the weather now?

"Why ... are you ... doing this?" I screamed.

My voice was torn away by the wind.

The thing circled around us, taunting me, growling out a rumble of thunder that dragged my memory back to the rabbit hole.

I *knew* that growl.

Dolly pinned her ears flat to her neck.

Let her protect you, Vandy.

A voice in my brain. Not words so much as a thought that wasn't mine.

Ma? My mind cried.

Let Dolly protect you.

I held onto my horse, anchoring myself to her stalwart strength. She was a solid presence I could lean into, and I twined my fingers in her mane.

I couldn't see a thing. This was a Hell that had no definition, and Dolly and I were somewhere inside of it. The world had disappeared into chaos, and all I could do was swear at myself for putting Dolly's life in peril.

Stupid, selfish pride.

"Where do you think you're going, Petruska?"

"I'm—"more coughing, "going home ..."

"Oh no you're not."

"Why are you ... doing—?" I couldn't finish.

"I am your nightmare," the thing answered gleefully. *"You think I don't know what goes on inside your mind? You think you can hide from me? You think you can call me into your world, only to abandon me? Poor little Petruska! You're no match for me. I will take everything you love away from you and then I will kill you. Kill all the Petruskas. One by one ... I got them all."*

I shielded my eyes with my arm. Sand stung like glass against my skin. My lungs weren't working, and I was running out of air. Tears streaked down my face, turning to mud on my skin, and stinging my sunburned lips.

I yelled into the storm. "I know your name! *Cel Care Ia—*"

"QUIET!"

The thing shouted at me through the wind, so loud it tore my thoughts into pieces.

Dolly had had enough. Somewhere in this wailing banshee of a storm, I heard her raise her voice. Her defiance turned into a squeal of madness.

She knocked me aside as she ran into the storm.

The lead rope zipped through my blistered hand, and I had to let go.

I screamed, "Dolleee!"

She ran at the thing circling us. She struck out with her front hooves, bellowing out a cry that only an angry mare can make.

The demon howled back at her.

Dolly bared her teeth and flattened her ears. I felt her lunge at the shadow moving through that wall of dust and heard it yelp when she threw her hindquarters around and kicked out with both feet.

"Fucking horse!"

The storm raged. It scraped up the desert and flung it into my face. This was an all-out battle for survival now, and I was lost inside of it.

There was no escaping the wind. No place to hide. The only thing I could do to save myself was bury my face in my sleeve and wait it out.

I hung on to Dolly and she kept me anchored to the earth. There were times when I thought the wind gusts would knock the legs right out from underneath me. I felt it pushing me, shoving me into Dolly's side. Felt her backing up to keep her feet dug into the ground, and her tail turned into the blasting sand.

No way of knowing how long the storm lasted. Felt like hours. I trembled against Dolly's shoulder, my eyes shut tight, breathing into my shirt, expecting *that voice* to invade my head again and drive a stake of terror through my heart. I would have cried, but I was just too damned *scared.*

I draped my arms around Dolly's neck and pressed my face into her mane. Even though I was the *last* person who had any right to call upon God to save me, I moved my lips in silent prayer.

Eventually, the wind died away. I felt a pressure building against my ears as the storm moved on, rolling away towards the east.

Silence fell, deafeningly quiet. Dust hung in the air. Sunlight peeked thinly through the choking clouds, making pillars of sand out of the shafts of light.

I opened my eyes to a desolate scene.

Dolly wasn't even gray anymore. She was covered in dirt, brown from head to toe. She coughed hard; a sound that came from the depths of her chest.

I had so much dust in my eyes I was almost as blind as she was.

I stumbled forward. My hands reached out for her. "Dolly ..."

Her cough worsened. She lowered her head, and her mouth hung open. Great, racking spasms gripped her body, and she staggered towards me.

I cried, "No, no... *no!*"

Dolly went to her knees.

I threw my arms around her. I had no voice left. My lungs were full of sand, and my breath sounded more like pathetic wheezing. "Dolly—" I coughed. "Please ... don't die on me."

She lowered herself to the ground and heaved out a groan.

I collapsed beside her, forgetting all about my own dim hurts. "Please, Dolly ..."

She put her muzzle into my cupped palm. I heard her voice carried across the great divide. *It's okay, Vandy. It's okay to let me go.*

I moaned. I hacked up dust. I still couldn't see very well. I could feel her body already getting colder. "Dolly ... don't go without me."

I'm tired, Vandy. I've lived my life. Didn't we have fun though? We loved the spotlight, didn't we?

Why ... why ... *why?* Why hadn't I listened to Jimmy and left her at home? Why had I dragged her out into the desert? Why couldn't I turn back time and make things right again? Why did everything I love have to *leave?*

I'll take everything you love away from you; the monster had promised.

My heart hardened. I screamed into the desert. "Your days are numbered, you fucker!" My battered lungs didn't like this, and I hacked up more mud.

Dolly lay propped on her chest. Her legs were folded under her, and her chin was pressed to the ground. She rested quietly. Her breathing grew more labored, and I knew she didn't have much time left.

I sat with her and stroked her face just the way she liked it. "I'm sorry, Dolly."

I heard her speak through the grief blanketing my mind. *There's another who waits for you at the end of the road. He needs you more than I do. Go. Don't look back. Remember, I'll always protect you. I'm always with you. As long as you carry me in your heart, I'll be with you. Look for me there, always.*

She rolled onto her side.

I tried to catch her, but she was just too heavy.

She groaned again and stretched her legs out straight.

When I raised my head again, the light had gone out of her eyes, and I saw that my dear old Dolly had died.

Chapter Six

I stayed with Dolly until the sun went down. I stroked her face until the fragile warmth of her body faded away.

Her legs were already stiffening. She lay on her side with her head flat on the ground. One sightless eye stared up at the dusty sky.

Sand had drifted over her.

I brushed it away from her mouth.

My heart was empty, my soul, drained. I felt nothing. I was dead too. I lay on one hip with my body resting in the hollow of Dolly's elbow. I laid my cheek on her shoulder and ran my hand along her side, wishing she would take just one more breath for me.

The sun sank into the drifting dust; a great burning globe that turned everything a burnished gold. It would be dark soon. And cold. The desert could turn frigid at night this time of year and I wasn't dressed for the elements.

Dolly's body was already chilled. I would have to leave her soon. I would have to leave her alone in the desert.

Not yet though ...

I pressed my knuckles against my lips to stifle the hitching moans tearing through me and buried my face in her mane.

I slept a little after that. I must have, because when I opened my eyes, night had fallen.

I tried to rub sand out of my eyes and only scrubbed the grit in deeper.

I was half-buried in sand too. I'd lost my coat and my crutches. I still had Ma's ashes though, in the satchel strapped across my body.

My horse was dead. It was cold enough to see my breath, and a million stars danced against the velvet darkness high over my head.

I rolled onto my back and lay in the crook of Dolly's shoulder, looking up at the sky. All I had to do was reach up with my hand and I would touch the stars. This was the closest I'd ever been to Heaven, and I wondered if I wasn't lost somewhere between the realms. I felt anchored to the earth, but there was a presence around me that made me second-guess my existence in this world. My body felt light. Hollow.

Why couldn't I feel *something?* Why wasn't I crying anymore? Screaming. Shaking Dolly, begging her to wake up.

A coyote yipped nearby. The night belonged to the predators, and I was standing in the way of a free meal.

I fumbled for the rock pressing into my hip and hurled it into the darkness. My aim was off, and it didn't go far. I heard it thunk along the ground and rattle against the loose gravel.

I screamed, "Get away!"

I sprawled across Dolly's lifeless body, lowered my face into my arms, and *tried* to cry. I forced air over my parched throat. I moaned. The sound I was making came from somewhere down deep in my belly, and it didn't sound like me at all. I covered my head with my arms and wailed. My nose ran, and I made myself sick. I couldn't spit the dirt out of my mouth fast enough and I tasted gravel. I didn't want to be *me* anymore. I didn't want this terrible pain burning through my heart. I didn't want to be here anymore.

I felt a light hand caress the back of my head.

I jerked as if something had stung me. I raised my head, sniffling. "Ma?"

It *felt* like her; like something she would do.

I gazed at Dolly's stiffening body and resolve hardened in my chest. I would be doing her a great disservice if I gave up and died out here in the desert. If the coyotes and the mountain lions didn't get me, the cold certainly would. Her sacrifice would have been for nothing.

Shock was creeping up on me. I recognized the deep tremors crawling up my spine and wondered if I was about to have another seizure. I hadn't had one in years. There was something about the heaviness pressing against my brain that warned me I was in trouble. I needed to get someplace warm, and soon. I needed water. Shelter. If not for my battered body, then for my wounded mind.

The only place I would find it was still miles away.

When I thought about leaving Dolly, I just couldn't do it.

I stayed by her side for a long time.

The desert would take her. It was the law of the natural world. It would consume her remains, and I couldn't bear it.

I ran my hands over her body, committing her to memory while grief made inroads through the dirt on my face.

"Goodbye, Dolly." I rubbed my nose with a filthy hand and swallowed hopelessly. I had no spit left to wash away the rawness in my throat and I ended up hacking up dust instead.

The moon crested a blurry horizon.

I saw the way back to the road. Cactus rose like silent sentries against the pale light rising in the distance.

I finally climbed to my feet and faced the moon. The desert was awash with touches of silver; here on a boulder, there in a dry riverbed. Pockets of shadow lay in between. There was nothing here that I could use to honor Dolly's sacrifice except what I could take away in my mind.

Something made me reach into the satchel at my hip. Ma's ashes were still intact. She rested in her Mason jar, safe alongside the baloney sandwich I'd never gotten around to eating.

My fingers recognized the familiar edges of my mother's tarot cards. I unwrapped the deck from the silk scarf and found the card I wanted.

I bent down and laid it over Dolly's heart, in the spot right behind her elbow.

It was my final gift to her.

The Moon.

The image of a galleon in full sail rode the still waters of a turquoise sea, centered in the swell of a full moon rising. The cheerful face drawn on the moon smiled up at me.

The Moon was number eighteen in the Major Arcana. When it showed up in a reading, it was a reminder to move through life's mysterious transitions with confidence and grace. I gave it to Dolly to help her on her way, hoping it would guide her home.

I stood over her body one last time. "You were a good horse, Dolly. I'll miss you." I bit down on numb lips. Silent tears welled and everything became a blur.

I turned away before I lost my nerve again and stumbled over the rough ground.

She had told me, *don't look back*.

I didn't.

Walking was hard. My left leg wouldn't support my weight. The splint helped a bit, but I'd lost my crutches, somewhere. No way I would get far without them. My heart might have been up to the task, but my body was exhausted, and the mechanics of getting back to the road posed a challenge.

I found my coat. I almost tripped over it. It was half-buried in a sand dune near the edge of the road. I saw one of the brass buttons glinting under the rising crescent of moonlight and stood there looking down at it for a moment or two. My mind was having a hard time focusing through the grief. After considerable thought, I realized that the coat belonged to me. I pulled it out of the shifting sand, shaking the dust off cautiously. I had to make sure it *was* clothing and not some animal that had died in the storm.

Like Dolly.

A fresh wave of loss hit me in the chest. I bent my head and ached.

I put my coat back on. I warmed up some after that. I put my cold hands into the pockets and still didn't look back.

I took another step. Then another.

I didn't get far. Only to the road before my leg gave out. I sat down in the dirt, leaning on one hip with my arms braced behind me while my mind fell apart. After that, it was simply a matter of sinking the rest of the way down, cradling my head in the cushion of my elbow, and drifting off to sleep.

***

A man driving a dusty old truck found me in the morning, still asleep at the side of the road.

I woke up when he shook my shoulder.

He must have thought I was dead. His look of apprehension turned to quiet relief when I yielded to his touch.

"Hey, kid." His voice was a pleasant baritone. "What are you doing out here? Did you get caught in the storm yesterday?"

I blinked up at him. "My horse ..." I croaked out. "She's ... dead ..." I don't know what I was saying.

I couldn't look. Just gestured in a vague direction over my shoulder.

He worried the corner of his lip with very white teeth and glanced up. He was young. No more than mid-twenties. Good-looking fellow. Smooth skin. Fresh-faced. Clean, unlike me. I was filthy and bruised and lost.

He wore a cloth cap, pulled down over blonde eyebrows. His hair was cropped tidily around his ears. It was the same color as Ellen's, kind of a pale honey gold. He had a strong chin. Strong shoulders. Strong *everything* from the looks of things.

"Wait here." He rose gracefully for a man of his stature.

He must have been a farmer. The watermelons in the back of his truck were a dead giveaway. He wore a faded checkered shirt, beige pants, and suspenders that looked far better on him than they ever had on Clarence Dawson.

He stepped over me and walked off, heading over the dunes that had blown in during the sandstorm.

I closed my eyes and rested. Time passed in fits and starts. I couldn't bring myself to accept the fact I would have to move at some point. I couldn't lie here in the dirt forever. Getting up wouldn't be a whole lot better than lying in the road, and then I would have to walk, which I already knew would be next to impossible without the crutches.

The sun was barely up. The air still hung onto the morning chill, and the shadows angling off the feet of some nearby cactus stretched across my prone body. I'd carved out a nice little bed for myself on the shoulder of the road and I was very reluctant to leave it.

The man came back. The look on his face confirmed what I already knew. My beloved Dolly was dead. He stood looking down at me, hands perched on narrow hips, probably wondering what he should do with me now.

He crouched down. "Come on. Get up. You can't stay here. What's your name, anyway?"

"Vandemere," I said. He looped his right arm underneath mine and lifted me off the ground. He set me on my feet. "Vandemere Davidson."

"*Davidson*?"

I stood on one leg, swaying precariously. I already knew what he was thinking. Yes, *that* Davidson.

"You're Del's boy, aren't you? The one who rides in the circus."

I nodded mutely.

"I'm Lester Simmons."

His eyes were a strange sort of gold. Not brown at all. More like a tawny yellow.

Lion eyes, I thought.

"Are you hurt?" he asked, noticing my one-legged stance.

I bowed my head. I wished he would stop asking me questions. I didn't want to talk. All I could think of was dear old Dolly lying in the sand back there under the scrub, and how she would never carry me into the spotlight again.

His eyes took note of my dispirited gaze. "I was taking some watermelons into town. I don't have a lot of gas in the tank but there should be enough to get you home."

"Home?" I echoed. "Home is in California. I don't think there's enough gas for that."

He gave me a strange look. "I meant, home to Del's ranch. It's not too far from here. That *is* where you were headed before the dust storm rolled in, wasn't it?"

I couldn't even manage a nod anymore.

He tried to help me over to the truck.

I balked.

He took his hands off me, finding me stiff and resistant. "You aren't scared of me, are you? Don't be. I'm just trying to help."

"It's not that," I said. "I ... had crutches. I lost them."

He looked at me like he thought I wasn't quite right in the head. "Okay. I'll go look for them."

He went back up the slight incline that led into the cactus scrub, meandering along the track towards Dolly's body, dragging his boots through the dirt.

I stared off into space and waited. Dolly was just another dead horse to someone like Lester Simmons. To me, she was everything. There should have been pain, but there wasn't. I was beyond feeling. Beyond thinking. Beyond coping. I was stuck in a body that refused to give up, no matter what I threw at it.

Lester reappeared at my side. "Are these yours?"

He handed me both crutches.

I was tempted to ask; how many other crutches could there be out here? But he was being so agreeable, I stayed silent.

I resumed my one-legged limp forward.

"Hey, where you going? It's this way." He steered me back towards the truck. "You sure you're okay? You not hurt somewhere I can't see?"

"Hurt?"

I *was* hurt. I was hurt in my soul, and I was hurt in my heart.

He kept one hand on my arm as he yanked the door of the flatbed open for me. The kindness of strangers always caught me off guard. I felt as if I ought to pay him back for putting him out of his way, but all I had were a few pebbles of turquoise, a shirt that probably wouldn't fit him anyway, and a couple of stale sandwiches.

"Do you want a baloney sandwich?" I asked, while he arranged my legs safely into the cab and laid my crutches across my lap.

A chuckle escaped him. "Thanks, but no." He muttered something about scrambled eggs and my brain all in the same breath, and slammed the door shut.

He went around the front and got in behind the wheel. It took him a minute to turn the truck around on the narrow track, then we struck off, back the way he'd come.

I closed my eyes. Rested my temple against the door frame. I gripped the strap of Jimmy's satchel with both hands, protecting Ma's ashes from God knows what. Time passed without me being aware of it, and I think I dozed off.

My face felt stiff and sore. My eyelids were stuck together. My left leg complained, and my lips resembled blistered meat. All things combined, I just felt old and worn out. Just like my poor old Dolly.

Grief hit me in the chest, as painful as a hammer.

Lester's hand on my arm nudged me back to a grim reality.

I straightened up and opened my eyes to full daylight now. Dust motes danced in the sunlight streaming in through the open window as the truck bounced over the deep ruts in the road.

He offered me a whiskey bottle, keeping one hand on the steering wheel.

"Go on, it's just water," he explained at my confused look. "You must always carry water out here in the desert." He recited this mostly for my own benefit. "Thirst will kill you faster than you can say John Adams. Drink."

I took the bottle from his tanned hand and drank. I swilled mud around inside my mouth, swallowed, and coughed.

I gave him his bottle back.

He eyed me sideways. I searched the Petruska *magie* for help and got nothing back.

Seems friendly enough, my mind reasoned. You can probably trust him.

“I’m sorry about your horse,” Lester said.

I looked away. I thought I’d gone as low as I could feel. Turns out, that wasn’t true. I hid my face beneath the collar of my coat and wallowed in misery.

I dozed off again, finding solace in unconsciousness.

I dreamt that the truck had stopped. The engine tinked and cooled. I dreamt we were parked on the side of the road. In my mind, I imagined the inside of the truck was as hot as an oven. The sun beat down on my face through the open window, and Lester Simmons was on top of me.

He had me pressed up against the passenger door. I was wedged between the back of the bench seat and the door. He held me there, using his body to trap me against the metal frame.

The window handle dug into my right kidney.

He had me in a bear hug. Had my elbows pinned tight against my sides. His knee was hooked over my thighs, preventing me from struggling. His voice came in whispered pants as he nuzzled my neck.

“Relax,” Lester breathed. His hand fumbled between my legs. “I just want to have some fun ...”

What the ...?

I woke up with a jolt.

Turns out, it wasn’t a dream at all ...

Hell, no!

I thrashed underneath him.

He returned the favor by pushing me against the door with his shoulder.

Lester Simmons wasn't so nice anymore. His brow furrowed, and his golden eyes blazed. He grabbed both my wrists and jerked me forwards until we were nose to nose.

I wasn't looking at Lester Simmons anymore.

The voice confirmed it. That screeching, whiney hiss was like a nail grinding against metal.

"*Where's your little pony now, Petruska*?"

I stared at the evil screwing Lester's pleasant face into an inhuman sneer and knew I was in trouble.

He tried to crush the bones in my wrists with his bare hands.

A scream crawled up my throat. I wrenched my face away, choking out a ragged cough. "I know who you are, demon! I know your name—"

"*Shut up!*" He bared his teeth like an animal. His lips curled back, and his spit sprayed across my mouth when he shouted, "*Demon? I'm no demon, Little Petruska. Poor, weak little Petruska. You think you know me?*"

"*Cel Care Ia—*" My voice broke over the pain. I bent forward. Knotted my brow against the mounting agony building in my hands. He wasn't going to stop until he broke both my wrists. "Let go of me!"

The creature gave my wrists a vicious shaking. "*Where's your pretty horse now, Petruska*?" He threw me hard against the door and climbed on top of me, or Lester did, I didn't know which. His knee pinned me to the seat. When he dug his weight into my bad leg, an explosion of pain pulled another scream out of me, and my breathless wails bounced around the cab of the truck.

He snarled over the groans bubbling out of my mouth. "*You have no horse now. I killed it. I'll kill you too. You're all alone out here. Alone in the desert. Just the way I wanted it. There's no horse to protect you anymore, little Petruska. No pretty pony to chase me away.*" His voice dropped for an instant. "*Fucking horse ...*" Lester's golden eyes pierced mine again. I would have covered my ears if he didn't already have my hands trapped in his brutal grip. "*You got lucky. I didn't count on the horse protecting you. I got rid of it. It's just you and me against the world, kid!*"

I clamped my lips down on a traitorous moan. I turned my face away when he moved in closer. He licked the salt stains off my cheekbone, and I felt him grinning; this monstrosity from the Underworld come to claim my soul.

I might not have had Dolly around to protect me anymore, but I wasn't entirely defenseless. I had a few tricks up my sleeve, and I wasn't above playing dirty. Not when it came to saving my own skin.

I gathered together the last few scraps of frail courage left in me and stared him dead in the eye. He had my wrists and he had me pinned against the door, but he'd forgotten one thing about me. He'd forgotten I was a circus brat. I'd been dealing with grifters and thieves and shady characters like him my entire life.

"Care to make a wager?" I asked this more shakily than I would have liked. "I have cards. I'll trade you: my life for yours. We'll play a game, just you and me. Two out of three. Winner takes all."

It confused him.

"*What?*"

That moment of hesitation was all I needed to tear my hands from his grasp. I used leverage against him, twisting my fists around until he was forced to let go.

I didn't think about the pain. I didn't think at all.

I drove my fingernails into the backs of Lester's knuckles. Grabbing all the fingers I could manage; I bent them backward until they snapped like chicken bones.

It was *his* turn to scream now.

I heaved him off me. Panic gave me strength I hadn't known I had.

My only thought was to get out of the truck.

I fumbled for the door handle behind me and jerked it upwards. The door gave way, and I spilled out, falling backwards onto the road. It was a long way down and a rough landing. I banged my head on the ground and scraped my shoulder on the way down. I was on my back *again*, but my coat protected me from the worst of it.

I remembered the satchel at the very last moment before impact—and Ma in it. I twisted onto one hip just in time to avoid crushing her in the fall.

Lester tumbled out after me. The ear-splitting screech he uttered almost stopped my heart. He was on me in seconds. I'd broken a few of his fingers, but it was *Cel Care Ia* I was fighting with now, not Lester Simmons, and a demon from Hell didn't care about a couple of mangled knuckles.

He clawed at my neck with fingers that flopped around, growling, spitting like a cat. He drove his knee into my stomach, and I wheezed out badly needed air.

The intimacy with which he held me down was worse than any torture he could inflict on me. I grappled with his frantic hands as he went for my face. I fought him off as best I could. I knew what was coming. He wanted my throat. He wanted to rip into it with his teeth. To spill my blood onto the desert sand. I was going to die out here and no one would ever know what got me.

An animal, they would say, expressions solemn when they brought my lifeless body to my father's home and laid me down in his hallway, probably the local sheriff from Scottsdale. Looks like something attacked him. Maybe a mountain lion. The desert's full of them.

Nope, I decided. Not today, you bastard!

I dug my fingers into Lester's jaw. I jammed the heel of my left hand under his chin, locked up my elbow, and pushed.

He pushed back.

He was so *strong*.

I scrabbled my right hand around in the loose gravel beside me, hunting for a sizable rock.

Something rolled into my hand.

I had only seconds to make out the wispy outline of Annie Lee standing next to me. There was no question in my mind she was responsible for kicking the baseball-sized rock across the sand.

She stuck her thumb into her mouth and watched with calm detachment as I fought for my life.

Lester pounded on me. He backhanded me hard in the mouth. He hit me again and again, savagely. A sickening crunch reverberated through my skull each time his fist connected with my face, but I was too dazed to feel anything besides the numbing pressure of bruising and blood.

I held him at arm's length with my left hand and closed my fingers around the rock lying next to me in the dirt.

I wheeled my arm around, and I hit Lester as hard as I could across the side of his head.

He rolled off me, and I could breathe again. I coughed. Choked on blood and downed most of it.

I gazed up at Annie. Her bright blue eyes held mine, and her little voice was an endearing comfort to my shattered soul. *Doggies won't bother your horse. I make sure.* She grinned around her thumb and faded back into the landscape.

I bit back a sob and wondered what I'd done to deserve her forgiveness.

A rock to the temple wouldn't stop a demon but it had certainly stopped Lester Simmons, and that's all that mattered to me.

I turned my head to squint at him. I worried I might have killed him. Lester had been kind to me. It wasn't his fault he'd been ambushed by a monster.

He was still alive, thank God. Still breathing, though his drawn-out efforts gurgled alarmingly.

I lay for a moment, coughing up dust and blood. My breathing sounded almost as bad as Lester's. I was starting to notice the various places where I was hurt too. My chest felt like someone had lit a bonfire in there. My arms shivered from exertion, and sharp bits of gravel pressed into the back of my head. My face was already starting to swell up like a lumpy mattress, and my lips felt like over-inflated tires. I think Lester might have broken my nose as well.

I still had the rock in my right hand. It was smeared with Lester's blood. Or mine; I wasn't sure. The sun pinned me to the ground, and I felt light-headed and sick.

Lester groaned.

He was waking up.

My heart jumped into my throat.

And here I'd thought I was done with fear ...

I lifted my head and somehow got my elbows under me. I was glad I was still wearing my coat. It cushioned my uncoordinated attempts to get moving.

I sat up all the way and crabbed my body forwards, shifting my ass along the loose gravel until I was at the open door of Lester's flatbed.

When I reached up for the running board, a terrifying pain shot through my lower back, and I let out a high-pitched cry.

My father would not have been pleased.

I thrashed around in the dirt for a bit, whimpering through swollen lips, and waited for the pain to subside.

Lester stirred.

I was running out of time.

I bent my good leg at the knee. I had only seconds to figure out the best way to pick myself up off the ground and get into the truck. Decided there was no easy way to do it.

I sat up, gritting my teeth on sand and the coppery tang of blood. I straightened the strap of the satchel better across my body and checked inside to make sure Ma was still intact.

She was still safe in her Mason jar, tucked in there with her tarot cards and Clarence's book to keep her company.

A savage thought crossed my mind. Where the fuck was Lieutenant Dawson when I needed him?

My crutches were still in the truck. I could see them lying on the floorboards under the dashboard. They might as well have been in the next county for all the good they did me.

I looked at my hands. They were in pretty rough shape. The rope burns I'd gotten from trying to hang on to Dolly's lead rope had turned my palms a strange, shiny-white, and the skin was already peeling off. My wrists were a bluish gray under all that filth, and I could already feel my fingers stiffening up.

My lip was split, and my nose was bleeding too.

Crimson raindrops landed in my lap.

Just go, I told myself. Go, or die out here. Those are your two choices, Petruska.

I glanced over at Lester. A smear of blood had clotted in his golden hair right above his temple, painting the side of his face red.

He opened his eyes and stared back at me.

Shit!

Fear was a great motivator. I pushed all the pain aside and hauled myself up into the cab of the truck. If I did any further damage to myself in the process, I certainly didn't feel it. Everything still worked … sort of.

Lester's keys dangled in the ignition. There had to be twenty keys crammed on that leather fob. I gave a passing thought for the man lying in the dirt, wondering; why on earth would a watermelon farmer need so many goddamn keys?

I wasn't sticking around long enough to find out.

I slammed the passenger door closed. My hands shook with the rush of terror as I slid across the seat. I knew how to drive. I was a bit out of practice, but how hard could it be?

I barely had time to stomp the clutch to the floor with my bad leg and crank the engine over before Lester appeared at the passenger side window. His ashen face was greasy with sweat, and there was a spiderweb of blood across his cheek.

He rested his broken fingers on the edge of the window and gazed at me with vacant eyes.

I forgot all about being brave and let out a strangled wail.

Lester Simmons surprised me that day. He said something that would change my mind about him. About a lot of things. Lester made me realize it wasn't just *me* who was fighting this entity. That I wasn't alone at all. That for all the evil in the world, there was still some kindness left.

My terror was reflected in his own unfocused thoughts, and I saw a battle going on behind his eyes.

"Drive," he said.

I put the truck in gear and hit the gas. The truck lurched forward, and the wheels spun around in the loose gravel, and I think I may have knocked poor Lester off his feet.

I drove.

Chapter Seven

I sat in Lester's truck, trying to come up with one good reason why I shouldn't turn myself around and go back to California.

What I *really* wanted to do was push Lester's date book and envelope full of receipts off the seat and sprawl across it. If only I could sleep away all my hurts, both physical *and* spiritual, life would be grand.

An organized huddle of buildings emerged from the dust cloud drifting past the truck. I looked around, praying my courage would come out of hiding and back me up.

It didn't.

The place had an air of understated style. No money spared here. From the circular flower beds blooming in the middle of a spacious courtyard, to the peaked roof of a covered riding ring tucked in behind the stables, everything was designed to impress.

Acres of wire fencing marched in straight lines away from the barn. A couple of tractors were parked by some out-buildings, all well-maintained. Behind them, a large structure for hay storage rose into the dazzling blue sky.

Some of the smaller pens clustered behind the barn held a horse or two.

I thought about Dolly, and grief stabbed me in the heart. I buried my aching face in my hands and waited for the moment to pass.

A man in blue jeans and a brightly colored shirt watched me. He lingered in the shadow of the stable doorway, sweeping a plume of dust out into the sunshine with a corn broom. Even from here, I could see was Indian. My guess was that he was probably Apache, but that could have been the *magie* talking. He wore a battered cowboy hat, and his long, braided hair fell in two tight plaits down the front of his shoulders.

Our eyes met.

I looked away long before he did.

The main house was to my left. It was like all the typical haciendas I'd seen over the years of traveling through New Mexico and the southern states, with its white stucco walls, and a flagstone walkway led to the front door. The shutters on the windows were a muted gray. The architecture was all smooth lines and graceful archways, with garden trellises covered in pink bougainvillea and *palo verde*, and date palms grown for shade. The landscaping around the house was tasteful. The paddocks were spacious, and everything was tidy and trim.

There was no question in my mind that I was sitting outside Del Davidson's home.

I couldn't recall how I'd gotten here. I remembered driving past a gate down at the road. There'd been some lettering on an ornamental wall, but I hadn't paused long enough to read it.

I hadn't needed the sign to tell me I'd come to the right place. My father had talked about building a ranch in Arizona for so long, I'd already painted a picture of it in my mind. I had imagined every detail, right down to the terra-cotta tiled roof, the brown chickens scratching for bugs in the dust, and the small kitchen garden just off the back path. It was all here; everything he'd ever wanted.

None of it had included me.

I thought about moving. I would have to get out of Lester's truck eventually. I couldn't sit here all day, looking suspicious. The man sweeping the clutter out the doorway of the stables had already made up his mind about me. It was only a matter of time before he came over, asking questions.

I fought with my own misgivings. I didn't want to see Del. I couldn't understand why I was so *scared*. I wasn't a little kid anymore, so why was I shaking like this? Dread sat like a stone in my chest and my throat was so dry I had to keep prying my tongue off the roof of my mouth.

I rested my left hand on the satchel tucked up against my side, feeling the outline of Ma's Mason jar through the fabric.

I shook my head. "I'm sorry, Ma. I can't do this ..."

I opened the door of Lester's truck and slid out anyway. I propped the crutches under my arms and slammed the door behind me.

The walk across the courtyard felt like a year in Purgatory. I planted my crutches in the gravel and limped slowly across the yard, concentrating on staying this side of upright under the shade of those beautiful palm trees.

I carried my mother's ashes up to the front door. Various injuries reminded me I was dangerously close to ruining my chances of ever riding again. My body wasn't coping well with the aftermath of Lester's attack, and pain chipped away at my already compromised constitution.

A horseshoe-shaped doorknocker seemed the best way to get someone's attention. My knuckles were far too tender to knock them against the wood.

Two small windows set at eye-level in the door gave me a glimpse of the hallway inside. Further back, I saw a spacious atrium filled with sunshine and living greenery.

I paused, facing aspects of my childhood I'd tried so hard to forget. I raised a tired hand and rapped the horseshoe a couple of times against the brass plate.

No one came.

A storm of anger was building inside of me now, replacing the dread.

I knocked harder.

The Native man in the barn stared at me from across the yard.

I stared back. In the seconds it took to acknowledge his interest in me, someone finally answered the door.

A whoosh of breeze swirled past me.

I locked eyes with a woman who looked a lot like the man out in the courtyard. She had light brown skin, dark eyes, a wide mouth, and sharp, arching eyebrows. But what stood out most about her was her *hair*. It fell down her back in tumbled, brown waves. It was very long, and thick like a horse's tail, going all the way to her waist.

Beautiful hair.

She had gathered the lengths into an oval clip made of silver and beaded turquoise at the back of her head. Silver rings studded with turquoise flashed on her fingers. She was dressed in a light cotton blouse with some embroidery on it, and the sweep of her printed skirt ended at her tanned calves.

She answered the door with a sunny smile. One look at me though caused her to step back. Her expression of welcoming curiosity turned into a wariness that didn't bode well for me.

I saw her glance past me. She was looking for the man with the broom, measuring the distance between me, *danger*, and him, *help*.

I spoke stiffly, trying to breathe through my clogged nose. "Is Del in?"

Tension bracketed her eyes. "He's napping."

Napping? Since when did Del Davidson ever take a nap in the middle of the morning?

"Can you get him for me?" My lip started bleeding again and I blotted it with a filthy sleeve.

She backed up until she had part of the door shielding her shoulder and most of her hip. "What do you want?" Her eyes went back and forth, first to me, then to the truck parked in the yard behind me. "If you're here to sell us watermelons, we don't need any."

I'd forgotten all about Lester's watermelons.

A voice called from inside the house. Familiar. Terrifying.

"Who's at the door, honey?"

Honey called over her shoulder. "Del? Could you come here for a moment?"

One name. All it took was one name to send my courage running for cover. I started to shake. My head pounded. There was a pressure mounting inside my lungs, and lack of oxygen trampled my courage into the dirt.

I heard the woman's apprehension hone her voice to a keen edge. She had no idea who I was, or what I wanted. Only that there was a black-haired stranger standing at her door, swaying precariously on a bum leg, blood all over his face, and wearing a coat of desert dust over baggy clothes.

She called out for my father.

"Del!"

One name nearly brought me to my knees.

He came down the hallway, a tall shadow of a man dressed in jeans and a clean, denim shirt. Sand-colored hair held a touch of gray at the temples. He had less of it than I remembered, but it was still familiar enough to invoke memories, both good and bad. His expression was calm, only mildly concerned by the woman's beckoning cry as he strode toward the door.

My body betrayed me. Panic bolted through me like an electrical shockwave, making my heart leap against my ribs like a wild animal. It thudded against my breastbone with so much force, I was sure it would break out of my chest. A tingling spread through my limbs, signaling a desperate need to escape, and I was already backing up.

He came on steadily.

He didn't recognize me right away. He hadn't seen me in well over five years, and I was definitely taller than he remembered. My welted face would have altered his memories of me, and his tone was sharp when he addressed the stranger standing on his doorstep.

"What is this?" He took stock of my disheveled appearance and fielded me with a look of pure disdain. "Why are you bothering us? Who are you?"

I panted through bloody lips. Stared blindly ahead. Everything was reeling.

I thought only of retreat. "I—I ..."

I backed up. The sun didn't feel warm anymore. The scent of all those flowers blooming in the beds beside the house reminded me of chloroform, and I choked on rising bile.

My father didn't know who I was, and it broke my heart.

Through all the panic, I remembered why I'd come here. I dug one hand into the satchel. Nerveless fingers slipped over the Mason jar.

Please, I begged silently, don't let me drop her.

I pulled Ma out of the bag resting on my hip and held her in front of me, praying my tenuous hold on courage and swollen fingers wouldn't let her down. "Bonnie died." I stammered this out. I couldn't see much more than blurry shapes rippling around me now. I felt like I'd died too. Like I didn't own my body anymore. I couldn't feel my legs, or my feet, but Petruska pride kept me upright, and I resisted the urge to keel over.

Something happened to the expression on Del's face. A lifetime of memories brought his world to a crashing halt, and whatever he'd lived with during all those years of absence came into focus in a single instant.

He stared at the Mason jar in my trembling hand, then brought his gaze back up to my face. "*Vandy*?"

I took a gimpy step forward and offered him the jar. "Take her." I choked on grief. I kept pushing her at him until he was forced to take the jar from me. Our fingers brushed against each other's, and we both recoiled.

I hated him *so much*.

I said, "She wanted you to have her ashes. Take her to the Grand Canyon and let her go. Those were her last wishes."

His face paled worse than mine.

I bent my head to hide my grief from him. I'd done what my mother had asked of me, and now I was free.

I slowly hitched myself around and turned my back on my father, just as he had done to me all those years ago.

The woman had seen all of it, of course. She knew my name, if not my face. She alone kept a level head.

"Vandy? Wait—*Del*. You *can't* ..."

She had only seconds to unravel a lifetime of trauma and secrets.

I had a pretty good idea what she was up against.

"Del! He's *hurt*. For God's sake! You can't let him leave like this ..."

And my father's voice overriding hers. "What is he doing here? Christ ... *look at him!*"

I kept Lester's truck fixed firmly in my sights. I limped towards it. Everything else was just empty noise.

The woman called, "Vandy, *wait!*"

"Lenora! You don't understand. He can't *be here!*" This, from my father. Harsh words from a heartless man. Everything I'd expected from him drove me away.

Lenora appeared at my side. She caught my sleeve and pulled me to a halt. "Don't go, Vandy." She was as breathless as I was. "Come into the house."

I shook her off and kept going.

She called for reinforcements. "Chuck! Don't let him leave!"

The man who had been sweeping out the breezeway was already loping toward us.

I stumbled to Lester's truck, but Chuck got there ahead of me.

"Do you want me to hit him?" Chuck asked, apparently game for anything.

"No! Goddammit! Take the keys!"

I snarled. "Get out of my way."

"He can't be here!" my father shouted from the house.

I wheeled around. A childhood's worth of pain and frustration boiled up in me, burning white-hot behind my eyes. "You ... fucking bastard!" My split lip cracked open and bled some more. "You *left* us! You left *her*. How *could you*?"

He came striding down the walkway toward me, his expression twisting into something horrible. “Is that Lester Simmons’s truck? Did you steal it?”

Lenora was still beside me. She faced Del down. “He’s your *son*, Del! Don’t let him go.”

I tried to meet him halfway down the path. I screamed at him, dragging Lenora with me. “Tell me why you left! *Tell me—*"

Chuck was caught in the middle, holding twenty keys bunched in his hand. “What happened to Lester?” he asked me, calm enough for everyone.

“How the hell should I know?!” My fists shook. God ... I wanted to hit ... *something* ...

Lenora barred the way. She got in between me and Del. Her brown eyes were round and pleading. “Vandy ... come into the house.”

My own bitter tears spilled over. I shook my head. “I can’t do this—"

“Lenora!” My father’s tone was sharp. “Let him go.”

“You’re not the boss of me, Del Davidson!” she shouted back.

I don’t know why *she* was crying. Her fingers were gentle on my shoulder, and I really did like her hair. I didn’t know this Lenora-woman from a fence post, but I was starting to warm up to her.

“This boy is *hurt*,“ she announced, and it shut my father right up. “Chuck, help me!”

Chuck approached warily, tipping his cowboy hat back off his eyes. “He isn’t going to bite me, is he? Seems a bit hostile if you ask me.”

I’ll show you hostile, I thought furiously.

My strength was flagging. The stitch in my side hurt so bad I could barely stand. All that yelling had given me a pounding headache, and everything around me turned an ominous gray.

My father conceded. Even though everything in him wanted me gone, he gave in to Lenora's demands. He stood, legs braced, his mouth a tight line, and he held my mother's ashes away from his body like it was a jar of vipers. "He can stay for a day. That's it. Then he has to go."

I looked him straight in the eye. "I hate you."

Lenora took a firm hold on my elbow, and Chuck was a warmer presence on my right.

Lenora raised her chin. For a moment, her dark eyes reminded me of my mother's. "Del, *move*."

I remember them helping me into the house. They parked me on the sofa in the sunken living room off the kitchen. Chuck peeled off my dusty coat and torn shirt, and Lenora got me a blanket. After that, things got hazy.

One day turned into three. I was put to bed in one of the spare rooms, given weak tea when I was awake, and visits from a doctor when I wasn't.

I started having seizures again, something that happened when my body was under stress.

I heard my father's voice from a long way off.

"He's had these fits ever since a scorpion stung him, back when he was a baby. I thought he would have grown out of it by now."

Typical Del. Only babies and sissies have fits.

I had dreams of Dolly. I dreamt she wasn't dead. To me, she was real. Alive. She ran through the desert, whinnying for me. I tried to go after her. I screamed her name, but she just kept running.

I saw a horse on fire. Saw him walking towards me. Everything around him was on fire too. It looked like a circus tent. Flaming bits of fabric dropped down from the burning roof, landing on the horse's back.

He shook them off like bothersome flies.

I woke up to the smell of something frying in the kitchen.

"He can't stay here," I heard Del say.

"I just don't understand you." This came from Lenora. Her frustration was palpable when she sighed. "His mother is *dead*. He's come all this way. His face is a mess, not to mention the rest of him. God knows what happened to him out there in the desert. Lester's still not talking. Really, Del, I thought I *knew* you. How can you be so cold-hearted?"

The light was too bright for my eyes. Sunlight slanted through a gap in the curtains, spilling across my body. Every inch of me hurt. I needed to pee in the worst way, but I was just too sore to move. Sore in the body, and sore in the mind.

"Just fix him up and get him out of here," said Del.

I pulled a pillow over my head and buried my sadness in sleep.

Chapter Eight

When I woke up again, the sunlight had crawled across me and moved on. The resulting gloom was a lot easier on my eyes. As long as I didn't move, the ache inside my skull was just this side of bearable.

There was a sense of quiet permeating through the house that had me wondering where everyone was.

I rolled onto my back and groaned.

"Feeling better?"

Shit.

I pried my eyelids open and blinked past the fog blurring my vision.

The man in braids sat in a chair in the corner of the room, resting quietly with one leg crossed over the opposite knee. To say he was looking at me would be an understatement. His eyes were keen on my face. He had skin like leather, a sharp, beaky nose, and he wore a black shirt and blue jeans, dusty with chaff.

I spoke around cracked lips. "It's Chuck, right?"

"Charles," he corrected. "But Chuck will do fine."

"Where is everyone?" God, it fucking hurt to talk.

"Out in the barn."

"I need to get out of here."

"Sure," he replied.

I frowned, but that just sent ripples of pain across my face, so I quit doing that. "You're not going to try and stop me?"

"Do you want me to?"

I paused, trying to figure out his game.

Concentrating for any length of time hurt my brain. It would be so much easier to stay where I was. I hadn't slept in a real bed in days, and the mattress cradling my sore body felt a hell of a lot better than sleeping on the side of the road. But I knew when I wasn't wanted. And I really needed to pee.

I shifted under the three layers of blankets and tried to move.

Everything spasmed and seized up. I swore and sagged back against the pillows. I watched the ceiling spin like a whirligig for a moment, then tried again.

Chuck watched my pathetic efforts with interest and made no attempt to help.

I squirmed around for a while, hissing out gasps of pain, and fighting with the blankets. At long last, I sat up and eased my legs over the side of the bed.

I hugged my left arm against sore ribs.

It had taken me the better part of five minutes to get this far, with a fair bit of swearing thrown in for good measure. At least now I was upright. And I was wearing clothes this time. Someone had dressed me in a pale linen nightshirt and sleep pants that might have been Del's, except they fit me pretty well, so maybe not. Still, clothes were an improvement over the last time I was bedridden; naked, and trussed up, stranded in the hospital in Oklahoma.

Someone had washed me and re-bandaged my leg, likely the town doctor. My left knee wouldn't bend at all, and a thick wrap of linen strips felt stiff and hot along my thigh.

I raked the hair off my forehead and winced when my fingertips grazed a scab crusted over the scrape on the back of my head. "Ow..."

Chuck nodded in sympathy. "You've got quite a nasty cut there. Lots of bruising along your ribs too. Your wrists are pretty banged up, but nothing's broken except your nose. Local medicine man says you've mangled-up your leg. He says that's an old injury. Says you've been walking around on it too much. If you ask me, I think you should be walking *more.* And I hate to break it to you, but your face looks like shit."

I probed my lips with careful fingers and ran my tongue around the inside of my mouth. I still had all my teeth, thank God, but everything throbbed and tasted like metal.

"Where's my splint?"

"In the other room."

"And my crutches?"

Maybe he would just go and get everything for me?

"Ask me nicely." Chuck grinned.

I flattened my expression so it wouldn't hurt so much. "I need to get out of here."

"You keep saying that. So go."

"I'm *trying* to."

He put his arms over his head and stretched like a cat. He had forty years on me at least, but he made it look easy.

He let his breath out in a rush. "Do you want something to eat? I don't know about you, but running away on an empty stomach always makes me cranky."

Heat rose in my cheeks. "I'm not running away. I'm going home. There's a difference."

"Says who?"

I refrained from glaring at him. "This conversation is going nowhere."

He shouldered my tone of voice without batting an eye. "There's a bad spirit after you. You sure you want to risk another meeting with it out there in the desert? You'll be all alone again. No way to fight him off. No horse to protect you either. Might succeed in killing you this time."

My jaw dropped.

He read my reaction with very dark eyes. "So, it's true then? You *do* have an evil spirit after you? I wasn't sure."

Despite a deep-seated resentment for anything that hinted at authority, my interest was piqued. I studied his posture, his relaxed jaw, and half-crossed legs, decided it was non-threatening, and challenged his position in our two-man tribe. "Maybe there is, maybe there isn't. What are you anyway, some sort of shaman? Are you a *Seer*?" I raised my chin in a show of defiance. "Prove it."

It might have been my imagination, but his smile lost some of its warmth.

He made a big to-do of closing his eyes, like I'd asked him to jump the moon, for Christ's sake. He proceeded to make strange movements with tough, brown hands. It looked like he was manipulating an unseen energy through the air around him. He broke into low, guttural, singsong notes typical of the Native communities we'd run across during the summer seasons on the road.

They never failed to send a thrill up my spine.

"I *can see*." He chanted out a throaty hum. He peeked through one eye and caught me staring. "Great Spirit tells me you have bad mumbo-jumbo after you. I have communicated with The One Mother and she has told me everything. And you talk in your sleep, by the way, so there's that too."

He laughed hysterically at my disgust.

I tightened my lips. Bad idea. Pain seared across my mouth, and I took it out on Chuck. "You don't want to help me? *Fine*, don't help. I lost my horse you know, thanks to that *freak* that's hunting me. Dolly was *everything* to me, and you're *laughing*?" My throat clamped up and my voice turned into a squeak. "That *thing* killed her! My beautiful Dolly ..." Grief ached, still raw in my soul, and I had to look away.

He grew serious again. "Sorry. I couldn't resist. White folks expect a show from us Natives. Easier just to give them what they want. I don't like conflict, so I tease them instead. Makes everyone happy, and I feel like I've won something when I probably haven't."

I sighed. "Can you *please* just go and get my crutches so I can get the hell out of here?"

He scratched his chin and didn't budge. "Stay for dinner. Lenora's cooking up some beef and gravy. And there's fresh tomatoes out of the garden."

Tempting.

I studied the terra-cotta tiles under my bare feet. "No thanks. I'm not wanted here."

"Ah," he commented wisely. "*The Martyr*. I had a look through your tarot deck. Didn't see that card."

Heat surged into my face. "Fuck you, Chuck. You think this is funny?" I retaliated by getting my *own self* up off the bed. My knees shuddered something awful when I stood up, and I wondered if I wasn't about to tumble headfirst into his lap. "I almost *died* out there. I had to leave my horse behind. I left her lying in the desert, and when

I dream, I see a horse on *fire*. What the hell does that even *mean*? This thing that's hunting me took over Lester's body and tried to *kill me!* It's already killed two little girls. Two little innocent children. And you're laughing ..."

He sat in his chair and watched me fall apart. "You named it, didn't you? Out there, in the desert. You called it out, and it had no effect at all."

I gaped at him.

He stated, "You've got it all wrong, Vandy, and it's going to get you killed."

The hair rose on the back of my neck. "What makes you say that?"

Something that looked a lot like blackmail flitted across his face. "Stay for dinner and I'll tell you."

"Why should I?"

He smiled, tiptoeing around my despair. "Because underneath all those bruises and bandages and bristling hostility, there's a hurting kid who just wants to know why his father left him."

I lowered my eyes and gulped past the searing burn in my throat.

Chuck's searching gaze scanned my face. "Look, Vandy, you don't know me from a hole in the ground, and you have no reason to trust me. One thing is certain though; I've walked this earth a hell of a lot longer than you have and I've come to know a thing or two about how the world works. If you don't stay and sort this out, you'll never know how close you came to flying. That's all you ever wanted to do, right? Fly?"

I said nothing.

His voice held no malice. "If you run away, all you'll ever be is an angry, broken-hearted *kid*. A kid that grew up thinking his father hates him. You'll end up a drunken, mean, son of a bitch who keeps taking it out on the people who want to love you. You'll never step into the shoes of the man you're meant to be, and that's just *sad*. I've heard the way Del talks about you. You are destined for *greatness*; you just can't see it. All that rage is getting in the way of your success. I know it. You know it. And that demon knows it too."

I teetered on the precipice of making the hardest decision of my life. I could feel the strain of secrets breaking their way to the surface. Trying to stop them was like trying to hold back the sea. I was just so damn tired of *hurting*. I felt like a wild bronco that had been whipped to exhaustion, but kept right on bucking, still *fighting*, even though every inch of it wanted to quit. It raged and fought because that's all it knew how to do.

Here was someone extending a hand to me, offering me a different life than the one I'd accepted as mine. The life I'd come to expect. A lifetime of rejection. A life starved of affection. Mad at the whole goddamn world.

I turned away so Chuck wouldn't see the war going on behind my eyes. "You don't know what it's been like ..."

He was suddenly beside me. He pressed his fingers gently into my arm. "Come with me. I want to show you something."

He helped me to walk. He let me lean on him. Each shaky step brought me closer to the truth I'd been searching for all these years. He had a familiar scent about him; comforting layers of horses and hard work, mixed in with herbal soap that got me thinking about Jimmy and home.

He helped me into the open kitchen space beyond the doorway of my bedroom where the living area revealed an atrium beyond, filled with potted plants. He took his time with me, letting me find my footing at each step. When I didn't think my leg could hold me anymore, he propped me up against one of the kitchen chairs and retrieved my crutches from a small alcove off the main room.

I looked at my hands. Lester's assault had left me with a band of rainbow-colored bruises circling both wrists. Blood had pooled into a darkened wash of gray and purple over my knuckles and turned the flesh under my fingernails a lovely shade of nasty.

After three days of aloe vera compresses, the rope burns on my palms were looking more like dried up snakeskin.

When I tried to make a fist, not much happened.

Chuck put my crutches back into the pantry. "Never mind. I'll help you."

A turtle would have crawled across the floor faster than I walked. My heart banged against my breastbone in time to the thin breaths I wheezed out. Sweat got into the cuts on my face and stung like shit. I felt about as beat-up as I probably looked.

Thank God Del wasn't around to see me creeping along like this.

"Where are you taking me?" I panted out.

"For a ride. Just to the road. You need to see something. Then you'll understand."

He ushered me down the narrow hallway, out through the door, and back into the sunshine, where the blinding Arizona afternoon left me dazed and squinting.

"Wait here," he told me.

I waited next to the circular garden while he brought his truck around. I made sure no one was looking and relieved myself against Lenora's tea roses. Felt ten times lighter, and the plants got watered too. Bees hummed through the flowers, and the air was stifling and still.

When Chuck pulled up to the flowerbeds, I climbed in beside him. "You aren't going to turn into something bad, are you?" I was only partly joking. "The last time I accepted a ride from someone in a truck, things didn't go so well."

He reached across my legs and opened the glovebox. He hunted up a jackknife buried in there under some paper receipts and some snarled up jute twine, and slapped it into my sweaty palm.

"Just in case," was all he said.

I shut my eyes and trapped the knife against my chest with my battered hands. The anxiety clawing at my throat had nowhere to go but up.

Chuck's eyes missed nothing.

He started the engine again and man-handled the farm truck into gear.

We lurched along the same worn-out track that had brought me to Del's doorstep three days ago and headed towards the main gate. The ride lasted maybe two minutes; down a rough path carved into the desert that would have taken me half the morning to walk it.

At the end of this drive lay the ornamental gate that announced to the world that the famous Del Davidson lived here. I vaguely remembered seeing it on my way in. The entrance consisted of two stucco walls, chest-high, curving gracefully on either side of the wrought-iron barrier. The gate was mainly for show, as anyone with half a mind to trespass could simply walk around it and continue on down the winding lane towards the cluster of rooftops in the distance.

Chuck wrestled the truck into neutral and shut off the engine.

He came around to the passenger side and let me out.

"I don't know why you brought me out here," I grumbled.

He stopped short of rolling his eyes. "Just *trust me*, for God's sake!"

I muttered something he chose to ignore and suffered the indignity of having to be helped out of the truck.

He walked me over the uneven ground and around to the other side of the gate.

He kept his hands on my shoulders and faced me toward the chalk-painted walls.

“Look,” was all he said.

I looked up, and finally saw the sign.

Black lettering, stenciled on what I would later learn was mahogany from the East Indies, spelled out, *Vandemere Ranch.*

My father had named his farm after me.

I didn’t understand this. Years of childhood trauma came crashing down on me. I thought he hated me. He certainly made that plain enough when he had come at me that day I’d ridden Samson and refused to do the backflip.

I had spent the last five years of my life hating him back.

Chuck stayed at my side. He didn’t try to make things better. Didn’t give me a lecture about giving Del another chance, or how I’d been wrong about my father all these years. He let me suffer without judgment and waited for me to come to my own conclusions.

All this time, had I been *wrong* about Del Davidson?

“You still want to leave?” Chuck asked.

I stared at the heat rippling across the horizon. *Nothing* would make me cry. Not even this.

“No,” I answered dully.

“Okay.” Chuck took hold of my elbow again, finding the one place that didn’t hurt. “Come on then. Let’s go home.”

Chapter Nine

Chuck became my ardent champion. He took me under his wing. If Del fixed me with a look that suggested I'd outstayed my welcome, Chuck intervened on my behalf. He always made sure I was somewhere else whenever Del came into the house: in bed, resting, or reclining in one of the wicker chairs under the palm trees in the backyard.

One night, while my father lingered over his evening coffee, I hid out in the atrium.

Liber Mortuorum rested in my lap. As far as I knew, Dawson still hadn't made any effort to get his hands on it yet. Part of me wondered if he was just too afraid of what it represented to chase it down. He was a man at odds with the supernatural. Experience warned me, if he didn't pick a side soon, chances were good the Petruska *magie* would do it for him. He would have to face his own rabbit hole someday. If I could do something to help the man out, perhaps it would mean that my own suffering had value.

That's why I'd stolen the book; in the hopes that I could lure Dawson into this insanity with me. So he would understand what it meant to be a Petruska. Maybe then he would finally *believe me* when I said I had nothing to do with Annie's death.

When he didn't follow me, the evidence of his doubt was tough to ignore.

Chuck said I'd been wrong about everything.

Had I been wrong about Clarence Dawson too?

I glanced up at a small shadow moving along the edge of my peripheral vision.

Annie was still with me. She played among the potted ferns, drifting between the earthly plane and the ethereal Divine. When our eyes met, she smiled at me.

I smiled back.

I reeled out a fragile thread of the *magie* and connected it to her shimmering energy field. *I'm coming, little mouse. Just be patient with me.*

She melted into the ether and stayed out of sight.

I thumbed through the ancient text. My fingers still weren't working very well. The bruises on my wrists had gone from dark purple to a faded grayish yellow. I still couldn't walk very far on a barely healed leg, and was content to hang out amid the plant life.

I studied the page Margaret had bookmarked with the tarot card. A lit candle near my elbow threw nervous shadows across the painted images laid out before me. Even the crickets outside had gone silent.

A monster looked back at me.

Cel Care Ia.

The One Who Takes.

Whispers and rumors rustled through my mind. I couldn't remember if Ma ever talked about *Cel Care Ia* specifically; one more secret among the thousand other things she'd kept from me. He lurked in the distant landscape of my heritage. He would have been passed down to me, just as the Petruska *magie* had been. He was a Romanian creation, with a Romanian name, but there were others like him. Every culture had its folklore. Every nation had its Elementals. They existed solely to cause strife. From what I'd heard, these faeries were linked to crop failures, and maybe the odd miscarriage and such. Mostly, they were miserable little creatures with mischief on their minds.

So why was this one bent on murdering me?

Could I be wrong about it being an Elemental? I'd named *Cel Care Ia* out there in the desert and it hadn't even slowed him down. I think I only made things worse. When I called to him, he *laughed* at me, and then he killed Dolly.

I couldn't understand how my heart could go on beating when the rest of me was so *broken*.

I let out a huge sigh, but it did nothing to salvage the wreck of my life.

I traced the inked script with stiff fingers. What was I missing? If it wasn't *Cel Care Ia* causing all this carnage, what else could it be?

The written words told me nothing.

I closed the book on my right hand, keeping it there between the pages to mark my place. I shut my eyes, inhaled a lungful of desert air, and sent feelers of *magie* out into the night.

Show me.

The response was shocking.

Flames engulfed me.

I saw ...

A horse on fire ...

I'm burning ... I can't see ... pain ...

I yanked my hand from the book with a strangled cry.

Lenora called from the kitchen. "You all right in there?"

"Yeah," I chimed back.

I was still in one piece. Still sitting in the atrium. Banal details greeted my startled gaze; plants in pots crowding around me, some cactus growing in gravel. Nothing had changed except now I had a tingling hand and echoes of it being blistered to the bone.

It *looked* okay. I still had five fingers and everything was still covered with skin.

All the air inside the atrium felt like it had been sucked out the windows. Shadows wrapped around me, pressing against my temples, and I felt another headache coming on.

Liber Mortuorum mocked me from my lap, witnessing my descent into madness.

I forgot all about it being a priceless artifact and threw it off my lap.

***

Lenora timed my meals between the daily chores. She made me breakfast only after Del had gone down to the stables. This relieved me from having to sit under his intense scrutiny. She was a great cook, and I think she was trying to make up for Del's sullen disapproval by overfeeding me. She heaped my plate with scrambled eggs, sliced tomatoes from the garden, and corn tortillas.

I could feel my strength returning. Physically, I was mending. Mentally? Debatable. I still had nightmares of chasing Dolly through the desert. Lester Simmons's face leered at me every time I closed my eyes, so getting a good night's sleep was wishful thinking.

The local doctor drove out almost every day to see how I was coming along. He was your typical small-town physician. Old. Gray.

Whiskery. White hairs grew out of his ears, and he wore the same uniform I'd seen on countless other doctors. Black coat, black trousers, dusty bowler hat pushed down on his balding head. I figured he came all the way out here mostly because he was curious about me. Whatever stories Del Davidson had been spreading around the county gave me a reputation I couldn't live up to in real life.

I sensed Dr. Franklin was as disappointed in my uncooperative sullenness as my father was.

"How did you break your leg?" He poked and prodded my sore thigh and cleaned the angry-looking wound with some linen rags and alcohol.

Sweat beaded on my upper lip. I'd had so much practice enduring varying degrees of pain, I took it all in stride. "I had an accident in the ring."

I didn't tell him about the tent pole coming down on all those people, or the monster chewing through the guywire. If I'd told him the whole story, he would have had no choice but to entertain thoughts of locking me up in an asylum.

He had a look at the cuts on my mouth, scrutinized the faded bruising around my eyes, pulled my shirt down so he could examine the large abrasion on my shoulder, and pressed a little too hard on the scabby wound on the back of my head.

"Does it still hurt?" he asked, seeing me wince.

"Like a bastard."

He made a disapproving sound in his throat and closed his doctor's bag. "Just try to stay off that leg as much as you can. And get plenty of rest."

Chuck and Lenora hovered in the doorway.

My father had found something to occupy his time down in the stables and was conspicuously absent.

"Keep me apprised of his condition," Dr. Franklin asserted. "If he spikes a fever, call me right away. Otherwise, he seems to be improving under your excellent care, Lenora."

I didn't need the Petruska *magie* to know Dr. Franklin had a thing for Lenora.

Lenora's usually pleasant expression looked forced. "Can I offer you some coffee, Dr. Franklin?"

"That would be most gracious of you, Lenora. Thank you."

Chuck put a damper on Dr. Franklin's efforts to have a cozy chat with her by making a lot of noise banging around the pots and pans.

An uneventful week went by. I hadn't realized how much I missed the circus until I didn't have it in my life. The only thing that kept me from going stir-crazy was the thought that it was the off-season anyway. Not a minute went by when I didn't think about going back to California. I missed Shorty's comical face, and Jimmy's stoic approach to life's problems, both big and small. After hearing absolutely nothing from either of them since I arrived here, it became painfully obvious the circus certainly didn't miss *me.*

Mostly, I just read some books and stayed out of everyone's way.

"Why is he still here?" Del asked for the hundredth time. He didn't even try to keep his voice down. It was sometime in the afternoon, two weeks after my aborted attempt at running away, and I was just waking up from a long nap in my bedroom off the main hallway.

He sounded as frustrated with this domestic arrangement as I was. "The sheriff is asking a lot of questions about him. I'm not sure how much longer I can hold them off. They want to know what happened out there in the desert. Lester's still not right in the head. Keeps yammering on about devils and dead horses. Vandy showing up here with Lester's truck is incriminating enough without both of them looking like they've been through a war. *Something* happened out there. It's not like Lester to lose a fight either. We don't need this kind of attention, Lenora."

"*We*? Since when did this become about us, Del?" Lenora's voice was sharp enough to draw blood. She must have been washing up the breakfast dishes because it sounded like she was taking out her irritation on the hapless china. "Maybe you could start thinking about your son for once? Have you even *asked* him what happened?"

I cast a weary gaze on Ma's ashes in the Mason jar. She did a great job holding down Clarence's copy of *Liber Mortuorum* on the nightstand next to my bed. Her presence tethered me to the life I'd left behind in California, and she kept me from giving in to a debilitating depression that tried to sink me into an abyss.

"*You* ask him," Del argued from the kitchen. "You're better at this than I am. I'll be in the barn if you need me."

"Oh sure," Lenora called after him. "Run away, Del. I see now where Vandy gets his stubbornness. You're going to have to talk to him *sometime.*"

My father muttered something that sounded a lot like, "Not if I can help it," and slammed the front door on his way out.

Chuck appeared in the doorway of my room. "You awake?"

I sighed. "I am now."

"Come down to the barn with me. You could use some fresh air. It's a beautiful morning. Shame to waste it."

"Are you always this cheerful first thing in the morning?"

"It's ten o'clock," he pointed out. "I've mucked the stalls and ridden two horses already, and I've harrowed the riding ring. You must have heard me out there. That blasted tractor sounds like a cannon going off. Come on. If you don't get up soon, it'll be too hot to do anything but hide in the shade. I want to introduce you to the horses."

"I suppose Del's down there too?" I suspected this was more of a plot to get me to face my father and less about stimulating my interests.

"It's a big barn. I'm sure there's enough room for the two of you to stay out of each other's way for an hour or so."

It still took me another ten minutes to finally drag myself out of bed. Muscles cramped up every time I moved, forcing me to hold my breath while my heart stuttered against my ribcage. My limbs felt like they were being drawn and quartered on some medieval rack.

Chuck watched me creak and groan my way into an old shirt of Del's. The linen sleep pants were easier to slip on over the brace, so I wore them instead of the faded blue jeans Chuck had lent me.

"We're going to have to do something about that," he stated mildly, bored of seeing me sweat out the pain. "Lenora's got breakfast waiting for you. Meet me down in the stables once you've finished up here."

Breakfast today was avocado slices on eggs, and toast.

I perched one hip on a stool at the kitchen counter and tucked into my food while Lenora studied me over a steaming cup of coffee. Curiosity was written all over her face.

"What?" I asked.

Her gaze flinched away. "Nothing. Do you always wear your hair like that?"

I shoved my forelock out of my eyes. "Like what?"

"Like *that*." She chanced another look at my bed-tangled mop. "Like a Gypsy."

I sipped my own coffee, and it did wonders to steady my nerves. "I am a Gypsy. Del must have told you by now, me and Ma are Romanian—*were* ..." I corrected, remembering my mother was now a pile of ashes in a pickle jar. "It's something I like to play up in the ring. People love it. Well, some did. That was before ..."

"Before what?"

I looked down at my half-finished eggs.

She was instantly remorseful. “I’m sorry. I didn’t mean to pry.”

I shrugged. “It’s okay.”

She waited for me to explain, but what could I say? Before I’d been accused of a child’s murder by a cop who, as it turned out, was a blood relative?

Annie’s parents certainly blamed me for it.

Should I tell her that I had a terrifying entity after me who could control the weather and send a dust storm after me? How it had killed my beloved horse? Should I tell her how it could jump into people and make them attack me? Break my bones and make me fall?

How long did I have before it showed up here? How long before *Cel Care Ia* jumped into Chuck and forced him to strangle me in my sleep?

If I breathed a word of this to anyone, it wouldn’t be the sheriff’s department showing up at the door, it’d be a padded wagon.

Lenora’s voice broke into my thoughts. “Can I fix it for you?”

“My hair? I guess so. Just don’t cut it.” I was very particular about my hair. I wouldn’t allow anyone near it with a pair of scissors. I usually trimmed it myself or got Dodger to do it. He’d been a barber before he became a clown, and he hadn’t lost his touch over the years.

I ate my breakfast while Lenora combed the snags out of my hair. It was weird, having someone else mess with my hair, but nice too. I liked the way her fingers felt when they brushed against the back of my neck.

Maybe her intention was to turn me into one of her Native relatives. Or her own kid. Did she have any kids? I didn’t feel it was my place to ask.

By the time she was done with me, my hair had been braided into a single length down my neck and held together with a knotted strip of leather at the end.

She threaded a dove feather into the braid and stood back to get a better look.

I'm not sure what she saw in me that day, but it seemed to please her. "Little Dove. You're quite the looker, you know."

"Now that the bruises have faded you mean?" I chuckled.

Her smile faltered. "What happened out there, Vandy? People in town are talking. It's only a matter of time before the sheriff comes to the door. Del's been telling everyone you're too sick to answer questions, but they're starting to get impatient."

I took my time answering. She deserved an explanation. She'd been kind enough to take me into her home even when my own father detested my very existence. I couldn't remember the last time someone had fretted over my welfare like this. The problem was, the details of that day out in the desert were mixed up with other memories, and I didn't know what was real and what was made up anymore.

I remembered some of it. I remembered the dust storm. Getting off the train in Tempe too, and the Bronson brothers. Dolly's death was forever burned into my psyche, but I couldn't recall Lester picking me up off the side of the road or giving me his truck.

I *did* remember the attack. I would hear the demon's high-pitched screech till the day I died.

I would *never* tell anyone about waking up with Lester's hand between my legs, or how he'd tried to kiss me. I didn't think it would be fair to Lester Simmons to brand him a homosexual when the whole incident was beyond his control.

As for the rest of it?

I gulped the dregs of my coffee down and said, "I don't really remember much."

When in doubt, feign amnesia. Works every time.

Lenora touched my hand. "When you're ready to remember, it will come."

I looked away, thinking, God, I hope not.

She helped me into my shoes and made sure my shirt was buttoned up straight. She brushed imaginary dust off my shoulders. The top of her head barely came up to my chin, but she moved with a self-assurance I could only dream of.

"Don't stay out there too long. You're not well, and it's hot out there. And don't let Del talk you into mucking stalls."

She and I both knew there wasn't a snowball's chance in Hell Del would keep me around long enough for *that* to happen.

I hooked my crutches under my arms and shuffled down the hallway.

Outside felt as if I'd stepped straight into a smelting oven. Heat closed in around me, coating me in sweat, and I had to ask myself if all this effort was worth it?

Chuck hailed me from the far end of the barn. "You made it!"

I limped into the main breezeway. The stable had two sections, but only one seemed to be in use. After looking off to my right, I decided there was no point exploring the empty stalls down that way.

I headed left, hitching my way along at glacial speed.

My father was just coming out of a stall about midway down the aisle.

His eyes locked on mine.

I kept forgetting how tall he was. Seeing his lanky frame striding down the center aisle towards me brought back memories I was trying hard to forget. Fear dried my mouth, and my heart fluttered behind my breastbone.

I paused mid-stride. I wracked my brain, trying to come up with something to say that would please him, but he brushed past me without a word.

I felt the wall between us getting bigger by the day.

I had to keep asking myself; how much could he really hate me if he named his ranch after me?

Chuck's smile more than made up for my father's rudeness. "Come over here. Take a gander at this lovely fellow."

I lumbered forward, reveling in all the familiar smells that brought me back home to the circus I missed so much. The sharpness of urine, and the salty tang of equine sweat, the unmistakable scent of horses combined with fresh hay and sweet feed ... it all flooded into my brain.

Chuck smirked at me. "I see Lenora had a go at your hair."

I panted my way down the aisle. "She accused me of looking too much like a Gypsy."

His eyes scanned me up and down. "I'm not sure the Apache style suits you either. I'd be careful if I were you, going out in public like that."

"Why do you say that?"

He wiped the dampness out of the groove of his chin with a gloved hand. "Oh, no reason."

I opened the *magie* a crack and got a whisper of something back. Something I didn't like. The man had secrets too, and he was making damn sure I couldn't pry the lids off them.

He was already changing the subject. "Come and meet Karma."

I limped over to the open stall door and looked in.

My first introduction to Karma did not go as planned.

The horse stood stock-still as I rounded the corner of his stall. All I remember is seeing a chunky black horse with a mane that went past his shoulder before everything tunneled in on me.

Fire ... everything on fire ... hot ... hurts ... my back is burning ... people shouting ... I walk through the fire ...

"Vandy?"

I came back with a jolt. I was still on my feet, thank God.

Things came back into focus. I realized my father had come back and was standing at my side.

He touched my elbow. "Are you okay?"

I looked up, startled. His energy surged into me, battering strong against my fragile boundaries, and it forced me to take a step back. "Yeah ... sure. Why wouldn't I be?"

His concern disappeared behind impatience. "You're not doing that *thing* again, are you? That stuff you and your mother were into. Mind-reading, and whatnot."

Whatnot? That *whatnot* had been instrumental in securing him a wife, *a family*, and here he was, dismissing it as if it was just another midway con.

I bristled. "What happened to this horse?"

"I don't think I like your tone of voice." Del's gaze was hard on mine. "*I* didn't hurt him if that's what you're implying. He was like that when I bought him."

Sensing another argument brewing, Chuck quickly intervened. "You can go in if you like. Just be careful of his scars. He's a bit touchy about them."

I dragged myself away from my father's disapproving glare and hobbled into Karma's stall. I half expected him to spook at the sight of my crutches, but he never moved. Not even a twitch. Even when

I brought my palm to his withers and felt the heat radiating off his burned skin, he regarded me with vacant eyes.

I ran my hand up under his mane and worked that spot on his withers they all liked to have scratched, pleased to see him wriggle his upper lip and arch his neck in pleasure.

Del watched me from the doorway. His expression was tough to read, even for me.

"Where did you get him?" I asked.

"He came from a carnival up in Canada. Something went wrong with part of his act. The burning hoop fell on him. From what I understand, it got tangled up in the harness and scorched his hide. I was in the prairies last year looking for stock and they sold him to me cheap."

I ran my hand over Karma's back.

He tried to twitch it away.

There were bald spots along either side of his spine, and he was missing a lot of hair over his rump. He hadn't been burned too badly. Not enough to warrant a trip to the stockyards, but his scars were evident. His skin had healed into shiny, thickened callouses, and the hair would probably never grow back.

I looked into his dark, round eye. Watched the squarish pupil for any sign of distress.

His delicate ears turned back slightly.

"I almost walked away from him," Del said behind me. "I must have been out of my mind when I bought him. He won't tolerate a saddle. He just runs away. I don't think the scars hurt him anymore, but his mind?" Del hitched his shoulders. "He's a gentleman for groundwork. Just don't try and ride him."

I half-turned and met Del's fleeting glance. "Then why is he here?"

A complicated mix of emotions crossed my father's face. "For some reason, the minute I saw him, I thought of you."

That set me back a pace. "Me?"

Del jammed his hands into his pockets and wouldn't look at me. "I thought ... well ... that you might come back someday. I thought you might need a nice horse to ride, so I bought him. Waste of money if you ask me."

It was the most he'd said to me since the day I arrived. He'd let his guard slip and must have instantly regretted it. This was a peace offering shrouded in insult.

I spit out a hard laugh. "What made you think I would ever want to come here?"

"You're here now, aren't you?"

I shut my mouth on all the arguments burning a hole in my gut.

Someone had to start to bridge our differences.

I turned to get a better look at the horse. He was solidly built, with sturdy legs, and a deep shoulder. For a stallion, he had a large, quiet eye. His hocks were clean too. No sign of curbs or spavins anywhere. He was all black, right down to his hooves. He had a lovely crest that would look nice under tack, and a broad forehead that suggested some intelligence there.

"He's pretty," I said, sensing this was exactly what my father wanted to hear. "Even with the scars."

Nothing could get past the wall my father had built up around his soul. Not even a compliment.

Del grumbled, "Yes, well, I saved him from the stockyards, so he owes me one. There's no such thing as a free horse. Costing me plenty in hay and feed. Chuck's been working with him. He won't accept a saddle, but he might work as a bareback act if we can get his mind to settle."

Poor Karma, I thought. You're just another casualty of my father's determination to prove his worth to the circus world.

I kept my anger in check this time. "Why is it so quiet around here? Where are all the clients? I would have thought you'd be booked solid by now, what with it being the off-season and all." I gave Karma one last pat on the neck and crutched my way out of his stall.

"I'm taking a bit of a break. Last year almost did me in. We had over forty horses in for training." My father moved aside to let me close Karma's door. His eyes challenged me. "I'm not as young as I used to be. I didn't book any clients in for this month. I might just take the whole winter season off this year." He looked like he was pitching for an argument, but I had no opinion one way or the other. He could do whatever the hell he wanted to as far as I was concerned.

"The only horses left belong to the ranch," he explained further. "Some of them are in training. Chuck handles that side of things. Lenora ... helps."

I'll bet she does, I thought, fuming.

I refrained from saying this out loud. Lenora had been nothing but charitable towards me, but I still had a lot to learn about forgiveness.

Chuck took my sulking in stride. "There's something else I want to show you."

More surprises?

I sighed inwardly.

I followed Chuck to the end of the corridor and out the back door.

Del left in the opposite direction.

The yard outside the backside of the barn was pleasantly shaded by a large overhang. It sheltered the machinery needed to keep a ranch running; tractor implements, harrows, and the like. The storage area was enclosed on two sides, with the opposite side of the barn left open to the elements. The ground was level and graveled for drainage, and the shaded overhang kept everything ten degrees cooler than the surrounding desert.

The back paddocks were visible through the open end. I could see a couple of horses lounging under a single tree. They dozed in the heat, swishing their tails and stamping at flies.

A few sparrows toughed out the heat in the exposed rafters over my head.

"What's this?" I asked, when Chuck presented me with what looked like a longish, low table, padded with horse blankets.

"I made it myself," he said proudly.

"Okay ..." I raised an eyebrow. "What's it for?"

"It's for you." He patted the thing like he was praising a dog. "Lie down on it."

I was instantly suspicious. "Why?"

"Because I'm going to put you back together again. Come on. Shirt off. On your stomach."

I didn't like the sound of this at all. "Is this going to hurt?"

"I'll have you crying by the end."

I started to limp off.

He barked out a laugh. "I'm joking! Don't run away. I'll go easy on you for today, I swear it."

"What exactly are you planning to do to me? And I'm *not* running away, just so you know."

He helped me out of my shirt. "You've been stuck in that brace for what, a couple of months now?"

"Yeah. But who's counting?"

"Take it off."

I would have to drop my pants to do that.

"The brace stays on," I stated tonelessly. I was still trying to forget Lester's hand cupped around my balls. Dropping my trousers for another man was the *last* thing I wanted to do.

Chuck held up his hands in surrender. "Okay, you're nervous. Understandable. Lie down."

I groaned and complained my way onto my stomach. I stretched out on the horse rugs and let my arms drop on either side of the bench. "It's already hurting ..." I bleated, feeling the strain in my shoulders.

Chuck slid an overturned bucket under the bench with his foot. "Here. Rest your hands on this."

I complied. I smelled the unmistakable stink of horse liniment wafting down on me and turned my head sideways so I could see what he was up to. "I sure hope you know what you're doing."

"No talking."

He rubbed the liniment between his palms and went to work, kneading the knots out of my spine.

"Everyone craves a human connection," Chuck said, noticing my apprehension in the tension carved into my shoulder blades. "Even you. Loneliness will kill a man faster than hunger. Without touch, we die. Maybe not the body. But the spirit? Yes."

For the next half hour, I floated away on a breeze of rubbing alcohol and cooling mint and something else mixed into the liniment that smelled a lot like Lenora's cold cream. I drifted on a sea of contentment. Any trepidation I'd had about having another man touching me melted away. I'd had so many doctors poke and prod me, stick me with pins and needles while they yanked on my bones that my instincts were honed to expect pain.

This was something close to bliss.

Chuck's hands could read my body like a roadmap. He brought me right to the point of painful manipulation, only to channel my resistance through his hands and bring me back down again. My muscles had been pushed to the limit of what they could endure without facing irreparable damage and walking with crutches had thrown my whole gait out of whack. It would take a lot more than one session on the table to straighten me out, but when Chuck was finally done with me, I was almost asleep and limp as a deboned fish.

"That's quite a nasty scar you have there." He traced the raised line of stitch marks under my right shoulder blade. "How did you get it?"

Tension instantly returned.

My voice was muffled by the horse rugs. "It's a long story."

He accepted my unwillingness to explain and backed off. "Every scar has a story to tell."

Ain't that the truth, I thought.

He rubbed more liniment into the base of my neck and pressed his thumb into the spot right where my spine connected to my skull. There was an insistent pain there. I squeezed my eyes tight and braced against it.

"Bad?" Chuck surmised.

"Bad," I agreed.

I changed the subject. "So, what's the deal with you and Lenora? Are you two related?"

"She's my niece. Her father is my brother, Hank Mescal."

I was going to have to work a little harder if I wanted more information.

I winced as he dug around in my flesh. "Hey, Chuck?"

"Yeah?"

"Why don't you ever go past the gate?"

I felt a hesitation slip through his fingertips.

I opened my mind a crack. *Careful,* the *magie* warned me. *Might be too soon for that.*

"Let me ask *you* something?" he said instead. "What did you see when you first laid eyes on Karma? I was watching you. You *left.* Only for a moment, but I saw it. Del saw it too. Where did you go?"

I decided to be polite this time. "I'd rather not talk about it, if you don't mind."

He kept me squirming on the hook. "You came here looking for answers, remember? How can I help you if you won't let me in? You can't fight this thing on your own, Vandy. That's what the entity *wants* you to do. It wants you to cower behind the lies. Hide in the shadows. You have to start trusting me, trusting *yourself.* You need to come out into the light—"

"All right!" God, I'd had enough preaching to last me a month of Sundays. I lowered my voice to something more civil. "If you must know, I've been having some ... *issues* ... with time. It keeps jumping ahead of me. One minute, I'm doing something perfectly ordinary. The next minute, I'm somewhere else. I can't remember how I got there, or what I've done in between. I know it sounds crazy ..."

He made no comment about the insanity reference, but he thought about what I'd said for a lot longer than I would have liked. "Could it be that your mind is trying to protect you from the violence of all this psychic stuff? That would make sense. You would need to keep a barrier between yourself and the magic. Especially if you're having problems controlling it."

"Who said I was having problems controlling it?"

"You did. When you talked in your sleep."

Goddammit.

I rested my cheek on the smelly horse blankets and dredged everything up from the muck in my soul, making sure grief didn't sneak up on me this time and derail my courage train. "My mother said if I didn't surrender myself to the *magie* then it would just keep taking over. But what she didn't know is that I've been ordered not to use it. I've seen what it can do. It can hurt people, Chuck. Cause their deaths. My mother called it a gift, but I know better. It's an evil, vicious thing. It masquerades as psychic ability. It followed my ancestors out of Romania, whatever *it* is, and it's attached itself to the family. Now that everyone is gone, it's stalking *me*. Killing little kids—"

My bravado failed me as the memory of Annie's death shuddered through my mind.

My voice trailed away.

Chuck's hands moved across my back, finding knots of pain everywhere. "Shit, Vandy, you're only what? Seventeen? You should be thinking about girls and shooting the lids off tin cans. Not going to war with a demonic spirit."

"I have to stop it." I heard the words coming from my mouth, but it was someone else saying them. Someone a hell of a lot braver than me. "I have to figure out how to use the *magie* without getting myself killed in the process. I don't know how I'm going to do that yet." I looked over into the corner where Annie sat on the ground, drawing funny little stick horses into the dirt with her fingertip. "One little girl is depending on me to get this right."

"Vandy?" Chuck's voice nudged me out of my musings. "Are you still with me?"

I faced forward again. "All the way to the bitter end, Chuck."

He didn't press me for more.

He wiped his hands on a towel. "That's enough for today. You're going to be sore in the morning. It's normal. I'll work on your leg next time."

I needed his help getting up off the bench. I grappled for my crutches, and I could already feel my wasted muscles complaining. "Can I ask you something else, Chuck?"

"You can try."

I stood under the roof of metal sheeting and open rafters and found the sudden silence unsettling. Even the sparrows had gone quiet.

I asked anyway. "What did you mean when you told me I had it all wrong?"

"When did I say that?"

I clamped my jaw tight to stop myself from mouthing off. He was deliberately picking at my vulnerabilities, trying to get me to open up, and I didn't like it. "That day you drove me down to the gate, remember? We were in my bedroom talking."

He set his capable hands on his hips and wagged his head at me. "You're not ready yet. You need time to heal. Get your strength back first, then we'll talk." He would have seen the worry flit across my face before I could tamp it down. "You're frightened, I know. I'm going to fix that too. I'm going to put you back together, and then I'm going to help you fight this thing."

I shielded my desperation behind teenage haughtiness. "I'm not scared."

He screwed the cap back on the liniment bottle and tucked it in his back pocket. "Well, I'm mighty glad to hear it."

"Then why are you keeping things from me?"

"Why? Maybe you should be asking *yourself* that question."

I watched him walk away; the man who promised to put me back together again. People were *always* walking away from me, and I had only myself to blame.

Chapter Ten

Deputy Sheriff, Tad Henley, arrived at precisely eight o'clock the next morning.

I was still asleep when my father rapped on my door. "Get up. There's a deputy here to see you. He wants to ask you some questions."

No *good morning*, or *how did you sleep*? He was as spare with his conversation as he was with everything else.

I don't know why Lenora put up with him.

"Shit." I muttered this low so he couldn't hear me, then called out loudly, "Be right there."

I reached for the brace hung over the chair beside the bed. My arm only got partway there before my muscles froze up like a rusted chain.

Chuck had warned me I'd be sore after the massage.

There was no way around it. I had to get out of bed, even if I had to hold on to the furniture to do it. I creaked and crawled my way out, and I *know* I whimpered a few choice expletives.

I wondered, when would I be free of this prison of pain?

I dressed myself in a clean shirt, raked my fingers through my hair, and buckled the brace around my leg. The day already felt old, and here I was, just getting up.

Del intercepted me in the hall. "How long are you going to keep using those crutches anyway? Isn't it about time you started walking on two legs again?"

I don't know why I was stunned. It was the same damn thing I'd been asking myself for months. Still, it was a knife to the guts coming from him.

My chest tightened into stone. I hid the fact that I was having trouble catching my breath behind an impassive façade. I would *die* before I let him see the hurt those callous words had carved into me.

My voice thinned. "What exactly do you suggest I do? Pretend none of this ever happened? Maybe I should I do a little dance for you. Would that make the great Del Davidson happy?"

His brows came down over keen gray eyes. "Don't be a smart-ass. I'm assuming this is only a preliminary investigation. Tell the deputy you don't remember what happened. With any luck, Lester will corroborate your story, and this will all go away."

I stared at his retreating back. I realized my mouth was hanging open. I shut it with a snap. My mind coughed up all sorts of nasty retorts I couldn't bring myself to say out loud.

Sometimes, I wondered if he was really my father at all.

There was no time to think up a suitable insult. Del hauled the door open, and there stood Deputy Tad Henley, looming large and imposing in the glare outside.

He wore the tan uniform and cowboy hat with that same entitlement I'd come to expect from everyone wearing a badge, and I took an instant dislike to him. He was out to ruffle some feathers, and by the look on his squarish face, he would enjoy every minute of it.

I looked past him.

Lester Simmons was in the Model A parked in the yard. The one with a big gold star painted on the side.

Lester met my glance briefly before putting a bandaged hand up to his face, shielding me from his shame.

Del's presence filled the doorway. "Would you like to come in, Deputy Henley?"

Henley hitched up his pants by the broad leather belt he wore around his paunch and declined the offer. He remained out there in the sunlight and squinted his beady eyes at me. "This your son?"

No way I could miss the surprise in his tone. I don't know what he was expecting. By the look on his face, it wasn't some lanky, long-haired Romanian Gypsy with only one good leg to stand on. He stared me down, then threw a skeptical glance back to Lester, who just sank lower down in his seat in the cop car.

Del pulled the door wider. "You're sure you wouldn't be more comfortable inside? Lenora's made coffee."

"That Indian squaw?" Deputy Henley flipped open his notebook and drew a pencil from behind his ear. "No, thank you. I'll pass."

That Indian squaw?

I gaped at Del. "Are you just going to stand there and let him get away with that?"

He scowled back. "Stop it."

Fury was a pressure building behind my eyes. I stared into Henley's black soul and met fire with fire. "Her name is Lenora."

My father stepped between me and the deputy.

I had to tilt my head back to meet his gaze.

"You don't know how things are done out here," he uttered tersely. "Mind your own business. Just answer the deputy's questions and leave the rest alone, all right?"

My face burned. "And how *exactly* are things done out here anyway?"

"Don't be an idiot," he hissed out. "I'm trying to protect you."

Deputy Henley wrote all this down in his notepad.

I passed my crutches to Del, a little more forcibly than I meant to, but it got my point across.

I faced Deputy Henley with both feet on the floor this time. I couldn't have taken a single step without falling flat on my face, but he didn't need to know that. Appearances could be deceiving, and I was banking on it. "What exactly can I help you with, Deputy Henley?"

"State your full name for the record," he grunted, pencil poised in hand.

"Vandemere Alexander Petruska."

Del interjected. "His name is Vandemere Alexander Davidson. Not Petruska."

I clenched my teeth while my mind seethed.

"Date of birth?"

"June 5th, 1922."

"That makes you, what ...?"

"Seventeen," I replied tonelessly.

He flicked a glance at me. "Place of birth?"

"In a circus trailer."

"I meant, what *city*?"

Del answered for me. "Des Moines, Iowa. I have his birth record if you want to see it."

"*I'd* like to see it," I started to say, but the deputy waved his hand like he was swatting at bugs. "No need."

I scowled.

He gave my father a sympathetic headshake that wrapped his opinion of me in a tidy little package. "Tell me what happened in the desert."

"I can't remember."

Hard eyes studied my bland expression. "You can't remember?"

"I must have hit my head, or something." I touched the back of my head for effect. "My memory's a blank."

"There's a dead horse out there," he pointed out.

My voice cracked; all beyond my control. "Yes. That's Dolly."

"So, you *do* remember some of it?"

Del's looming presence behind me was all the convincing I needed to bite my lip and stay silent.

The deputy pressed on. "Did Lester have anything to do with the horse dying?"

Grief was another wound that hadn't healed yet and it showed up in the pitch of my tone. "Why do you ask that?"

"Just doing my job," he said.

It took a conscious effort to steady myself. "No, he didn't. Dolly was old. She had a bad heart. We got caught in the dust storm." I left the part out where she had died defending me from a rampaging demon.

I was struck with a sudden image of her; my old Dolly lying on her side, her white coat gone all dirty where it had once gleamed under the spotlights, her body resting on the desert sand, and her milky eye staring sightlessly into the sun.

Sadness drove a red-hot poker deep into my chest.

All I wanted was my horse back.

I bent my head and grieved.

Deputy Henley seemed oblivious to human misery and carried on. "Did you and Lester get into a fight? He was found wandering down the road, dazed and bleeding. Did you hit him with something?"

I looked past Deputy Henley to the car out front.

Lester Simmons hunkered down in the front seat.

I asked, "Is he okay? I mean ... he's not hurt badly, is he?"

"He'll be fine," Henley grunted. "He's got some broken fingers. Doctor Franklin sewed up a gash in his head too. He'll have a scar though."

I got the distinct impression that Deputy Henley had already decided this was *my* fault.

"My son showed up here with blood all over him too," Del put in. "Maybe you ought to ask Lester if he did something to *him*, instead of the other way around?"

"Is this true?" Henley's sweaty gaze searched mine. "Did Lester hurt you?"

Hurt me? He pinned me down and grabbed me between the legs, and then he tried to kill me. Yes, he hurt me—*badly*. But it wasn't him. He didn't have a choice, and if I tell on him, he'll be run out of town. I know it, and he knows it too. You only have to look at him to see the shame in his eyes.

I didn't say this out loud. It wouldn't have done either of us any favors to speak that kind of truth.

I put on my best grifter's face. "No. He was kind to me. He let me borrow his truck. I needed a ride here to the ranch and he told me to take it. I don't know how he was injured. We parted ways after ... well, after my horse passed away." I choked a bit on that. "I'd come a long way on the train. I wasn't prepared for the heat, or the storm. It was too much for Dolly ..."

The deputy had no use for anything that hinted at emotional weakness.

He trained beady eyes on my father. "I'm going to have to be honest with you, Mr. Davidson. If this boy showed up on my doorstep banged up like that, I'd have to assume he must have done something to deserve it. It's my opinion that your son attacked Lester out there in the desert and stole his truck. Lester probably gave your boy those injuries defending himself. For some reason, he's being very unhelpful at the moment." Henley gathered his disgust into a scowl and aimed it at the man sitting in the car behind him.

Lester only sunk down lower.

He turned back. "Did you know your son is wanted for murder?"

I forgot all about my bad leg. I forgot my father was standing beside me and that I'd been warned to behave myself.

"You lying son of a—"

My father put his hand on my chest.

I leaned against it. "Arrest me then." I held out my hands and offered them to the deputy. "Go ahead. Slap the cuffs on me. You can't though, can you. Because I didn't do anything—"

Del's fingers fisted into the folds of my shirt. Anger got mixed up with thoughts I didn't understand; the way his knuckles tightened into the fabric, his palm damp from something I couldn't put a name to. A glimmer of fear seeped through his flattened expression.

Shut up and let me handle this.

I heard his voice speaking in my head.

My gaze jerked up.

My father stared straight ahead. As always, he was dressed impeccably, wearing a clean cotton shirt tucked into dark blue trousers, his collar pressed into a crisp point. The vee of his throat was as tanned as an old shoe. He shaved every day without fail, and his neatly trimmed hair made my own look like a tornado had gone through it. He was precise in everything he did, never once showing an inkling of trepidation ... until now.

A slow trickle of sweat made its way along the corner of my father's eye. "I know about the little girl, Deputy Henley. I've been in contact with Lieutenant Dawson and the Oklahoma City Police Department. I know for a fact there's been no warrant issued for my son's arrest. You're just trying to scare him into confessing to something he hasn't done."

I steadied myself against the hand that restrained me and remembered to shut my mouth this time.

Waves of anger radiated off Henley's braced shoulders. His eyes were narrow and mean. "There's no warrant *yet*. He is, however, in possession of some stolen property. At the very least, I could charge him with theft."

"Or," Del countered, "I could *give* you the book and you could pass it along to Lieutenant Dawson, and then you can brag about how you solved the crime of the century to everyone in town."

Deputy Tad Henley stood in my father's shadow, hitching up his belt, and he made a point of letting his hand linger on the weapon holstered on his hip. Del's insult must have drawn blood under the badge on his chest. He was accustomed to using it as both his shield and the ironclad justification for his bullying. His pupils shrank into dots and his sallow skin was bathed in sweat. I could smell the stink of wounded arrogance coming off him. I think if I'd been alone with him, trapped in some back room in the sheriff's office, my chances of coming out of this interrogation with my limbs intact would be thrown into serious question.

"Lester Simmons has refused to press charges against your boy." It pained Henley to say this. "Rest assured, the minute I have grounds to arrest him, I'll be back here with reinforcements."

Del was a lot more accommodating. "I'll get the book. Wait here."

"Don't—" I whispered.

He shot me a look that kicked me right back to my childhood; the Del Davidson who ruled my existence without any of the responsibility that came with parenting. To say that I was angry was an understatement.

He left to get the book. He left me in the direct sights of a man who wanted nothing better than to beat me just because he felt like it. The metal star Deputy Henley wore over his heart was the only alibi he needed to lord his power over those who had none. He reminded me of Sal in a lot of ways, and frankly, I was sick of looking at him.

"I can't find it," Del said, coming back at last. He glided down the hall and stood at my side again. There was nothing in his expression to suggest he was lying. He glared at me. "Where did you put it?"

"It was on the nightstand next to my bed. Right under Ma's ashes." It was tantamount to swearing the truth with my hand on a Bible.

"Well, it's not there now," Del insisted.

This was just more ammunition Henley could use against me. He watched me argue with my father, and I could almost hear him thinking, *give me five minutes with him. I'll knock some respect into that mouth of his.*

I leaned my hand against the wall and propped myself up. "If you give him the book, we'll never see it again. He'll keep it for himself and say I stole it." I cast a withering sneer at Henley. "Wait for Lieutenant Dawson to get here. It belongs to him. This pig will just wipe his ass with it."

"That's some boy you got there," Henley drawled. "You must be so proud." Civility was clearly not his strong suit, but Del must have earned some respect with the locals over the years and it was indicative of his clout that Henley limited himself to sarcasm.

"My son hasn't been well," Del offered as an explanation. "He broke his leg some months ago. An accident in the ring. He's still getting over it."

Henley licked the end of his pencil and scratched something down in his notepad. "I heard about that. It's very nice of you to offer him a place to stay during his convalescence."

"Thank you. This has been hard on all of us."

I snorted.

Tad Henley rounded on me. "You make sure you thank your father for letting you stay here. I've heard about you, Vandemere Petruska. All you circus clowns... you're all the same. Circus comes to town and trouble follows. Upsetting good, honest folk. Nothing but a bunch of crooks and con artists if you ask me." He jabbed his pencil towards my face. "You should get a haircut too. You're not at the circus anymore. You'd do well to remember that *freak*."

My smile was dangerously calm. "Don't call me that."

He bared his teeth and grinned, filing my reaction away for future use. I'd given him a weapon to use against me. I'd let him get to me and he knew it.

My father interrupted me before I could talk myself into an early grave. "We'll find that book, Deputy Henley. I'll turn it over to the Oklahoma City Police Department. You have my word."

Anyone else would have taken this as a sign the interview was over. Henley, however, gave no indication he was leaving, so Del was forced to ask, "Is there anything else I can help you with?"

Henley hitched up his pants again and sniffed. "The boy's story matches up with Lester's. I'll have to clear it with the brass, but there's nothing more I can do here. If I were you though, I'd keep your son on a short leash from now on. Scottsdale can be rough on an outsider. I'd hate for something to happen to him. Good day, Mr. Davidson."

He took his sweet time sauntering down the flagstone path back to his vehicle. We both watched as he got in beside Lester and rolled away in a cloud of dust.

I unleashed all my pent-up anger on Del as soon as it was safe. "You didn't need to defend me like that. I've been taking care of things ever since you left. Don't think you can start being my father now just because I'm living under your roof."

All the things he wanted to say to me were piling up like storm clouds behind his silence. I only knew this because the same thing was happening to me. We would never get past this animosity without someone conceding, and neither one of us had the guts to go first.

His mouth trembled but his eyes remained stern. "I should never have left you with your mother. She ruined you."

His statement sent shockwaves through me. I had no idea how badly words could hurt until they were uttered by a man who should have loved me for all that I was and all that he had decided I wasn't.

My vision swam. "Why do you hate me so much?"

He held out the crutches, daring me to take them back.

I fell victim to his cruelty all over again and choked on my own defeat. "Burn them. Crutches are for sissies, right? You were the one who taught me that."

Chapter Eleven

I escaped to the sanctuary of the stable as often as I could. As long as my father wasn't around, the hours spent around the horses calmed the anxiety his presence needled under my skin.

Chuck was a lot nicer to talk to. He didn't seem to mind me getting in the way of his routine and I think he liked the company.

When I wasn't pestering the horses, I spent many hours lying prone on Chuck's medieval rack, trying not to whimper as he kneaded the knots out of my spine.

Liber Mortuorum had miraculously showed up the day after Henley's visit, despite us having looked everywhere for it. It was back on the nightstand right where I left it, but no one believed me when I said so.

"*I looked there,*" Del insisted. I heard him talking to Lenora through the walls between us. "If it was on the nightstand, I would have seen it. Vandy must have hidden it and brought it back after the deputy left."

Of course, he would blame me.

I should have paid more attention to this psychic anomaly. As with everything else in my life, I had to learn things the hard way.

I finally got to see the spiritual side of Chuck Mescal. A week after Henley's visit, he laid me out on his torture table like Christ at the crucifixion and decorated my body with tumbled stones of white quartz and some of Ma's turquoise.

I squirmed. "This is stupid."

"No talking." He dragged some more buckets over to support my arms and proceeded to put a few grains of desert sand on each of my upturned wrists. "Just *trust* me. Close your eyes."

I did what he asked.

He placed a polished stone of amethyst on each of my closed eyelids and set about smudging me with a raven's feather and some sweetgrass and sage.

I felt myself being transported into a mysterious world of Apache *magie* that rivaled my own. He hummed a throaty chant over my prone form and blew smoke into my face. It might have been wishful thinking, but I sensed the chains of anxiety releasing their hold from around my mind.

I took a deep breath; something I hadn't been able to do in months, and let it out in a long, slow sigh.

Everything was going well until Chuck placed Dawson's copy of *Liber Mortuorum* on my chest.

Instantly, I stiffened. "What are you doing?"

"You said you weren't afraid of anything," he reminded me.

"Yeah, but ..."

"*But* nothing. It doesn't matter if you lie to me, Vandy. What *does* matter is that you're lying to yourself. Pay attention to what your body is telling you."

It was no surprise to anyone that when I got scared, I covered it up with anger. "I don't want to do this."

He put both hands on my shoulders and pinned me to the bench.

This was too much like the rabbit hole. Too much like being buried alive. He was going to use the book as a source of connection to the Underworld and I didn't like it. He was going to ask me to tap into the *magie*… after I'd been warned repeatedly *not to*.

I threw off his hands and bolted upright. The crystals scattered, and Dawson's book landed in my lap. "I said, I don't want to do this!"

He pressed me. "What did you see just then?"

"N—Nothing," I stammered. "Why? What did *you* see?"

He had that shuttered look about him. The one people get when the laws of nature become unreliable, and they can't wrap their minds around a different perspective. "Nothing."

Neither of us wanted to call the other's bluff.

I handed him Dawson's book. "I'm leaving."

Chuck's reprimand chased me out of the storage shed. "You can't keep running away from this. Eventually, you're going to run out of desert!"

***

Running was the furthest thing from my mind. Without the crutches, I was forced to limp at a laborious pace that wouldn't get me anywhere fast. I made the trip across the yard every morning one slow step at a time, looking for things to grab hold of to keep myself from capsizing. I had to test my weight on my bad leg first before I committed to putting my foot down, expecting to fall on my face at any moment. Each time my leg held, I wasn't sure if I should cheer or cry. The pain was horrible, but it was no worse than the words my father had uttered to my face. As much as I smarted over Del's hurtful words, I forced myself to accept the truth. I couldn't depend on a pair of crutches for the rest of my life, so I put on a brave face every morning and stared down a dubious future without them.

I still wore the leg brace, but even that came off after Dr. Franklin's next visit.

Thanks to me, it would be the last time we'd ever see Dr. Franklin at the house again.

He took his sweet time checking me over. I didn't really need a doctor's visit. The bruises and scrapes had long since disappeared, and the hole in my thigh was almost healed now, though I still had a long, granular scab over a wound that oozed yellowish fluid into the pad of bandages.

"Normal for this sort of thing," Dr. Franklin assured me.

"Coffee, Dr. Franklin?" Lenora was already setting the cup and saucer down in front of him. He made himself at home at our table, admiring the view through the towering panes of glass that overlooked the miles of desert beyond.

"You know I can't say no to your coffee, Lenora." He turned away from the heat-rippled landscape to give me a devious wink.

I sat in the chair next to his, only because I didn't trust Dr. Franklin to mind his manners if I left him alone with Lenora. I suspected the visit was more about his attraction to Lenora and less about my health.

I narrowed my eyes at him.

"I have some biscuits in the outside oven," Lenora replied. "They should be done now."

He pinched her bottom as she walked away.

I heard her breath catch in her throat. Her expression froze, and her eyes widened.

Dr. Franklin smiled, showing off a full set of crooked teeth. “Nice and firm,” he said to me. “Just the way I like my women ...”

I slammed my hand down over his fingers where they rested on the table and bent them backwards. Not too hard. Just enough to get his attention.

He threw his head back and yelped. He looked more surprised than hurt.

“You touch her again and I’ll break your fingers,” I said coldly.

He ripped his hand from mine.

“Vandy!” Lenora’s eyes were round with shock. She pressed her hands over her mouth. “Dr. Franklin! I am so sorry!”

“Don’t apologize to him!” I snapped back.

“How dare you!” Dr. Franklin rubbed the ache out of his fingers and vented his rage on me. “After everything I’ve done for you, *this* is how you repay me? Stupid boy. I should have known better." He pursed his lips like a woman and wagged his head at me. “Everyone kept telling me not to trust you. Seeing as you were Del Davidson’s son, I thought you might be salvageable. Serves me right.”

“He didn’t mean it, Dr. Franklin,” Lenora wailed.

“Yes, I did,” I returned mildly.

Dr. Franklin rose from the chair so abruptly it scraped across the flagstones. “You should be more careful, young man.” He aimed a thick finger at my face, tempting me to have another go at it. “The desert can hide a lot of mistakes.”

I laughed. “Oh yeah? So can I.”

He gathered up his black bag and stormed out of the house, but not before he called me a filthy Gypsy, and a freak, and a lot of other unflattering things, most of which I’d heard before, from far better people.

"Why did you do that?!" Lenora cried. "Dr. Franklin is married to the sheriff's *sister!* Do you know how much trouble he could make for us? For you?"

I didn't understand her anger. "Dr. Franklin is an idiot."

"You shouldn't have threatened him like that, Vandy. You come from a different world. You don't know how things are out here." She teetered on the verge of tears.

"Why are you mad at *me*? You let him handle you like you were nothing better than an old cow."

Her whole body shook. Everything vibrated from the top of her head, right down to her bare toes. "You *don't know*, Vandy! How can you? You're ... you're a ..."

I felt the blood seeping out of my face. "I'm a what? *Say it*. I'm just a dirty Gypsy, right?"

She held my gaze defiantly. "You're *white*."

My mouth fell open.

She grabbed Dr. Franklin's cup and saucer from the table and almost dropped it. "I know what you're thinking; oh, the poor, helpless Indian woman. She needs a white man to defend her. Heaven help me! When you cause trouble with Dr. Franklin, we all pay for it. Mind your own business from now on, all right?"

Where the hell was this anger coming from?

"I didn't protect you because you're an Indian," I argued, half rising in my chair. "I protected you because you're a *woman*."

"And you'll get yourself killed because of it!" she hollered back. "I can't let that happen again. *I won't*. Just leave it alone!"

I sat back down again, stunned into silence. Shame warmed my cheeks, worse than a slap. I'd been so focused on my own righteous indignation; I'd forgotten all about hers.

Lenora gave up fighting back her tears and fled through the back door, running off to feed her chickens or rip some weeds out of the garden. Neither Lenora nor Chuck ever went further than the gate down at the road, but behind the house, the desert held no borders.

She wouldn't go far. It was too hot, and she hadn't taken any water with her.

You must always take water with you out into the desert.

Where had I heard that before?

But Lenora was a lot smarter than I was. She would hide in the shade, talk to the hens, and leave the desert alone.

Chuck was the one who liked the open spaces. Sometimes, I would see him way off in the distance; a shadow moving through a liquid horizon. He would saddle up one of Del's horses and ride out into the blistering heat, coming back long after the sun sank into the west.

As luck would have it, he was still in the barn and not somewhere out in the barren wilderness.

I hobbled into the breezeway at a snail's pace, minus the crutches and brace.

Chuck spotted me from the end of the barn. He came down the corridor, all smiles. He seemed to never get tired of seeing me walk into the stable every day on two legs when my own father couldn't stand to be in the same room with me.

He took one look at my ashen pallor and the smile faded from his face. "What happened?"

I sighed. "I messed up."

He cocked his head. "That bad, is it?"

"Worse," I wailed.

"Come with me," was all he said.

Chuck waited patiently at the end door while I negotiated my way down the length of the barn, taking things step by step.

Karma was far more interested in me than he was in eating. He stuck his lovely head over the door and swiveled his ears towards me.

I stopped at his stall, glad of the rest, and I reached out a hand to him.

He shrank back, still unsure of me.

Chuck had always been the one to ride him. I'd seen him walking the horse out past the fence border until they were just a black speck in the distance. The stallion had been a jangle of nerves the whole time. When they came back an hour later, Karma's chest was lathered with sweat and his nostrils flared with every gasp.

"You could have a chat with him," Chuck suggested, coming back to stand at my side. "Find out what he's so afraid of."

"It's not that easy." I refrained from mentioning the *last* time I tried connecting to an animal trapped in a cage, I'd ended up in a field a mile from home with a child's abduction branded on my back. "He's not ready to let me in yet." I sent out tendrils of *magie* into the ebb and flow of Karma's energy even though I wasn't supposed to, and I came up against a huge wall of resistance. "He's stuck somewhere, and he doesn't know how to let go."

Chuck chuffed out a laugh. "Sounds like someone else I know."

I offered my palm to the stallion, but he politely declined and went back to eating his lunch.

Chuck led the way through the end door and over to the padded bench. At his unspoken word, I laid down on the horse blankets. This daily ritual challenged my endurance. I rested on my back and stared up at the rafters while Chuck went to work on my leg.

He tested the stiffness in my knee, bending it cautiously. "Tell me when it's too much."

I winced and sucked in a short gasp. "That's too much."

He went ahead and bent it some more.

I almost fell off the bench. "Shit! Chuck, not so hard!"

He'd numbed himself to my complaints long ago and dug his fingertips into the spasming muscles in my calf. "You ditched the brace, I see," he said unnecessarily.

I held my breath. Answered tightly, "Yeah—I figured it was time." I felt like the Tin Man from *The Wonderful Wizard of Oz*. I could almost hear the creaking in my joints.

"So? What happened?"

I covered my face with my hands so Chuck wouldn't see me grimacing. "I'm an idiot. I'm so sorry, Lenora."

A ripple in the *magie* told me Lenora had followed me down to the barn. She'd slipped into the storage building behind me and plonked herself down on an overturned bucket while I wasn't looking. She'd come in on silent feet, and her presence comforted me in a way that reminded me of my mother.

"How did you know I was here?" She was intrigued but not quite ready to forgive.

Chuck chimed in. "I told you, Lenora. He has a gift."

"A curse, you mean." I dragged my hands away from my face and let them rest down at my sides. "I never thought ... well, I'm sorry if I hurt your feelings, Lenora. I thought I was protecting your honor. Sometimes the *magie* leaves me stranded." I sighed. "I'm just another stupid white man who doesn't know when to keep his big mouth shut. Is there anything I can do to make it up to you? You can call me a dirty Gypsy if you want to. Call me anything you like if it will help."

Chuck went to work on a tight tendon beside my kneecap. "Who called you a dirty Gypsy?"

"Every ... one ... does." I dug my fingernails into the bench as he unearthed nuggets of pain.

"That's not very nice. If I call you a dirty Gypsy, I'm no better than my enemy. Hate can't be defeated by more hate. That only leads to war. Believe me, Lenora and I have seen plenty of *that*."

"Is that why you don't go further than the gate? I had a run-in with the Bronson brothers when I got off the train in Tempe. I can see why you're nervous. People in town are just looking for an excuse to run you out of town. If it hadn't been for Daniel ..."

"Daniel *Bronson*?"

"Yeah. He remembered my name from Del's stories. He asked me to show him a trick or two. Dolly could have done a nice turn for him. But me? Not so much. He gave me this bandanna as a gift." My hand went to the folded band of cotton I'd tied around my neck. "Once you get past that rough exterior, he's really very nice. People have already made up their minds about the Bronson brothers. If they would only take the time to get to know them, they would see they're not so bad."

"Are we talking about the *same* Bronson brothers?" Chuck bent my knee towards my chest and pulled a whimper out of me. "Because if we are, they're the meanest sons-of-bitches in the west."

"See, that's what I'm talking about. You don't know them like I do. They're actually a nice bunch of thugs, once you talk them out of busting your head in."

He laughed, but Lenora remained cautious.

"Be careful, Vandy," she said. "Chuck's not joking around. You stay away from them. Especially now that you've made Dr. Franklin and Tad Henley mad. They don't like outsiders. You go into town and there's bound to be trouble. Stay here with us, where it's safe."

"You made Dr. Franklin mad?" Chuck asked.

"It's nothing," Lenora said quickly, keeping it just between her and me.

I turned my head and gave her a bleary smile. "I sorry, Lenora. I hope I haven't done anything to call out the torch and pitchfork brigade. Or a posse. Del's going to kill me when he finds out."

The joke about the pitchforks made her laugh. She sat on the metal bucket like she'd been doing this all her life—watching the world go by from a safe distance. She had one leg crossed over the other so she could rest her chin in her hand. Her eyes peered out from behind a guarded expression that never went away, no matter how hard I tried to make her smile. She wore a white blouse and pretty skirt today. Her hair flowed down her back in soft waves, with pieces of it gathered behind her ears in a pair of matching silver combs. "Well, at least you're man enough to apologize. Most people wouldn't. I accept your apology."

"Most people wouldn't."

Her laugh was genuine this time. "You're a funny kid."

I blushed. "I can do tricks too."

"On horseback?"

"Not yet." Sadness crept in and hollowed out my confidence. "Card tricks. If you get my tarot deck for me, I'll show you."

She left on two lovely legs that worked better than mine and went back to the house to hunt up my mother's cards.

"Your knee is seized up bad," said Chuck. He worked at the hinge in my left knee until the joint stopped creaking. "You still have a long way to go. All those weeks in traction turned your joints to jam. Your muscles are weak, and your right leg is all in knots from being overworked."

"Tell me something I *don't* know. Where did you learn all this anyway?"

"From a Chinese prostitute."

"*What?!*"

"*What nothing!*" His grin threw shades of indignation at me. "I'll have you know I've had my share of lady friends. I don't look like much now, but back when I was young, I was quite the charmer."

I sputtered, "*Well* ..."

"What about you?"

"What about me?"

"You got a sweetheart? A good-looking kid like you must have a girl in every town. Or are you a heartbreaker? The love-em-and-leave-em kind of cowboy."

My memories glanced off Sylvia Reinhart's disdain for me and landed squarely on Ellen Dawson. She'd been in my thoughts more times than I cared to admit. I'd put it down to homesickness, and grief over losing Dolly, and my mother. There was a hole in my heart that needed patching up, and Ellen was just the one to do it.

"No," I answered finally. "There's no one. There *was* a girl, but I think she's probably forgotten about me by now. I was mean to her. Not *that* way," I added quickly, when Chuck's brows arched. "She said she liked me. I pushed her away." I almost told him about Grace too, but her suicide was still a shameful stain on my soul, and I wasn't brave enough to face it yet.

"Why did you do that? The love of a good woman doesn't come around more than once or twice in your lifetime. What are you so afraid of? And don't say *nothing*."

I shrugged, looking up at the sparrows bouncing around in the spiderweb of rafters over my head.

Where would I even start?

"Oh ... you know. Things."

He loosened the spasm coursing through my right calf while I burned at the stake. "You can trust me you know, if you want to get things off your chest."

My courage retreated back into its shell. “So you can use it against me?” I spat out a bitter laugh. “I don’t think so.”

Chuck’s expression perfectly summed up his unbending humanity toward me. I’d insulted him with my thoughtless comment and his only reaction was to draw a curtain across his hurt feelings and ease my leg back down. He’d been unfailingly kind to me and here I was treating him like dirt.

I wanted to run and hide from the shame.

Chuck looked like he wanted to say something more, but Lenora arrived just in time with the tarot cards still wrapped in my mother’s silk scarf.

She handed them to me, sparing me from further interrogation.

I hung my legs over the side of the bench and darted my eyes away from Chuck’s hurt expression.

Lenora giggled like a little kid as she watched me shuffle the cards at breakneck speed. “This is so exciting!”

I smiled even though my heart wasn’t in it. “It’s just a grifter’s trick. I use it sometimes when I’m short on cash. Can’t make much of a living on what Jimmy pays me. It’s easy to find a townie or two to dupe behind the big top. Sucker gets his money’s worth in entertainment, and I get to lighten his wallet. Works out fine for everyone.”

“So, what you’re really doing is robbing the public,” said Chuck.

Nice of him to put it so bluntly.

“It’s not *stealing*," I countered, “It’s gambling. There’s difference.”

He made a derisive sound in his throat. “If you say so. Last time I checked, this state had laws against gambling and grifter’s tricks. Not to mention you’re underage.”

Lieutenant Dawson’s voice echoed in my head. I was suddenly aware of the miles between me and anything familiar. Homesickness always caught me off guard, and I had to scramble to put up defensive walls around the sudden onslaught of emotions. I still mourned for my mother. Grief from her passing left a void in my soul that couldn't be filled with words of condolence, no matter how sincere. Dolly's death only compounded the emptiness. I'd lost the two most important constants in my life all within weeks of each other, and I was still reeling from disbelief. My mother's love had been wrenched from me at a time when I needed her the most, and the loss was a physical ache that never went away.

I was just really good at hiding it now.

I cut the deck into two piles and laid them down on the horse blankets. I don't think anyone noticed my fingers trembling.

"There's a card missing from the deck," I explained. "I left it behind ... somewhere." I avoided Lenora's searching look. God, those words were tough to get out. "I can make do with what I have."

Lenora drew closer. Her hair fell forward over her slim shoulder when she leaned against my side. "How does it work?"

"Tap your finger on the half-deck you want me to work with."

"Either one?"

"Any one you like."

She hemmed and hawed over the two halves for a moment, then tapped the left pile. "This one."

I picked up the cards and shuffled again.

Tarot cards floated between my hands.

Her eyes tried to keep up—and she wasn't mad at me anymore, so I put some extra flair into the performance.

"How do you do that?" she asked, in breathless awe.

I gave her a sad grin. "Magic."

I finished up and fanned all the cards so that the corner of each one showed equally. I kept them face down. "Now, pick any card. Don't let me see it."

Lenora's excitement was contagious. She drew a card and pressed it to her breast.

Even Chuck was interested. "Which one is it?" he asked, looking over her shoulder.

She let him see it.

He nodded in appreciation. "Nice."

I joined the two halves of the deck back together again and asked her to place her card back on top, which she did. I shuffled the whole deck once more. I felt my mother's presence in the cards. Felt her watching over me. I blinked hard enough to send the tears back where they came from and straightened the deck until I had them in a solid block again.

I asked Lenora to remove the top card.

"Don't show me," I instructed. "Take a peek at it. Is it the card you picked?"

She kept her hand over the card as she glanced at it. I could see her disappointment. "It isn't. This card says *Strength*. Mine was different."

"Are you sure?" I gave Chuck a wink. "Maybe you should look at it again?"

She did as I asked and gasped. "What? How—?"

"A magician *never* reveals his secrets," I replied, laughing. It was nice to see her smiling again.

Her eyes were huge. "That's amazing, Vandy!"

Suddenly, I was very pleased with myself. "It's just a trick. Was I right?"

"Yes! This is the card I picked out." She turned the card around and held it out to me, beaming.

It was *The Moon*.

Chapter Twelve

I stared at the card for what felt like an eternity.

Lenora touched my arm. "Vandy? Are you okay?"

Logic deserted me.

"I ..."

I put a hand to my temple. Was I dreaming? I took the tarot card from her. Realized my mouth was hanging open and shut it quickly. "This shouldn't be here. I left it ..."

I drew in a ragged breath. "Who did this? One of you? Did Del put you up to this? Sounds like something he would do. Let's put one over on the circus *freak,* huh?"

Chuck looked as confused as I was. "What?"

I practically shoved the card in his face. "*The Moon*. It's not supposed to *be here*."

"You're not making any sense," Chuck argued. "Where did you leave it?"

I couldn't answer. Not with both of them looking at me like I was missing a few marbles. I would have to explain everything. I would have to tell them about Dolly's sacrifice and Lester's attack, how *Cel*

Care Ia had used him to take me down. Saying it out loud would shatter me with a grief I was trying so desperately to forget.

Lenora wasn't put off by my strange, sudden anger. She put a light hand on mine. "You're obviously upset about something. Tell us, what is it? Let us help you."

I couldn't, of course. It wasn't the Del Davidson way, to ask for help. But she looked so worried; I gave her a wan smile. Her kindness was more than I deserved. "Don't pay any attention to me. I don't know what I'm saying. I think I just got confused is all." I placed *The Moon* back into the tarot deck and wrapped the square of blue silk around it. I would need time to decipher its sudden appearance. Time with the *magie*. Time with my mother.

I stayed in my room for the rest of the day, listening to Lenora's hens gather outside under my window. Their contented crooning kept the loneliness from becoming unbearable.

When I couldn't sit up any longer, I rested in bed on my back. Every inch of me had a different kind of ache, thanks to Chuck's Chinese prostitute and her giving ways. But I *was* making progress. It might have been my imagination, but it seemed I could bend my knee better after Chuck worked on it. There were times I even kept my balance for longer than a minute without any support. Giving up the crutches had left me teetering between panic and terror. I was like a toddler learning to walk all over again. I suffered a new kind of hell every time I thought my leg wouldn't hold me and I was nowhere near a chair, or one of Lenora's rose bushes. But I hadn't actually *fallen* yet. Strength was a state of mind, and I had to trust it to lead me back to life.

Strength.

Sometimes, it came from the unlikeliest of places.

I held the tarot card up over my head, gazing at it until my arms ached. I lay in the stifling gloom of a curtained afternoon while *The Moon* looked down on me.

Had my mother had something to do with its sudden reappearance? Was she trying to send me a message? Letting me know she was looking out for me.

When the card got too heavy, I let my hands drop to my chest. I pressed *The Moon* against the sad beat of my heart and searched the corners of the room for any trace of her.

My gaze fell on her jar of ashes next to the oil lamp. "Ma?" I whispered. "Can you hear me?"

I didn't expect her to answer. She hadn't come to me yet in a way that I could recognize. My experiences with the dead varied from slight vibrations to all-out war. My mother would need to learn how to reconnect with me. She needed time. Unfortunately, time meant nothing to the dead, even though it meant *everything* to the living.

"Ma? Please, talk to me." The lump in my throat felt like a hot coal. I missed my mother and Dolly so much it damn near killed me.

I fell asleep listening to the clatter of Lenora getting dinner on the table, and if I dreamed of death, it remained mercifully buried in my subconscious mind.

***

At Chuck's insistence, I stopped sleeping in till all hours of the day. I took to rising early. Most mornings, I tottered across the yard before sun-up. There was a certain kind of peace in the routine that drew me to the barn at dawn, and if it meant I could spend a few hours away from Del's disparaging looks, then I was willing to sacrifice a few extra hours of sleep.

My father had smoothed things over with Dr. Franklin. I think it involved a fair bit of money. I expected a lecture when he came home from town that day but all I got was the usual austere disinterest from a man who might as well have been a stranger.

The desert more than made up for my father's indifference.

I never realized how much I'd missed it since we'd visited Scottsdale back when I was a child. I'd forgotten what the desert *smelled* like. How the sunrise painted the eastern sky in a riot of color. How the air held a perfume of earthy notes and creosote that lingered in the back of my memories.

We'd gotten a few storms lately; some real bangers that shook the ground and woke everyone up in the middle of the night. After it rained, the land came alive with new growth and prosperity. It reestablished the ground water levels, and the windmill at the corner of the property didn't have to work so hard to flush the water to the surface. We filled buckets and barrels to the brim. I started taking baths in the horse trough outside in the paddocks when it got too hot to stay in the house. The horses didn't seem to mind as long as I cleaned it out afterward.

Lenora's roses warmed to the new dawn. I stopped to bury my face in their sweet blooms on my way to the barn, more to rest and wait out the pain than anything else, but it was a good excuse to stop and admire the scenery.

Chuck put me to work in the stable. He gave me Karma to look after. For the first week, it took me the better part of two hours to clean out the soiled bedding and pitch it into the wheelbarrow. I still couldn't do any heavy lifting, so Chuck had to trundle the wheelbarrow down the aisleway for me and up the ramp into the wagon parked behind the barn.

Nothing like shoveling manure to put a little humility into my soul.

It gave me a lot of time to think.

My muscles were so weak that my arms shook when I lifted the bedding fork, and I had to pace myself so I wouldn't run out of steam before the stall was clean. But beyond all that, I saw a glimpse of the person I used to be starting to surface out of the wreckage.

"This is so frustrating!" I complained. Sweat ran off me, and Karma only highlighted my discomfort by swatting me across the face with his tail.

"Give it time," was Chuck's usual reply. "Think of where you were a few weeks ago? Focus on how far you've come, not on how far you still need to go."

It didn't help that Chuck could muck out the whole barn in the span of time it took me to clean one stall. He could throw hay around without breaking a sweat, haul a sack of feed over one shoulder like it was a pillow, and leap onto a horse's back from a complete standstill. Before my accident, that was something I'd done a million times in the ring and thought nothing of it.

He noticed my wistful expression one day as he walked Karma around the mechanical rigging Del had set up in the center of the covered ring. The gears were flaked with rust, and the ropes hanging off the pulleys reminded me of dead snakes. Cobwebs fluttered in the crook of the mechanical's arm, moved by some imaginary breeze, and the thing looked like it hadn't been used since last year.

Karma, who was used to open spaces, eyed the metal contraption like it was a troll getting ready to attack him. He jigged sideways under Chuck's light seat and rattled the bit against his teeth. The worried look in his eye bothered me. This gateway into his mind showed me a conflicted mess of bad memories and trauma, and I think he was more afraid of life than I was. He was trying so hard to be obedient and the combination made for a very unhappy horse.

"Do you want to try sitting on him?" Chuck asked.

It took so few words to send a chill of anxiety shivering through my innards. "God no!" I collected myself and spoke in a more reasonable tone. "I don't think so. Not yet. My leg ... you know."

Chuck brought Karma to a halt in front of me. The air stilled. Birds chirped in the rafters and my heart banged like thunder in my ears. "You could use the mechanical."

My harsh laugh startled poor Karma.

I lowered my voice. "I would sooner die."

Chuck's gaze roamed over me in a kindly way. His seamed face held no judgement, and his unlimited patience reminded me of Jimmy. "I think it would be good for you to get back on a horse. There's no substitute for riding. It works every muscle in your body. Good for the soul too. Come on. I won't let you fall; I promise. I'll even stay at his head."

Something dark wrapped its cold fingers around my brain. "I said, I don't want to."

He gave Karma a reassuring pat on the neck and backed off. "Okay. You're not ready. I understand."

He wheeled the stallion around with a touch of his leg and cantered off, leaving me to gaze in envy and wonder what it would feel like to sit on such a beautiful animal as that.

Stop it, I told myself.

I couldn't help thinking about poor Dolly. The thought of her lying alone out in the desert, her body disintegrating under the Arizona sun poisoned my mind. Putting Karma in place of her memory made me feel like a traitor. And I would be lying if I didn't admit I'd felt pangs of nervousness squirming in my belly when Chuck offered me the ride. Every time I thought about the accident that had broken my leg; a sourness lumped in my throat. My heart quickened against my will. My mind replayed those slow, torturous moments of dodging the flying cable and tumbling off Dolly's back so often a sickness invaded my mind. It turned me into a coward. I revisited the memory of crashing to the ground in front of a thousand spectators over and over again, and I just didn't think I could survive another round with that kind of pain.

As determined as I was never to accept another horse into my life after Dolly, Karma slowly won me over. He was a perfect gentleman while I cleaned his stall. He seemed to anticipate my movements. He stayed out of my way, giving me space while I wielded the bedding fork around his feet. He didn't seem to mind when I spent half an hour shaking out the fresh straw, and he was careful not to step on my toes when I balanced myself against his shoulder after my back gave out.

Chuck never asked me again if I wanted to ride him, but I worried the idea around in my mind like a loose tooth.

I wondered, what if I *did* try to ride him?

"You all right in there?" Chuck asked, the following Monday. I'd been in Karma's stall for ages, and I think he worried I might have passed away in there.

He found me resting against Karma's shoulder. The stall was airless. Suffocatingly hot even with the window open. Pain was a constant companion. Even now, it radiated across my kidneys like the jab of a knife blade. I braced myself on my good leg and leaned on the horse for support. "I'm just taking a break."

The actual truth was, I'd been trying to read Karma without giving myself away to the demon who wanted me dead. Consequently, I was a bit distracted by all the images scattered inside Karma's mind.

Chuck had this uncanny way of seeing right through the lies. "You're using the *magie*, aren't you."

I glowered at his pathetic efforts to keep a straight face. "Shut up. I'm just letting him know that he's safe now."

He lifted an eyebrow. "Do you think that's wise?"

I used my sleeve to sop the sweat off my forehead. "What do you mean?"

"Telling him he's safe? What if you can't promise him that?"

Doubt slipped between my defenses. "Why do you ask me these things?"

He hitched up a shoulder. "You're the one with the *magie*. I just think you ought to be more responsible with it."

I'm sure that pregnant woman I read for months ago would have probably said the same thing.

I turned back to Karma. When I looked into his mind, I saw only flames.

"He can't forget the fire," I said. "It's all he thinks about. His burns have healed, but his mind is still stuck on the flaming hoop."

I ran my hand over the bald patches on his spine. The hair had tried to grow back, but it was sparse. Coarse, and prickly. I merged the *magie* with his energy, moving my palms an inch above his back. There was a current rippling around him. It was faint. Resistant to my hands. It felt like my fingers were moving through water. "His scars tell a story," I concluded, harking back to something Chuck had told me.

Chuck remained silent behind me. He'd come down to the barn that day dressed in faded blue jeans, cowboy boots, and a cream-colored shirt worn through at the seams. His characteristic braids fell past his shirt pockets. His deep brown eyes were watchful and intrigued.

I stepped back carefully, ever mindful of my mutinous leg, and noted a change in Karma's eyes. After I'd infused the *magie* into his apprehension, there was a quietness there now. He stared at nothing, unblinking, unthinking.

He really was a pretty horse. He was as black as a crow, except for the bald spots. He might have had some carriage horse somewhere down his lineage, judging by the high set of his neck. I'd overheard Del saying he was mostly Percheron but had some French-Canadian horse in him too. His mane and tail took an immense amount of work to keep tangle free. He had a lovely, chiseled profile, large, expressive eyes, and his legs were surprisingly clean of blemishes. He was broad across the back too, with a substantial rump.

A perfect back for standing on.

"I think I'd like to try riding him."

The words left my mouth before I could stop them. Once they were out, there was no stuffing them back in again.

"Don't look so smug," I grumbled when Chuck's face split into a wide grin. "I just want to sit on him. I'm not even sure if my leg will tolerate it, so don't get your hopes up."

He went to get Karma's bridle off the peg in the harness room. The stallion was tacked up without fanfare, and Chuck led him out of the stall.

I followed them down the aisle, moving at a slug's pace to the common breezeway where the side door led into the covered ring. My leg worked better if I slid my foot along in the dirt. I'd adopted this method of walking after leaving the brace off for good. That way, I didn't have to rely on absent muscles to lift my leg or bend my knee. I could just drag myself along, leaving tell-tale signs in the gravel that Vandemere Petruska had passed this way. It got me to where I wanted to go. Certainly not in record time, but I had hoped my father would be pleased with my progress.

So far, he hadn't said anything, or noticed.

Chuck stood at Karma's head. "How do you want to do this?"

"Have you got a ladder?"

Chuck mulled it over.

I smirked at him. "I was joking. I wouldn't expect Karma to stand for that. Why don't you start by giving me a leg up."

Doubt settled in the creases on Chuck's forehead. "It's probably going to hurt," he warned me.

I sighed. "What else is new?"

I sidled up to Karma's shoulder and reached my arms up over his withers.

This wasn't going to be pretty.

I bent my left knee as far as it could go and grimaced.

Chuck cupped his left hand under my knee and took hold of my ankle with his right.

I gritted my teeth. "Ow, ow ... God—" Pain jolted up my thigh and into my back. White-hot, and sickening. "*Wait—!*"

"I haven't done anything yet!"

Karma's eyes were ringed with fear. He stayed perfectly still, but his muscles twitched when I leaned up against him. He tried to shake me off like I was an annoying fly. His ears swiveled nervously, and I could feel his heart banging away inside his chest.

"Poor horse," I murmured. "You don't deserve this."

Chuck eased my leg back down. "Do you want to try again?"

"In a moment ..."

I rested against Karma's elbow and panted out the minutes until things subsided.

Sunlight lay in crisp squares all along the west side of the covered ring, beaming through the open gaps in the kickboards. The mechanical stood dead center in the ring, taunting me with its wheels and pulleys and safety ropes.

"It's not a crime to work on the mechanical," Chuck said, reading my thoughts.

"Tell that to my father." I shook my head. "No mechanical. That's the rule."

Chuck smoothed Karma's mane with a brown, leathery hand. "He's not the same person he once was, Vandy. If you would just *talk* to him, you might find out he's on your side. He didn't tell you the whole story about why he didn't want to take on any clients this winter. Ask him. Talk to him. Remember what you said about the Bronson brothers? You said, if people would only take the time to get to know them, they might find out the Bronson boys are just misunderstood. Those were your exact words. Remember?"

I didn't want to talk about Del anymore.

"Just ... help me get up on this damn horse."

He tipped his head back and laughed. "Okay, you win. But I'm not giving up on you."

Ellen Dawson had said the exact same thing to me once, and in a moment of weakness, I had pleaded, *don't*.

I shook that hopeful part of my past out of my mind and positioned myself behind Karma's left shoulder again. "You're going to have to do most of the heavy lifting," I said, already preparing myself for the misery I was about to feel. "And I might scream."

Chuck took up my leg. "Ready?"

"No. But go ahead."

"On the count of three?"

I shut my eyes.

"One ... two ... *three*."

There was a lot of heaving and gasping, and elbows getting in the way. I *know* there was a lot of swearing.

I clambered up Karma's side, grabbing hold of his mane to pull myself along.

Chuck threw me across the stallion's back like I was a sack of flour. I lay on my stomach, my legs hanging on one side, elbows dug in for purchase on the other. I spat out curses like they were spare change from a vending machine and stared down at the sandy floor below me.

Karma's withers dug into my ribs on the left side.

I remembered to *breathe*.

Poor Karma. He stood frozen like a statue, his front legs braced, probably wondering what sort of amateur was climbing onto his back. He was such a gentle soul, but I could feel the tension running through his backbone.

"I can't do this," I wailed.

"Yes, you can!" Chuck grabbed hold of my right ankle and forced it over Karma's rump.

"Chuck, *stop!*"

"You're almost there!"

It felt like I was being ripped in half. Muscles I hadn't used in months howled in pain.

"Get me down," I begged, "*Please*, Chuck! I can't take it—"

He gave my hips one last shove, and suddenly I was astride. Sort of.

I lay across Karma's withers. My chin was buried in his mane and my legs were locked up behind me. My balls were crushed underneath me, and I might have been digging my toes into Karma's flanks, I wasn't sure. He would have been well within his rights to buck me off, but he accepted the strange arrangement with white-ringed eyes and simply awaited further commands.

"Sit up," Chuck insisted, giving my knee a quick shake.

"I can't! I'm *stuck!*"

Thank God no one else was around to see this. Del had gone into town earlier and Lenora was somewhere in the garden, digging up beetles for the hens.

"You're so close, Vandy! All you have to do is sit up!"

I pulled my legs down and nearly passed out. Maybe if I *had* fainted, it might have convinced Chuck to let me off this damn horse! My left thigh threatened to snap like a wishbone on Christmas morning, and the muscles in my lower back were being pulled in different directions.

I missed my old body. I missed the suppleness I'd taken for granted all those times it accepted the punishing schedule of life on the road and never let me down. The indifference of youth mocked me.

Would I ever get back to normal again?

Slowly, *very* slowly, I sat up. Not quite all the way. My back just wouldn't allow it. My muscles had seized up after all the months of bedrest and to force them into submission would have been stupid. But I *was* up. I was sitting on a horse again, and suddenly, the world looked *different*.

Chuck beamed up at me from the ground. "You did it, Vandy! Well done!"

My face glowed under all that sweat. I tasted salt on my upper lip and grinned. "Yeah. But I'm going to pay for this tomorrow."

"Do you want to walk around some?"

I hesitated. So far, Karma hadn't put a foot out of place. His back was tense under me, and if I was reading him right, he didn't know what to make of my nervous apprehension.

I grabbed a handful of his mane. "Okay. But just go slow."

We walked. Slowly at first. Then, as wounded muscles grew accustomed to the rhythm of Karma's stride, a familiarity began to take hold of me. My body *remembered*. I was still in pain, but I was surprised to find it didn't matter so much anymore. *This* was the world I was supposed to exist in. This was who I was meant to be. Not that damaged shell limping around on crutches and dragging a foot through the dirt. My father had taught me how to *fly*. It was high time I stopped complaining and lived up to his expectations.

Something loosened around my heart. I hadn't been aware of its brutal grip until it released its hold on me, and a sudden warmth spread through my bones.

I still ached for Dolly. When I looked down, I expected to see a white mane cascading over a silvery neck. Instead, there was a black horse nodding gently with every stride.

For a moment, I was okay with that.

Chapter Thirteen

I didn't tell my father I was riding Karma. I didn't want him to know. I didn't want him coming to the ring to watch me sitting on the beautiful horse he'd bought for me—the *old me*, only to see Chuck leading me around at a slow walk like a child on his first pony.

The last time Del had seen me ride, I'd been on Samson. I'd been invincible back then. Unbreakable.

I barely remembered that person.

I rode Karma every day as the sun came up and my father was none the wiser.

When I wasn't riding or mucking stalls, I was back on Chuck's torture table. There were times when I had to force my mind to go somewhere else while he pushed me to the edge of what I could take. Every day brought a new kind of hell, but amid all the pain, a transformation was taking place. I was still limping, and probably would for the rest of my life, but I wasn't dragging my foot in the dirt anymore. Working in the barn had done wonders to build up the muscles I'd lost during my convalescence.

I waited for my father to notice the changes in me. I wasn't expecting a pat on the shoulder. A kind word would have sufficed.

He gave me nothing.

Sometimes, I would stare at him from across the dinner table, thinking if I could just make him uncomfortable enough, he might glance up and acknowledge my presence.

He was definitely uncomfortable. He would fixate on the food Lenora put in front of him and bury his thoughts so deep even the *magie* couldn't dig them to the surface.

Lenora seemed uneasy with the silence. When I tried to read her, all I could see was a cloud of trepidation swirling in her mind. She'd been that way since the incident with Dr. Franklin. Most nights, she pushed her food around on her plate and leaned her chin on her palm like my mother used to do when she was in a pensive mood. Her dark eyes would glaze over, her thoughts too far away for even me to see.

Chuck just ate as fast as possible, then retreated to his room.

"Sheesh," I said once, trying to lighten the mood, "I can barely get a word in here."

My father took his plate in hand and left the table.

I thought I was beyond being hurt by him. It's not like we had any kind of meaningful relationship. I was old enough that I didn't need a father around to guide my progress into adulthood or protect me from the perils of the world. I could do that for myself. And anyway, since Lester Simmons's attack, the entity had left me alone. I was stronger now. Even if the thing did show up, I'd be ready for it. Or so I thought.

Stupid.

Despite my attempts to clad myself in armor, there was an ache in my soul that never went away. My father had taught me to fly, and now he wouldn't even look at me.

I was headed in for breakfast after helping Chuck in the barn one day, when I met Del coming out of the house. Time had marched steadily into early December, but instead of cooling down, the temperatures climbed into the low hundreds. Even at this early hour, the sun felt like it was about to set my hair on fire.

I might not have needed the crutches or the brace to walk anymore but I still needed to concentrate on where I was putting my foot down. I wasn't watching where I was going, and Del's shadow suddenly loomed over me.

I looked up. I saw something in his eyes I wasn't supposed to see. He let his guard down for a split second and I caught a glimpse of a complicated tangle of emotions struggling to make sense behind his pale, gray eyes. The *magie* collided with his guilt and shame and I almost buckled under the weight of it.

I heard his voice ringing inside my head ...

It makes me sick just looking at him.

He's lost his mother and his horse ...

Why can't I help him? Why can't I stop hating him?

My father must have realized what I was doing and instinctively recoiled. He quickly shuttered his thoughts away and a familiar hardness flattened his eyes.

He brushed past me. His elbow grazed mine as he went, and I felt him jerk his arm back as if I'd burned him.

I turned on the path and called after him. "Del?"

He ignored me.

I ran my tongue around the dryness inside my mouth and tried again. "Hey, Dad?"

He walked away.

"Why won't you talk to me?" Suddenly, I was that little kid playing in the dirt again, gazing up at the man who had thrown me into the wind and promised to catch me every time I came back down to earth.

The place between his shoulders stiffened.

He got into the Packard and drove away from me as fast as he could.

***

"I don't even know why I'm still here, Chuck," I said wearily. "I should just go home."

I sat astride Karma as he picked his way around a mixed clump of teddy bear cholla and ocotillo. His steps barely jostled me now, and the pain grinding away in my thigh seemed to lessen with each passing day.

My walks around the covered ring had graduated to short treks into the desert. We usually headed out in the morning before the sun got too hot. Pockets of chill competed with the rising heat coming off the sandscapes, burning off the mist as the day dawned bright as a silver dollar.

We'd gone about a mile now.

Behind us, Vandemere Ranch was a dazzle of rooftops gleaming in the Arizona sun.

Chuck rode his own horse, Saguaro, a sorrel gelding with some white on his face and hind legs. That horse could be as prickly as the cactus that grew around Tucson. As we rode knee to knee down the dusty trail leading into the vast desert, Saguaro pinned his ears if Karma so much as looked in his direction.

"You said it yourself: the circus isn't going anywhere for the winter," Chuck reminded me. He gave Saguaro a nudge with his calf to keep him out of Karma's way. "Stay here with us until the spring."

"Give me one good reason why I should."

He grinned. "Arizona suits you."

I expressed my thoughts in one dramatic sigh. I assumed he was referring to the improvements resulting from all those hours he'd spent working on my battered body. I wore an old pair of blue jeans over my scarred leg and a cotton shirt with the cuffs rolled up. I'd pulled off my gloves to pick at a stick-tight caught in Karma's mane, revealing calloused palms that hadn't been there before. Beneath the faded clothes, my shoulders were starting to fill out again. There was even a hint of definition to my biceps and forearms. I was still skinny, but Lenora was working on that too. She was a great cook, and I was always ravenous, so we made a good team.

I'd gotten quite tanned working in the Arizona sun. With a bit of color in my cheeks, I looked halfway alive again. My hair was getting so long now that I had to braid it down the back of my neck to keep it out of the way. I used the bandana Daniel Bronson had given me to keep the front from falling into my eyes. Every morning, I knotted the square of cotton cloth around my head, and Chuck said I could easily pass for an Apache scout as long as no one looked too closely.

"Or a dirty Gypsy," I'd shot back.

No brace or crutch anywhere in sight.

Arizona might have suited some people, but I missed the circus, and I was thinking it was high time I went back.

Chuck objected when I voiced my plans. "But I like having you around."

"You just like having help in the barn."

His eyes crinkled up in the corners. "True. But I've noticed a change in you. It's good to see you laugh. You're not the same person you were when you first arrived on our doorstep."

"God, I should hope not." I thought back to that wretched excuse for a human being I'd been when I'd first staggered up to the door of Vandemere Ranch and cringed.

"I'm proud of you," said Chuck, without a hint of sarcasm.

"Well, you'd be the only one."

"Stop doing that."

I reached down to flick a fly off Karma's neck. "Stop doing what?"

"Stop sabotaging yourself. I'm not saying it's your fault that you feel this way. I see the way Del acts around you." He pushed his cowboy hat back off his brow and scratched behind his ear. "Can't understand it myself. If you were my boy, I would shout it to the world. If you could only see yourself the way I see you, you would be astounded."

My face warmed. "I wish you *were* my father."

His smile faded. His gaze darted away like a nervous hare. "Well, that's a fine thing to say, Vandy. I appreciate it." His words didn't quite match up with the glint of shame in his eyes.

He stared out into the desert like he was searching for a place to hide.

I let him be. He would tell me his secrets when he was ready to. For now, the sun was warm, and the air was heavy with the scent of growing things. I was glad to be mobile again, and even though it wasn't Dolly under me, I got to experience the desert from the back of a horse. Missing Dolly left me feeling like I'd lost a limb, but riding Karma gave me something back—a glimmer of the capable circus rider I'd been before everything had gone to shit.

We rode in silence, the stillness broken only by the occasional bird call or the horses snorting dust out of their nostrils.

I scanned the endless vista, squinting when the sun got in my eyes. Many of the world's problems had been solved on the back of a horse and I was beginning to understand why. There was something about the connection between man and beast that merged the two together. I trusted Karma to pick the safest way through this maze of cactus while my own mind was free to wander.

I was thinking about how these open spaces were the furthest I could get from the rabbit hole. It was easy to dismiss the desert as a whole lot of nothing. It was a brutal place of dust and sand, and a heat that would kill you if you didn't take it seriously. A place of sudden storms and furious winds. A desolate place to a person like me.

The desert had almost destroyed me. It had taken Dolly away, and it had taken my father away too, setting me adrift. It would have been so easy to hate this place, and yet, once I looked past the anger in my heart, I saw beauty everywhere. Prejudice didn't always start or end with men. I'd changed my mind about Arizona. Now that I'd gotten to know the desert a bit better it was going to hurt to leave it.

"I dunno, Chuck," I said at last, "I'm thinking I should just go back to California. I need to start training again. It's going to take me months just to work up to some of the easier tricks."

"You could train here," Chuck suggested. "Del was talking about taking a trip up to the Grand Canyon next month. Didn't you say your Ma wanted to have her ashes spread out there?"

It was a low blow to bring my mother into this. I retaliated with a scowl. Just when I'd gotten up the courage to leave, Chuck tightened the screws.

"She never said she wanted *me* to throw her into the Grand Canyon. Del could do it. I got her here. Let him finish it."

"Don't you want to see the Grand Canyon?"

"Course I do. I've wanted to see it my whole life. Del talked about it all the time when I was a kid. Always going on about how you have to see it to believe it. Damn near drove Ma and me nuts."

"Then stay."

I shook my head. "I've made up my mind."

Persistence was a palpable ally and he used it to his full advantage. "I know you can get through to Del if you just keep trying. He always talked about you like he was missing a chunk out of his soul. *That's* why he didn't take any clients on this season. I bet you didn't know that did you. His heart just wasn't in it anymore. All those years without you? It broke him down. I saw it with my own eyes. He trained so many riders, but they could never measure up to you. I think he just gave up."

"Did he ever say anything to you?" I asked. "About why he left us?"

Saguaro stubbed his toe on a protruding rock and nearly went to his knees. Chuck sat out the bobble like it was nothing and waited for the horse to right himself.

"Not to me," he answered at length. "I don't think Lenora knows either or she would have told me. It must be something pretty awful—" He realized too late what he was about to imply; that maybe *I'd* been the one to drive Del away after all. I caught him staring into the distance, averting his gaze so I wouldn't have to see the guilt rising into his conscience.

We fell into a thoughtful silence. Our horses walked side by side, kicking up the dust. Nodding heads made peace with the space between them.

Sunlight tripped off my shoulders and onto Karma's scarred back. I was careful not to dig my seat bones into his spine. He guarded his memories of the fire with the tenacity of a bulldog, but he was such a kind-hearted soul; I was honored he let me ride him at all. He carried me without a trace of nervousness. His mouth was soft in my hands, and he never once pulled at the bit. His sweat smelled like creosote. Sharp and tangy. *Familiar*. A clean smell that drifted through my consciousness and put things right.

I twined my fingers through his mane and his ears swiveled back.

Ahead of us, the trail beckoned, straight as an arrow.

"I think I'd like to try cantering," I told Chuck. By the look on his face, I must have shocked the hell out of him that day. "Nothing too crazy though," I warned. "Let *me* set the pace."

"Why don't you try standing up on him?" Chuck's laugh was light and full of mischief. "The old boy looks pretty quiet there. Come on, Vandy. Show me a bit of what you've got?"

Innocent words.

The effect was almost immediate.

I heard a booming voice in my head, screeching. "*You're going to die, Petruska! I'll make you fall again and the whole world will hear you scream this time! I'll break you just like I did before. Go on. Stand up on the horse. I dare you.*"

The desert dissolved into a nightmare as images flooded my brain. I was flung into the past with all the violence of an explosion. I wasn't just remembering the accident. I was *re-living it*.

All the blood drained out of my face and my tenuous hold on reality went with it.

I felt like I'd been kicked in the head by a mule. Like someone had pulled the plug out of me. Everything I needed to *live* poured out of me and I slumped over Karma's neck. Terror seized the air up solid in my lungs. I fought it. Tried to stay conscious. Stay *alive*.

Chuck's voice was a distant holler over the slam of my heartbeat pounding inside my head. "Vandy! What's wrong?"

I *tried* to tell him. A vice tightened around my throat. I shook my head, trying to clear away the things assaulting my mind. I tried to force the words out, but they just wouldn't come.

Karma took one look at all that chaotic energy coming at us like a speeding train and froze.

Chuck jumped off Saguaro. "Shit ... *shit!* Vandy! What's wrong?"

He caught me as I slid sideways off Karma.

I fell to the earth. My eyes stared vacantly up at the sky. My feet thrashed around in the dirt.

"Can't *breathe—*" My hands flailed against my throat.

Chuck laid me out on the ground at Karma's feet and fumbled for the buttons on my shirt collar.

I fought him. I didn't mean to. I was so desperate to fill my collapsing lungs with life-giving air that I panicked. I lay on my back in the dust, expecting to die right then and there, and my eyes looked to his for help.

Chuck's weathered face swam before me. He held me by the wrists so I couldn't claw at his chest. "Vandy! Tell me what's wrong!"

Darkness in my mind. Insanity tried to crush the bones in my chest, trapping my heart against my breastbone. Pinching off the blood.

Sweat ran in rivers down my sides.

"*Dying ...*"

I saw myself falling off Dolly again. Heard the whistle of the cable slicing past my head. I felt the punch of pain driving the wind from my body when I landed in the sawdust. I heard the sickening crack of my bones breaking.

The searing pain was back in full force. Acid in my veins. But I wasn't under Jimmy's big top this time. I was somewhere else.

Everything is on fire.

Smoke fills my lungs. I'm on fire. A scorching wind wheezes in and out of me and I hear the entity laughing …

"Come burn with me, Petruska. Come feel what I felt. I was born out of fire. They created me. You Petruskas … you left me to burn. Now, it's your turn."

Poor Chuck. He was trying to hold onto two horses and help me at the same time.

I coughed violently and threw a punch at his face. "Let … *go* …"

He wrestled me onto my right side. When I tried to sit up, he threw a leg over me and pinned me to the earth. I would have run away from this blind madness if it hadn't been for Chuck. I know now that he was just trying to stop me from hurting myself, but at the time, his efforts only fueled my hysteria.

"Where are you?" he shouted. "What are you seeing, Vandy? *Tell me!*"

The desert remained impassively quiet while I panted and fought and kicked at him. Dust rose around me like smoke from a bush fire. My mouth was full of it. I was down in the rabbit hole again. Caught in the dark. My throat was clogged, and my lungs burned.

The earth caved in on me.

"Can't … *breathe* …"

"Yes, you can!" Chuck insisted. "It's *not real!"* He renewed his grip on my right wrist when I bucked underneath him, and he pressed my palm flat in the dirt. "*Feel the earth.*" He dug my fingers into the pebbled surface. He was panting as hard as I was, and he had a tough time getting the words out. "*Feel the desert!* Feel her heartbeat! Let her speak to you. The desert is the only thing that's real, Vandy!"

Tears streaked my face as I rocked my head from side to side. "*Dying* …"

"You're *not* dying!" Some of Chuck's spit landed on my cheekbone. "Use the *magie*, Vandy! This thing is trying to trick you! It wants you to think you're the cause of everyone's suffering, so you'll give up. Use your gift. Don't be afraid of it. Look at me ..."

"Can't ..." I moaned.

"You can! This thing is a *coward*. It uses others to attack you. It steals your memories and uses them against you. Don't listen to its lies. Stay with me this time. Don't go away. Take deeper breaths." He threw me onto my chest like I was made of rags instead of flesh and bone and kneed me in the small of my back. "The desert will save you, Vandy. *Feel her*. The earth is a living being. She has a heartbeat. Let her help you. You can't keep running from this. Let her *breathe for you*."

I inhaled dirt and coughed wretchedly.

The light was fading behind my eyes.

I was going away ...

Chuck gave me everything he had. He pressed my chest against the desert floor until my heart thudded against the ground. "You want to see the Grand Canyon, don't you?"

I wept. "Yesss ..."

His words were little more than a terse gasp. "Then look into my mind. Use the magic. Let *me* take you to the Grand Canyon ..."

Suddenly, it was my mother's voice I was hearing. The desert ceased to exist. One minute, I was dying; wallowing in the throes of hysteria that knocked the sense clean out of me. The next thing I knew I was standing on the edge of a great chasm of rock and cloud.

This was the game we used to play when I was a child and my mother's laughter rang clear in my head.

Look, Vandy! Can you believe it? It's just like your father always said it would be!

I lifted my eyes to the distant land and gaped. Before me, great vistas filled with mountains and majesty were topped by a vast plateau that went on and on for miles.

The canyon was as deep as it was wide. I stood on the precipice of immense beauty, staring in wonder, and something broke inside me. This was a joy that had no name, and I trembled in stunned awe.

I looked down. A thin ribbon of water glinted far below; the mere memory of a mighty river that had once carved a path through this land, running through the floor of the canyon on its way south to Mexico.

No words could describe the feeling that swelled inside my heart. As I stood in the presence of God, I knew then how insignificant I was as a human being.

There was nothing between me and certain death if I fell. I didn't care. If I fell, the wind would catch me. There was no need to fear. My mother had taught me how to read the *magie* but my father had taught me how to *fly*.

I looked across the canyon at the rainbow hills. Was this even *real?* Laughter bubbled up from the depths of my soul. Freedom had never felt so grand! Wind blew through my hair, and I filled my lungs with the scent of pine trees. Never had I breathed air so sweet.

My mother's voice sang on the breeze. *Listen to the wind, Vandy. I'm always with you. Remember what you're seeing. Whenever you're afraid, remember the canyon. Remember me.*

I held my hands out to the wind. Grief should have been a shard of glass in my soul but all I felt was a profound happiness.

Am I in Heaven, Ma?

If this was death, I didn't know why I'd ever been so afraid of it.

It's not your time yet, Vandy. Our family did a terrible thing. We loosed an evil onto the world and you need to put it back where it belongs.

How, Ma? How am I going to do that? I don't even know what it is.

The father knows. You just need to have faith, bebelus. Trust the magie. *Trust it to lead you to the truth.*

I closed my eyes. I left my body on the edge of the cliff and drifted over red rock hills. I soared over pillars of gold, sailing on wings made of wind. Sunlight painted the weathered shores with purples and crimsons, and I felt untethered from the earth. Nothing evil could live in a place like this. Grief had no hold on me and I drifted above the canyon walls on a current of air.

The father knows.

Knows *what* though?

Have faith …

Someone was calling me.

Sharp barbs of consciousness hooked into my mind, pulling me out of the vision.

"Vandy …"

The sound prodded me out of the dream, louder this time. More insistent.

I came back to earth in stages. I became aware of my body again, only to realize Chuck was on top of me. I heard panic constricting his throat and his panting breaths sounded thin and raspy.

I blinked up at him.

Sweat dripped off the end of his nose and his eyes were wide and staring. His braids swung forward, framing his weathered face and horrified expression. Everything about him was covered in dust.

I must have scared the absolute shit out of him.

Chuck held me down in the dirt until my breathing calmed. I think his weight helped more than anything. It forced me to take deeper gulps. Things slowly came back into focus, and my mind finally acknowledged that I was looking at the world from the ground up.

Everything looked different down here in the dust. Cactus towered over me. The sky was a cloudless blue bowl arching over my head.

I shifted under Chuck's weight. Confusion scrambled my brain and fear stabbed through my chest like an icicle.

I croaked, "Chuck? What's happening?" I had a bad moment when I remembered Lester's attack on me. I wondered if I might have misjudged Chuck's intentions in getting me alone out here in the desert. "Why am I lying in the dirt?"

He eased up on my wrists. "You don't remember?"

"Remember what?"

I struggled to sit up.

Chuck climbed off me.

I braced my arms and pushed myself up out of the dirt.

I was hit with an all too familiar dizziness. My head felt like it was stuffed full of rocks, and there were the usual gaps in my memory.

"Did I have another seizure? Feels like I did ..."

Chuck scrutinized my wan expression from a squatted position beside me. His face had aged ten years. Whatever had happened scared him, and here I was, looking to *him* for reassurance.

"Are you okay?" He put his hands on either side of my face, turning me this way and that, checking for blood. "*Christ*, Vandy. Does this sort of thing happen often? You were fine one minute, riding along nice as you please, talking about trying a canter on Karma. Then I mentioned something about showing me a trick or two and you went all crazy on me."

"I was riding Karma?"

Not Dolly?

I raised my eyes to the black horse standing watch over me. The two horses waited nearby, sheltering me from the worst of the sun. Saguaro couldn't have cared less, but Karma bent down to nuzzle my shoulder. His dark, liquid eye studied mine, and it was the first time I saw potential behind the fear in him. I would have hugged him if I could. He wasn't Dolly, but he was doing his best to fill the hole left in me by her passing.

Everything crashed back into place. All of it. Annie's murder. The accident. The months of pain that followed. The endless loneliness of my stay in hospital. Grace's death, and the circus leaving me behind. On top of all that, I had a demon hunting me. *Cel Care Ia*, who could and *would* kill me in the most despicable way he could think of, even if he had to break every bone in my body to do it. He'd already killed two children. He would kill again if I didn't find a way to stop him.

He had killed my mother too.

God, I thought, my poor *mother*. The pain of breaking my leg was nothing compared to the agony of losing my mother. I'd lost my horse. My father. My job. Everything that *meant* something to me was gone.

I'd spent a lifetime hiding the pain behind a wall of indifference. To the rest of the world, I was a tough, mean-hearted circus brat. A *dirty Gypsy*. But truth was, I was *scared*. Scared of what the world might think of me. Terrified of my father rejecting me again. Scared of showing him what I could do with the *magie* and giving him even more ammunition to hate me.

Karma lowered his head until he was eye to eye with me. He saw through the lies and the deceit and scars that had healed over the wounds in my heart as only a horse could do. He lipped at my hair where it fell along the crook of my neck, blowing warm breath against my damp skin. He could never replace Dolly, and yet, here he was, asking me to accept him with as much love as I could spare. I had done nothing to deserve his affection, and yet he was offering me his unfailing devotion as a gift I hadn't earned.

He nuzzled my hair and tried to lick the salt off my face.

I pushed him away.

His gentleness was the thing that undid me.

Tears flooded my eyes. One blink and they would spill over. I dashed them away with the back of my hand before Chuck could see this terrible weakness in me.

I grabbed a fistful of his shirt to steady myself. "I remember now, Chuck! The father *knows*."

Whatever Chuck saw in my wild eyes spooked him. He tried to back away from me. He was making odd, crab-like movements in the loose ground that got him nowhere. His blue jeans were white now from the dust and I couldn't tell what color his cowboy boots were anymore. Everything about him was just ... pale.

"The father knows?" he echoed.

"The father knows!" The words were burned into my mind. "Tell me what this thing is, Chuck." Not a question this time. "It's not *Cel Care Ia*, is it. It's something else. It's only *masquerading* as the wolf-demon I keep seeing. You've known this right from the start, haven't you. And you never *said anything?*"

He tried to pry my fingers off him. His face looked ... I don't know ... *stricken*? Defensive?

"You weren't ready," he hedged.

We must have looked a sight; two men sitting in the shadow of horses, facing down a monster. Chuck, a nervous wreck, and me, barely conscious.

"You were too weak," he maintained. "Too vulnerable. Naming this *thing* would have called him to us. He would have set his sights on you, and you were already so *hurt*."

My own voice rattled inside my chest. Dust made me cough. "You told me once that I was wrong about everything. What did you mean by that? If I'm wrong, tell me. Be the father I never had. For God's sake, Chuck, someone has to *save me*."

He thumbed away the errant tears that traced lines through the dirt on my face. "That's just it." His voice broke over shards of despair. "I don't think I *can* save you, Vandy."

I searched in vain for something to anchor me. All around me, the desert offered me nothing in the way of solace or protection. I saw danger in every clump of cactus and piled rock.

There was only Karma. He stood over me the same way Dolly used to do, fluttering his nostrils across my ashen cheek.

I shifted into a position that didn't hurt so much and braced myself for what Chuck was about to tell me.

"At first, I thought it was a Shapeshifter. A Skinwalker." He checked my expression for signs of delirium. I think he still half-believed my mind was broken and that he was talking to a crazy person. When he was satisfied I was still with him, he continued. "Generations of Navajo storytellers have fostered a belief in an entity that can change at will. A Skinwalker can take the shape of an animal—a coyote, or a buffalo. Whatever serves its purpose. Now, this isn't my culture, but I've heard stories. The elders used to say it was human once, before it was corrupted. It's a powerful being. They're damn near impossible to get rid of too."

Figures.

"I had a look in your book," Chuck stated. "Near as I can tell, your *Cel Care Ia* ... is that how you pronounce it? It's similar to a Skinwalker. At first, that's what I thought we were dealing with here, but now I'm not so sure."

I said nothing. There was a steady beat of pain thudding against the inside of my skull, churning up a nausea that roiled around in my guts. I hung on grimly to the scrambled eggs I'd eaten for breakfast, but part of me wondered if I wouldn't feel better if I puked it all up and just got it over with.

"I don't know *what* this is," Chuck admitted grimly. "It's not a Skinwalker, that's for sure. I caught a glimpse of it that day I smudged you in the barn. Whatever it is, it's smart. It knows when someone's getting too close, and it knows how to hide in the shadows."

"So, there's no way to fight him?" Hopelessness got mixed up with shameful misery and my heart sank. I should have been better at this by now. Should have been more committed than ever to driving this fucker out of my life. Every time I started to make progress, the bastard would come along and knock me on my ass again.

"Don't give up, Vandy." Chuck climbed to his feet. He must have been getting as stiff as I was from sitting in the dirt so long.

He held a hand down to me.

I clasped my fingers around his and he pulled me up.

The horizon tilted and my legs barely held.

"You still have one thing in your favor." He dusted me off a little harder than necessary.

"I'm not dead yet?" I tried to laugh but it sounded more like desperation.

Chuck's calm never wavered. "Think about what you just said."

"What? That I'm still alive?"

He nodded. His dark eyes pierced mine. "You're *still alive.* After everything that's happened, you're still here. The entity has tried everything to stop you from hunting it down. It's gone after the people you love, your mother, your horse. It's taken two little girls, one of which you're taking the blame for. Yeah, I know about that," he said, seeing the shock on my face. "Del's been in contact with Lieutenant Dawson. He knows you're here in Arizona. He doesn't like it apparently, but there's not much he can do about it. He followed you to California. Did you know that?"

I didn't.

"He wants his book back."

I sorted out Karma's reins and crossed them over his withers. "If he wants it that bad, he can come and get it."

I felt the weight of Chuck's gaze lingering on the side of my face. "That's why you took it, isn't it. To make sure he followed you. He's your protector in all of this."

"He doesn't believe in the *magie*," I said. God ... I couldn't remember ever being so tired. And why did Arizona have to be so *hot?* "Dawson's got some skills of his own, and he knows about hunches. Don't ask me to explain it, but if I have to go into battle with this thing, I'd feel a lot better having Clarence Dawson watching my back."

I stood against Karma's shoulder, feeling my legs shake like a newborn colt's while the blistering sun tried to melt my hair. I mopped up the sweat running down between my brows with my sleeve and wondered if this is what it felt like to be a hundred years old.

Chuck had more wise words for me. "I think you're doing a swell job standing up to this thing on your own. If you think about it, this thing's done everything it can think of to bring you down, short of murdering you with its bare hands."

"*Jesus*, don't give it any ideas ..."

Chuck's expression was grave. "I think it's *scared* of you, Vandy. It knows you're coming for it. It knows there's something in you it can't control, so it's upped the ante now."

When I didn't respond, he tried a different approach. "What's the one thing you have that a demon might want?"

I pressed my forehead against Karma's shoulder, and I had to count to ten just to keep from passing out in the heat.

Chuck mistook my silence for indifference. "Don't you get it? It's the *magie*. As long as you've got the *magie* on your side, you can defeat it."

Frustration hardened my voice. "I don't even know what *it is*, Chuck! If it's not *Cel Care Ia*, and it's not a Skinwalker, then what the hell is it?"

The father knows ...

Chuck's hand whisked across my back. "It's okay, Vandy. We're going to figure this out, I promise."

You and me against the world, as Shorty would say.

"It's just ... so ..." I shook my head, pressing my lips over the rest of it. Bad enough I'd made a fool of myself already thrashing around in the dirt like I had. I would *not* give in to temptation and *cry*.

Chuck stepped back and gave me the space I needed to pull myself together.

"Do you want help mounting up?" he asked. A safe question. One I could answer without bawling.

I sniffed quietly and brushed sand off my mouth. "If you wouldn't mind. And Chuck?"

"Yeah?"

"I'd appreciate it if you didn't say anything to Del about this. It's just that ... I need some time to sort it all out. If he knew about my ..."

"Fit?" Chuck supplied, helping me out in more ways than one.

"Yeah, let's call it that. He'll bring Dr. Franklin back out here. Then everyone in town will know about me. They'll say I'm in league with the Devil, or that I'm prone to raving."

A freak is what they would call me.

It wouldn't take much to convince my father I was sick in the head. At best, he could send me to a psychiatrist, where I would be forced to con my way out of a straitjacket. At worst, he could have me committed to an asylum, where all manner of horrors awaited me.

It's funny how one's place in society could be altered by that single word; *insane.*

It didn't matter to *me* what people thought of the Petruska *magie*, but Chuck and Lenora might suffer even more stigma by consorting with a crazy person. It was clear they had enough to worry about without someone like me compounding the problem.

"I won't say a word," Chuck promised. "But personally, I think you're making a mistake not telling your father. I think you're wrong about him. If you would just *talk* to him, you might—"

"Chuck, if you even *think* about finishing that sentence, I'm going to have to sock you in the mouth."

"Okay, okay." The corners of his lips twitched over a grin even as the hope in his eyes dimmed. "I know when I'm licked. Come on. I'm about to fry in this heat. Let's go home."

Chapter Fourteen

I got Shorty's letter three days later. I took it to my room, eager for news. The postmark from Fresno was dated two weeks prior, but it had gotten mixed up with some other papers stacked on the breakfast table. The smallish envelope was buried under some feed bills and out-of-date editions of the *Arizona Republic*; war had broken out overseas, and Britain and France were joining up with Poland to fight the Nazis.

It was the war inside this house that concerned me more.

I tore open the envelope and scanned the folded note tucked inside.

Dear Van,

I hope my letter finds you well. Jimmy got your address from some of your Ma's old things. You were supposed to send a wire to Jimmy to let him know that you made it to Arizona safe and sound. We never heard from you. Now we don't know what to think. Are you okay? Please write back and tell us you are fine. Everyone is so worried.

I'm writing to tell you that Jimmy is getting a jump on the competition this year. He wants to iron out the kinks before we put the show back on the road. We'll be in your area in mid-December. Yup, the circus *is coming to town! We will be in Tucson around the 15th. If you can get yourself there, we will pick you up and you can ride the circuit with us. We'll be touring the Southwest until spring rolls around. Jimmy's talking about rustling up some contacts south of the border. Mexico could be fun! Anyway, I hope you can make it. It'll be just like old times. I hope your leg is getting better. I'm sorry I didn't visit you more in the hospital but places like that always give me the heebie-jeebies. I hate the smell. It makes me pass out.*

That's all for now.

Your pal,

Shorty.

I gnawed on my lip. I'd forgotten all about my promise to let Jimmy know I'd made it to Arizona in one piece. I hadn't realized until now that people were actually *counting* on me to be more responsible. I'd always taken it for granted that my mother would keep the peace between me and Jimmy. Now that she was gone, I had only myself to blame for worrying him.

I read the letter three times. The circus was coming to Tucson! A scant hundred and twenty miles away. They were due in town on the fifteenth and here it was, the tenth of December already.

I hid the letter in the bottom of Jimmy's old satchel and wondered how to break the news to Chuck.

The next morning, I rode Karma around the property right as the sun broke over the edge of the world. Sunrises in Arizona would stay with me forever. I brought Karma to a halt and watched as a rim of fire burned through the shadows dimming the path ahead of us.

Fire. One of the four major energies making up the tarot. I'd always associated fire with the suit of Wands. Passionate, transformative, and always on the move, Wands hinted I could be headed for trouble. Fire could devastate, sure, but it could also bring new growth. New beginnings. I'd seen it happen. I'd seen firsthand what a forest fire could do to the land.

Californians lived in fear of forest fires. I'd seen the scorched earth and blackened trees still smoldering after a thunderstorm had just put out a wildfire. But coming back the same way in the fall, I'd seen flowers blooming on the forest floor and tiny seedlings sprouting up everywhere. Destruction had brought new life to the land. Adversity, I realized, didn't always have to be a bad thing.

I ran my hand along Karma's neck while he waited for instructions.

"Do you want to be a circus horse?" I asked him. I felt I owed it to him to offer him the job. No one ever asked horses what they wanted. Their fates were thrust upon them by men who used them as a means to an end. The west had been tamed from the back of a horse. I'd hoped that in some small way, I could make it up to all the horses who had laid down their lives in the service of man by giving Karma the freedom to choose.

He didn't answer me right away. He was too busy watching a small herd of deer browsing on some desert willow nearby.

They didn't seem to mind us being so close. They moved like ghosts through the rags of mist that lay over the land. I wouldn't have even known they were there if it hadn't been for Karma picking up on their presence and stiffening his back underneath me.

I could *hear* his heart banging away under my leg. It sounded like a tympany drum, but he barely twitched a muscle. He took good care of me, and I trusted him with my life.

I didn't know it then, but at the end of everything, I would have to.

***

"You've been awfully quiet lately," Chuck said.

I sucked in a tight breath and held it longer than usual, focusing on the sparrows twittering in the rafters while he eased my bad knee toward my chest. I was back for another torture session on the bench.

"I guess I've got a lot on my mind." I was thinking about how I was going to cross a hundred and twenty miles of desert without anyone noticing I was gone.

"Your leg's getting better," Chuck assured me. "Turn over. I need to work on your back next."

I complied. I got myself rolled over without falling off the bench. I lay with my head turned to the side and rested my arms on the overturned bucket under the table.

Chuck used the heels of his hands to knead the knots out of my spine.

"I'm going to miss your Chinese prostitute," I sighed.

"You still thinking about heading back to California?"

"Not for a while yet." I didn't like the lies coming out of my mouth. "But I can't stay here forever, Chuck. You know that. I belong with the circus. It's the only life I've ever known. I wouldn't know what to do with myself if I had a different job. Once a circus brat, always a circus brat."

There was a profound sadness in the way his fingertips moved across my skin. "I guess it's not really fair of me to ask you to stay. I really wish you would. The thing is ... well, I've gotten kind of attached to you, Vandemere Petruska. Or Davidson—I can't make up my mind which one you take after. I never had a kid of my own, see."

"Why not?"

He hesitated. I sensed him hitch his shoulders back, like the weight of the world rested on him. "I never wanted children. There are things you don't know about me. Things that might change your mind about me if you knew. I just didn't think it was right to bring a child into that sort of business. Then you showed up. You were so ... *damaged*. And now look at you. You're the closest I've ever come to having a son of my own. Maybe I've done a bit of healing too, thanks to you. So, yeah, I want you to stay. I know you won't, but don't say I never asked you."

Tears stung the back of my eyelids.

Oh my God, Petruska. You're such a sissy ...

That word was ingrained in my soul in bold letters, and it would take a lot more of Chuck's kindness to sand them out.

I sat up and swung my legs off the bench. "Is that why you never go past the gates? Why you never go into town?"

He took a seat beside me. We sat hip to hip, staring at the hulking shapes of tractors and grain seeders. The stink of oil and metal was as comforting to me as the animal smells coming from the stables on the other side of the breezeway.

I studied his profile while he wasn't looking. I was going to miss that face. I was going to miss his graying hair plaited in the two braids hanging down over his shoulders. The wrinkled ears. The rumbling voice that welled up from his lean, well-muscled chest. The hawk nose and the tanned mouth, and the lines in his cheeks that mapped out a hard life.

His dark eyes glinted. I don't know why, but they reminded me of the surface of a lake. How waves would catch the sunlight and sparkle, hiding secrets in the depths below.

"I know about the man from Sedona," I said.

He glanced up sharply, frowning. His eyes darted about, trying to find something safe to land on. Beneath it all, the familiar look of shock and dismay cut me deep.

I'd seen it before. The fear scuttling across their faces when they figured out *how* I knew. Didn't mean I had to like it.

"How long have you known?" he asked.

"For a while."

"And you never said anything?"

"Well, I was trying to be more responsible with the *magie*, like you said."

He looked everywhere but right at me. I could feel shame coming off him like the ripples of heat that danced along the Arizona horizon.

"I beat that man nearly to death, Vandy." His head drooped as his mind stared into the past. "And you *knew that*? You still talked to me? *Trusted me*?"

"I didn't always trust you, Chuck," I admitted. "But I was never *scared* of you."

All those times he had put his hands on me. The way he'd pieced together the remnants of my tattered soul and made me walk again. How he'd brought me to the brink of weeping while he worked the pain out of my broken bones. I'd known all along the damage those brown hands were capable of, but never once did I think he would hurt me.

Because of the *magie*.

Because, sometimes, I got it right.

I picked at a loose thread on my blue jeans. "I guess we're all running from something, huh?"

He was still beside me. He hadn't inched away. I felt him shaking, vibrating under the surface of the secrets he kept, and his nervous energy was like a glowing brand next to my arm.

"I'd say it's more like *hiding*," he muttered back.

"Does Del know?"

Chuck cleared the thickness out of his throat. "He does. It's why he took us in. Lenora came first, then me. Del knows my brother, see. Lenora's father. He knew him from a horse trade he made a few years ago, up in Sedona. Del stayed with Hank for a few days—that's her dad. Del got to know Lenora a bit, and Lenora got to know Del even better. Well, I guess I don't need to say it, do I? What happened next."

No. He didn't need to say it.

"She's married you know," Chuck said. "Still is, by law. Her husband, Otis Bristol, is a mean son of a bitch. White man with a drinking problem shacks up with an Indian woman and there's bound to be trouble. Otis was always finding some excuse to pound on her. She put up with it, but then Del Davidson came around. He offered Lenora an opportunity to leave Otis and get herself to safety."

I said nothing. The whole time my mother was dying of cancer, Del had been living the good life. In the eyes of the law, he was still married to Bonnie, and Lenora was still married to Otis, and yet this snag in the fabric of morality hadn't stopped them from enjoying each other's company.

I was trying really hard not to be angry. I didn't want to slip back into my old way of thinking. I'd come too far now to tear down the glorious memories I had of Arizona, just to lose it all to damn, stupid pride.

I stared at my hands, thinking it would be so easy to slam them into something hard. What's one more broken bone anyway.

The old me would have done it.

I unclenched my hands and breathed a deep sigh of reconciliation with past traumas; something I should have done a long time ago but just wasn't ready.

I heard my mother's voice whispering inside my head. *You're the best thing I ever gave to this world. Never forget that Vandy.*

Chuck didn't notice my internal battle. He sat hunched over beside me on the bench and went on with his story.

"After Del left Hank's place, Lenora finally worked up the courage to get out of her marriage. Otis went crazy. She hid out at the ranch in Sedona until things cooled down, but Otis wasn't about to let things be. He followed her to Hank's place and busted his way in. I was there that day, thank God. Hank's old, you know. He's no match for Otis. Otis went through Hank to get to Lenora, and she hid behind me, so Otis went for me instead. He's a tough bastard when he gets riled up, let me tell you. For a moment there I thought I was a dead man. Lenora was screaming. Hank had cut his head on the edge of the fireplace. Otis was bellowing like an elk in rut. *Shit* ..." Chuck's eyes watered as painful memories played themselves out in his mind.

I waited.

He exhaled shakily. "I had to fight back. It was fight back or die. Otis would have had Lenora all to himself then and I wasn't going to let that happen. So, I started swinging at him. He got some good hits in. He's a big guy, and he was in a blind rage, so I doubt he even felt a lightweight like me knocking on his face." Chuck's gaze dropped to his hands. He turned them over, flexing his fingers as if they still hurt him.

I noticed small, whitened scars still visible there.

"At first, I was only fighting to protect Lenora. That's what I tell myself. But the truth is, I was angry. Otis was punching the shit out of me, and every blow hurt like hell. Something in my mind turned. Suddenly, it wasn't about Lenora anymore. I wanted to kill him. I forgot who I was, Vandy. I had one thing on my mind and that was to get back at the guy. I beat Otis until I couldn't lift my arms anymore, then I went at him with my boots. Lenora finally had to pull me off him. All that rage ... it *scared* me. It's *in me*, Vandy. I know it's there. I can't ever let it out again."

"So, you stay here on Del's ranch and hide away from people," I said, when the silence stretched between us. "Did Otis survive?"

Chuck's tone flattened. "He did. I mean, look at me. Got no weight to throw around. I did some damage, though. I broke a few bones in Otis's face. He was in the hospital for a while."

"What about you?"

He grunted. "Couple of cracked ribs. Lots of blood. Gave me a headache that hurt for a month." He stared into space. "Busted bones are one thing. It was the three months I spent in jail that damn near killed me."

"*Jesus*. Otis had you arrested?"

His nod was barely imperceptible. "I was looking at some hard time for beating on a white man. I tried to tell the judge that Otis started it, but no one ever listens to an Indian." Chuck did a good job of keeping his tone on an even keel, but I could hear a shakiness trying to come to the surface. "Anyway, Del pulled some strings with the county prosecutor. My lawyer cut a deal, and I was released, but not before the guys in county lockup made my life a living hell. After I got out, I came here. I was remanded into Del's custody. Judge's orders. He's responsible for me now. I owe him big time."

I thought about this for a moment and came to some rather unappealing conclusions. "Sounds like you've traded one prison for another."

He drew in a shaky breath. "Well, it's a pretty nice prison."

We sat in silence for a spell. Here I was, thinking about leaving, when all Chuck could think about was staying put.

And chains. Chains that kept him tethered to a violent past and some acreage of land that belonged to someone else. Just another white man dictating what an Indian could and couldn't do.

I offered him a crumb of hope. "You won't ever let it out again, Chuck."

He breathed a small laugh. "Is that the *magie* talking or you?"

"Maybe a bit of both." I pinned my gaze on him while the sparrows in the rafters tried their best to crap on us. "Thing is, you know it's there. Otis doesn't. That's the difference between you and him."

I tried to put it another way so he would understand. "We have these elephants at the circus. Omari's the bull elephant. Nia and Eshe are the cows. The elephants are always chained up. They're chained, and the chain's attached to a stake in the ground. To put things into perspective, if Omari ever decided he'd had enough of circus life, he could pull that chain up out of the ground and run. And how would we ever stop him? It's the chain, see. He knows the chain is there. He respects it, so he never tries to escape. But it's not the chain stopping him. It's what's up here." I tapped my temple. "Control is just an illusion. It hasn't occurred to Omari that he's stronger than that flimsy chain, or that he could break away any time he wanted to. But he doesn't want to break it, so he doesn't try, Chuck. That's *you*, see? You don't *want* to break the chains you've put on yourself. Otis does. *So, trust* yourself. Trust yourself like I do. And if you ever doubt yourself, remember I told you the *magie* knows, and the *magie* says it won't ever happen again."

Chuck's expression crumpled. He blinked rapidly and his nose started to leak. "You mean, I should have faith?"

I grinned. "Yeah. Exactly. Have faith."

I saw him rub a quick knuckle under his nose.

He caught me looking and laughed it off. "How did you ever get to be so smart?"

"From you," I answered.

His eyes teared up again. "God ... dammit." He wiped a knuckle across his eyes and cleared the gravel out of his throat. "Sorry."

"Now we're even," I said, trying hard not to sound smug.

He sighed. He tested his voice and found it steady again. "Lenora told me what you did for her. How you stood up to that bastard, Franklin, and defended her honor. Not many people would have done that for someone like her. That took guts. I'm proud of you."

"She's scared."

He sniffed into his sleeve, blotting his nose dry. "She doesn't want to see you get hurt. She's scared of all the Dr. Franklins in the world. She's seen what can happen to someone who stands up to them."

"What about Otis? Is he still in the picture? Can he still make trouble for Lenora?"

"So far, Otis has left us alone. He knows we're under Del's protection. Your father is very well respected around here."

"Until I came along."

It dragged a chuckle out of him. "It's not Otis I'm worried about. You stood up to Dr. Franklin. Franklin is married to the sheriff's sister. They could make trouble for Del if they wanted to. They could run Lenora and me out of town. This is my home now. I like it here."

One more reason for me to leave.

He must have sensed my attention wandering. He noticed my thoughts drifting, squinting at my temple like he was trying to see inside my head. Chuck had his own kind of *magie*, different from mine, but the language was the same. His came from the earth. From the desert. From the living things that crossed his path, whereas mine came from the Petruskas. He had shown me this connection when he'd pressed my palm to the desert's heart and told me to feel it.

Feel the heartbeat, he'd said.

I'd felt it, and I would never look at the desert the same way again.

I wasn't surprised when he asked, "What did the desert show you that day, Vandy? Do you remember?"

I paused for a moment to put my thoughts into words. "I think it showed me a way out."

It was his turn to gape at me. He studied my profile the same way I'd memorized his. He would have seen that I was a Petruska through and through. I carried the same precise jawline as all the other Petruskas before me. The same dark brows. Same black eyes set with thick lashes, and I had my mother's cheekbones. I had my hair loose that day, but Daniel Bronson's bandana did a fine job of keeping it out of my eyes.

No sign of Del Davidson anywhere.

"What does that mean?" Chuck asked. "A way out of what?"

I glanced at my hands. Saw them trembling, so I clenched them into fists. Then I remembered I wasn't going to do that anymore and slowly released them.

I packed my fears away in the furthest corner of my mind.

Chuck was still waiting for an explanation.

I answered finally. "I'm not sure. Bad things are coming, Chuck. The question is, do I sit here and wait for it? Or do I go forward and meet it head on. The consequences will be the same no matter which one I choose." I scuffed the toe of my shoe back and forth in the loose gravel just to give myself something banal to focus on.

"Then why choose at all?"

Why choose? The answer was as simple as it was complex.

One was the coward's way out, and it involved running away. The other would send me into the fires of Hell. There was peril in both, and if I was being honest, I didn't know which choice scared me worse. Going back. Or going forward to meet the Devil himself.

Coward or brave? Was I a Davidson, or a Petruaska? Either way, I was probably going to die.

The only question burning in my mind; at the end of all this madness, which one did I want to be remembered as?

Chapter Fifteen

I didn't tell anyone I was thinking about leaving. I hadn't shown Shorty's letter to anyone. No one knew the circus was already in Tucson, waiting for me to show up. If I decided to stay at Vandemere Ranch, I could just go about my business, and no one would ever know how close I'd come to abandoning them.

I started writing a letter to Chuck. I wrote out all the details of Annie's death, and how I blamed myself for all of it. If only I'd used the *magie* sooner, I might have been able to do something to stop it from happening, but I hadn't. Not in time anyway, and I could never forgive myself for that. I wrote about Grace's suicide, and how I'd nearly died of loneliness all those weeks I spent in the hospital until Ellen Dawson made me laugh again.

I miss her, I wrote.

I sat for a moment, staring at the words, and the implications of falling in love with someone who probably never wanted to see my face ever again.

I scratched it out.

I wrote instead ...

When I first came here, I hated Arizona. Arizona took everything away from me. But then Arizona gave it all back. I have Karma now. And I have you and Lenora. And best of all, I have myself back.

I have *myself* back.

I put the letter away, unfinished.

I went to the barn, looking for Chuck. I never got tired of seeing his expression light up when he saw me.

If only my father would look at me the same way.

He called from the far end of the aisle. "Just in time to help me sweep!"

"I need you," I said.

His smile faded. "What's wrong?"

"It's nothing like that. Do you have a moment? I want to take Karma back out, only I want to ride him in the ring this time."

"Okay." He spoke in that easy way of his. "But why do you need my help? Is your leg bothering you again?"

"It's fine."

His eyes narrowed. "What are you up to?"

"You'll see."

It took some convincing to drag Karma away from his dinner. Once I got his nose out of the pile of hay mounded in the corner of his stall and slipped his bridle on, he was all business.

I attached a pair of side reins to the leather harness and made sure nothing was so tight that it constricted his movements. I wasn't sure if he'd ever worn a bareback harness before, and there were his scars to contend with. But he barely batted an eye when I clipped the side reins to the bit and led him down the aisle and into the covered ring.

Chuck swung the end door closed so the circle was complete. Regulation size. Forty-two feet in diameter. The same sized circle I rode Dolly and Copper around back home under the big top.

Chuck stood under the arm of the mechanical, hands on his hips, giving me the once-over with keen eyes. I was wearing blue jeans and a light flannel shirt this morning. I had my hair tied back and Daniel's bandana knotted around my head. Not exactly circus attire, but my shoes were rubber soled. And I wasn't sure how far I would get with this anyway, so they would have to do.

"Do you want to work on the mechanical?" Chuck asked me, starting to get a sense of what I was out here to do. "Del's gone out, just so you know. I'm the one responsible for you now. I don't want you to get hurt."

"No mechanical," I stated, as kindly as I could. It wasn't Chuck's fault I'd turned out this way. That's the thing about habits. Del wouldn't know I'd used the mechanical, but *I* would, and that's all that mattered in the long run. "Just help me up."

He cupped one hand gently under my bad knee as I bounced lightly on my right foot. I'd gotten better at mounting up, thanks to Chuck's marvelous talents for putting people back together again.

He clamped his other hand around my ankle and tossed me aboard Karma's back.

I landed with a muffled grunt. I settled in behind the pommel of the harness and worked the stiffness out of my lower back with a few painful stretches.

"How's the leg?" Chuck asked. "Good?"

I caught myself grimacing, and quickly smoothed the discomfort out of my expression. I rubbed my thigh. I could feel the thick, puckered scars right through the material. "It's cranky, but I'll live."

"Tell me what to do."

I nudged Karma forward with a touch of my heel. "Stand in the middle. Pay attention to his rhythm. Listen to his feet in the dirt. It should sound just like music if he's doing it right."

I couldn't believe how shaky my voice was. Fear tasted like metal in my mouth, and my forehead was already damp with sweat. My armpits were slippery, and a cold finger of moisture slid down the length of my spine. I couldn't have swallowed even if I'd had enough spit to do it.

Chuck stayed in the center of the ring while I walked Karma around him. "You're sure you're up to this?" He kept glancing over at the doorway as if he expected trouble to show up … mainly in the form of Del, who was nowhere near, thank God.

"I—I don't know." I was back to taking shallow breaths again. My vision tunneled in on me and blood throbbed in my ears. "Let me sit on his canter first. See how that goes."

Chuck sent Karma back out to the edge of the circle with a clap of his hand.

The stallion picked up speed, easing through the transition from walk to canter without so much as a hitch in his step.

I got my first taste of what this amazing horse could do.

I'd never sat on a horse like this. *Ever.* His feet skimmed over the sawdust as if they barely touched the earth. He moved under me like a rocking horse, knees near to knocking his chin, and his hocks were deeply collected. The side reins rounded his frame, and his gait was so smooth I could have carried a glass of water and never spilled a drop.

So why was I so terrified?

I fixed my gaze on the space between his ears.

Time slowed down.

Karma cantered the circle, waiting for me to ask him to do more.

"Vandy?"

I heard Chuck's voice over the soft, blowing breaths of the stallion who moved between my legs. I was stuck in the memory of falling. Of seeing myself crashing to the ground in front of half the town. Remembering the pain—

"Vandy!" Chuck's call was harsh, dragging me back from the brink of panic. "Look at me."

I couldn't feel my limbs anymore.

"I ... don't think I can do this."

I let Karma slow to a walk. Fear scrabbled at my throat, invading every nerve, giving me a shaking I wouldn't soon forget. It was as if I'd been pulled from an icy river and left to die on the shore; I was *that* cold.

Chuck stayed beside me. He kept pace with Karma as we walked around the perimeter of the circle. He rested his hand on my knee, and I prepared myself for a lecture. "Your body remembers how to do this. All you have to do is stand up."

I tried to pull in a shaky breath, but it just got stuck in my throat. "I *can't* ..."

"Yes, you can." Chuck studied the terror on my face and adjusted his voice accordingly. "Do it in stages. Don't think about doing the whole trick. You'll only sabotage yourself that way. Just think about kneeling on him first. Stay in that position until you're comfortable with it. You can do that, can't you? Look, we'll just start from a walk. Karma will take care of you. He's a good horse. I'll stay right here beside you. I won't let you fall."

I gulped sickly. Someone else had promised me that before, and stupidly, I'd believed him.

The sun went behind a cloud ... or maybe it was just my eyes. The ring was thrown into shadow. The circular roof clanked as the metal contracted around the rivets, competing with the thundering pulse in my ears.

I wiped the sweat out of my eyes with my sleeve, silently begging my heart to stop racing. Dizziness wouldn't do my balance any good.

I shifted my position behind the handholds and gave Karma an apologetic scratch on his crest. "Sorry, Karma. You don't deserve this ..."

Chuck stayed right with me. "Do it from a walk first," he repeated, trying to reassure me the only way he knew how.

I shook my head. "I have to do this the proper way, at a canter. It's what I'm used to. It'll be easier for me to lean into the motion." I dried my palms on my thighs, then wrapped my fingers around the metal handles on the pommel again.

Chuck stepped back.

I touched a heel to Karma's side, and he leaped into a canter.

Someone must have spent a lot of time with him, up there in Canada. He had a solid foundation of training, and he knew his job. He kept a steady pace while I sat astride him, and he waited patiently for me to clear the images of imminent disaster out of my mind. Waited for me to do *something*.

I quieted my seat. I took my time linking up with Karma's stride. I needed to familiarize myself with his deviations and thoughts.

His ears were forward and relaxed. Whatever reservations he had about a saddle rubbing against his scarred back melted away when I sat on him bareback.

Whether he would tolerate me standing on him was still up for debate.

I pushed all the other stuff away and focused solely on what my body was doing.

The only thing that existed was me and this horse.

And fear ...

The circumference of the ring had me leaning to the inside. I compensated by straightening my shoulders. I put more weight on my outside seat bone, and Karma adjusted his stride to match my questionable balance. He lightened his inside leg, curving his spine under me as he followed the pitch of the circle. His mane flicked over my hands, brushing my wrists, and I hung onto the handholds until my fingers ached.

It's now or never, my mind reasoned.

Slowly, I bent forward.

I brought my bad leg up first, knowing it would cause me the most grief.

I watched Karma's ears for any signs of concern.

He never altered his stride. He never showed a glimmer of fear. He was as scarred as I was, and yet, he *trusted me*. It was only fair that I return the favor in kind.

I knelt on my bad knee. Pain carved a deep knot between my brows, and I set my jaw against it.

Chuck noticed. "Relax your jaw," he instructed. "Breathe."

I breathed.

We glided over the sawdust.

I brought my right leg up under me next.

Sickening laughter invaded my consciousness. *Stand up, Petruska! Stand up: I want to see you fall!*

Cel Care Ia was back.

A switch in my brain flipped. This time, instead of being frightened, I got mad.

The *magie* in me fought back.

Shut up! Leave me alone! I'm sick of you following me around. I'm sick of your threats. You hide in the shadows while you make other people do your dirty work. Show yourself or fuck off. Christ, do one or the other!

Gleeful laughter. *You want me to show myself, Petruska? Consider it done.*

"Vandy!"

Chuck's shout brought me out of my head.

I was still kneeling on Karma's back. Still braced against my hands while he cantered underneath me. My wrists shook, the tendons in my arms locked up stiff.

The sparrows still flitted through the timbers above. The sun had come out from behind the cloud and the ring was bathed in brightness again. Dust motes curled and danced.

The only thing that had changed was my determination to see this through.

I steeled myself against the spasming weakness in my lower back. My left leg wasn't happy about having to stay in this new position, and I still had that bastard's laughter ringing in my head.

I armed myself with the power of the *magie.*

You sick son of a bitch. You want to see me fall?

Well, I *had* fallen... and I'd *survived.* I'd survived the months of hell that fucker had put me through. I'd survived the grief of losing my mother. I'd survived the accusations Mrs. Lee had slapped into my face. I'd survived Dolly's death, and Grace's suicide, and a train ride to the middle of nowhere. I'd survived my father's indifference even after I *begged* him to notice me. If I could survive all *that*, standing on Karma's back ought to be a walk in the park.

I trusted my body to remember. Trusted Karma to take care of me. I closed my eyes and gathered my feet under me. First the left, then the right. I paused there for a moment, crouching on Karma's back.

He never once deviated from the rhythm I set for him.

I locked my toes under the harness. Willed my shaky knees to bear my weight. Then I simply let go.

I stood up.

I won't say it was the best Liberty Stand I ever accomplished. My form was off, and the setup wouldn't have fooled anyone. I wobbled precariously above Karma's withers, getting ready to grab for his mane if things took a turn for the worst, but nothing bad happened.

Nothing bad happened!

I opened my eyes to a dizzying height. I looked down at this amazing black horse cantering under my feet and felt such a lightness in my soul it was almost painful. Joy bubbled up from my belly, so intense it seared the inside of my chest. I had to laugh just to release it. I spread my arms to the breeze whistling past my ears, and a huge smile broke across my lips—

"What in the hell are you *doing!?*"

My father's yell brought me back down to earth.

The spell broke apart. I lost focus. My feet slithered and slipped, and I scrambled for a handful of Karma's mane to save myself.

I didn't fall, but I *did* sit back down with an ungraceful thud.

I slowed Karma to a walk, both of us breathing hard.

Del strode into the ring. His head swiveled to drive a furious glare at me before he stormed over to Chuck's side.

I doubt very much Chuck had ever seen my father this upset before. He took a step back, holding his hands outstretched, his palms visible—the defensive stance of a man under attack.

"Why isn't he on the mechanical?!" my father bellowed, gesturing frantically at the metal arm hovering above Chuck's head. "How could you let him do this?! Do you want him to break his goddamn *neck* this time?!"

I couldn't believe what I was hearing. For my entire life, all I'd ever heard about was staying *off* the mechanical. *Now* he was changing his mind.

I shouted. "Stop yelling! It's not his fault, Del!"

He turned his rage on me. "Get off that horse."

My own face burned. "No."

He stared me down. His eyes were terrifying. Cruel, and cold. Black beneath the brim of the tweed cap. His fists were shaking, a tangible reaction to the fury in his mind.

"You don't get to tell me what to do, Del," I said stiffly. "Not anymore. You lost that privilege when you walked out on Ma and me."

Chuck looked torn. I didn't need the *magie* to understand his dilemma. He was stuck between wanting to protect me and running to call Lenora, who might have been able to talk some sense into my father. I knew he'd be thinking about the chains around his mind and how he was going to stop himself from breaking them again.

"I own that horse you're sitting on." Del's voice was deadly calm now. Precise, and mean. "You're on private property. Get off the horse right now, before I call for the sheriff."

Numbness spread through me. Anger turned to dismay in one shattered heartbeat. My mouth trembled and my eyes watered. "Why do you hate me so much?"

He turned his back on me. "Pack your bags and get out. Go back to California, where you belong."

I bent forward and worked my right leg over Karma's hindquarters, managing to kick him in the hip in the process. I slithered off his back, landed as best I could on one leg, and covered the distance between us in three strides.

I grabbed Del by the arm and pulled him around. "Say it to my face! *Say it!* Tell me why you hate me!" My throat cramped up, turning my voice into something I didn't recognize. Another me I didn't like. My eyes stung too, but *nothing* would make me cry in front of him.

He wrenched his arm out of my grasp. "You're behaving like a child."

"You ... *left us!*" I panted. "You left me to take care of Ma *by myself*. I was *twelve*. She never got over it you know. She never got over you leaving us. She drank—because of you. She slept with so many men ... because of you. She got sick because of *you!* You know what she told me, right before she died? She told me ... all she ever wanted from you was a safety net. You were supposed to be our *safety net* ... and you turned your back on us! Ma *loved you! I* loved you! I loved you with all my heart—and you broke it. How does that feel, Del? Does it make you happy? Knowing you destroyed us?"

"Don't be stupid." He jerked his chin at Chuck. "Take him into the house. I'll see to the horse."

Chuck raised his hands. "Sorry, Boss. I think you need to hear this. It's about damn time you listened to him."

Del seethed. "You forget your place, Chuck."

He shrugged tight shoulders and jammed his hands into his pockets where they couldn't do any harm. "No, I haven't forgotten anything. You probably saved my life. I *know* you saved Lenora's. If it wasn't for you, I don't know where I'd be. Probably hanging by the neck in some prison cell up north. You have a big heart Del, which is why I can't for the life of me understand why you won't talk to your own son. He deserves so much better than what you've given him. He's a good boy. If you would just *talk* to him, you'd see that."

I wasn't finished. I'd waited *years* to tell my father exactly what I thought of him and I wasn't about to waste my chance. "What happened, Del? You were so... *nice* to me. What changed?" I was still madder 'n hell and it showed up in the stranglehold ratcheting around my neck. "Why did you make me eat that cactus fruit? To humiliate me? I was just *a kid*." A thin moan got past nerveless lips. "You *laughed* at me."

"I don't know what you're talking about. What cactus fruit?" my father asked.

I stared at him. He didn't remember it. The incident had left deep scars on my soul, and he didn't even remember doing it.

"This is ridiculous." He started to walk away, but then brought himself up short. He turned back to me and arranged his expression into something that resembled pity. "Look, I know I haven't done right by you. I wish things could have been different between us, but sometimes you just have to cut your losses. You deserved better, I know. And I'm really sorry about your mother. It hurts, I'm sure, but it's best if you leave here. Just ... move on with your life, Vandemere. I can't give you anything more than that."

"You're sorry?" I gasped. "You're *sorry?*"

"Put the horse away." Del threw orders at Chuck like he was nothing more than an indentured servant.

He turned his back on me again headed across the ring towards the door.

Tears spilled down my face, scorching my skin. Tears I couldn't hide anymore. My sobs bounced off the tin roof overhead and my tongue tripped over the words— "You ... said you would ... always be there to catch me, but you *lied."* I sniffed back snot and slashed my hand across my eyes. My breath shuddered in and out of my chest. "I fell, Dad, in front of all those people. I *fell*. You ... weren't there. You *promised me*. You ..." more useless gulping. No way to salvage my pride now. "You were supposed to be my *safety net*." I scrubbed more tears off my face with my sleeve. "You ... taught me to *fly*, and then you let me fall. How ... *could you*?"

He paused mid-stride. I saw him bend his head. Saw him take a careful breath.

I hid my face behind my hands. Realized my voice was trapped in there now, so I dropped my arms back down and let him see the pain he'd caused. "What did I do to make you hate me? Tell me ... so I can fix it. If I did something wrong, please *tell me*. Just ... don't hate me anymore. I ... need you. I ... don't want things to be like this—"

He turned around. His eyes were as watery as mine. "Good God, Vandy. What would ever make you think it was something *you* did?"

I scrubbed a hand under my streaming nose. My voice was all hitchy now. "Because ... I wouldn't do the backflip ... off Samson that day."

He made a sound in the back of his throat, a wretched sound from a broken man. "No, *no*, Vandy ... it wasn't you. It was *never you*."

"Then what? Was it Ma? Was it the game we played? The *magie*? I know you never liked us doing ... that stuff."

He paced. There was agitation in every step he took. He kept his eyes on the ground, then thought better of it, and turned to face me. "That's not it. There's a reason why I left. If I tell you ... well, it's just best if I don't."

Chuck remained silent and watchful. I knew he was still thinking about chains. How the ones we couldn't see were often the hardest to break.

"Why can't you just be honest for once?" I argued. It was so odd, how I could be inconsolable one minute and back in control the next. "I'll ... go back to California. I was planning on leaving anyway. I—I know I've caused a lot of trouble for you. But I deserve the truth. Tell me why you left. It's the least you could do to make up for abandoning me and Ma. All this time, you've been living on this beautiful ranch with Lenora, no responsibilities to us, or to Jimmy, or the circus. All this time, I never asked you for anything. I'm asking you now ... for this *one thing*. Tell me the truth. Why'd you leave?"

His anger suddenly deflated, leaving him stone-faced and grave. "Don't you understand? I *can't*." He paced out his frustration before me and fixed his eyes on the sawdust again, as if begging the earth to open up and swallow him whole. He was fighting a war with something I couldn't see. He stayed well back of me, afraid to come near, and his gaze kept glancing off me like bullets. "Please, Vandy. Go home. It's for your own safety. I'm sorry it has to be this way. I know you don't understand, but I'm trying to protect you."

"Protect me?" I barked out a laugh as sharp as glass. "What kind of shit is that?"

He pressed the back of his hand over his lips as if it would stop the words from escaping. "I don't hate you."

"Then *what*? Tell me!"

He stopped his infernal pacing and rounded on me. He faced me in his impeccably clean trousers and checked shirt, the skin showing through the vee of his collar gone ruddy from the sun.

I had to look up to meet his eyes. I kept forgetting how tall he actually was. The long, lean legs and squared up shoulders set him apart from the rest of us, and his boyish features were still handsome even after all these years.

"Vandy ... please, *go home*." His tone was colorless, strained to the breaking point, and for once he seemed genuinely concerned for my welfare.

Silence beat down from the rafters. Even the sparrows had gone quiet now.

I called upon the *magie* to help me. I needed *something* to help me understand this. *Anything* ... I was desperate.

At first, he wasn't going to let me in. There wasn't a person or animal I could read if they wouldn't open that door and let me through. He had lived with my mother long enough to know how to erect a barricade around his thoughts to keep her from getting too close to his personal truths.

He covered his face with his hands, just as I had done, and I heard him groan softly. When he took them away again, my heart sank. "I'm sorry, Vandy. I just can't tell you. Hate me if you want, but please ... just go. I've ... tried ... so hard—" He couldn't finish.

I took a small step towards him. Then another. When he didn't retreat, I walked right up to him.

I took his left hand into my own, opened his palm, and placed it over my heart. My lips felt like they belonged to someone else, but I had to get this out before I lost myself in the grief again. "It's okay, Dad. I know you're scared. Can you feel my heartbeat? *Feel it*. I'm still alive ... because of *you*. I'm still here ... because you walked away. I don't blame you anymore. I *did*. God, how I blamed you ... but it's okay now. I don't have to be angry anymore. *That's* what was killing me. That's what it wants. It's the anger that destroys us. I know that now. It's something Chuck taught me. He gave me my life back, Dad. He taught me to walk again. He got me up on Karma even when I thought I would never ride another horse, *ever*. He took me into the desert and he showed me the way out."

I expected rage. At the very least, I expected Del to push me away. I would have forgiven him if he had. I wouldn't have blamed him for throwing me away. *I* would have done it if it were me.

He kept his hand pressed against my heartbeat. I could feel tremors vibrating through his body, and his own heart was beating so hard I could hear it drumming away inside his chest. He had sweated right through his checkered shirt. His hair had turned to dark spikes under his tweed cap and sweat dripped off him like rain.

"I know it's bad," I whispered. "It's not your fault. It really isn't. You can tell me, Dad. I won't be mad at you anymore. You need to say it. Otherwise, we're both lost."

"Vandy ..."

His eyes told me no. He wouldn't admit it. How could he? He knew what it would do to me if he loosed the secret he'd kept from me all those years ago, but I made him say it anyway.

His betrayal was the only thing that could save me now.

I begged him. "Tell me."

He drew in a frugal breath. He found safer things to look at, and he finally told me the truth. A truth so painful, I think a part of him died that day.

He said, "I left ... because I wanted to hurt you, Vandy. I wanted to hurt you every second of every day. From the minute you were born, my mind was filled with terrible things. I was so *scared* ..." He swallowed with difficulty, and his forehead creased with shame. "I was so *afraid*. I would lie awake at nights thinking up ways to break you. How I would *kill* you. Things no father should ever *dream* of doing to their own child—I thought them. There wasn't a moment that I wasn't picturing myself slamming my fist into your face, or wrenching your arm out of your shoulder, or throwing you against the wall just so I could hear your head hit the plaster.

"At first, I hid it. For those first few years, I was able to control it. This *thing* that was inside of me wasn't as strong back then. You were just an infant. It wanted me to hurt you, but I wouldn't let it in. You were so small. You were *a baby*, for Christ's sake! But the older you got, the stronger *it* got. It wanted me to do things to you. Horrible things.

"I thought I must be out of my mind. I thought, if I just stayed away from you, things would get better. But they didn't get better. They only got worse.

"That day when you rode Samson? That was the closest I'd ever come to losing control of myself. Of *it*. *The Madness*, I called it. What else would it be, other than insanity? I was so *angry* ..."

Tears streamed down his face, but he didn't make a sound. He looked everywhere but right at me. He made sure he would never have to see the pain his confession mirrored in my eyes. Pain he put there himself. "I could have killed you that day, Vandy. I *wanted to.* In my mind, I saw myself knocking you down. Saw myself kneeling on your wrists. I saw myself wrapping my hands around your throat and crushing the life out of you until you stopped breathing. If it hadn't been for Samson ..."

I clutched my head. I threaded my fingers into my hair and pulled. Every word he said left its mark on me; lashes that flayed my soul, leaving me wounded and bleeding.

"So, you see ... I *had* to walk away. I had to leave so I wouldn't hurt you. I had to get as far away from you as I could. To protect you from *me.* Your own father." His whole body shuddered. "I thought I had done the right thing. I thought it was over. I hadn't had those feelings once since the day I left. But then you showed up here ... and it all came back. All those hateful things I thought I'd left in the past came back. I thought; if I could just make you *leave*... but you were so injured. Chuck and Lenora took such good care of you. I thought; give him a chance. Give him time to heal, then he'll go."

I said nothing. I stared at my feet. Yes, I was still breathing. Still living. Still standing up. I existed, but beyond that? Only time would tell.

"What about now?" I asked, in a dull voice. I had dropped my hands down to my sides again. "Do you still want to hurt me?"

His silence was like a knife to my chest.

He didn't answer.

Didn't have to.

I moaned. "Then why tell me to work on the mechanical?"

His honesty was brutal as it was swift. "Because it's broken. The arm is rusted out in a few places. I haven't gotten around to fixing it yet. Chuck wouldn't have known. I thought ... one day soon, you would ..."

"Try to ride," I finished for him.

The world got very bleak.

"Vandy?" I heard Del speak my name but it didn't seem connected to me anymore. That name belonged to someone else. The person I'd been a moment before. Someone filled with joy, and standing on Karma's back ...

"You wanted the truth," he said. "I warned you. Please ... say something?" His hand was suddenly on my shoulder, buoying me up. "Son? Can you look at me, please?"

I lifted my gaze. I think my father was a little confused with what he saw there. Or rather, what he *didn't* see.

He peered into my vacant eyes. "I knew this would be too much, but you *asked me*. You aren't having another fit, are you?" He flicked a worried glance in Chuck's direction. "Go get Lenora."

"I'm okay," I said, halting their panic. I looked around but I don't remember seeing much. "I'm going to ..."

I stumbled away and nearly ran straight into Chuck.

He put out a hand to stop me from falling over. "Good God, Vandy ..."

I mumbled, "It's okay, Chuck. I just need," I choked on the bitterness rising into my mouth, "some time. Can you take care of Karma for me?"

He was struggling too. Searching for the right words that would somehow make this all go away. "You shouldn't be alone right now."

The look he gave Del was chilling.

I smiled; a fake grin meant to reassure him. "I'm fine. I just need … need to … go …"

I barely felt the ground under my feet. How I ever made it to the door was a mystery. My thoughts blurred. My mind was a mirror smashed upon the ground. All that was left of me were shards of glass. Fragments reflecting the memories of my childhood in bits and pieces.

No way to put them back together again.

I walked out of the barn and made it all the way across the yard. I couldn't feel my feet anymore. My legs carried me forward, but they may as well have belonged on someone else's body.

The sun pressed down on me. It sharpened my shadow into a separate form of myself; another *me*. The one that walked beside me. Darkness against the light.

Hopelessness invaded my body like a disease; a hard mass of ugliness that grew from the hole in my heart, sending tendrils of sickness into my chest.

I thought about the cancer my mother had suffered; how she'd kept her fear a secret so I didn't have to suffer right along with her. I hadn't realized until now how she'd tried to protect me from it. I'd been too caught up in my own anger to notice her sacrifice. Too busy being a smart-assed circus brat, thinking I was so much better than everyone else. Her pain was *my* pain now. Her desperation had become my own. I knew now why she'd sent me here, to Arizona. Why she'd wanted me to face my father. It must have half-killed her to do this, knowing what she was sending me into, and yet, she'd done it, and so bravely too. My own fortitude paled before hers. She'd never once complained as the cancer hollowed out her bones and pulled her spirit apart, and yet here I was, stumbling blindly. I wasn't strong like her. I wasn't strong enough to do this. I was going to war, and I needed to be held accountable for my mistakes … something I wasn't exactly known for.

I'd treated people horribly in the past. Now I would have to atone for my sins.

Have faith. My mother had said this to me, and I'd told Chuck the same thing.

The desert had shown me a way out. It had shown me I was capable of greater things than what I'd accomplished in the past. It wasn't too late for me. Not yet. I was still salvageable. I was a mess, sure, but deep down, I still believed there was some good inside of me. I believed I could finally face the evil my family had called from the Underworld, maybe even survive it.

And if I failed?

Well, at least the people who really mattered to me would know that I tried.

Chapter Sixteen

I went to my room and stayed there. I heard hushed voices out in the hallway. Some real. Some imagined.

Lenora tapped on the door. "Vandy, honey? Do you want some supper?"

I schooled my voice into a semblance of normalcy. "I'm not very hungry, thanks."

"What about a cup of tea?"

"No, I'm fine."

She went away after that.

Dawson's book, *Liber Mortuorum,* rested in my lap. I *had* gotten it all wrong. I'd been duped by a grifter's trick, only this one had come in the form of a vengeful demon who had done everything it could to deceive me into thinking this was all my fault.

It had been staring me in the face all along. I just needed the *magie* to see it. When dear old Margaret had bookmarked the page in *Liber Mortuorum* while I'd slept beside her on the Greyhound bus heading back to California, I'd been blinded by the obvious. The painted image of *Cel Care Ia* had been so terrifyingly familiar I hadn't even thought to look at the opposite page. I'd fixated on the beast with knives for hands and porcupine quills in his mouth because that's who the demon *wanted* me to think was my enemy.

I studied the painting on the opposite page.

Vigolii.

He was nothing more than a shadow. Man-shaped. Faceless. The picture showed him as an empty space tucked into a crowd of brightly painted circus performers. There were jugglers, and fire-eaters, and jesters marching across the page—all oblivious to his presence. Drawing upon my limited knowledge of my mother's native tongue, I was able to read enough of the text to get an inkling of what he was; what he could do. A couple of Romanian words stood out to me. *Dăunător*, and *rău*. Not the words you wanted to see when researching the demon bent on murdering you. Those words translated into *bad* and *injurious*. He was a manifestation of Death. In his presence, no one was safe. He was darkness against the light. A shapeshifter. Chuck called him a Skinwalker, but he was more than that. He was a Shade. A fallen Underling of Hell. He had worn the face of *Cel Care Ia* to fool me. An Elemental might make your life miserable, but a Shade would kill you. He had played the ultimate con on me, and I'd fallen for it.

Why hadn't my mother just told me the truth?

Even as that question raged through my mind; I already knew the answer. In my arrogance, I would have tried to confront *Vigolii* without the *magie*. He would have killed me, just as he'd killed Annie, and Dolly, and the other little girl, Cassie Lamont.

Fury smoldered behind my eyes, mingling with a grief that threatened to grind me into dust... but I still had a job to do, and time was getting on.

I closed the book and left it on the bed. I didn't need it anymore. Where I was going, it was bound to get damaged. Dawson would come looking for it soon enough and I planned on being far away by then.

I packed my belongings and put everything I owned into the satchel Jimmy had given me. There wasn't much to speak of. Just my mother's tarot cards, and the turquoise I'd kept as reminders of her. A couple of shirts and an extra pair of pants.

I left the letter I'd written for Chuck folded up on the nightstand where someone would find it in the morning, next to my mother's ashes.

My fingers lingered on the Mason jar. I whispered, "Stay with me, Ma. I need you. I'm scared."

I wove Lenora's dove feather into the braid behind my ear and knotted Daniel's bandana around my neck. I stuffed Shorty's letter down into the bottom of the satchel before pulling on my coat. I adjusted the strap of the satchel across my chest, then I sat on the edge of my bed and waited. I waited until the house was silent and dark, and everyone had gone to sleep.

Moving as silently as a ghost, I let myself out.

The December moon spilled its brilliance over the roof of the barn. It bathed the ranch in amber radiance. The air was still, the earth barely breathing. The heat left over from the day warmed me as I brushed past Lenora's roses.

I moved through the half-light. I'd prepared myself for a quiet escape. My black coat would hide me from prying eyes, and the moon would show me the way into town. I hadn't had anything to eat since earlier this morning, but the dread in my stomach did a fine job of taking my appetite away.

I remembered to take water with me this time. I stopped long enough to fill a jar with a screw-down lid from the bucket Lenora used to water her roses with and tuck it into the satchel.

I crept into the stable.

Most of the horses were outside in the paddocks for the night. A few we'd brought inside after suppertime; a couple of mares who didn't like being outside for more than a few hours and one gelding that belonged to a client who had skipped out of paying his bill, so I think the horse was Del's now.

And Karma.

In the letter I'd left for Chuck and Lenora, I'd written ...

I have Karma. I'll take good care of him. I'll write to you to let you know where you can come get him. Please don't follow me. I'm sorry I couldn't say goodbye in person. I hope you understand why I'm doing this. Even though it looks like I'm running away I'm really not. There's something I need to take care of. Tell my father—

I hesitated. Ink dripped from the end of my pen onto the paper, leaving a black bubble that remained whole for a moment before it seeped into what I'd written. Blowing on it just made it worse.

I left things unsaid.

I signed off.

Chuck, I'll never forget your kindness.

Yours very truly,

Vandy Petruska.

Not Davidson. I'd never been a Davidson. My father's admissions had stuck *that* knife between my ribs, leaving little doubt in my mind that I was a Petruska to the core.

I walked past darkened stalls. My goal was to make as little noise as possible. A human in the barn usually meant something was up, that maybe food was coming. Horses could make a ton of racket if they thought they were going to be fed.

I needn't have worried. Every horse was lying down. I heard snoring coming from the gelding's stall, and even Karma was a dark shape nestled in the deep bedding I'd piled around his stall earlier that day.

I got his bridle down from the peg in the harness room and moved to his stall door. "Come on, old fella. Time to get a move on."

He thrust his front legs forward and heaved himself up on all fours.

I waited until he'd shaken the straw off his back, then slipped the bit between his teeth and pulled the bridle over his ears.

Sensing excitement, every horse woke up and came to the door of their stall to peer out.

I led Karma out of the barn before they could figure out I was stealing a friend away.

There was the small matter of mounting up on Karma's back. My strength hadn't returned enough to vault on from a standstill, so I had to find a place to get myself as high up as possible to throw a leg over. Lenora's flowerboxes worked perfectly. I positioned Karma close to the raised boxes, clambered up onto the corner, and used my free hand to help guide my right leg over his back. The rest was easy. I settled in behind his withers and gathered up the reins before touching his side with a light heel.

We headed down the lane with the full moon rising over my shoulder. The desert spread out on either side of me, casting shadows across the landscape that hid my intentions and muffled Karma's footfalls.

Annie went on ahead of me. To anyone else, she would have looked like nothing more than a tattered rag of mist floating over the dirt track leading down to the front gates. I connected the *magie* to the lightness surrounding her, and she led me towards home.

Time to go, little mouse.

I bid a silent goodbye to Vandemere Ranch, vowing never to return again.

***

I asked a lot from Karma that night. I made him canter most of the way, slowing to a walk long enough for the sweat to dry on him and his wind to settle before nudging him forward again. There wasn't much time, and we had a lot of ground to cover before the rising sun gave us away.

He kept up that beautiful, rocking-horse lope for miles at a time, carrying me through the darkness without complaint.

I was conscious of his efforts, and I never let him run to the point of exhaustion. He was doing this for me, and I made sure he had enough time to rest and gather his strength before I asked him to canter again.

My own pain was a choice I put up with. I wasn't used to riding this long and my muscles were showing signs of fatigue. Sitting astride Karma was torture, but I took it all in stride. I was making him do this, so it was only fair that I should suffer too. I set my teeth against the grinding ache in my bad leg and focused on the silver road cutting through the desert instead.

The entity spoke to me that night, in whispers and rustling wind.

I returned the favor.

I'm coming, I told him. *Just like you wanted me to.*

I'm waiting for you.

I'll make a deal with you. Strange, to be bargaining with a demon. *Leave me alone until I get there. No more threats. No more possessed train conductors promising to set me on fire. Those things are beneath you. I'll fight you on my terms. Otherwise, I'm turning around and going back.*

You're giving me choices?

I'm giving you options.

Sad, little Petruska. You have no idea what I have planned for you. I agree to your terms.

Karma shook his head and his stride faltered.

I stroked his satin neck. "It's okay, Karma. Nothing bad will happen to you. I promise."

Screeching laughter pierced my thoughts, splitting my consciousness into a million sparks of light.

I pressed the heel of my hand against my temple and drove *Vigolii* out of my head.

You forget who you're dealing with, Demon.

You're going to burn, Petruska.

Oh, probably …

I sensed his hesitation. Placid submission was something he wasn't used to, and I think this threw him off his game. *Vigolii* was used to feeding off my fear. My panic. He had even tried to devour my soul, that day he attacked me in Dolly's stall. His very presence heralded death, and when I wouldn't play by the rules, he got confused.

I sent him a clear message. *I know your name now. Go on. Gather your strength. I know how much energy it takes for you to attack me. Rest up, while you still can.*

He left me alone after that. I didn't believe for a moment that I was free of this. My mother hadn't been the one to start this war, but her family had been the ones to bring it across the Continent and the Atlantic to America.

Bonnie Petruska had seen to it that I was armed with the knowledge of how to send this thing back to where it came from. It had been her dying wish to see me return to Arizona and confront Del Davidson about why he'd left. It was through that terrible truth that I had learned what the entity was afraid of. I knew his secret now. I knew how to fight him. It would come at a cost though. Already had. *Vigolii* had taken my mother's life. He would probably take mine as well, but I was going to do my damnedest to keep that from happening.

The moon rose higher. The light changed from a rosy glow to a brighter white, turning the desert into shades of black charcoal and lighter gray. The air was cool, and I was glad of my coat.

There was no definition to the landscape. Just clumps of shadow here and there. Black hills merged with the greyer tones in the distance. Bats flitted against a legion of stars shining far above me, and the air was fragrant with nighttime blooms.

We rounded a bend in the road.

Karma came to a sudden stop. He dug his toes in the dust and gaped at a group of javelinas that had just come into view. They moved across the paleness of the desert floor, rooting through stones along the edge of the road; dark shapes merging with an even darker background.

Karma's heart pounded between my legs. His head shot up, blocking my sightline, and he held his breath for an instant before letting out a great snort of terror.

The javelinas ran for their lives.

Karma pranced on the spot for a few moments before wheeling on his hocks and bolting back the way we'd just come.

His spook nearly unseated me. My aching bones cried out for mercy. I grabbed a handful of his mane as he pelted down the road, and the wind screamed across my ears.

He ran himself out. I was finally able to wrestle him down to a walk. I pulled him around and sent him back up the road. It took some convincing, but once he decided it was safe to pass the spot where the peccaries had disappeared into the brush, he trotted forward again. He held his tail flagged over his rump, lifting his feet like he was walking on hot coals instead of dirt.

He really was a marvelous horse. I pictured him performing under the spotlight, his black coat luminescent in the glow, me on his back, dressed in satin and spangles.

The image dissolved into tattered remnants of hope. With my body broken the way it was, I doubt I would ever manage even a simple vault from the ground, let alone the dreaded backflip that had cost me my career.

Still ...

I stifled a wry smile. I was about to go into battle with a demon who wanted me dead, and here I was, dreaming about showing off for spectators. It made me wonder: after everything that had happened, had I really changed at all?

I sat aboard Karma while his gorgeous stride ate up the miles and talked myself into a grin. Maybe there was still some circus brat left in me after all?

I raised my chin a little higher. It was good to have the old Vandemere back. Now, all I had to do was find a way to keep him from dying.

Chapter Seventeen

The sky paled as day dawned over the desert. Cactus emerged out of the gray light, heavy with dew. Prickly branches were beaded with enough silvery pearls to put Sylvia Reinhart's sequined costume to shame. Sheets of mist lay low over the desert floor, clinging to glistening spiderwebs as a bank of cloud hid the sun's ascent, and the sky turned a milky white.

I couldn't ask anything more from Karma. He'd given me everything he had, and still I'd pressed him. I knew he was tiring, so I let him walk the last stretch into town. His lowered his head, dragging his toes in the dust. I let out more rein so he could stretch out the weariness from his spine.

There came a point where I just couldn't take the pain of riding anymore. I stopped Karma in the middle of the road and eased myself off his back. I had to lean against his side to let the quivering agony work its way out of my leg before I could even think about continuing on foot.

Walking wasn't much better than riding.

I hadn't seen a single soul the whole night. I'd ridden past some open gates along the way; skeletons in iron that spelled out the names of the property owners, and there was always a long, dusty road of ruts leading deeper into the desert where someone's homestead lay back there. I'd seen cows milling about. Seen sheep too. But no humans.

I thought about Dolly.

I couldn't remember the exact place where she had died. I wasn't about to go traipsing all over the desert looking for her bones either. It didn't stop me from wondering, at what point during the night had I ridden past her?

I kept my gaze forward and my attention on the road and I asked her to forgive me for putting her life in such peril.

You deserved better, I told her, in case she was listening. The desert will take care of you, just like it took care of me.

I sighed wearily. I knew in my heart she wasn't confined to the earth any longer. I just really missed her. She'd been my partner under the big top, and outside of it too. She'd been my constant companion in this crazy, mixed-up chaos that had been my existence up till now, and she'd been the one to anchor me to a life of possibilities inside the circus ring. Not having her with me cast my confidence into serious doubt.

Believe in the magic, the voices in my head told me. *Dolly isn't really gone. You just need to have faith.*

But that was the trouble with faith. You had to go into it blind.

So blindly, I went.

***

I walked Karma along the banks of the Salt River just as the sun cleared that mountain range of cloud. The harsh sky hurt my eyes and I was starting to boil under the black coat.

The butte was visible now, appearing as ragged-edged monolith through a transparent wash of fog. I could just make out the railway bridge that spanned the river too, a meshwork of iron anchored to the rock on either shore. Roosters crowed from unseen backyards, and there were signs of life along the road.

I led Karma over the land bridge, rather than asking him to slosh through the muddy currents of the Salt River to get to the other side. A truck rattled towards us, kicking up a plume of dust, and I moved Karma off to the side to let it go past.

As with most hick towns in the US, Tempe came with its share of public watering troughs. After wandering through the narrow streets and back alleys, I found a working spigot that trickled into a cracked enamel basin and let Karma drink his fill.

I leaned my shoulders against the stone wall behind me, bone-tired, arms crossed over my chest. I kept an eye out for trouble. There didn't seem to be many people about so early in the morning, but I was a stranger in a small town, and I was in possession of a valuable horse. Consequently, I wasn't about to turn my back on curtained windows and prying eyes.

After Karma was done drinking, I cupped my hands under the spill of water and flushed the dust off my face. The water tasted like rust, but I refilled the water jar anyway, and stowed it safely away again.

Karma lipped at a few sparse blades of grass that poked through the edge of the basin.

For me, hunger would have to wait.

The satchel was a cumbersome weight against my hip. I made sure it was secure across my shoulder before buttoning up the front of my coat and brushing the filth off my cuffs. I might have been called a dirty Gypsy from time to time, but it didn't mean I had to *look* like one.

I found the train depot easily enough. I remembered the way, sort of, and only got lost once. We walked past sun-bleached store fronts and utilitarian façades soaking up the glare of the ascending sun while the town of Tempe slowly came to life. Proprietors opened their doors. Swept the dirt off slatted porches. People in drab clothing went about their business, and I heard a church bell tolling off in the distance.

Cars rumbled along the road.

One even slowed to get a better look at us.

The man behind the wheel looked a lot like Dr. Franklin.

Apprehension tugged at my already frayed nerves.

There was a woman with him, gray-haired, and clad in a floral dress. She stared at me and pointed through the window.

I smiled, thinking I could win her over with my charm, but a dog chose that moment to rush out from behind a picket gate to bark at us. By the time I had shouted at the dog to warn it off, the Franklins had already moved on up the street and disappeared around a corner.

All ephemera of a day in the life of a small town.

The streets we traversed were just a continuation of the desert, only with few less tumbleweeds and boulders to navigate. The whole place had an air of faded glory of lawlessness and dusty dreams, but to the people of Tempe, it was home, and home was a place you fought for.

I tied my horse to a hitching post outside the train station and went in to inquire about the cost of a one-way ticket to the Tucson.

The lone proprietor of this whistlestop eyed me up and down. "Four dollars for you. Eight dollars for the horse."

That was four dollars more than I had in my pocket. I was leaving a trail of breadcrumbs to a place I wasn't even going to, and it was going to cost me dearly.

I drummed my fingertips on the surface of the counter. "When's the train coming?"

The man behind the glass partition blinked at me.

I stilled my fingers.

The train station was little more than a one-room shanty that stank of wood polish and old boots, and the look on the clerk's face warned me I wasn't welcome here. He was the picture of a typical employee of the Union Pacific Railway Company, in his pin-striped shirt and arm bands. Pale, bulbous eyes scanned my face, noting my long, braided hair and black overcoat, and it was obvious by the press of his mouth that he didn't like what he saw.

He shuffled some papers in front of him and licked his thumb to wet it down. "You must have an angel on your shoulder. The train's due in twenty minutes."

An angel? More like the Devil at my heels.

I had twenty minutes to figure out how I was going to make another four dollars to pay for this charade.

I dug myself into a deeper hole than the one I was already in. "Hey Sir?"

He glanced up.

"I changed my mind," I said. "I want to go to Flagstaff instead."

The clerk sighed pointedly. He didn't come right out and say, *make up your goddamn mind, kid*, but I could tell he was thinking it. "Then you'll have to wait for the train coming out of Maricopa. It's due in at noon."

More breadcrumbs.

"Will it get me close to the Grand Canyon?"

"Close enough. And it's more expensive. Five dollars for you. Ten dollars for the horse. You want the tickets or not?" His colorless tone told me he was already bored with my presence.

"I want them. Can you excuse me for a moment? I'll be right back."

He shrugged his indifference. "Whatever you say, kid."

I went back outside to ponder my situation, only to find Dr. Franklin and the woman in the floral dress leading my horse away.

"Hey!" I yelled. "*What the hell?*"

Dr. Franklin rounded back. His fear of horses was evident in the way he gripped Karma by the bridle. He kept his arm locked straight out, holding the stallion as far away from himself as he possibly could.

"You!" He pulled his upper lip into a snarl. "Caught you red-handed! Bad enough you attacked me. Now you're stealing this horse too. I'm sure Mr. Davidson will thank me for rescuing this animal."

I crossed the platform in less than three strides and planted myself directly in his path. "Give him back!"

Franklin assessed the threat in my expression and spoke to his wife. "Go get Jeb."

The woman put her birdy-claw hands on her narrow hips and gave me one last chance to redeem myself before she ran for help. "Listen you. I'll have you know my brother is the sheriff in this town. We're not looking for any trouble here. It's obvious you don't own this horse. Go on now. Go about your business and let us do ours."

Anger tightened its grip around my windpipe. "I want my horse back!"

Franklin's wife seemed perversely pleased with my reaction. "I've heard about you. You're that kid from the circus. Del never stops talking about you, how you're such a fancy-pants trick rider. Jumping through fiery hoops and all." Her sneer grazed me, cutting me to the bone. "You don't look like much of a rider to me. More like a clown,

I'd say. It's too bad a fine man like Del has to put up with a son like you."

The old me would have handed it right back to her.

The new me tamped out the sparks of rage and cooled his voice. I wasn't going to be *that* person anymore, but God ... it took some doing to bite my tongue.

"I know you don't like me," I said. "I've seen how outsiders are treated around here. I get it. I don't look like you and it scares you. I'm just a dirty Gypsy. A circus freak. People like me can't be trusted around decent folk like yourselves, right?"

Mrs. Franklin snorted her disapproval.

I pasted a bland smile on my lips. "But you know what? It goes both ways. I don't like *you* much either."

I felt kind of bad for saying that. I was still getting used to wearing the skin of a changed man so things like that were bound to slip out.

She gasped dramatically.

I turned to Dr. Franklin, keeping one eye on Karma, who was shifting around and not liking this new situation we'd gotten ourselves into. I dragged the new me to the surface, and put him on like a costume. "I owe you an apology, Dr. Franklin. I'm very sorry I treated you poorly that day I tried to break your fingers, but you shouldn't have put your hands on Lenora like that."

That got the questioning glance from Mrs. Franklin I was hoping for.

A sudden understanding took shape behind her deep-set eyes. Age had worn away her beauty and left her with sagging jowls and wiry hair that could not be contained under the hat she'd chosen to wear that day. To me, she was a lost woman. I read the hopelessness beneath her scowl, and I actually felt sorry for her. The floral dress and the stylish hat were meant to offset the boredom of being a doctor's wife. She'd been promised a life of privilege and had gotten tumbleweeds and dirt instead. There was nothing for her to do in this town except present herself on her husband's arm, and even that had come into question now.

In some ways, she was a bit like me. She was a performer too. She had a job to do, and she was bound by the constraints thrust upon her by narrow-minded people. I wondered; had she wanted a different life than the one fate had handed her?

"What's he talking about, Jan?" she demanded.

Dr. Franklin squirmed under the threat of exposure. "You shut your mouth, kid."

Karma pawed his impatience into the dust and came very close to stepping on Franklin's foot.

Dr. Franklin jumped away from Karma's aim and rattled his bit with a rough hand. "Hey, you. Mind your manners!"

Karma rolled his eyes.

I blurted out, "Stop it! You're scaring him!"

"Jan, this is ridiculous," Mrs. Franklin huffed. "We're going to be late for church."

I was reduced to bargaining with the man. It was either that or employ my fists, and I was better than that now, wasn't I?

I donned my best grifter's face. "Just give me back my horse. I promise I won't say another word. Circus honor."

"This is stolen property—"

"He's not stolen! My father bought him for *me*. If anyone is stealing him, it's *you!*"

I moved in to tear the reins from the doctor's hands, but Franklin was ready for it. He put up a knee to block me. "You see that, Harriet? See how he tried to attack me? I told you he was trouble."

People had started to notice us. A man in dusty blue jeans and gray shirt must have heard the ruckus and joined us on the platform. Another woman, sheltering her delicate skin under a white parasol, crossed the narrow dirt laneway to stand close by. I thought she was quite pretty. There were spots of rose-petal blush warming her cheekbones, and her eyes were as blue as the turquoise Arizona was famous for. Her chestnut hair fell across one shoulder in tidy ringlets, and I caught the glint of a gold cross on a chain half-hidden under the neckline of her dress. When I read her energy, I found her elusive and wary.

I pulled the *magie* away from her and honed my focus. I had about fifteen minutes left to think up a way to earn four dollars and get my horse back before the train arrived. I had an audience now and time was not on my side.

"How about we make a little wager?" I sweltered under my coat and too many layers of clothing, but my hand was steady when I thrust it into the satchel at my hip. "If you win, you get to keep Karma. If I win, I get him back, plus four dollars."

My mother's tarot cards rested against my fingertips. Shorty's letter was still there too, along with the turquoise stones rattling loose under my spare clothes. I had eight dollars in my pocket and a long line of Petruskas standing with me on this.

Have faith ... they whispered.

Faith is about all I have, I told them.

Dr. Franklin rolled his lips inward until his mouth nearly disappeared. He stood in the gathering sunshine, dressed for church; in a brown suit, and bowler hat tamped down on his gray head. "Four dollars? That seems a bit steep to me. What makes you think I would give you anything, let alone four dollars?"

Karma leaned his nose toward me. His eyelids wrinkled with worry. He would have sensed my agitation, and he was looking to me for guidance.

I wanted to reach out to stroke his broad forehead, but Dr. Franklin was standing in my way.

In the end, the man left me no choice.

I turned to the crowd. "Ladies and gentlemen ..." I summoned up my best barker's voice, hoping no one would notice the underlying squeak of panic. "Allow me to introduce myself. My name is Vandemere Alexander Petruska." I made a sweeping bow for entertainment's sake. "I am a fourth-generation bareback rider. This here is Karma." Another theatrical gesture guided their attention toward my horse. "My Romanian ancestors crossed the continent of Europe on a horse very much like this one. That horse's name was Vandemere too, so now you know the origin of my name. I am the only son of Del Davidson, a name I'm sure you are all familiar with. My mother, God rest her soul, was a mystic and a fortune-teller. I am my mother's heir to the Romanian *magie*. That's Romanian for magic by the way. I have the gift of Sight, just as she did!"

A ripple of tepid interest rolled through the crowd.

I held up Ma's tarot cards for everyone to see. "I have been instructed by the ghosts of my forefathers to read Dr. Franklin's future. If you'll allow me the privilege of your time, I will attempt to guess the very card Dr. Franklin will pull from this deck of cards. I will read his past, present, and future ... all for the modest sum of four dollars.

"And you have to give me my horse back," I added, muttering low, so only Franklin could hear me.

"This I've got to see," the woman under the parasol drawled.

"Me too," the man in a cowboy hat said, though he was more suspicious than entertained.

"Do it, Franklin," a station worker insisted. Instinct had me guessing he didn't like Dr. Franklin any more than I did.

Dr. Franklin attempted to massage the tension out of his jaw and darted his gaze about, looking for an escape route. "This is ridiculous," he said, echoing his wife's sentiments.

I shuffled the cards with a deft hand, letting them dance between my palms. I challenged the laws of gravity with practiced illusion, and the small crowd applauded.

I could do this trick with my eyes closed.

I cut the deck in half, looking for a place to put them down. Decided I was fresh out of overturned pickle barrels, so I just held them in my hands instead.

I offered the fan of cards to Dr. Franklin. "Pick one."

He studied the cards in my hands.

Karma shook a fly off his face and some of his saliva flew into the crowd.

Franklin looked back up and challenged me with a smug grin. "I don't want to play this game."

A nauseous chill crept through me. "But ... you *have to.*"

Karma tried to rub his temple on Franklin's sleeve.

Dr. Franklin cocked his fist and aimed it at Karma's eye.

I jumped forward to stop him. "If you don't want to play, fine! Why don't I just read you your fortune instead?"

He withdrew his hand. "You're wasting my time. Come on, Harriet. Let's go."

I turned back to the crowd, hating myself. Hating what I was about to do. I was about to destroy another man's life, and my mother would not have been proud of me.

"Dr. Jan Franklin," I called out. "Born in March of 1867. The seventh surviving son of Agnes Green, married to Joseph Franklin, a poor, immigrant farmer from Bulgaria."

He stopped dead in his tracks.

I added another nail to the coffin.

"Dr. Jan Franklin, having grown up on nothing but turnips and potatoes, decided to leave his parents' dugout in North Dakota and head west to California like so many others before him. He went to seek his fortune in gold. But the gold didn't pan out for you, did it, Dr. Franklin?"

Harriet Franklin stood in the glare of the hot sun, gaping at me with a half-opened mouth.

"But that didn't stop you. ... am I right, Dr. Franklin?" I felt the weight of truth pressing against my chest. "You decided, since you were dead broke, there had to be another way to make a living. A comfortable living. A *respectable* living. One befitting a man like yourself. *You*. Jan Franklin. Not that other one who ate turnips and potatoes just to survive. So, you became a Doctor of Medicine. Except you never actually *trained* to be a doctor, did you? In fact ... you're not really Jan Franklin *at all*."

He came at me, swinging a fist at my face.

I ducked it easily, surprising the hell out of him—and myself, for that matter. The force of that missed opportunity sent him reeling in a circle and he staggered sideways.

His eyes were shot with a panicky rage. "You ... you *shut up*."

My own lungs strained to take in air. Standing under the beady eye of a glaring sun was turning my brain to mush, and it was getting increasingly more difficult to keep my sightline level with the horizon. "Give me back my horse and I will."

He stared me down. "What *are you*?"

I shrugged. "Just a no-good dirty Gypsy. What are *you*, Dr. Franklin? Or should I ask ... *who* are you?"

A man outfitted in jeans and chaps spoke with a voice that sounded like a rusty sawblade. "What's the kid talking about, Franklin?"

He laughed nervously. "Nothing ... nothing at all."

I rounded back to the crowd. "It might interest you all to know that Dr. Franklin here isn't really who he says he is. Many years ago, he had a claim partner in California named Jan Franklin, who *was* a licensed physician. The two of them worked a creek up in Shasta before the real Dr. Franklin passed away under mysterious circumstances. The gold was long gone by then, but some claim jumpers still held out hope of striking it rich. Like our Dr. Franklin here." I swept my arm around in a grand gesture that pinned the crowd's attention on the man's flushed face. "Or should I call you Goran Nikolov? That *is* your real name, isn't it?"

Franklin shoved Karma's reins at me. "Here. Take your goddamn horse. You win. Just ... *stop talking!*"

The smile on my face wasn't at all pleasant. I mean, he *did* ask for it. "But I haven't finished telling your fortune yet."

Karma, glad to be back in my possession, sidled over to me and nuzzled my ear.

Sweat trickled down Franklin's cheek. "Is it money you want?" He dug into his pocket and came up with a wad of cash. His hand shivered like an aspen leaf in the wind as he counted out bills. He held out ten dollars. "Here."

I packed Ma's tarot cards away and carefully separated four dollars from the ten he was offering.

"Consider it charity," I intoned, but it was really blood-money. Extortion would have been the proper term. I didn't like myself very much right now.

In the distance, a train whistle hooted.

"And one other thing..." I said, before Dr. Franklin could scuttle back to his wife's side. "I want you to stop putting your hands on Lenora. In fact, I want you to stop harassing the women of this town altogether. You're abusing your power as a doctor to get what you want, and it needs to stop."

The small crowd on the platform suddenly took a very keen interest in what I was saying.

Franklin looked around at the muttering spectators. "He's lying!"

"No, he isn't."

This came from the woman with the parasol. Her eyes held mine for a brief moment before going on. She uttered her confession through trembling lips. "It's all true."

Anger and shame flitted between her brows.

There was something ethereal about her. Something off. Watching her dab at her mouth with a gloved hand, I wondered if I was doing the right thing by including her in this.

Another approaching distraction pulled my focus away from her.

Footsteps clomped across the platform, sounding a lot like a team of Clydesdales in full harness.

I shifted impatiently.

Now what?

The crowd parted to let four men through—big brutes in dusty overalls and hobnailed boots.

The Bronson brothers.

The tension that collected on the platform was palpable. A few people decided it was a good time to leave. Others jammed hands into their pockets and ducked scared eyes to the ground.

Harriet Franklin stood at the edge of the platform, watching silently as her world came tumbling down.

Only the woman with the parasol remained upright and brave. She kept her eyes on me. She had both hands on the parasol handle now, and I saw her chin quivering.

Dr. Franklin just looked relieved.

"What's the trouble here?" the elder Bronson asked. He walked right up to me, already working the cricks out of his knuckles.

"Thank God ..." Dr. Franklin breathed. "This boy has just robbed me! He's a thief and a liar. I know for a fact this horse belongs to Del Davidson. I caught him stealing it. I was just trying to return it to its rightful owner when he accosted me. You need to teach him some manners, Emrys. You and your kin! Take him round the back there and show him how we keep the peace here in Tempe." This was said with a pugnacious jut of his chin toward the shadows behind the train depot. "I'm sure there's a reward in it for you if you do a proper job of it."

To me, Franklin muttered, "Now you're in for it. You're going to wish you'd never been born, Vandemere Petruska." His voice was so cold, I almost expected to see it frosting in the morning air.

I turned to the four men closing in on me. "Oh, hey there, Daniel. How's everything these days in the Bronson camp? Good?"

Daniel, standing tall at his brother's shoulder, grinned. "All good, Vandy. And yourself?"

"Couldn't be better," I returned. "I kept meaning to thank you for the handkerchief you gave me." I made a show of exposing the bandana I'd knotted around my neck so he could see I still had it. "I wear it every day."

Warmth crept into his eyes.

Every inch of him was designed for fighting, from his broad shoulders and chiseled biceps, all the way down to his scarred fists. I had no doubt his reputation in this town had been hard won. Scars of a violent past were stamped on his face, and I wouldn't have wanted to be on the receiving end of those hammers he had for hands. Out here, it was survival of the fittest, and I was just a skinny kid asking for trouble.

But just like Daniel Bronson, Arizona was a place of contrasts. There was beauty in her desert soul, as well as cruelty. Like the heat that danced across the horizon. Unbearable in the daytime, terrifying after dark. There were sandstorms to deal with, and a shortage of water, and seeing as there were thorns on every surface, it wasn't a place for the faint of heart. But it was also a place of healing. In the short time I'd been here, living beneath an unmerciful sky, I'd come to learn that Arizona was a land of immeasurable kindness, if only one took the time to get to know it better.

Like Daniel Bronson.

And me too.

Dr. Franklin's gaze bounced between me and the Bronson brothers. I don't think he could believe what he was hearing.

"Is there something we can do for you, Vandy?" Daniel asked.

Karma rested his chin on my shoulder, and I gave him a nice scratch under his mane to reassure him. "I was just telling these good folks how Dr. Franklin was going to try to do better in the future." I spoke in that same flat voice I normally reserved for people of authority. Cops, sexual predators masquerading as public servants ... that sort of thing. "He made a mistake. He was just saying how very sorry he is. He was saying he's decided to stay here in town after all. He's not going to run away and hide like he wants to. He says he's going to apologize to all the women he's frightened and hurt, and he's not going to do that anymore. Isn't that right, Dr. Franklin?"

Franklin's unblinking stare went right through me. The grayish pallor beneath the glaze of sweat trickling down the bridge of his nose told me he was doing some serious thinking.

I hoped, in some small way, he was feeling a bit of what those women had felt after he'd broken their trust and sentenced them to a cruel, silent shame.

Harriet Franklin's shoulders drooped. The bright façade she'd worn over her hopelessness faded like a mist in the morning sun. Now, she just looked worn out and tired, and ready to go home instead of to church.

"You're a terrible person, Vandemere Petruska," she told me.

Nothing I hadn't heard before.

I held up well under her words.

Tough to do, that.

"I can be," I agreed. "But I can be a good person too. I can be mouthy, and stubborn, and a down-right pain in the ass. I used to be an amazing rider before I broke my leg, and I loved to show off in front of a crowd. I love all my horses, every one of them, and I loved my mother more than anything else in this world. I'm just a crazy, mixed-up bag of flaws and mistakes, stirred up with a whole lot of heart. All I can do is try harder next time. It's all any of us can do, really. Just keep trying."

Harriet fished around in her handbag for a clean handkerchief and blotted her nose with it. "I don't have to listen to this."

"No, you don't," I said. "But I think you should. I'm trying to change your mind about me if you'll just hear me out. I was a lot like you, see. Before I got here, I was angry, and I was hurt. I didn't like myself very much. I *was* a terrible person. But you know what? People forgave me. Good people, like Chuck and Lenora Mescal. They don't deserve to be treated unfairly. They were nice to me, and they forgave me even when I pushed them away."

Harriet rolled her eyes heavenward. "Spare me, Lord ..."

I went on doggedly. "All these years, I blamed the bad things happening in my life on everyone else. I drove my father away. My mother was sick too, and I just made her life more difficult. I told someone the child his wife was carrying wasn't his." I cringed at the mere thought of this. My stomach did a sick roll when I recalled the look of utter defeat on the poor woman's face as I ruined her chances for a happy home. "I did it because I was angry. So, yeah, that does make me a terrible person. I've said some terrible things, and I'm ashamed of myself for doing it. But I learned something while I was here in Arizona. Something that changed *everything*. No one ever told me I needed to forgive *myself* too. It's not too late for me, Mrs. Franklin. I know that now. It's not too late to turn things around, same as it's not too late for Jan here. This town needs a good doctor. He needs to stay here in Tempe and take care of everyone, just like he took care of me. He's not going to bother the women anymore, and he's going to do much better in the future. Right, Dr. Franklin?"

He didn't answer.

He looked a hundred years old, standing there on the platform with his hat in his hands. He'd stolen another man's identity and used it to create a career. He'd been corrupted by his position in the community, and he'd decided at some point that it was his right to demand sexual favors from the women who couldn't stand up to him for fear of being run out of town, or arrested by Harriet's brother Jeb, or accused of something terrible by their husbands. When I searched his thoughts, I saw a man who was sorry for *himself*, not for the women he'd hurt.

It wasn't up to me to forgive him. That would have to come from the women he'd assaulted. Women like Lenora, who would have tanned my ass if she knew what I'd done here.

Harriet slipped her arm through her husband's, defiant enough for both of them. "I've heard enough. You should be ashamed of yourself." It was the typical response of someone who was dealing with too much of their own guilt to think about someone else's.

The Bronson brothers stood back and allowed them to leave.

Daniel stood by while Harriet put her husband in the car and took her rightful place behind the wheel. "You sure you don't want us to rough him up some?" Daniel asked. "We can make it so nothing shows."

I had hoped to find some kernel of sympathy for the man who'd left a swath of voiceless, wounded women in his wake, but all I got was the tattered remains of that other person I was trying so hard *not* to be. "Nah. Leave him alone. When it comes to retribution, I'm sure Mrs. Franklin won't leave that field untilled."

"You're sure?"

"I'm sure."

The woman with the parasol had difficulty tearing her gaze away from Dr. Franklin's retreating car. She approached me and Karma one cautious step at a time, as shy as a frightened deer mouse.

I thought Karma would spook at her parasol, but he stood his ground like the wonderful, brave horse he was.

I was surprised when the woman put a hand on my shoulder and planted a kiss on my cheek. Her breath felt like ice against my skin, and her lips were as light as a down feather. "That was a marvelous thing you did."

My cheek tingled where her mouth had grazed me. I stood in the shadow of her umbrella, our bodies nearly touching, and I felt her *magie* jump across the space between us. Her presence merged with mine. It ran along my nerves like an electrical current blitzing through a copper wire; not exactly pleasant, but I accepted it anyway.

I lowered my gaze. "Then why do I feel so crummy?"

Her smile held a vague sadness. "You need to stop blaming yourself for everyone else's mistakes. He's been getting away with this for years.

All we wanted was for someone to *believe us*. The women in this town prayed for an angel to come and save them, and here you are."

My face reddened all the way to the roots of my hair. "Ma'am, if you were praying for an angel, then God must be off his rocker sending someone like me."

She didn't laugh. "You should be very proud of yourself, Vandemere Petruska. It's true what they say about you. You *are* destined for greater things."

She walked away after that, a lovely ghost in a pale blue dress ... and I was the only one who saw her outline scatter into particles of light.

Chapter Eighteen

The train pulled into the station at exactly seven-fifteen.

Daniel's brother, Emrys, handed me a slip of paper. "That's a ticket for Flagstaff," he explained. "You're getting on the wrong train, kid. This is the train that goes to Tucson."

"I know," I said. "This is the train I want."

When he scanned the determination behind my eyes, a look of understanding dawned across his face. "You want me to keep this private? Just between you and me?"

"If you could," I answered gravely.

His ruddy expression remained placid and kind. He had a jaw like granite, and dark brows that slanted over deep-set blue eyes. Eyes that had seen too much of the world to know a smokescreen when it was staring him in the face. "I'll let the boys know your plans."

I nodded my thanks. "If anyone asks, tell them I went to see the Grand Canyon."

He shoved me so hard I nearly fell over. "Yeah, yeah ... see you around, kid."

Daniel kept pace with us, taking one stride for every three of mine. "You look a lot different from the first time I saw you."

I led Karma down the length of the platform where a cattle ramp was lined up to the door of one of the boxcars. "Arizona has been good to me."

He considered this and smiled in agreement. "If you're ever in town again, stop by for supper. Ma's a decent cook. We'd be happy to have you over."

Judging by the furtive looks he was giving me; this wasn't something he did very often ... invite people over for dinner. I suspect most people would have taken it as a sign to run in the opposite direction, but I was moved by the gesture. "I doubt I'll ever come back here," I said. "But if I do, I'd be honored, Daniel. Thank you."

He kicked a pebble off the platform. "Well, you're kind of a big deal around here. Halfway to famous even. You going back to the circus? After the Grand Canyon, I mean." He winked at me.

I schooled my expression so he wouldn't see the shame burning behind my eyes. "Um—"

The steam whistle saved me from another bald-faced lie.

Its shrill scream nearly broke my eardrums.

Karma scooted forward, his hooves scrambling on the bleached boardwalk.

I called over my shoulder. "Bye, Daniel!"

He waved back, a tough hulk of a man with an even bigger heart. "Bye, Vandy! If you ever need help, we're only a holler away!"

Karma and I had the boxcar all to ourselves this time. He scrambled up the cattle ramp, nearly running me down in the process, and I remembered to sort out some details with the conductor before he locked us in.

"How long before we get to Tucson?"

"Train gets in at six o'clock. Gotta make a few stops along the way," the man answered.

Of course, it did. A direct line to Tucson would have been too easy.

I sighed. "You staying with the train, or are you making a shift-change here in Tempe?"

"Staying with the train." He pulled on the lever-chain to raise the ramp. "Sorry. Gotta lock you in now."

"Let me off in Tucson ..." I blurted out, just as the ramp was slammed in my face. "And my horse needs hay! I paid for it!"

"I'll see what I can do at the next stop," came his muffled reply.

Darkness after that. Darkness, and bands of light where the day got through the slatted sides of the boxcar, and a stench that forced me to breathe through my mouth.

No one had cleaned up after the cattle who had ridden in the boxcar before us. The floor was slippery as hell, and the thick layer of sloppy manure had to be a foot deep in spots. This ungodly soup ran in rivers towards me whenever the train negotiated a bend in the tracks, and I spent most of the ride dodging this unsecured, liquid mess, dreaming up at least half-a-dozen other ways I might have traveled around the country in style. The stuff made wet, slurping noises every time Karma shifted his feet, and any thoughts I might have had about lying down and sleeping off the exhaustion that chiseled inroads into my mind were thoroughly squashed.

When the conductor mentioned we had to make a few stops, what he was really saying was we would stop at every single train platform along the route.

Every. Single. One.

Once, we even stopped in the middle of the desert for no good reason that I could see, other than to annoy me. The train sat idle, panting out steam while the sun climbed higher, wasting precious time going nowhere.

Karma still had hay left over from an earlier stop and he'd drunk half a bucket of water from the pail that hung at chest-level. I had already pulled his bridle off. I kept it hooked it over my shoulder, along with the strap of Jimmy's satchel containing the souvenirs of my life. He found solace in eating and was content to wait out the delay.

I was the one who fretted and cursed under my breath.

I suspect Karma must have come by train from Canada to Arizona. He was a patient traveler ... unlike me, who just wanted to get this over with.

The conductor had provided me with a bottle of root beer and the cheese sandwich his wife had packed for him. I was starting to feel a bit light-headed from not having slept at all. My eyes felt like they'd been scratched with sandpaper, and my left leg throbbed with a tedious ache that had me fighting back a groan.

We started up again without warning.

The train jolted forward. I lost my balance and ended up banging my shoulder against the front of the boxcar, with a surprised Karma landing in my lap for good measure.

He did his best to avoid trampling me. He went to his knees, his head bobbing wildly, and he would have done anything to keep from flattening me.

I don't know why, but the strained worry in his dark eye cut me deeply.

His kindness baffled me. Why would he want to protect me at all? Humans had put scars on his back. They had trained him to canter in endless circles and perform stupid tricks, all for the sake of entertainment. They had turned him into a toy. Something to be played with. *Shine the spotlight on him and watch him dance ...*

Bitter tears threatened to leak from my eyes, and my nose streamed.

I wrapped my arms around his head, and he returned the favor by pressing his face into my chest. I sniffed when my nose leaked. "I'm so sorry, Karma." Part of me wanted to bawl like a little kid, but the other part of me refused to let go. I hadn't quite made it to a point in my life when crying came easily, and I still carried the memory of my father's cruel words like a yoke across my shoulders; a burden that shouldn't have been mine to bear, but there it was.

I rested my cheek on Karma's knobby temple and sighed. I was just so tired. Tired of all of it. "I should never have asked you to come with me," I told him. "This is my fight, not yours."

He lifted his head. He was a shadow against the narrow spears of sunlight that got through the cracks in the boxcar. I guessed he was about sixteen hands at the withers. A little shorter than my Dolly had been. He was a dark horse to her lightness. There was solemn resignation in the way he swiveled his delicate ears back and forth, and he lipped at my damp face to comfort me.

He spoke in a language I could understand, having been around horses all my life. The connection I had with these magnificent animals went well beyond the average horseman. My survival depended on correctly reading their signals, and I trusted them with my life. I had to. There was no other way I could do what I did without the faith I had in their willingness to carry me through a literal ring of fire.

But what right did I have to ask him to do this?

No right at all.

I centered my thoughts and aimed them like a beacon into Karma's mind.

I used the *magie*. I used it, and I didn't care if *Vigolii* didn't like it. I gathered together as much divine protection my weary soul could muster and went forward into the swirling chaos that reeled around my beautiful horse.

He wouldn't let me in at first. My questions were an invasion against his defenses, and he backed off nervously. Horses communicated through energy. Through subtle signals that fed information along psychic threads. Their very survival depended on connecting to the world around them, picking out the threats in the atmosphere and reading their environment for any predator trying to sneak up on them. It was one of the benefits of living in a herd. There was safety in numbers, and it helped to have many eyes on the alert. Centuries of domestication had bred a lot of the wildness out of them, but it would only take one thoughtless act to bring it right back to the surface again. I was trespassing into uncharted territory, and I wasn't sure what Karma had in store for me.

I spoke to him in a language only a horse would understand. I formed my questions around an image of fire, hoping he would show me how to help him release the memory of the flaming hoop falling on him.

He sent things back to me. Truths that turned my entire world upside down.

All this time, I'd been wrong about him. Wrong *again*. If only I'd used the *magie* sooner, I would have realized it wasn't *the fire* he was afraid of. It was something else. Something that changed *everything*.

I was the one to back out first, not him.

Karma went back to eating his hay as if nothing profound had ever happened between us.

I gripped the side of the boxcar with whitened fingers and slowly died inside.

My mother leaned in to whisper in my ear. *The father knows.*

I hung onto the side of the boxcar and pressed my forehead to the backs of my hands while the mucky floor under my feet slopped back and forth.

I didn't understand this at all. And how was I still standing up?

I felt detached from my body. Weary beyond words. Utterly spent. Any bravado I had used to cover up my lack of courage seeped into the shit I was standing in.

I shut my eyes and tried to block it all out.

I whispered to the air, "Oh God, Ma. *We* did this? All this time, and you never once thought to *tell me?*"

She wouldn't answer. Maybe she didn't want to. The grievous thing my ancestors had done carried a shame that had traversed many generations. This trauma now sat squarely on my shoulders, and maybe she was frightened of that too. Maybe she was afraid to come out of the shadows and show herself to the demon who had tortured her for years. Maybe she wasn't strong enough yet to face it. Scared of what it might do—to her, and to me.

Whatever the reason, she refused to help me.

I was on my own.

The one thing I thought I wanted *so badly* was to be left alone, and *Vigolii* had seen to it I'd gotten exactly what I'd asked for.

***

Tucson beckoned in the distance; an impressive sprawl of commerce and farming, and a major attraction to the health conscious who came here looking to take in the dry, desert air. The Southern

Pacific Railway had opened up this gateway to the west, and it was because of the railway that Tucson had thrived. It was a multi-cultural community made up of Mexicans, some Chinese, a lot of European immigrants, and a smattering of local Native tribes.

The city rose out of the desert like a welcome mirage, stretching into the rocky hills surrounding it.

Karma and I disembarked from the train.

On a different day, I might have lingered to take in the sights. Tucson was a golden oasis in a desert of thirst, offering food and drink on every corner. I saw theaters, white-washed and dazzling. Saw a lot of hotels. Saw sophisticated architecture befitting the discerning tastes of the wealthy patrons who came to take pictures of the desert and carry them back to their brownstones in Manhattan or cottages in the Hamptons.

Cars sputtered past me. A steady stream of vehicles clattered up and down dusty streets, and the corners were crowded with well-heeled men and women. Tall buildings took on the deepening gold and amber hues of dusk as the sun began to set. Shadows lengthened in shades of twilight, bleeding into purples, and blues. The air was gentle against my damp forehead, reminders of why the world had come here in the first place. I smelled the desert underneath the stink of exhaust fumes and wished it could have done more to ease my spirit.

I got some funny looks as I led Karma along the street. It might have had something to do with my long hair, or my black coat and blue jeans still reeking like cow. Or the dove feather stuck in the piece of string I'd used to tie my hair back. It might have had something to do with the emptiness in my eyes as I stared out at nothing, every limping, purposeful step bringing me nearer to home.

I suppose I should have known better. I thought I would get further than I did. My mind was still unbalanced from what I'd seen inside

Karma's mind, and I should have done a better job of talking myself back from that semi-conscious state of stunned disbelief. Should have slapped myself out of it.

Instead, I walked on blindly.

I think on some deeper level, I felt I deserved it; what was waiting for me at the end of this road.

I had to ask someone where the circus was set up.

A man pointed me in the direction of the Catalina Mountains humped along the horizon on the outskirts of town. He was faceless to me. A voice with no name. The information registered without really leaving an impression.

More walking.

I walked until I thought I couldn't take another step. Pain warned me I was pushing my luck with barely healed bones.

Thinking back on it, I probably could have found something to stand on and hopped onto Karma's back. I could have ridden him the rest of the way.

I just couldn't do that to him. Bad enough I was leading him into battle. I just couldn't find it in my heart to *ride* him there.

The fact that he followed me into it willingly made me all the more determined to keep him safe.

Tucson was a huge, mixed-up maze of streets and back alleys. A warren of tall buildings and endless blocks running for miles in all directions. I wasn't prepared for navigating my way through this unfamiliar urban sprawl. The *magie* left me with a vague sense of home, along with some general directions given to me by a man in a hurry, and it took me the better part of two hours to finally clear the city limits.

I walked into the desert.

The sun sank behind the jagged peaks of the Tucson mountains. Darkness came on fast. Night fell early now that we were nearing the end of December. Christmas was just around the corner, but Arizona seemed to have forgotten about that. The desert traded snow for heatwaves, and any sense of excitement I might have had for the festive season dried up and died in the blistering heat.

I found the circus. It was easy to spot it; a dreamscape of excitement calling across a desolate plain.

I led Karma across a field strewn with parked cars. Automobiles gleamed under the pinkish moon just coming up over the eastern mountains. When I looked past the cars, I saw the striped peaks of Jimmy's big top rising from the desert floor.

Outlined in dazzling lights, the circus called me home. A beacon of magic, and memories of my childhood. Starlight pricked the night, studding the darkness with a million distant diamonds. Music tinkled over the field, and I recognized the strains of the opening parade.

I should have been glad to finally come to the end of what had been a very long, very arduous journey. I rested gritty eyes on the familiar landmark and tried to dredge up a sense of peace into my tired soul, but all I got back was dread. A heavy, sickening fear that put dust in my mouth and struck terror into my bones.

Voices in my head urged me to turn around. They argued I couldn't do this. Told me I wasn't strong enough, brave enough, or smart enough. I staggered under the weight of the responsibility that had been thrust upon me and knew I would never be enough of *anything*.

I wanted to run. God, how I wanted to run.

Annie's ghostly form drifted ahead of me.

She smiled.

Almost there ...

Karma stayed at my side. His dark eye searched mine, looking for reassurance.

I couldn't give it to him.

I wrapped my right hand around the cheekpiece of his bridle and held myself up.

We crossed the field, each step built upon the previous one, threading a way through the parked cars by the light coming off the big top tent. I came back to the only home I'd ever known. I came back to Shorty, and Dodger, and Jimmy, who had been like a father to me. These men had guided me through a difficult time in my life, and I don't think I ever thanked them for it. I think it was fair to say that I actually loved them, especially Jimmy, who never once turned his back on me no matter how bad things got.

I prayed he thought the same of me as I did of him because I was going to have to trust him to help get me out of this.

Someone watched me come in. A shadow darted through the silent cars, melting back into the darkness. Word was out that I was back, and all I could do was resign myself to my fate.

I made my way around the far side of the big top. An undulating wave of cheering came from the crowds inside the circus tent, and the band played a merry tune. Smells sparked familiar memories. Elephants. Sawdust. Popcorn. Caramel apples. Frankfurters cooking on a charcoal grill. Cotton candy ...

I thought about the little girl with fluffy blonde hair.

The father knows.

Oh, God, Annie ... Why couldn't I have known sooner?

She faded away. Gone from my mind, and my sight. She had done what she'd set out to do. The rest was up to me.

I had every intention of going in search of Jimmy to tell him I was back, but I wanted to put Karma away first. He was as exhausted as I was, and probably hungry too. I had it in my mind to find a stall for him. To search out some hay and water, and fluff up a nice deep bed of straw for him to rest in. I skirted around the big top and headed for the animal tent first.

I never made it there.

I rounded the stable tent, thinking; all of Tucson must have turned up for the evening performance ... and walked straight into an ambush.

Chapter Nineteen

Menacing silhouettes merged out of the dim light of the stable tent, approaching on silent feet.

Karma sounded the alarm. His sudden snort roused me from my sleepwalking. He'd come to a halt, unsure of this new threat advancing out of the darkness. His ears pointed at the three shadows who slowly turned into men I knew by sight.

I looked at them one by one, wondering if this wasn't just a trick of my already strained imagination. Dismay finally registered in my wandering brain as the faces slowly identified themselves. "Hey, Sal. Mr. Lee? What are you doing here? You're a long way from home, aren't you?"

Sal Lorenzo blocked my path. Him, I could understand. He *would* be here. But Matthew Lee? Annie's father? Why was *he* here?

Grim understanding settled into my belly.

Sal sneered. "Brave words from a cornered rat."

He should have been in costume by now. Instead, he was dressed in dark clothing; black trousers topped with a long-sleeved shirt. A cloth cap hid his pale hair. He was wearing the same heavy gloves the guying-out crew used to protect their hands from steel cables.

He stank of hard liquor and menace.

He slowly uncoiled a bullwhip from his belt and slid his gloved fingers along the handle.

Jake was here too.

I'd forgotten about Jake Topher. Never thought he'd last this long. That mistake would cost me.

I looked past them, searching for an escape route, or help. No luck. Just that god-awful coffin Sal used in his magic act, propped up on a wheeled handcart behind him.

Suddenly, I knew exactly what they were planning to do to me.

The voices in my head shrilled. *Wake up!*

"Oh, no ..." I said, scrambling backwards.

Sal glanced at the two men. "Get him."

Karma threw himself into the fray. He struck out with a foreleg, teeth snapping on air, ears pinned flat to his neck. He lunged at Sal, just as Samson had done to my father five years ago.

This time, I managed to stay on my feet.

"Christ!" Sal sputtered, dodging Karma's savage hooves. "Shoot that damned horse if you have to!"

"I got no gun!" Jake threw back.

Something sparked deep in my brain. This wasn't *Vigolii,* or Chuck's Skinwalker. This was Sal Lorenzo getting back at me for every transgression he'd ever suffered due to my very existence, real or imagined.

I shook the self-pitying fog clear of my mind and prepared myself for a fight.

It's amazing what a little adrenaline could do for a person.

Jake Topher made a grab for Karma's reins.

"Leave him alone!" I ran at Jake. I jammed my shoulder into his stomach and sent him flying backwards. I hit him with everything I had; something I should have done a long time ago, in retribution for taking advantage of my mother.

We both fell hard. I heard Jake's breath grunt out of him as I kneed him in the ribs—not entirely unintentional.

Music blared from inside the big top. The striped canvas was close enough to see movement against the spotlights dancing around inside the tent. Safety had never been so close, and yet so far away.

Sal caught Karma's trailing reins as the stallion veered away from the commotion. "Fucking horse. I'll show you who's boss around here." He swung the bullwhip away from his side and traced a circle through the air with his arm.

I couldn't get there in time. I had Jake underneath me, and Matthew Lee made a grab for my elbows from behind. I got tangled up in all those arms and legs, and I still had the satchel with my belongings strapped across my chest, hindering any chance to flounder to my feet.

I didn't see the whip cut into Karma's flank, but I heard it. Heard the snap of leather on flesh.

What was meant to vent Sal's frustration actually turned against him. Instead of subduing the stallion, whipping him only scared him worse.

As strong as Sal was, Karma was a lot stronger.

He scuttled backwards, eyes rolling. His hooves scrabbled through the dust as Sal tried in vain to hang on to him. Finally, he broke away.

Matthew Lee piled on top of me. He grabbed a fistful of my collar and dragged me off Jake.

I twisted madly and tried to kick him in the crotch with my heel.

He took a handful of my hair and slammed my temple into the dirt.

Colorful sticks of dynamite blew up behind my eyes.

He dug his knees into my kidneys. When that didn't hold me, he put his full weight over the old break in my thigh and leaned in hard.

I screamed.

Matthew Lee's hand drilled into my cheekbone. "You shut up! I told you what I would do to you if I found out you killed my Annie!" His plain, ordinary face looked anything but ordinary now. His light brown hair fell over his eyes—gone all black now, and I knew there would be no talking myself out of this one.

He was only doing what he'd promised. What he'd threatened to do outside Jimmy's office that day Dawson had questioned me about Annie's death. No one would blame him for wanting me dead. A quick dispatch of the perpetrator was in order. If the law wouldn't do it, Matthew Lee would spare them the trouble of putting me out of my misery.

Except he and I both knew I hadn't killed Annie.

The father knows ... my mother had said.

"*You did it!*" I inhaled dirt and coughed it back up again. "You son of a bitch! *You* were the only one who could lead Annie away from the circus and not get caught! No one would have thought twice about her *father* stealing her away. I *saw you* ... at the gate that afternoon with Dawson ..." My voice rose to a screech when he knelt harder on the break in my bad leg. Pain ripped through me. Scary. Unbearable. Inescapable.

Cheerful band music played in my ears.

I stopped fighting. I lay still, panting. If I continued to resist, Lee would break my leg again. I *couldn't* go back to that. I quieted my breathing and shuddered under his weight.

Jake got himself righted again.

I played dead, and waited ...

Karma was still on the loose. He didn't know what to do. His conditioning told him to stay close to me, the one person who meant something to him. He trotted around us, looking lost, his reins trailing along the ground.

I spit sand out of my mouth. "Karma ... go!"

"Shut up!" Matthew Lee shoved my face into the ground even harder and I ate another mouthful of dirt. It was the rabbit hole all over again, only this time there would be no Farmer Castleman to pull me out.

The bullwhip cracked over my head. It circled through the darkness in a whistling arc, and Sal got Karma across the back this time.

I wailed, "*Please* ... don't hurt my horse ..."

Sal spoke from somewhere above me. "Get him up."

Matthew Lee rolled off me.

It took both Jake and Mr. Lee to wrangle my arms and legs back under control and haul me to my feet.

Karma was still hanging around. Despite his extensive training, he was still a herd animal at heart. He was expecting me to tell him what to do, to reassure him, to catch him and lead him to the safety of his stall.

I wasn't in a position to do any of that.

Something inside the big top tent sent the crowd into hilarious laughter. I recognized the music right away. Shorty was doing his pony act. The one with the flaming hoop. The one where he would pretend to jump through it. The one I used to do for real.

Dodger would wait until the flames were extinguished before pulling the smoldering hoop back up into the rigging.

Sal tapped me under the chin with the handle of the bullwhip, dragging my attention back to him. "I knew you'd come." His boyish face contorted into a dangerous mix of arrogance, hurt, and spite.

"Shorty's been going on and on about sending you letters, begging you to meet up with us. God, if I have to hear your name one more time …" Sweat was a sparkle of dampness across his forehead, illuminated by the frugal light coming from inside the tent. Gleaming on his upper lip. His eyes were black pits of rage sunk into the sockets, and the angles of his face were carved out of shadows. "All I ever hear is, how's Vandy? Where's Vandy? When is Vandy coming home? Even my own father won't shut up about you."

I spit out dirt and blood. "Do you want to trade?"

Stupid, stubborn Petruska pride. Why couldn't I just keep my mouth shut?

He shook out the bullwhip. "It's too bad that cable only broke your leg. It was supposed to kill you." He glanced at the two men holding me. "Take off his coat."

They stepped away to yank at my clothes.

I saw an opportunity to fight back, and I took it.

I don't remember the exact sequence of events. I launched my weight against the hands that held me, breaking free one moment, caught again the next. There were grunted shouts. Muttered curses. There were blows and kicks. Punches thrown. Some from me, most of them from Sal.

Explosions of pain burst behind my eyes. My head rocked backwards each time Sal smashed his knuckles into my face.

I fought, losing ground. Took one too many hits to the gut. Swallowed a lot of blood. Thought I'd never breathe again.

I fell to my knees, fingers splayed in the dirt, coughing, and sick …

Sal yelled. "I said, *hold him!*"

Hands grabbed me. Fingers locked onto my wrists. Violence in the way they kept my arms outstretched from my sides while I sat back on my heels.

They made me kneel on the ground.

My head sagged forward. I watched the blood drip from somewhere on my face and spatter into the dirt in front of me.

They'd gotten my coat off. One of them had thrown the satchel away, leaving my back feeling very exposed.

Nothing between me and the whip but a thin layer of flannel.

"I've waited a long time for this," Sal panted. "Years and years."

I thought I was ready for it. I'd come through the worst kind of shit life could throw at me and survived it, so the odds were good I would survive this too. I mean, it's not like Sal was going to murder me. Hurt me, yes. But murder? That was crossing a line neither one of us would come back from.

I constructed fortresses around my mind so I wouldn't have to look at the horrific reality looming on the horizon, and braced myself ...

Sal didn't hit me with the tasseled end. He used the butt-end of the whip instead. Just like Jimmy had done to him after the farmer had pulled me from the rabbit hole. He stood over me, a towering pillar of hatred and bone.

Matthew Lee held onto one of my arms while Jake levered the other one against his knee, wrenching it backwards so hard my elbow screamed.

Sal raised his arm high over his head.

No amount of teenage arrogance could prepare me for this.

He brought the handle of the whip down across my shoulders with every pound of muscle he owned.

A searing brightness branded a stripe across my back, white-hot at first, ebbing into a pulsating fire that dispersed the impact across my spine.

I gasped and stiffened. I squeezed my eyes shut. Gritted my teeth and whimpered through my nose.

I *refused* to cry. I would go to my grave before I gave Sal the satisfaction of raising that kind of reaction out of me.

I sensed his arm wheel back, and he hit me again.

My whole body spasmed this time. Pain was an iron smashed across my back. It scored a welt of agony into the point of my shoulder blade, and I bit down on the wail that tore up my throat.

Sal leaned back on his heel. He wound his arm up and dealt me another blow, making sure it landed on top of the one before.

It felt like a million wasps were caught under my skin.

My forehead knotted up, and I gasped against tight lips.

I heard Jake say, "I don't have the stomach for this ..."

He really was a coward.

Sal aimed the whip handle at Jake this time. "You stay like I told you to! Hold him!"

Matthew Lee hoofed me in the stomach just because he felt like it.

I coughed the last dregs of air out of my lungs. There was a moment there where I thought, I'm done. No amount of reasoning could convince my lungs to inflate again. I opened my mouth on emptiness and gulped hopelessly. I fought hard to grab the barest sip of air in. A pinch of breath that would keep me from dying. *Anything*.

I would have fallen flat on my face if they hadn't been hanging onto my arms.

I wish I could say I was brave. The whip handle came down on my back again and again. Every blow was a new version of Hell. I thought I would pass out from the pain. I certainly *wanted* to.

The whip handle had a knot on the end of it. It was there to keep the hand from slipping off. Every time I felt that knob cut into my back, I shut my eyes a little tighter and wondered if I had been too quick to dismiss the idea of dying.

I counted the blows in my head.

Surely, he would stop after ten.

He didn't.

Sal drove the toe of his cowboy boot into my side. "I want to hear you scream!"

I felt something give way. A rib bone sprung there. Just another burst of pain to add to all the rest.

Another slam on my back brought me one step closer to unconsciousness.

I tried to get away. I tried to send my mind somewhere else, but it wouldn't go!

Sal shrieked. "*Scream*, goddammit!"

Another punishing crack across my spine sent a shockwave thudding through my body.

More laughter from the crowds inside the tent.

Horrible ...

Sal got mad. He wanted me to cry, beg, and when I didn't, he smashed the whip handle across my head this time.

Pain stunned me. Blood ran down the side of my face. A raging fire blazed across my temple and stars danced in front of my eyes.

I lost count of how many times I heard the hiss of leather sing past my ear. How many times I braced myself for another battering ram of pain.

Sal's arm finally got tired.

No Del Davidson around to step in and stop the madness this time.

"Now ... you know ... how it feels," Sal said at last, his lungs heaving. He dropped the whip and wiped saliva off his mouth with a gloved hand.

The bullwhip lay like a black snake in the grass beside me, glistening wet with my blood.

They needn't have worried about me trying to escape anymore. I rested on the ground, twitching, my back all cut up and raw. Every feeble breath was a cruel reminder I was still alive, still awake.

My mind wandered off. I was in an ocean of pain, and I was hearing voices from the depths. There was a piccolo whistling a tune in my ears, and my head was stuffed with cotton. The sand cradling my body was still warm from the afternoon sun. Or maybe it was just me? I felt awful. Sick. Feverish and shivery. My shirt stuck to me, and everything stung and throbbed.

Sal unbuckled his belt and tossed it down.

It landed on my back.

I jerked instinctively and forgot I wasn't supposed to whimper.

"Tie him up," Sal said. "Put him in the box."

Oh, God. *No ...*

Jake was the one who defended me. *Jake,* of all people.

"*Jesus ...* Sal. You can't be serious? You know how he is with cramped spaces."

I heard the change in Sal's voice. Knew that *Vigolii* was back in charge. I'd know that grating, high-pitched cicada whine anywhere. "*Oh, yes, we know how it is. Now, the real fun begins.*"

Darkness staggered into my brain, and I never heard the rest.

Chapter Twenty

Consciousness came back in stages. Sound threaded its way into my brain. Muzzy at first. Slowly building to a crescendo. Filling my head with a strange roaring.

It *sounded* like waves crashing over the sand when we used to go walking on the beach as a family.

Was I back in California?

My body had no shape. I free floated through space. Disconnected thoughts tried to make sense of the sound. To put a name to it.

I frowned.

No. It didn't sound like water after all. It sounded like ... *cheering*.

Pain bled into my thoughts, tolerable as long as I stayed still. I took stock of things, wondering if the skin on my back wasn't embedded with broken glass. It certainly felt like it was. A persistent ache of nausea rolled around in my guts. No way I could go back to sleep with all these needles of misery stabbing into my body. A dull throb pulsed along my hairline too. My lips were swollen against my teeth. My shirt felt stiff, and it tugged on raw flesh when I stirred back to life.

Bad idea.

I stayed still after that.

I heard music. Darkness pressed into me, hemming me into a space I didn't seem to fit into very well.

It took me a moment, but I finally sorted out which way was up. I discovered I was curled up on my side, slightly flattened, and I couldn't have moved a muscle even if I'd wanted to. My left shoulder was mashed up against something firm and unforgiving and my arm was all tingly from me lying on it.

My hands were cold. Someone had bound them behind my back. My wrist bones were digging into each other, and everything had been tied together with a strap of some sort.

There was a piece of cloth jammed between my teeth. It filled my mouth and tried to choke me. I did my best to spit it out, but someone had made damn sure it wasn't getting out that way by knotting it round the back of my head.

A nasty piece of business that.

I gagged hard and felt it all the way down in my sore belly. I worked the sodden fabric clear of my airway with my tongue until I could breathe again.

I lay there panting.

Scary.

There was another strap around my ankles, binding them together just above the boney knobs.

Sweat itched along my hairline. Clammy. Definitely not nice.

More of this mental inventory revealed a very lumpy face. Things felt misplaced. Hot, and aching with a dull monotony. My cheekbone felt twice its normal size, and everything hurt.

My bent knees were butted up against a firm surface. The soles of my feet were pressed up against something solid too. The top of my head leaned against what felt like a wooden panel and my spine felt compressed into itself.

I cracked one eye open. Looked past swollen eyelids at an inky blackness.

I knew exactly where I was.

Everything came back to me in sick, sudden clarity. I was in that damn coffin Sal used for his magic act. The one with the false bottom.

I recognized the beat of the music outside. Heard Shapiro barking up Sal's act.

"Ladies and gentlemen! I welcome you back to center ring—"

The crowd was rowdy. Clapping. Eager, and deafening.

I felt the coffin shift a bit as Sylvia got in on top of me.

She wouldn't know I was there.

Oh, *shit!*

I couldn't move. Not even an inch left or right. The space under the false bottom wasn't big enough for a man to fit in there, not even a bone-rack like me, and the sides held fast. I couldn't even bang my head against the side to warn Sylvia I was trapped underneath her. I was surrounded by solid wood, packed in tight, with an unsuspecting girl on top of me and no way to tell her I was even *there*.

It was only a matter of time before Sal started stabbing his banderillos into the box. Sylvia would press the switch to unlock the false bottom to get herself out of the way, only this time, it wouldn't work.

If the banderillos didn't kill her first, the final plunge of Sal's sword certainly would.

I screamed around the cloth in my mouth. I pressed my feet against the bottom of the coffin and pushed. Ended up bruising the top of my head on the panel instead.

Can't breathe ...

I went insane.

I was down the rabbit hole again. There would be no rescue this time. I'd told everyone I was going to the Grand Canyon. No one knew where I was except the men who had put me here.

And Karma.

The father knows ...

I can't do this, Ma! Why did you ask me to do this?

The music played louder.

Sylvia howled when the first of Sal's knives pierced her breast. She lay trapped on the board on top of me, writhing madly. The whole box shook on its flimsy legs, and Sylvia cried out. "*Stop* ... it's not working!"

It wasn't Sal trying to kill her. It was *him*.

Vigolii.

Hysteria threw a bucket of ice water over me. My heart tried to beat itself to death against the cage of my ribs, and I fought to get my hands free. I wrestled with the strap around my wrists. Twisted my hands as hard as I could. The leather never even budged, not even a hair, and I managed to rub off a few layers of skin for my troubles.

I sucked as much air into my lungs as I could and let out a muffled scream.

No one heard it.

I panted against the cloth in my mouth while the sides of the box held me down. I shut my eyes and prayed.

Another banderillo went through the slit in the box.

Sylvia's shrill bellowing turned into a pain-smothered gasp. More cheers and excited applause rolled over the coffin. The crowd thought she was playing it up for dramatic effect! This one glanced off her shoulder. A lucky break for her. Not so much for me. The knife stuck into the thin, wooden panel between us, pausing there for a second or two before it went all the way through.

I felt the cold shock of that razor-honed point going deep into my bicep.

My garbled scream never made it past the rag. I raged against an unseen foe—the panic in my mind. It drove logic from my brain, and I used every mental trick I could think of to break free of it.

God help me ... I'm going to die in here ...

Think of something else! Think of the desert. Think of the Grand Canyon.

That was my mother was talking to me now.

No one knows I'm here, Ma ...

Think of a way out, Vandy!

I'm sorry, Ma. I'm just not strong enough.

Sanity tried reasoning with me; there *has* to be a way out of this!

Wetness pooled into my flannel shirt, running warm along my arm. I was pinned down by the banderillo blade and losing blood.

That *thing* pretending to be Sal would use the sword next. One thrust into Sylvia's heart and it would all be over for the both of us. *Vigolii* would use Sal's will to drive the sword right through Sylvia and into me.

It suddenly occurred to me that I was smelling smoke.

It wasn't just Sylvia doing all the screaming now. I heard a lot of shouting, and not the good kind either. I heard the clang and clamor of many shoes pounding along the benches. People running ...

Smoke drifted into the coffin, stinging my eyes, and getting into my lungs.

Sylvia's wails took on a feverish pitch. "For God's sake, someone *help me!*"

And the one thought rolling around in my brain?

No one knows I'm here.

Except Karma.

I lay quiet after that. My efforts to break out of the box left me weakened and spent. I breathed in the smoke. Retched behind the gag until my eyes streamed.

I listened to the panic going on outside.

Something big was on fire.

It *had* to be the tent.

I pictured the whole damn big top on fire; probably set ablaze by the smoldering ring Shorty had used in his act. I could see it in my mind's eye. Dodger would have pulled the hoop aloft after the flames had burned themselves out, except they *hadn't* gone out. Some of the embers must have flared up when no one was looking, sparking a fire in the canvas roof.

People were stampeding away, leaving poor Sylvia locked in the coffin with a banderillo stuck in her breast. She was still very much alive, and her cries were terrible to hear.

No one came to help her.

Without help, we would *both* die.

Smoke filled the box. It triggered another fit of coughing. The rag in my mouth stifled the violent spasms coming up from the depths of my belly and my screams sounded more like dried-up heaving.

I tried beating my head against the side of the box. I was hoping I could knock myself out. I would have done anything at this point to numb the terror. It would have been nice to slip into unconsciousness and sleep through the whole thing, but I just couldn't *move*.

My eyes streamed and stung.

My body just kept right on living. A deep sense of self-preservation battled against my mind's grim acceptance of death. Such was the dichotomy of good and evil.

I suppose if I had had more time, I could have composed a final exit speech. I could have planned out some sort of eulogy I would take to my grave. I pictured myself standing in front of all the circus folk who had come to my mother's funeral, only this time, I saw *myself* in the ashes instead of her. I saw myself as others might have seen me, a young man with hair to his shoulders, a dove feather tied behind his ear. A confident soul beneath the black coat, speaking from a gentle heart ... lessons learned far too late.

I wondered what Jimmy would say at *my* funeral.

'Poor Vandy. He died a virgin.'

Yup, *that's* what he'd say.

There is a way out, Vandy. My mother's voice fluttered through my mind like raven's feathers. *All you have to do is look.*

I'm dying, Ma.

Even at the end of things, I had to argue with her.

You have to live, Vandemere. You have to undo what we did.

I'm not strong enough ...

Yes, you are. They're coming to help you, Vandy. Trust the magic. Trust your horse ...

I thought about the Grand Canyon while my chest filled with smoke. Dizziness scattered my thoughts, but I hung on grimly. I coughed. Inhaled more smoke. Died a little more. Above me, Sylvia was coughing too. Not screaming anymore.

I thought about the Grand Canyon. How I never got the chance to see it in person. I thought about Ellen too. I thought about Ellen *a lot.*

I wanted to see the Grand Canyon with her. I wanted to run my fingers through her honey-colored hair and feel the sweetness of her mouth on mine. I wanted to kiss her freckled nose and give her shit for eating all my potatoes like she had done when I'd been abandoned in an Oklahoma hospital. I wanted to stand beside her, hold her hand in mine, and share what I'd seen in my mind the day Chuck showed me the Canyon. I wanted to stand on the edge of that precipice, throw my arms wide to the wind, and *fly* ...

I wouldn't be able to do that if I was dead.

I felt my consciousness slipping away ...

I made up my mind—with very little debate—that I was going to try to live through this. I wasn't that helpless little kid who got stuck in the rabbit hole all those years ago. I was seventeen years old! Nearly eighteen, for God's sake!

Time to start behaving like a grown man.

My body had other ideas. I'd taken in too much smoke, bled too much from the gash in my arm, and suffered a savage beating from Sal. There was only so much a person could take before the body gave up.

Just when I'd decided I wanted to live, death came stealing in on silent feet.

Sorry, Ma.

Dammit ...

This was the last thought I had before the darkness swallowed me whole. Nothing to be afraid of now. Dying, it seemed, was quite painless after all.

***

I floated, weightless for a moment, then I came back down to earth with a sudden jolt. A soft bed rustled under my limp body. Sweet, blessed air blew down on me, drying the sweat on my face, and inflating my lungs.

"Vandy?"

Voices called me back. Urgency in the tone.

I coughed and wheezed. My limbs didn't want to work, and for some reason my back *really hurt*.

I was breathing ... sort of. Not much air was getting through. Enough to bring me around though.

"Vandy... you gotta wake up!"

I came to, still hacking, and felt someone pinching my upper arm.

"Ow ..." I complained, in a wrecked voice. Not exactly the most philosophical discourse from someone who had just risen from the dead.

"He can't stay here!"

God, where had I heard *that* before?

Memories of my father's hatred for me rubbed salt into my wounds.

I opened my eyes, squinting past the bruises and the sting of tears. I was expecting to see Del standing over me, but it wasn't him. Instead, I got an eye-full of Apache Indian.

"Chuck?" I stammered.

He wasn't looking at me. He was gazing upward, as were Jimmy, and Shorty too, all of them standing close by, watching the fire eat up the canvas roof. Great rents appeared high above me, letting in a glimpse of an inky night. Half of the upper canopy was already gone. Some of the guywires had snapped from the heat, and the grid holding up the trapeze buckled and groaned.

Fire crackled like paper.

Dodger knelt at my side. He was busily knotting a rag around the slice in my bicep, stanching the steady stream of blood. It was the same rag that had been stuffed into my mouth; Daniel's bandana put to better use. To some, a clown in a laughable costume and floppy shoes putting pressure on a weeping blood vessel might have raised some eyebrows, but I was so accustomed to this oddity my mind didn't even register the absurdity of the situation.

Under the grease paint smile, Dodger's face was grave.

Shorty patted my hand. Even from my vantage point on the ground, I could see the white paste starting to melt over his gnome-like face. "It's okay, Vandy. You're safe now. We've got you."

Beyond them, Karma stood guard.

My beautiful horse. My brave Karma. If it hadn't been for him ... well, I wasn't going to think about that right now.

They told me later how he'd run off into the parking lot after Sal's ambush. No one had been able to catch him. Some townie had gone to find Jimmy to tell him one of his horses was running loose out in the field, looking to get itself killed. When Jimmy went to investigate, he didn't recognize the stallion as one of his.

That's when Chuck showed up in the Packard. He, of course, knew straight away it was Karma, and that I wouldn't be too far away. A plan to find me was set in motion, and Karma's strange antics told them where I was.

He'd come down the chute at a full gallop, knocking people down and scaring the rest of the fleeing patrons half to death. He ran into the fire, looking for me. I wanted to believe it was the deep connection we shared that led him right to me, but I was about to be proven wrong about that too.

Karma had stood over the coffin, his bridle in tatters, and it was because of him that I'm still here to tell the story.

I saw him now, standing off to the side of me. His ebony coat was painted in flickering orange.

A horse on fire ...

"We can't stay here," Chuck repeated, blinking hard against the smoke in his eyes. "The whole place is coming down."

My voice was hardly more than a croak. "Where's Sylvia?"

"She's outside." Another familiar voice came striding out of the ashes. "She's safe. The blade missed her heart. We have to get *you* out now."

I looked into the face of Lieutenant Clarence Dawson and thought, well, how about that! He *did* follow me after all.

They tried to lift me out of the sawdust.

The welts on my back screeched in protest.

I gasped, "Stop ... *stop* ... put me down ..."

They dropped me in the tanbark.

The flames heating up my peripheral vision turned an ominous gray.

I grabbed for Jimmy's hand and panted, "Find Sal. He's ..."

"He made it out safe, Vandy," Jimmy said.

I coughed. "Not ... what I meant ..."

But Jimmy wasn't listening. He was staring up at the flames currently destroying his beloved big top, shocked, and stone-faced, watching his livelihood going up in smoke.

Clarence Dawson stepped in and took charge of things, same as he always did. "The fire brigade is on its way. Some of the animals are still in the stable tent. If you want to save any of them, we need to go *now*."

Bits of flaming canvas turned into liquid fire and dripped down on us. Everything that *could* burn did. The wooden benches. The sawdust floor. Even the plywood circles were beginning to char.

Clarence turned his attention back to me. "If you can't walk, we're going to have to carry you out. Tell me what hurts so we can make it as painless as possible."

I lay on my bed of sawdust in the center ring, my lungs full of soot, and I had to push the words out. "It's the father ..." Another fit of coughing had me hitching back tears. "Matthew Lee ... he's the one who took Annie."

Above us, the entire framework of scaffolding and cables pinged and snapped. One by one, steel wires whipped through the smoke. Flames crawled along the painted canopy, gaining ground.

Dawson coughed into his sleeve. "It doesn't matter right now, Vandy. We need to get you out."

He looked so earnest; I tried my best to please him. "I can walk," I said.

"You're sure?" Jimmy asked. He shielded his eyes against the smoke with a shaky hand. I think he'd shut his emotions down by then. His circus was in ruins. His son had saved himself instead of Sylvia, and it didn't take a genius to figure out who had stuffed me into the coffin. Sal's belt was lying nearby, taken from my wrists after Jimmy and Dodger had lifted me out of the coffin, and Jimmy's bullwhip had been used to bind my ankles. The devastation on my boss's face was tough to look at, but unlike my own father, he refused to abandon me.

I nodded.

Jimmy and Dodger each slid their hands under my shoulders. I steeled myself against a shudder of pain as they lifted me and set me on my feet.

Jimmy peered into my face. "Good?"

Somehow, I pulled off the ghost of a smile. "Good enough."

Another terrifying growl rumbled over our heads. One of the steel girders broke from its moorings. The cable holding it snapped with a loud whizzing noise as the support structure heeled toward us, groaning under the pressure of keeping the tent aloft.

"Heads up!" Shorty cried.

Everyone scattered for their lives. Everyone except me and Karma.

I closed my eyes and braced myself. I half-expected to be impaled by the heavy beam as it curved towards me. I felt the earth shiver when the girder slammed into the ground. It fell very close to me, carving a deep rent into the sawdust floor, sending a flurry of sparks into the night sky through the fiery rips in the tent.

Karma was too terrified to move.

"Go," I said to the others. "I'll lead Karma out."

Something heavy fell behind us. Metal girders broke apart and the whole tent leaned over, putting more stress on the guywires outside.

There was something strange about the light. An eerie brightness stabbed into my eyes. I felt the ground slipping out from under my feet, and the air popped like a bubble bursting.

I turned.

Karma stood unmoving before me.

Flames danced on his scarred back.

Fire ... burning around him.

A horse on fire.

Everything was burning. Sound dissipated into silence, and time stood still.

I stepped outside of everything familiar. Stepped into a different reality. I was by myself now in this strange, alien place. All the others had gone. I was alone now, with Karma. Trapped inside the burning big top.

Sal's Spanish sword lay close to my foot. The blade reflected the flickering roof back at me, glowing red. The glass jewels in the hilt looked a lot like blood.

I bent down to pick it up. The welts on my back cracked open and started bleeding again. I made a pitiful sound that got caught in my mouth. I decided I really ought to be tougher than this and shut it down.

I dragged the sword up out of the sawdust with two hands on the hilt and used it to support myself while I straightened up again.

It was heavier than I expected. Sal had always bragged that it had been forged out of many layers of Spanish steel. The hilt was solid brass, and it had been plated in twenty-two karat gold.

I transferred the sword to my left hand. Blood from the slice in my right arm dripped off the end of my fingertips.

I wrapped my hand around the hilt. It was almost too much for me to lift, and I was weak from losing all that blood. I left the point stuck in the sawdust floor for now, saving my strength.

I used a bloody wrist to brush the hair off my forehead so I could see better.

Karma lowered his head. His eyes were hidden in shadow behind his thick forelock. His ears were pointed at me, held stiffly forward.

He was quiet. Waiting.

I reached up and moved his forelock aside so I could see his eyes.

Fathomless liquid pools stared straight ahead, unblinking.

"Come out and face me," I said.

Chapter Twenty-One

Vigolii spoke from the fire.

"HAVE YOU HAD ENOUGH YET?"

The sound boomed like thunder against my ears.

I dropped the sword and clapped my hands to my head, crying out as knives of pain carved an unbearable agony into my mind. His voice speared through my brain, nearly sending me to my knees. I heard it inside my head, and I heard it with my ears, a deafening screech that tore through my consciousness.

"POOR LITTLE VANDEMERE. SUCH A LOST LITTLE BOY. ARE YOU READY TO BURN WITH ME?"

I pressed my hands over my ears. "Show yourself, demon!" My own voice was a puny thing. Small and pathetic.

"DEMON? I'M NO DEMON. YOU OUGHT TO KNOW THAT BY NOW."

The entity circled around me, prowling like an animal, watching every move I made.

Karma stood in front of me, unmoving. Nothing showed in his eyes. A bit of breeze swirled by and lifted a few stray hairs of his mane, and a bright orange glow flickered across his scarred back. My brave, brave horse.

I took my hands away from my ears. My right palm felt sticky. When I looked at it, it was smeared with blood. The cloth around my bicep was already soaked in red. Dizziness tilted everything to one side.

"I did what you asked," I said. "I brought you back to the place where it all began. The least you could do is come out and face me."

"I'M RIGHT IN FRONT OF YOU. ALL YOU HAVE TO DO IS LOOK."

The voice crashed through the smoke, splintering the air around me. I staggered back a few steps and something very close to a sob rose in my throat.

"PICK UP THE SWORD, VANDEMERE. SAD LITTLE BOY... IT'S WHAT YOU CAME HERE TO DO, ISN'T IT? TO END ME? YOU PETRUSKAS. YOU'RE ALL THE SAME. YOU HIDE BEHIND THE MAGIE. *THEY THOUGHT IT WAS A GAME. SOMETHING TO BE PLAYED WITH. FOOLS! THEY WERE THE ONES WHO CALLED ME—"*

"To *protect* them," I reminded him.

"TO PROTECT THEM, YES. AND HOW DID THEY REPAY ME?"

I hid my face in my hands. I wasn't supposed to cry. I was able to stop myself, thank God. I blamed my fragile emotions on blood loss and the steady beat of pain glowing white-hot across my back.

I lowered my hands back down to my sides again, taking a moment to arrange my bloodied face into an expression of calm. "You shouldn't have gone after the children. What harm did they ever do to you? They were just innocent kids."

"INNOCENT? NO HUMAN IS EVER INNOCENT. YOU SHOULD KNOW THAT BY NOW, VANDEMERE PETRUSKA."

Karma stood like a statue. A piece of burning canvas dropped from the skies and landed on his croup. It would have been a terrible thing for him to suffer, but he didn't twitch a muscle.

I sprang forward, swiping it off with my bare hand. If I burned my fingers, I certainly never felt it.

"Get out of my horse!" I shouted at the air. "He doesn't deserve this! I did what you asked—"

"PICK UP THE SWORD!"

I felt strangely detached from my body. It was someone else's hands reaching for the sword again, lying half-buried under smoldering embers of sawdust.

I pulled it from the ashes.

The hilt was so hot I almost dropped it.

I dragged the tip through the dust until I had a good grip on the hilt, then raised the whole thing to my waist, holding the blade at the ready out in front of me.

"I know who you are," I said. "*Vigolii. Shade*. You really had me going there for a while."

"I AM *SHADE!"* The thing laughed at me. *"I AM A MANIFESTATION OF EVERYTHING INSIDE OF YOU! YOU MADE ME, LITTLE PETRUSKA. I AM EVERY WICKED THOUGHT YOU EVER HAD, COME TO LIFE!"*

I touched the point of the sword against the center of Karma's chest.

It wasn't me doing this.

I had no choice.

My voice was surprisingly steady. "And I will un-make you now."

The glee in *Vigolii's* taunt chilled the marrow in my bones. *"I'M A PART OF YOU. IF I DIE, YOU DIE TOO. IT WILL TAKE A*

BLOOD SACRIFICE TO SEND ME BACK, AND YOU DON'T HAVE THE GUTS!"

Yeah... he was probably right.

"I know what they did to you. The Petruskas. My family." My face was streaked with blood and tears, mixed with a rain of sweat. "That doesn't give you the right to take the children. You shouldn't have made them suffer. And to use the fathers? How could you?"

The ear-splitting voice screamed. "YOU *HATED THE FATHERS! I WAS ONLY DOING WHAT* YOU *WANTED!"*

"I *didn't* hate them."

But we both knew it wasn't true. I couldn't hide behind the lies anymore. Not if I wanted to live through this.

"SAY IT!"

"I ... hated the fathers." I moaned. "You're right. I *hated* them. I hated the fathers. I hated the ones who stayed behind. The ones who took care of their families. Fathers who sacrificed everything they had to put food on the table. I hated what I didn't have. I ruined a pregnant woman's life just because I was angry. Her unborn child had a father who *stayed*. I was so jealous ... but you shouldn't have taken the children away."

"YOU WERE THE ONE I WANTED. YOUR MOTHER WAS ALREADY DYING. SHE WAS NO FUN. YOU *WERE SUPPOSED TO COME TO ME THAT NIGHT. AND WHEN YOU DIDN'T, I MADE THE FATHER SUFFER."*

I stood before Karma, holding the sword to his chest and swaying on somebody else's feet. *I* was the accuser now. "You ruined ... so many lives ..."

"YOU DID TOO! YOU RUINED SO MANY LIVES!"

It mocked me. It threw my own mistakes back in my face.

"Yes ..." Pain strained my voice to the breaking point. "The pregnant lady, and the other woman who just wanted a man to love her. And Dolly too. I should never have brought her to Arizona with me ..."

"I KILLED YOUR HORSE."

"Dolly sacrificed herself for *me—*"

"I KILLED IT."

"*Why?!*"

"TO MAKE YOU PAY!"

"Stop yelling at me!"

A disembodied voice stalked around me. It growled, softer now; a thousand times worse. *"Have you had enough? Are you ready to burn for your crimes?"*

Something big gave way to the left of me. One of the outside guywires snapped as the big top heeled over. The cable was under so much tension that when it broke, it came zinging through the canvas, tearing a hole through the flames.

It sang past my face, missing me by an inch. If it had hit me, it would have knocked my head clean off my shoulders.

Another girder collapsed, sounding like a banshee when it bent and buckled. It got caught up against one of the other fallen support beams at the furthest end of the tent, blocking the chute.

My only escape route was gone.

Under different circumstances, I might have been able to shimmy myself to safety under the bottom of the big top, but Jimmy always made sure the guying-out crew pounded extra stakes into the ground, securing the bottom of the tent. No one was going to sneak into *his* circus for free. So now I was stuck in here. Caught in the fire with no way out. For me, or for Karma.

"Well?" Vigolii taunted me like a hungry wolf, waiting, watching. A predator taking its time with a mouse ...

I worked some spit into my mouth and took a better hold of the sword. "I don't want to do this ..."

"TELL THE STORY."

Bastard ...he was going to make me say it just to torture me.

I drew in a breath. Hacked up blood and soot and inhaled more smoke. I called up the images I'd seen in Karma's mind when I used the *magie* to read him back on the train, the history of a family *Vigolii* had used to fuel his hatred of the Petruskas until it burned his soulless heart into blackened ash. *My* history. *Vigolii* had held up a mirror and shown me what the Petruskas were capable of, using Karma as a conduit to a past that should never have included me.

"TELL IT!"

I did what I was told. I recounted the story I'd seen in Karma's mind. The one *Vigolii* had put there when he'd stolen Karma's body and used him to ferry me across Arizona. Bringing me back to the circus. To the place where it all began. I relinquished the secrets Karma had tried so hard to keep from me, the trauma I'd attributed to the accident that had scarred him. All this time, he'd been carrying a demon's bloodlust inside his mind, and here I'd been thinking he was just remembering the flames on his back. I told the story of the Petruskas—and quietly died inside.

"My family, the Petruskas, came from Romania nearly half a century ago. They left with the clothes on their backs, and a trick horse named Vandemere, fleeing the Cossack invasion and religious persecution. People called them dirty Gypsies. People hated them. Hated the Petruskas. Hated what they didn't understand. So much prejudice—just because they followed a different way of life. Because they rode horses and tinkered with magic and didn't abide by the rules of society. It made them outcasts." I shook my head. "They accused the Petruskas of terrible crimes. Made up stories about how they liked to steal babies right out of their cribs. Take them away into the night and drink their blood. They sent soldiers after them. Men with guns ..."

"Go on."

"My family ran for their lives. They were frightened of the hate. Everywhere they went people threw stones at them. Hurt them. No one cared if they were starving. Domenico put on shows for the townsfolk, but no one would pay him. The only food my family got was what the people threw at them. Scraps off the ground. Not enough. It was never enough. Domenico worried he wouldn't be able to get the family out. Not without some kind of protection."

I hesitated.

"Say it."

I licked blood off my busted lips. I used my tongue to trace the meaty wound Sal's knuckles had cut into the corner of my mouth—one more scar I had to look forward to. "One night, Domenico called the family together. They used the *magie*. They shouldn't have done it ..."

I stopped. It was just too much.

"Tell it!"

The tip of the sword wavered against Karma's chest. My arms were getting really tired now. I could feel the strain buzzing across my shoulders. Felt the tremors assaulting beaten muscles. My thready pulse kept time with the welts throbbing along my spine ...

"TELL THE STORY!"

The sound nearly broke my eardrums.

"All right! I'm doing the best I can, for Christ's sake ..."

An energy swirled around me. Threatening me. Raising the hair on the back of my neck.

He was looking for a way in …

I went on grimly. "They used the *magie* …and they called you. Domenico needed to protect the family, so he gathered them together and they delivered you from the Underworld. You are the manifestation my ancestor created when he drank from the poisoned well. The *soul-force* of all the Petruskas who came before me. Luka Petruska was hardly older than I am now when he created you, and he died young defeating you. He saw what you were capable of, and he drove you out. Sent you home. But then Domenico needed help, and stupidly, he called you back. He gathered the family together and they raised you from the dead—"

"And I came."

"And you came."

"And I protected them."

Blood pooled in my mouth. I felt it dribble from my mangled lips. It was just one more irritant to add to the torture I was forced to endure. "And you protected them. Just like you're protecting me and Karma from the fire right now."

"One word from me and you're ashes, little Petruska."

My fate was at the mercy of an angry Immortal, and he wasn't about to let me forget it.

"You protected the Petruskas all the way to America," I said. "They called you from the Underworld and they bound you to Vandemere. You needed a vessel and Domenico knew Vandemere would hold you. You carried the family all the way across Europe to England *through him*. You brought them safely to America. You saved them. Saved *me*. I wouldn't be here if it wasn't for you. I was named after you, you know. My mother called me Vandemere … for *you*."

Sadness in the shrieking voice. *"I LOVED THEM!"* His voice quieted. He choked out a sound like a sob. "*I … loved them*."

I swallowed past the burn in my throat. "I know you did."

"YOU. KNOW. NOTHING!"

My eardrums took another beating.

"You can't make this go away by killing me," I argued. "At least let Karma go. Hate *me* if you want to, but hasn't Karma's done enough for you? *Prove* to me you're more than just a hateful Shade. Show me you're capable of greater things."

"*Prejudice—all of it! You think a Shade is unworthy of love; a thing invented by violence and death? What do you humans know? You assume the worst from EVERYONE! Even you, Vandemere Petruska. You, who has known the wickedness of men. You think you can stand there and judge ME? You're just as weak as all the rest of your kin.*"

My mind was losing ground fast. Every time I came up with a way to talk myself out of this, *Vigolii* would change the rules on me. He was playing the ultimate grifter's trick on me and I was the one who was on the *fooled ya* side of things now.

It didn't feel none too good either.

Vigolii's howl beat against my temples. *"The Petruskas gave me a physical body! They gave me a HOME! A place in this world! They were the only ones to ever show me any kindness. They pulled me out of the fires of Hell and bound me to the horse. They danced upon my back, and the people cheered. The Petruskas loved Vandemere, and in turn, loved ME. A Shade. They offered me a glimpse of what it was like to be worthy of such a gift. When Vandemere died, their love for me died too. Stupid Petruskas! They told me they loved me, and I believed them! I trusted them! I protected them all the way to America, and do you know what I got in return?"*

Sudden tears blinded me. I bent my head on a terrible truth.

He waited for an answer.

The air crackled with silent thunder.

I said it. I said it, because if I didn't, Karma and I would both die.

"They left you to burn."

Silence.

Silence ... and fire roaring like a lion over my head.

"FINISH THE STORY!"

I let the *magie* in. I let it take over, because it was the only way out of this. I let it speak *through me*. I opened my mouth and let the words come.

"There was another fire. Just like this one. Domenico scraped up enough money to put on a show for the high society in upstate New York. There was even a proper tent this time. The Petruskas hired a quartet to play for the patrons. They had music, and they had better costumes. My great-aunt Nikita did ballet on the back of the horse named Vandemere and the whole of society cheered."

"I did everything they asked of me."

"You really were an amazing horse."

"Tell me the rest."

I spat out blood when it clogged up my voice. I didn't even sound like *me* anymore. Vandemere Petruska barely existed now. If my father had been around to witnessed this, he would have berated me for being so weak.

"No one noticed the small blaze starting in the corner of the tent. Someone had thrown away a cigar. It ignited the tanbark. It set fire to the canvas. The Petruskas had oiled the material to make it rainproof and the fire got out of control. People panicked. Everyone stampeded for the exit. Most got out. Some didn't. Some people were trampled to death. Some died from the smoke before the fire ever got to them. The Petruskas ..." God, this was awful. "The Petruskas were the first to get out. They found a loose spot and crawled under the tent. They escaped to safety ... but they left you behind. They knew they wouldn't be able to save you *and* themselves, so they were forced to make a terrible decision. They left you. Left you to burn. After everything you did for them ... they *left* you."

"Do you know what it's like to burn to death, Vandemere Petruska?"

I was about to learn firsthand *exactly* what it felt like to burn to death.

"If it makes any difference, I would have *died* trying to save you," I said.

Silence bridged the distance between us. At least *Vigolii* was thinking ... pondering the implications of my loyalty towards an animal that had perished long before I was even born.

"Look," I said. "I know what it feels like to be angry. I know you want to get back at me for what my family did. You have every right to be mad, I know—"

Something hit me upside the head.

I sighed. It was just another pain on top of all the others.

The entity was getting physical now.

Not good.

The sword was so heavy; it quivered at the end of my grip as my strength failed. I tried to drop it, but my hands just *wouldn't* let go. I was trapped in *Vigolii's* power. He had control over my arms. Over *me*.

I coughed up a froth of blood and ended up swallowing most of it.

As soon as I had enough breath to speak again, I went on. "You tried to lure me away from the circus that day, didn't you? You used Annie to get to me. You got into her head somehow and tried to make her to lead me into the field so you could tear into me—only it wouldn't be *you* doing the slaughtering. It would be Matthew Lee. You needed a *body* to hurt me, so you jumped out of Annie and made yourself at home inside her father. Get someone else to do your dirty work for you, right? I was supposed to go with Annie that night. I was supposed to follow her away from the circus so you could get me alone, and then you would make Mr. Lee kill me, but Dolly got in the way. Dolly, and the ghosts of my ancestors. When I channeled Apollo after the show and chased the deer through the jungle, it was Domenico's way of getting me away from you. The Petruskas *saved* me. They wouldn't let you get to me, so Matthew Lee led Annie away instead. It was supposed to be *me*. I was the one you really wanted. And because you're so angry, you killed her anyway. You did the same thing to Clarence. You sent that little girl to get him. Cassie Lamont. She was supposed to take him by the hand and lead him away so you could get rid of him too."

"The other Petruska."

I licked parched lips. "He doesn't believe in the *magie*. He asks too many questions. He lives in a world of logic. You can't use fear against him. He would never submit to the craziness I've had to deal with all my life. He wouldn't go with the little girl, so she led her own father away instead. It's always the fathers, isn't it? You had to kill *someone*. Make the Petruskas pay. All because Domenico tethered you to Vandemere, showed you love, and then ripped it away from you." I was mad now too. I couldn't help it. I was going to die in a fire, along with my horse, because of something my great-grandfather had done, and it wasn't right.

Blood dripped off my chin.

I had no hands to wipe it off.

"You use people to get what you want. You made my own father *hate* me. Use the fathers, right? Make *them* pay. My father wanted to *kill me*. I saw it in his mind the day he pulled me off Karma and told me to leave the property. I used the *magie* to read him. I saw *everything*. Do you have any idea what that did to me? To be rejected like that, over and over. How is that fair? And all those things he said he wanted to do to me? It *destroyed* him. He thought he was out of his mind. Do you even *care*? He never laid a hand on me, but he may as well have stabbed a knife into my heart."

"And you hate me *now."*

God ... I just wanted this to end. Why wouldn't it just *end?*

"I *don't* hate you. How could I hate you? My family left you to die in a fire. No wonder you're angry."

"You want to kill me."

"The old me would have wanted to," I agreed. "I hate what you've done, don't get me wrong. But I can't hate *you*. I won't. You've suffered so much. My family did a terrible thing and for that I am truly sorry."

Silence.

"I don't want to hurt you," I said to the smoke. "Hate only fuels more hate and that's how wars get started. Someone told me that once. A man with a big heart. Carrying around that kind of anger makes me no better than my enemy."

Laughter in the billowing clouds, and a voice that sounded way too much like Sal Lorenzo's. *"Brave words from a cornered rat. You have the power to end this, Vandemere Petruska. All you have to do is lean on the sword."*

"No!"

"Kill the horse and send me back. It's that simple."

I moaned. "I... can't. I won't do it."

Karma took a step towards me. When I searched his liquid eyes, all I saw were flames reflected back at me. No fear or confusion there. His ears remained passively sideways. Saliva dribbled from his slack lips, and he hadn't even blinked when he felt the prick of the sword scratch his flesh. His mind had wandered off somewhere and I wasn't sure if there was any way of getting it back.

Maybe it was kinder to leave him where he was ...

I tried to back up, but I couldn't make my feet move. "Stop it!"

I dug the hilt of the sword into my belly to keep the business end of the blade from cutting into Karma's flesh.

"Kill the horse."

"No!"

"Then you'll both die."

"I can save you! You don't have to stay in this world. You're not bound to the family anymore. We don't need protection. You can go home."

"I'm giving you a choice, little Petruska. I'm giving you options, just like you gave me."

I never knew a soul-manifestation could sound so much like a petulant brat. I bit back a moan while this thing *raged* at me.

"Your ancestors never gave ME a choice! They left me to die. But you? I'm giving you a way out. Kill the horse and I'll save you. Or stand here and burn."

Not great options.

The voice paced around me.

"I give you something. You give me something in return. You said that once, true?"

I'd had no idea how those words would come back to haunt me.

Karma leaned his chest into the sword point.

My hands held the hilt steady.

I hate to admit it but I did whimper a bit.

"I have an idea," I blurted out. "Why not take the *magie* instead?"

I'd gotten *Vigolii's* attention now. Had him considering a different fate than the one he had in store for me.

"It's what you really want, isn't it? Kill all the Petruskas, right? Make them pay for leaving you behind. Make them suffer. Without the *magie*, I won't be able to see you coming. I'll be vulnerable. I'll give it to you one on condition. You have to let Karma go."

"You would give me the magie*?"* He actually sounded shocked.

Tears made inroads through the soot on my face. I didn't mean to cry. I just couldn't stop myself. Everything I needed to survive was leaking out of me and I just didn't have the energy to care anymore. "I give it to you freely. No questions asked."

"But ... you won't be able to defend yourself." It was odd, listening to an Underling of Hell trying to work out a scam. *"You would sacrifice yourself for the sake of a horse?"*

"He's not just any horse." I adjusted my hands on the hilt of the sword, getting a better grip on things. My right hand was slippery from all the blood running down my arm and I couldn't make much of a fist so the left hand had to do most of the work. "You can have the *magie* all to yourself. Think how powerful you'll be. You can make the whole *world* pay for letting you burn."

He took a long time to reply, calculating his next move. *"It's a trick."*

"It isn't. You can have it. It's brought me nothing but grief. I would gladly give it to you, but you have to let Karma go. That's the deal. Take it or leave it."

"If you give me the magie, *I'll save you too."*

"Well, that would be damn decent of you," I said, keeping my voice steady. Not too high, not too quick. An easy conversation between a demon and the damned.

"Why would you do this? Without the magie, *you'll be nothing. You'll be ordinary."*

"Ordinary?" I spit out a wry chuckle, remembering dear old Margaret's words. "Excuse me, but I will never be *ordinary*. People have called me terrible things, yes. But you would know that, right? You've been with me all these years. They called me a dirty Gypsy. *A freak.* I hated that. I hated *them*. It wasn't until I went home to Arizona that I realized how happy I was to be different. So yeah, I might be a dirty Gypsy and a freak, but I was never *ordinary*. I'm proud to be a Petruska. Proud of my heritage. It makes me unique. Makes me different from everyone else. Domenico gave the *magie* to my mother and my mother gave it to me. *Me,* of all people." I found it odd that I felt the need to explain myself when two lives hung in the balance.

"I loved them," Vigolii repeated, driving that stake home.

"I know you did. They know it too. They want me to tell you how sorry they are. They want me to send you home. It's where you belong."

"I don't want to go home. I like it here. Besides, there's no love in Hell ..."

He stopped.

Stopped *dead.*

Flames burned up the canvas roof high over our heads, screaming along the panels of the painted temple that used to be my home. The wind howled, swirling up the flames into a tornado of hellish heat. I'd heard that sound before, when *Vigolii* had cloaked himself in the dust storm out in the desert and killed my beloved Dolly. The sound of Death come a-calling.

A gulf of silence betrayed him.

"That's what you're most afraid of, isn't it," I said. "Living without love."

A pause.

"I fear nothing." It was said without emotion. Spoken by a fallen soul who only wanted what he couldn't have.

It was too late for him to take it back. Too late to renege on his confession. *A magician* never *reveals his secrets*. In his arrogance, *Vigolii* had shown his hand to me. Told me the truth. Delivered the thing he yearned for. The thing he killed for. Would *die* for. Even for a Shade like *Vigolii*, a life without love was no life at all.

In the end, he was nothing more than a sad, little Petruska, same as me.

I used the last bit of strength I had left to pull my shoulders back and stand a little straighter. "Take the *magie* and go. I dare you. Go after Lieutenant Dawson if that's what you want. He's got a son you could torture. That ought to keep you busy for a few years, right?"

He mulled this over. *"You'll trick me."*

"I won't. All you have to do is break the tether binding you to Karma's body and jump into me. I'll do the rest."

"If you trick me, you die."

I took a firmer grip on the hilt of Sal's sword with both hands and tried not to think about all that blood running down my arm. "I won't trick you."

I hoped wherever she was, my mother would forgive me for what I was about to do.

"You swear you'll give me the magie*?"*

"All you have to do is jump," I promised.

My legs kept trying to buckle at the knees. There was a chill spreading through my body that couldn't be warmed by the fire. I was cold from the inside out, and I was running out of blood.

And time.

I stood before Karma and pointed the sword at his chest while the big top burned all around us.

"Okay, deal."

Vigolii gave me no warning. There was no great long speech about how he wanted to stay out of Hell, and that I'd better not be lying to him. No more howling about how the Petruskas had hurt him, and used him, and turned him into a shield against all mankind's prejudices. He'd said what he'd meant to say, and in the end, he just ... *jumped*.

A great shadow leaped out of Karma's body. It had no shape. No sound. I saw a dense cloud of *something* block out the blinding glare of fire right before it shrouded my eyes in darkness.

I barely had time to turn the sword around and aim the point of it into my own stomach before *Vigolii* swept into me.

It felt like a house had landed on me.

I staggered back.

The sword sliced into my abdomen. It sank into my body just at the point below my breastbone, going all the way through and out my back.

For a moment, shock kept me from feeling anything at all.

Then ...

Pain ... oh, dear Christ ... the *pain* ... like nothing I'd ever felt before.

I did my best not to scream.

It wouldn't have helped anyway.

The shadow broke apart. It turned into blackened rags of mist that spun around me, hissing like water on hot coals; the only sound *Vigolii* was able to make before he dissolved into nothing. In the end, the evil I'd manifested with my hatred, and my hurt, was nothing more than smoke too.

An acrid stench burned my nose. It scorched my consciousness—what was left of it anyway. I couldn't tell what was fire now and what was just me dying.

I looked down at the ornate sword hilt stuck in my belly. It was so absurd, seeing a murderous trinket poking out of me like that, that I actually coughed out a laugh. I don't know why. My insides were all torn up, and I couldn't see for shit.

Insanity, maybe?

I pulled my busted lips into a crooked grin. Raised my eyes and spoke to the air where *Vigolii* had just been. "Looks like you forgot who you're dealing with—" A savage pain speared through my insides, stopping my voice. What was meant to be a defiant taunt sounded more like a broken sob.

There was no one around to hear it anyway.

Vigolii was gone. I didn't feel the need to apologize for tricking him either. He'd forced me into a dangerous game and I'd fought back. Fought for my life—and Karma's. Gambling for souls was a sport without rules, and God knows, I'd learned from the best.

What I'd failed to mention during our negotiation, was while *Vigolii* was busy being distracted by the thrill of stealing the *magie* away from me, goading me into thinking he had me trapped into his web of deceit, I'd snuck around behind him and infiltrated his lies. I'd used my mother's *magie* to weave myself into his hellish game and had seen the trickery laced into his promises. As much as he'd played the ultimate con on me, I'd doubled it back on him. It was never *Vigolii's* intention to let me off the hook. I knew that now. He didn't just want the *magie*. He wanted my body to go along with it. He needed a vessel to exist in this world, and I was the one he'd set his sights on. *I* was the one in the spotlight. *I* was the one who desired love above all else. Of all the Petruskas, I was the strongest—because of what Luca Petruska gave me. Me—of all people. The one destined for greater things ... but that's a story for another day.

Vigolii couldn't take possession of me without getting the *magie* out of me first. The *magie* would stop him. The *magie* was the weapon he feared most of all. Feared, and desired. As long as I controlled the magic, he wouldn't stand a chance in taking me down. He would have to convince me to offer it freely, and once I fell for his honey-tongued assurances and handed over my power, he would crush me like a bug.

It wouldn't be *Vigolii* who waged war upon the earth then. It would be *me*.

I had to stop him. I had to slam the door on him, and if it meant running a sword through my guts to keep him out of me, then it had to be done.

Didn't mean I had to like it.

I'd seen it all. I'd harnessed the *magie* and spooled it into his mind. Seen he was a liar, and a cheat; all of it he had learned from me, of course. Once a circus brat, always a circus brat. Grifting was my specialty after all, and I was an old pro at it.

Sadness crippled me worse than the blade stuck through my insides. Sadness, and guilt. I'd been the one to condemn *Vigolii* back to Hell, and I'd be lying if I said I was happy about it. My family had done a terrible thing, and someone had to take responsibility for it. That task had fallen to me. Evil like that had no place in this world. That's what I told myself anyway. Made it easier to justify what I had done.

Funny, the things that run through your mind when you're busy coming to grips with your own mortality.

I dropped to my knees. I spat out a weak moan. Retched on blood and focused on hitching out some feeble gulps that passed for breathing.

I planted a bloody hand in the sawdust to brace myself up.

Sending a Shade back to the Underworld seemed ... I don't know, anticlimactic? All that nonsense leading up to it; there had been a lot more drama than I thought necessary, but that was the deal you got with demons. All that talk and shouting and, *you're going to die, Petruska!* I was more of a *let's just get this over with* sort of circus freak, and not really into dragging things out forever.

I fixed a bleary stare on the embers smoldering on the ground while my life leaked out of me in spatters of red.

I may have overestimated my ability to survive this.

Above me, the remnants of the big top creaked and groaned. Flames peeled back the canvas walls, and thick fingers of smoke wrapped themselves around my face. Heat was the enemy now. I was in stuck in an oven going full blast, and I had a pretty good idea now of what it meant to burn in the fires of Hell.

I gripped the hilt of the sword with my right hand and tried to pull it out.

It moved, a little ...

Pain doubled me over. I crumpled forward until I was balled up in the sawdust, pressing my forehead against the back of my hand so I wouldn't burn my face in the embers stirred up by a roaring wind.

I stayed on my knees, spitting out a few ineffective whimpers. The sensation of having a solid object pushed through my body was quite indescribable. All I could really do at this point was hold my breath and gather what little strength I had left into something that passed for courage. There was still more to do, and sitting here feeling sorry for myself wasn't helping one bit.

Karma approached me, merging like a ghost out of the billowing smoke. His topline glowed red from the fire, and his footsteps made no sound at all.

He lowered his head. His eyes searched mine. Eyes that caught the firelight, blinking against the smoke. He was just a horse now. He was trembling, and his hide was streaked with sweat. Fear was the thing that drove him to my side, and he wanted to be close to me for comfort.

"Karma ..." I put a bloody hand up and grabbed a hank of his mane. I tried to pull myself up, but my legs just wouldn't hold me. I collapsed at his feet again and threw everything I had into one unhelpful, terse, tirade of misery. "God ... damn ... fucking ... *hell* ..."

I still had to get Karma out. I had to save him. Save *us*. I needed the sword to bust us out of this freak show. Needed to pull it out of me so I could use it to cut a hole in the side of the tent.

No sense in sending *Vigolii* home if I perished right along with him.

Besides, what kind of Petruska would I be if I let my horse burn?

What kind of *Davidson* would I be?

I dragged my face out of the ashes and rocked back on my heels. I considered the futility of the task before me and looked Death square in the eye while the fire raged closer.

I wrapped both hands around the hilt of the sword and tried to pull it out of my gut again. Even got as far as drawing it out an inch before I folded like a house of cards.

I never realized being brave came with that much *pain*.

Karma was still waiting for me to tell him what to do. He pushed his broad forehead into the crook of my neck and hid his fearful eyes from me.

I draped my arm over his powerful neck, sobbed into his delicate ear, and bled some more. "Sorry Karma ... to put this on you ... but you're gonna have to help me up."

He did something amazing then. Something totally unexpected.

Someone must have taught him ...

Karma placed his right foreleg straight out in front of him and folded his left knee back, tucking it underneath his body. He lowered himself until his muzzle was touching the ground. He bowed his head until it was level with mine, presenting his back to me. A gift offered at the end of things ...

I hadn't known he could do that trick.

They did things all right up there in Canada.

I screwed my eyes shut and slowly pulled myself up against his side.

My life ebbed out of me. Blood ran over my left hand where I held it tight over the sword hilt. Gleaming wet threads glistened over my knuckles ...

It would have been so easy just to stay where I was and let the fire take me. It would have certainly been a lot less painful, for sure. Standing up with three feet of Spanish steel run through my insides required a certain amount of dedication and willpower.

I slid my right leg over the hollow place behind Karma's withers and eased myself onto his back. Every time I moved, the sword sawed back and forth through my insides. I didn't know this kind of hurt even *existed*. A thin, primal wail tore out of my mouth before I could stop it. I would remember that sound for the rest of my days, although I would never speak of it.

I half-lay across Karma's back with my legs draped on either side of him. I buried my face in his magnificent crest, and I had to sit a bit sideways to accommodate the sword hilt.

Stupid, really, to think I had any chance of coming out of this alive. I didn't feel brave, so I settled for just being calm.

I did it for Karma, not for me. If I stayed where I was, he would stay too, and that just wouldn't be fair. He deserved a chance to live even if I wasn't going to, so I happily accepted the ride out.

I tried not to fall off as he scrambled to his feet again.

He picked up a slow canter, taking care not to jar me any more than he had to. His strides were pure silk, and I didn't feel a thing.

Odd … that I wasn't aware of my body anymore. Even the pain wasn't so bad now. I was just cold. Freezing actually, and my face was already numb to the flames.

Karma circled around what was left of the center ring, keeping up that seamless rhythm that rocked me to sleep. He dodged bits of flaming canvas where it had set the ground alight, gathering speed.

I threaded nerveless fingers through his mane and rested my cheek on his magnificent crest, letting him carry me through the fire.

I barely felt him leave the earth.

He must have jumped. To me, it felt like flying. He bore me through the chaos of smoke and fire towards the chute—the only way out—and he cleared the broken girders blocking the exit in a single leap. Blistering heat licked my cheek, only for a moment, then we were outside.

Easy as jumping through a hoop of fire.

He bore me out into the clearer air. Into the flickering night and the spray of fire hoses, where people were calling for me. Searching for me.

I slid off Karma's back and fell into waiting arms. I think I said something like, "It's done." I couldn't be sure of anything now.

In my delirium, I saw shadowy figures leaning over me. I mistook them for the faces of my ancestors. I expected them to berate me for using a grifter's trick on an immortal Shade, but they had nothing but love and admiration in their eyes.

I saw my mother standing slightly to one side. She was clothed in tatters of mist and rain, although it was probably just water from the hoses. Her long hair fell around her pale, moonlit face.

I called for her. I stretched my hand into the ebb and flow of firelight, reaching for her hand as she held whitened arms out to me.

My body had turned into ice now, and I couldn't feel the heat dancing across my face anymore. "I'm coming, Ma!"

I might have only said this in my mind though.

She swept me up into her frigid embrace.

If she answered back, there was no *magie* left in me to hear it.

Chapter Twenty-Two

I woke up someplace quiet. Lost in peaceful shadows. My body was cocooned in warmth even as my groggy mind wondered where the hell I'd landed myself into now.

My thoughts drifted lazily ...

I pried my eyes open a crack.

"I'm getting really tired of visiting you in the hospital," Ellen said.

I smiled. My lips were smashed up and scorched from the fire. My face had taken a walloping, so my attempt at a grin ended up pretty lopsided.

"How do you feel?" she asked, chuckling at my dancing eyes. "They've got you doped up pretty good. You want something else to go with that, horse boy? Whiskey? Money?"

I couldn't answer. My throat was still raw from all that smoke and heat. The fact that I woke up *at all* was still something of a shock.

I tried to use the *magie*. I tried to tell her; *I want you to stay with me. I want you to marry me. I want to see you standing at the altar in a blue silk dress with lace around the cuffs. I want you to come with me to see the Grand Canyon. I want you by my side for all the days of my life. I want you to love me and to never let me go. All you have to do is say yes and I'll be your safety net, forever and always.*

The *magie* was gone.

I remembered now: I'd given it away. A deal was a deal. In exchange, Clarence Dawson, his first-born son, and me, the last three remaining Petruskas, would get to live their lives in relative peace.

I fumbled my right hand free of the blankets and reached out to her.

She wove her fingers into mine.

When I drew her closer, she lifted the blankets and got into bed with me, arranging herself so she wouldn't put any pressure on the thick layers of bandages going around my abdomen. The nurses had me propped up with pillows on my left side so that the delightful pattern of blackening welts on my back wouldn't interfere with my naptime, but there was just enough room in the bed for the two of us to lie face to face.

She draped her arm across my shoulder and cradled me to her chest. She brushed the hair back from my forehead and kissed my swollen eyelids one at a time. "What am I going to do with you, Petruska?"

I drifted off, safe in the haven of her arms, and content.

***

They told me it was a miracle I survived. My doctor said he'd never seen anything like it before.

"In all my born days," he said.

Those were his exact words.

He said I must have had an angel on my shoulder.

"Not an angel," I'd told him. "A tarot card."

He held up *The Chariot* to squint at it. "Is this some sort of *Ruskie* talisman you people carry around with you?"

"I'm not Russian," I explained patiently. "I'm Romanian."

I was well aware of the hole sliced into the card where the Spanish sword had gone through it. One of the nurses had already shown it to me, after she wiped the blood off it, that is.

"Why was this thing under your shirt, anyway?" the doctor asked.

"For extra protection."

"From a piece of cardboard?"

"From a family."

He still didn't understand.

When the sword had gone clear through me, it hadn't punctured a single vital organ. It had sliced a pathway between my diaphragm and stomach and glanced off my spine without nicking anything important. It was as if all my innards moved out of the way when the blade slid into me. The doctor told me it went through the tarot card, passed all the way through my body and out the other side, but I already knew that.

He stared in wonder at my hospital chart. "How *on earth* are you still here?"

I shrugged. "My mother told me to have faith ... so I did."

The hospital in Tucson was a hell of a lot nicer than the one in Oklahoma. No one threw a shoe at my head or tied me down with restraints. The walls here were painted a cheerful blue, and the windows overlooking the cactus garden two stories below were curtained in buttercream linen. There was a faint odor of bleach in the air, but I much preferred that to a nose full of smoke any day of the week.

I slept right through Christmas.

I had a steady stream of visitors marching through my room. Doctors and nurses, and curious medical students. Mostly, they came to gawk. I was the patient who'd had a sword run through him with nary a mark to show for it.

They all agreed it was a mystery how I survived, but I knew better. I'd counted on my mother's magic to protect me, and a host of Petruskas had backed her up.

Every morning, a nurse would come in, fluff my pillow, and place a tray across my lap. She lifted a metal dome, revealing my breakfast as if she were performing a magic trick. Eggs, accompanied by toast with marmalade, a couple of strips of bacon, and a cup of tea lay before me.

Ta da!

"I've never seen anyone eat so much with a hole in his guts," the nurse quipped as I tucked in.

My voice was still somewhat of a croak. "I have to eat this fast before Ellen gets here."

She fixed me with a sly grin. "Yes, the one who takes all your food. Is she your girlfriend?"

My own smile was still a little awed. "You know, I think she *is*."

***

Chuck stomped into my room later that afternoon. "You had better start explaining yourself, Petruska."

He'd caught me sleeping. Dozing, and coughing. I was still hacking up ashes from the fire and was told that my lungs would need time to heal.

It was still better than dying.

He leaned against the windowsill where Ellen usually perched, glaring at me with very dark eyes. His arms were crossed over his chest and his expression warned me he was more than a little upset with me.

I rolled over and struggled to sit up in bed.

"Do you need some help?" he offered, somewhat grudgingly.

"I can do it."

"Some stitches and lots of rest," was what my doctor had prescribed. "Soon, you'll be good as new."

At this point, I would be happy with slightly tarnished.

There was no comfortable position available to me, so I just rested my back against the pillows and worked on keeping a straight face. The whip weals on my back stung brightly, as if a million fire ants were burrowing into my skin, and I had to clench my jaw just to stop myself from swearing a blue streak.

"How did you know where I was?" I asked, sliding that in first before Chuck could work himself into a dither. "I told everyone I was going to the Grand Canyon."

His eyes were flinty. "If you didn't want anyone to follow you, why did you leave Shorty's letter on the nightstand for us to find?"

My mind did a mental somersault. "I *didn't*."

He uncrossed his arms and reached around to the back pocket of his blue jeans, producing an envelope I recognized right away. It was folded in half, still warm from being carried around next to his ass all day. When he tossed the envelope into my lap, it unfolded itself to me, face up.

Sure enough, there was Shorty's handwriting ... addressed to me.

I frowned, which was difficult to do given the fact I had a pattern of ugly bruises striped across my face. "But ... that's impossible." I picked up the letter and turned it over just in case this was a trick, a grifter's ploy to get me to confess to something I didn't want to. "I didn't leave this behind. Where's the one I wrote to you? It was six pages long."

Chuck leaned over to pull my satchel off the shoulder of the wooden visitor's chair near my bed. "I never saw any letter like that on your nightstand. Only Shorty's note, saying how the circus was coming to Tucson." He placed the satchel carefully across my knees. "The envelope with the story you wrote me is still in your bag. Check it yourself if you don't believe me."

It's not that I didn't believe *him*. I just couldn't wrap my mind around what he was implying.

"I swear on my mother's ashes I didn't leave Shorty's letter behind," I insisted.

"Well then one of us is lying."

I looked inside the satchel.

Everything was still there. All my earthly belongings: pants, extra shirt, Ma's tarot cards, and the letter I'd written to Chuck was tucked underneath all of it.

"You ought to thank the spirit guides the wrong letter got left behind," said Chuck, getting huffy again. "Otherwise, we'd be looking for you somewhere in the Grand Canyon right now, and you'd be a pile of ashes."

I stared at Shorty's letter in my hand while my brain short-circuited.

Chuck saw the dismay on my face and took pity on me. "I read your letter a few days ago while you were recovering from the surgery. It was addressed to me anyway." He leaned back on his hands, surveying me from the windowsill with a much more approachable expression.

He waited for me to direct the conversation to whatever I was comfortable with.

I took my time debating between telling the truth and not speaking at all. It was too soon to go back there yet. Too many wounds. Some on the outside. Far too many on the inside.

I changed the subject. "I see you finally went past the gate."

He nodded. "For you."

I felt the tears start behind my eyes. I sniffed them away. Told myself, I will not *cry* ...

Chuck grinned and understood.

I moved on to safer topics. "How's Karma?"

"Right as rain. He lost a bit more hair off his rump. We've been treating him for some superficial burns, but he'll be fine."

"He got me out," I said. "Even though he was afraid of the fire, he got me out."

Chuck's patience reached the end of its tether. "What happened, Vandy!? Why did you even *come here?*"

"I couldn't put you and Lenora in danger like that! Because of *me*." It didn't take much to start me coughing again. I barked violently into my hand. My healing innards didn't like it and my eyes watered from the pain.

Eventually, I got my wind back. "It wanted a war ... so I gave it one."

"Alone?"

"I wasn't alone."

"No." His tone was tight with anger. "You had Karma. You trusted your life to a *horse*, Vandy."

As had all the other Petruskas who had come before me.

"How did you end up with that damn sword run through your stomach anyway?"

When in doubt, fall back on selective amnesia. Works every time.

"I ... don't know." The stammer in my voice wasn't all pretend. "There was so much smoke ... I couldn't *see*. I must have fallen on it by accident. After you all left, I tried to follow you out of the big top. Things got a bit crazy after that. I couldn't breathe. I was dizzy, and I tripped. That damn sword ..." I shook my head, playing up the act. "I guess I impaled myself on it somehow."

He didn't believe me. "And what about the bruises on your back? Are you going to tell me you impaled yourself on Sal Lorenzo's bullwhip too? The doctor counted twenty-three marks on you. Four of them are on your head, and you took two more across your face. You suffered one hell of a beating from someone. You'll need to speak with the authorities. They're waiting for you to recover before they question you."

Dread was a bitter taste in my mouth. "About Annie?"

"About Matthew Lee."

"Oh." I reached for the glass of apple juice the night nurse had left on the tray beside my bed and took a sip, hoping to cool the glowing coal rammed down my throat. It gave me time to collect my thoughts and pack them safely away. "Will Lieutenant Dawson be there too?"

"We're in Tucson, Vandy," Chuck reminded me, as gently as he could. "It's out of his jurisdiction. The local police will be the ones asking the questions. They'll want to know about the fire and who attacked you. You're their key witness. Matthew Lee will be extradited back to Oklahoma for questioning. They'll want your testimony for that too. If you know something, you need to say it. Clarence has offered his support. He's family, right? And you're still underage. I wouldn't bet on your chances of coming out of an interrogation unscathed with the local boys here but having Lieutenant Dawson in your corner will help.

"It's going to be okay, Vandy," he added, seeing my courage crumbling. "You're not alone anymore. We'll help you. *I'll* help you. You don't have to face this by yourself."

It was getting really hard to stop my expression from giving too much away.

"I understand now why *you're* here, Chuck. If you say I left Shorty's letter behind, then I guess I have to believe you. What I don't get is how Clarence ended up in Tucson too?"

"That was Ellen's doing. She's ..." he paused.

His silence stretched into awkwardness.

"Yeah," I said. "She's a handful."

Chuck made a noise somewhere between a laugh and a snort. "She got it into her head to follow you to California. After you left the hospital in Oklahoma, she stewed about it for months. Once she decided you were the only man for her, she took off after you. She bought herself a bus ticket to Fresno, with Clarence hot on her heels. He was determined to bring her back—by the scruff of the neck if he had to, he was *that* mad. Ellen got into Fresno barely a day ahead of him. Jimmy told her you were in Arizona. She had just enough money for another bus ride to Scottsdale, and when she got there, someone in town pointed her in the direction of Vandemere Ranch."

He paused again to collect his thoughts. "I have to say, it was a shock when she turned up on our doorstep. It was on the morning you left. She told us she was your girlfriend. She was very ... convincing." The color deepened in his face. "I haven't heard such things come out of a girl's mouth since I spent a week's wages for a night with my Chinese prostitute."

That's my Ellen, I thought, chuckling through smashed lips.

"I was just about to start looking for you when Ellen arrived," Chuck said. "I lost time sorting her out. That's when her father came banging on the door. The whole thing seems like one giant coincidence to me, but I think you know better." There was a shrewdness behind his raised eyebrow that left me feeling very exposed. "I'm thinking there were other forces at work here. Something in the wind making sure we all rallied together to save you from yourself. How else can you explain it?"

He waited, and I realized he was expecting an answer from me.

I had nothing to offer.

Frustrated with my silence, he sighed hard. Weariness bracketed his mouth and he had to keep blinking just to keep his eyes open. The nurses told me he hadn't slept much these past few days and had rarely left my side while I hovered between life and death.

"Who are you protecting, Vandy?" he asked.

I toyed with the empty glass, turning it round and round on the tray beside me. "I'm not protecting anyone. I just think I should speak to Clarence first. I need someone who can advise me ... you know, about the law. I don't want to say anything yet. Not until I figure things out." I glanced up. "I hope you're not mad at me, Chuck. I *want* to tell you. I will, soon. You deserve to know the truth. Believe me. *Trust* me. I want you to know how grateful I am that you decided to come after me. I owe you my life."

He shrugged out his embarrassment, pleased just the same. "Actually, it's Clarence you ought to be thanking. When the fire brigade brought you in here, you were on death's doorstep. You'd lost so much blood ... you were as pale as a gutted trout. That bullfighting-stick nicked a blood vessel in your arm, and you were bleeding all over the place. Combine that with the sword in your guts... well, no one thought you were long for this world. The doctor had to perform a blood transfusion before they could even take you to surgery. I've never heard of such a thing. Apparently, it's a common procedure they do now. Clarence was the obvious choice. He's a blood relation, so they hooked him up to you and bled him dry."

I could feel my pupils dilating. "I have Clarence Dawson's blood *inside me*?"

Chuck laughed at my horror. "Two pints of it."

I reached up to massage the knot out of my forehead, remembered how much that was going to hurt, and groaned instead. I don't know why, but the thought of Clarence's blood singing round my veins made me cringe. I'd just gotten *rid* of a demon who tried to use me for evil purposes. Now I had tiny bits of Clarence Dawson taking up residence inside my body too? It was just so ... *gruesome*.

Maybe if I asked politely, I could convince one of the nurses to bleed him out of me.

I took my hand away from my face and shifted against the pillows.

It had to be asked, so I asked it.

"Where's Del? Did he come with you?"

The set of Chuck's jaw warned me of the impending bad news. "He's ... not doing so good, Vandy. He's still in Scottsdale. Lenora stayed with him. I know, it looks bad. It's ... complicated."

I struggled to keep the disappointment out of my face. Stupid, to think he would come ...

"I'm sorry," Chuck said, reading my thoughts.

"It's okay," I said, but it really wasn't.

***

I was still in the hospital when the local sheriff's department organized a team of investigators to spearhead my interview. There was talk of releasing me from the hospital, but I was still having trouble breathing, so the medical staff decided to keep me around for another couple of days for observation.

Clarence Dawson, still pale from donating his blood to me, slid into the chair next to mine. He'd dressed for the interview, wearing an authoritative suit of brown wool, his hair combed back, eyes gone flat and chilly. He sat down beside me, taking up space at the table the hospital administration had provided us in a room normally used for staff meetings.

I faced an interrogation team of uniformed police officers, a couple of detectives, members of the sheriff's department from Tucson, and some from Oklahoma as well. The captain of the fire brigade was in attendance too, and the local fire marshal. They were all shuffling papers on a table similar to ours; all of them tight-lipped and already on the defensive.

Jimmy was allowed to attend the meeting. Seeing as it was his circus that had gone up in flames, he could be called upon as a witness to add credence to my statement. He was to sit along the back wall and only speak when spoken to.

It was the first time I'd seen him since he'd pulled me off Karma's back the night of the fire. I was shocked by his appearance. His hair was unkempt, and he had a week's worth of whiskery growth on his jowls. His clothes hung loose off his boney frame. His eyes were dull and his spirit seemed tired. He looked out at the world with an apprehension that rubbed off on me.

When I'd asked if Chuck could join us too, everyone in the room had laughed in my face. Prejudice, it seemed, had a staunch foothold in the city of Tucson.

I bore the full brunt of their suspicious natures as I sat before their court. My singed hair hung unevenly around my face but at least the bruises across my eyes and the bridge of my nose had faded somewhat.

Most of the vivid purple had bled into a mess of yellowish gray. The blisters and cuts on my lips were healing nicely as well.

I'd dressed myself in a turquoise-colored cotton tunic Chuck had found at a local trading post, one geared mostly to tourists, but he assured me the Romanian authenticity was close enough. Someone had done a wonderful job of embroidering a pattern of multicolored beads down the front. I wore a pair of ill-fitting black trousers, a wide sash tied loosely around the bandages hugging my midsection, and thick socks on my feet. I'd woven the dove feather into a lock of burnt hair behind my left ear as a symbol of solidarity to Chuck Mescal.

I walked into the meeting under my own steam. All eyes followed me across the room, and I hoped I was representing my heritage with the honor and dignity it deserved.

A Petruska, through and through.

The lead investigator started the proceedings.

"State your full name for the record."

"Vandemere Alexander Petruska."

"The name on your birth certificate says Davidson," the man reported.

"Then why'd you ask me?"

Dawson laid a fingertip on my wrist, grounding me to his presence. "It's just a formality, Vandy. Standard procedure."

I felt the weight of a roomful of eyes on me. My voice tasted like dust in my mouth. "I haven't been a Davidson for a very long time."

"Petruska is a Russian name, isn't it?"

"Yes, although my family's original surname was Pusoma. Petruska is the name my great-grandfather Domenico took after being run out of Budapest nearly a century ago. He would have been around my age at the time. He was born of the Roma clans. His surname was Pusoma back then. They were performers. Traveling Gypsies."

I hadn't known any of this until *Vigolii* had shown me the truth about my past. I'd seen the Petruska history play out like broken pieces of a silent picture film after I'd connected to Karma's mind, the day we rode through the desert on a train bound for Hell.

I omitted the part about how I'd gotten this information from a horse; a horse, and a demon Shade, who was using Karma's body to get close to me. These strangers didn't need to know about the *magie*. How I'd used it to look into Karma's mind that day on the train and witnessed my own death.

They wouldn't have believed me anyway.

I told them, "My family's actual bloodline begins with the Roma people of Hungary before they immigrated to Romania. When he was a young man, Domenico had enough foresight to recognize that having a Roma name would target him for persecution. He understood the trouble it would bring down upon his children, so he changed his last name from Pusoma to Petruska, thinking it would help avoid detection in the war."

"You mean the war that's going on now?" the man asked. "The war in Europe?"

I nodded. "Yes, that one."

"But... how would he know about a war that hadn't happened yet?"

"I can't really say."

"Can't? Or won't?"

They all waited for me to pick one. When I didn't, the collective assembly shifted and tittered among themselves.

One of the investigators took pity on me, an older gentleman with kind eyes. "You would be wise to take your father's last name from now on, son. Hitler's war isn't going to turn out well for the Roma people."

"It's not going to turn out well for a good many others either," I agreed sadly.

"You don't mind if we call you Vandemere Davidson, do you?"

"It's a good name," I answered.

The questions got a lot harder after that.

When the committee foreman asked who put the marks on my back, I said I didn't know.

Behind me, I sensed Jimmy sitting up straighter in his chair.

"You don't know?" This one had shifty eyes and spidery hands that couldn't seem to stay still. He leaned forward in his chair, looking like he wanted to eat me.

"I can't remember," I clarified.

A gray-haired secretary in a white blouse and wool skirt committed my words to paper for the record.

The man sputtered. "Well, that's not good. Who else was there that night? Can you provide us with names?"

"I don't recall."

He spread his palms wide. "Listen kid. If someone beat the shit out of me like that, I'd sure as hell remember who it was."

"It's kind of a blur."

Clarence whispered into my ear. "Vandy? What are you doing?"

I stared straight ahead. "Can I ask a question?"

The committee spent some time getting more comfortable in their chairs.

"You can," another man said. He was from the sheriff's department; a thick-set man, around forty years old. He looked a lot older than that though, showing off a bright metal star on his lapel. "I can't guarantee you'll get an answer however."

I asked anyway. "Is Matthew Lee in custody?"

More shuffling around and knowing glances between them.

"He is," the sheriff replied.

"And Jake Topher? What about him?"

Hard eyes looked into my soul. "Why do you ask about Jake Topher?"

Would they have heard my heart pounding under the blue shirt? Would they have noticed my throat tightening, or my fingers starting to shake?

"I owe him some money."

They weren't buying it. As for evidence? Clarence had told me they had nothing. Only my blood on Jimmy's bullwhip, a belt that no one admitted belonged to them, and my own testimony.

"Jake Topher has disappeared."

"He's got family in Tennessee," someone else explained. Someone with more clout. A man in a tailored suit, with a crisp, white shirt underneath, and a silk tie with a pin. "Say the word and we'll pick him up. It's as easy as that."

"You think he'll stay in Tennessee?" I asked.

"The local boys are keeping an eye out for him," the man assured me. "Did he have anything to do with the attack on you?"

"I can't remember," I said.

A collective mutter hovered over the group.

"What *do* you remember?" This came from the fire marshal.

"I remember seeing flames."

"Do you know who set the tent on fire?" the marshal asked.

"The fire started when Shorty's hoop touched off a spark in the canvas."

"You witnessed this?"

"Yes."

"With your own eyes?"

How could I tell them? How would I explain I'd been stuck in a box when I used the *magie* to see the tent catch fire? Why would they believe me? Believe in the *magie*?

"The fire was started by accident," I said.

The sheriff angled his bulk forward to study my wan expression. "And where were you when you witnessed this?"

"Looking up," I said.

They asked me about Annie Lee.

I told them the same thing I'd told Clarence, months ago; that I'd seen Annie in the stable tent hours before she went missing.

They picked my statement apart until there was nothing left but the bones.

Clarence stayed close to me, whispering encouragement in my ear when I needed it, backing off and letting me talk when I didn't.

They tried to trick me into changing my story. They made me tell them the events backwards. They made up lies. They accused me of taking Annie away from the circus. They said they had evidence to support their claims. When they couldn't break me, they asked Jimmy to verify my whereabouts and confirm my alibi, which he did. He told them about finding my other shoe in the field more than a mile away. He said it wasn't possible for me to lose it there *and* get back in time to take Annie.

"You have Matthew Lee in custody," I pointed out. "You must suspect him of Annie's murder, otherwise he'd be out by now."

The man in the expensive suit sat back in his chair and watched my reactions. "You're afraid of him, aren't you. I can see it in your eyes."

Exhaustion thinned my voice. "You need to release him."

This provoked creaking chairs and sputtered protests.

The man in the fine tailored suit introduced himself as Detective Tom Gordon, second in command, and affiliated with the Tucson police department.

"What makes you say that?" he asked me.

Clarence leaned in close to my ear. "Be careful, Vandy. You're treading on thin ice."

Wise words. Too bad I didn't listen.

"Matthew Lee didn't know what he was doing—"

Dawson's fingers dug into my forearm. "Vandy ... *stop.*"

I stopped. I rubbed my eyes wearily. The cracks in my resolve were beginning to show. I couldn't think straight anymore. I kept trying to connect with the *magie* to help me read the room, only to remember I was on my own now. I'd never realized how much I relied on it to see my way through life until I'd lost it.

My safety net. I'd lost my safety net ... and I was floundering.

Clarence Dawson addressed the dour-faced group. "If you'll allow it, I'd like to speak on the boy's behalf."

They talked among themselves for a moment, and I watched Detective Gordon nod in agreement.

He turned back to Clarence. "State your name for the record."

"Lieutenant Clarence W. Dawson, Oklahoma City Division, badge number three-oh-five." He offered them a glance at his credentials, a shield and identification card tucked into a leather billfold, which seemed to satisfy them.

Gordon waved him on. "Please, continue."

I thought he would address the committee. I *thought* he was going to stand up and tell them I was out of my mind. That I was suffering from some sort of psychosis left in the wake of too many blows I'd taken to the head.

He's from the circus, he would say. One of *them*, you understand. This kid tried to trick me once. He's good at it. They're all the same, you know. You can't trust anyone from the circus.

Instead, he faced me and took my hands in his own. "Vandy, this isn't your fight anymore. I know you think you're doing the right thing by not speaking up, but you need to start telling the truth. It's just evidence. No one will judge you. No one will blame you. If you won't do it for yourself, do it for Annie Lee."

The look on his face chipped away at my armor. I glanced away so he wouldn't see the tears brimming in my eyes. "It's because of me that all this happened."

"It's because of you this thing is *gone*," he returned.

I blotted my eyes with my sleeve.

"I know you want to save Matthew Lee," Clarence murmured, "but it's out of your hands now. Let us do our job."

I heard Detective Gordon speak over the cold beat of my heart. "We just want to get your side of the story, Vandy. Any information you can offer will help make our case against Annie's father more compelling."

And condemn the man to a life behind bars? Maybe even a death sentence? If it hadn't been for *me*, Matthew Lee would never have stolen his own child away from the circus. It was because of me that he acted on behalf of a murderous Shade, breaking poor little Annie's skull like that.

All my fault.

I couldn't do it. *Wouldn't* do it. A man's *life* was at stake here, and I was all out of grifter's tricks, and cons. The arrogance I'd once hid behind had been beaten out of me and it would take some time before my mind healed from the trauma of it.

I felt my only recourse was to remain silent.

They questioned me for hours.

I stuck to my story; that I couldn't remember any details.

No one warned me about the pictures.

Christ ... they *had pictures?*

They laid them all out in front of me. I looked at the black and white photographs and my soul collapsed. Those grainy images would haunt me for the rest of my life.

The big top was gone. That familiar landmark of red and white striped canvas was nothing but a ghost now. What had once been my home, my church, and my refuge, was now a huge square of charred field with a few blackened girders rising out of the ashes.

There were people standing around in the photos. The urge to gape at someone else's misfortune might be a thrill to some but it left me burdened with an unforgiving grief and feeling lost. It was a side of humanity I didn't much care for. This was my *home* that had gone up in flames after all.

All the animals had survived, thanks to some quick thinking by the guying-out crew. They'd enlisted anyone who could handle a horse to lead them all away from the fire. That included some of the townies and a few firemen as well.

Omari and his two girls were in some of the pictures, safe and unharmed.

Most of the outlying tents were gone. Some of the midway rides had buckled in the heat. A couple of the trucks Jimmy used to cart everything around were unrecognizable. Not much was left of Jimmy's circus but a few smoldering embers and a lot of broken dreams.

They'd taken pictures of me as well, without my permission, I might add. The medical examiner had stood over me while I was being prepped for surgery, committing my injuries to permanent record, to be studied and discussed by anyone with a passing interest in my case.

"This is a travesty," one of the investigators said, not unkindly. He gestured to the pictures, and the woman taking dictation stared at a spot on the wall instead. "Who did this to you?"

I stared at the pictures. I couldn't believe it was even *me* under all those blackened welts and bruises. "I ... can't remember."

Clarence brushed his hand against my shoulder. "Vandy."

I heard his disappointment in me summed up in one word.

I gulped. "I don't feel well."

"Why are you protecting him?" Clarence's whisper was so low I almost couldn't hear him. I could feel the heat of his breath on my cheek. "I don't understand you."

I couldn't look at him. "You wouldn't," I said, with great sadness.

After that, I just stopped talking.

I found out later from Chuck that Matthew Lee had already confessed to leading Annie away from the circus. The local police detachment in Tucson had arrested him in town the day after the fire. Apparently, he'd gone to a tavern after leaving me for dead, drank himself into a state, and started a fist fight with some of the patrons. He was charged with disturbing the peace, payable with a fine. That is, until he started talking about some hellhound messing with his mind. He'd blabbed about how it had commanded him to bring his little girl out past the parking lot back in July, where he said he saw an animal that looked like a large wolf-thing carry her off in its jaws.

In hindsight, it made my interrogation seem somewhat of a farce. I know the detectives were only using my testimony to determine if Matthew Lee was criminally responsible for Annie's death, but it didn't make my interrogation easier to live with. If only I'd corroborated some of Matthew Lee's story instead of clamming up, he might have avoided incarceration altogether.

His defense team played up the insanity plea at his arraignment hearing. If he was found to be criminally insane, the judge would have no choice but to sentence him to a lengthy term locked up in an asylum.

I'd heard about those places. I knew what happened to people who were deemed unfit to live among normal folks. If you weren't crazy when you went in there, you certainly were when you came out. *If* you ever came out. It was a place where they put the freaks like me, and sick men like Matthew Lee away to keep the rest of the world safe.

Knowing that my silence had condemned a man to a mental institution hit me hard. My impotent anger turned into a depression that put me off talking for a few days. The burden of guilt for what I'd done to everyone—to Jimmy, Matthew Lee, Annie, and even little Cassie Lamont, left me staring vacantly at the walls, only half-listening to Ellen taunt me with insults about my burnt hair while she ate my lunch.

"If you don't start talking again pretty soon, they're going to have a psychiatrist look in on you," she warned me. She used a piece of bread to mop a smear of gravy off my dinner plate and shoved it into her mouth. "I heard the doctors talking about you this morning. One of them mentioned a stint in the looney bin." She chewed noisily, swallowed hard, and licked her fingers. "Said it might do you some good. I don't mind visiting you in the hospital, horse boy, but I draw the line at coming to see you at the crazy house."

I spoke, finally. "It's all my fault."

She swiveled around and set the plate down on the windowsill.

I remember how the sun glowed around her as it rose past its zenith against the half-opened blinds. How it turned her eyes the color of the ocean. She'd worn a pleated skirt that day that fanned across her shins, and a forest green sweater hugged the swell of her breasts.

Something about the way she looked at me warned me she wouldn't be tolerating any of my self-loathing nonsense.

She approached my bedside and put her hands on either side of my face. "Look at me, Vandy."

I really didn't have much of a choice.

She looked me straight in the eyes. "I wish I could say I know how you feel, sweetheart, but how could I?"

I smiled. "Did you just call me *sweetheart*?"

She brushed her lips across my mouth. "It's nice to hear your voice again."

A warmth spread through me, lessening some of the chill that held me in its frigid grip. "I've never been called sweetheart by a girl before. Only freak, and dirty Gypsy."

"Anyone ever calls you that again, they're going to regret it."

The determined set of Ellen's well-defined jaw told me they would too.

I felt her sigh across my face, and she got all thoughtful on me. "I don't know what to say to you, Vandy, or what to do to take your pain away. I wish I did. I don't understand any of this ... this mind-magic stuff you do." She tried everything to straighten my hair but I think it was a lost cause by now. "Here's the thing, dearest. You've been through a terrible ordeal and it's bound to leave some marks on you. Clarence and I have been talking. He's told me about that creepy thing your family summoned up from the grave. Now, I don't pretend to know what sort of creatures live in Hell, or even if I believe they exist—"

"They do," I assured her, *vehemently*.

She pressed cool fingers over my mouth. "Let me finish. The thing is *you* believe in them. And if you believe in them, then I will too. I haven't known you that long, but I know you wouldn't spin me a tale about demons and bad spirits just to impress me. I can see how much you've suffered because of it. And I know you wouldn't run a sword through your innards for no good reason."

I looked away. Looked at the small bouquet of daisies slowly wilting in the glass of water sitting on the same wheeled trolley that held all my pills and pain medications.

There was a tightness in Ellen's voice that hadn't been there a moment before. "Don't do that."

I rounded back to her. "Don't do what?"

Her blue eyes reminded me of a turquoise sea. Of secrets beneath the surface and the challenges presented to those who decided to swim in its currents.

"Hide your feelings from me," she said. "Like you did just now. I'm trying to tell you; you don't have to face this alone anymore. You've got *me* now. Through thick and thin. I *want* to see your sad eyes, Vandy. I want to know what you're thinking. Nothing you could do would ever scare me off. I've seen you at your worst and I never once thought about abandoning you. *You* were the one who pushed me away, remember?"

I remembered.

She made me shift over so she could sit down on the edge of the bed. She leaned over me, her weight braced on one arm. She stroked my face until the tension building a mountain of pain behind my eyes went away.

When I fumbled for her hand, she hung onto it like she was getting ready to pull me out of quicksand.

"I'm glad you never gave up on me," I said.

She touched the back of my hand to her lips, letting her eyelashes flutter across my knuckles. "You should know what you're getting yourself into. I have scars too. Scars you can't see, but they're there all right. I don't know if Clarence ever told you this, but I was abandoned on the steps of a Catholic church when I was only a couple of days old. I spent my childhood growing up in a convent."

I glanced up sharply. "You? In a convent?"

A smile twitched at the corners of her mouth. "Hard to believe, I know. I spent ten years in that religious hellhole before I was sent away to live in at St. Joseph's Orphanage, in Bethany. As terrible as the orphanage was, it was better than anything the church dished out. The nuns warned them I was an ungrateful brat. Those evil women did everything they could to turn me into a good girl, but I showed them."

A hardness worked its way into the knot between her brows. Memories welled behind her stern expression, and I could see her eyelashes getting damp with unshed tears.

This was a side of Ellen Dawson I had only glimpsed once before. The vulnerable side of a tough, self-assured girl she rarely allowed me to see. I didn't have the *magie* anymore to read her thoughts and adjust my reactions, but even *I* knew one wrong word, one slip-up, and it would send her scurrying back behind that unbreakable wall of lies and insults she used to shield herself from the ugliness of her past.

Chuck might have known what to say at a time like this, but me?

Then again, Chuck might have just stood back and waited for her to continue. He would have given her some time to get her emotions under control. Let her talk when she was ready, like he did the day he stood with me at the gates of Vandemere Ranch.

I stroked my thumb across her palm, hoping it would be enough to reassure her she could trust me. That her secrets were safe with me.

She tucked a length of hair back around her ear—the only clue to her nervousness I got without using the *magie*. "I blamed Clarence for coming to my rescue. I spent the past three years making his life miserable. The nuns told me I didn't deserve an adopted family who cared about me. They never let me forget my own mother left me on the church doorstep so I guess I believed them. There must have been something wrong with me, right? Some reason why my mother didn't want me. Like, maybe I cried too much. Or I cost too much to feed. Or maybe she didn't like the way I looked."

She sounded so defeated, I had to say something. "Well, I love the way you look. To hell what everyone else thinks."

She raised her beautiful blue eyes to mine. "Why did you do it, Vandy?"

My smile lost some of its shine. "Do what?"

"You *know* what. Is this something I'm going to have to worry about? You trying to die on me all the time?"

It took everything in my power not to pull my gaze away. I met her eyes unflinchingly while the rest of me wanted to run. "I'm sorry if I scared you. I wasn't trying to kill myself. Honest, I wasn't. It won't happen again. It's just that... well, things got a little crazy there. I didn't know what else to do. The entity... *Vigolii*... wanted the *magie* in exchange for Karma's life, so I gave it to him the only way I knew how."

"By running a sword through your stomach?"

I shut my eyes. I just couldn't bring myself to look her in the face and continue to lie to her. What happened inside the big top was between me and something I had created. I would suffer the guilt of *Vigolii's* destruction upon those who had no choice for the rest of my life. Like little Annie, and Lester Simmons, and poor old Dolly. It just didn't seem fair to put that burden on Ellen too, so I made up a story that would appease her; a simple tale that would lessen the concern welling in her eyes. A grifter's trick. I might have only been seventeen years old after all, but I was a pro at this.

"It was an accident," I told her. I was suddenly very tired.

I heard Ellen ask. "What about your magic?"

I pried my eyes open again and spoke with an effort. "I don't have it anymore, if that's what you mean?"

She took some time to mull this over. It was a lot to put on her, especially so soon in our relationship. But if I knew one thing about Miss Ellen Lyla Dawson, it was that she didn't back down from a challenge.

After a moment's reflection, she came to a decision. "You'll get it back, Vandy. I can't explain it, but I don't think your magic is gone. I would know it if it was. I think it's still inside you. There's a sort of... I don't know, a *specialness* about you." She smirked when she caught me grinning. "Shut up. I'm trying to explain it!"

I'm surprised she didn't stamp her foot like she usually did when I toyed with her affections.

A flush of embarrassment surfaced across her freckled nose. "What I'm *trying* to say is, we have a lifetime to figure it out. I want to be with you, Vandemere Petruska. I want to go where you go. I want to watch you ride your horses and see you do your tricks and jumps. I want to be there when you stand up on your beautiful Karma and throw your arms wide in the spotlight. I'm going to tell everyone around me; that's my man out there."

I smiled a soppy grin. My heart was filled with such a warmth, I could have floated along the ceiling like an untethered balloon. I felt the sun shining through my heart again, *finally*, and for that one precious moment, everything was just... well, *right*.

Two days later, with Ellen and Clarence backing me up, I was able to convince my doctor I hadn't run a sword through my belly deliberately and he released me from his care.

I was free to go.

Ellen asked if I needed help getting my things together.

I said I didn't.

She made a face and told me she would wait for me downstairs then.

Chuck had brought the Packard around. He and Clarence would escort me to a public livery stable outside of Tucson where Jimmy had rented stalls for the horses who'd escaped the fire. I was to be reunited with Karma and Copper at last. My spirit had taken a beating over the past twelve days but the thought of seeing my horses again put a song in my heart and a spring in my step.

The nurses gave me one final hit of laudanum before breaking the news that I was on my own now. I tiptoed around a sleeping giant of pain, hoping he would stay that way long enough for me to pack up my belongings and walk out of here without any help from the nurses. Chuck had bought me some better shirts to wear, since my other clothes reeked of smoke and had little holes burnt into them. I dressed myself, albeit stiffly, in a soft linen shirt, and I tucked the tails into a pair of wool trousers. My hair was still a bit of a disaster. I had a swath of bandages wrapped around my midsection too. Sal's boot had left me with a dislocated rib that gave me kick me in the side every time I moved, or inhaled too deeply, and I had a riot of deep bruising across my back. I sported some colorful marks on my face that had the uncanny shape of a whip handle, and the slice in my bicep itched with a pain that reassured me it was healing without any infection.

Could be worse, I told myself. I could be *dead*.

I adjusted the strap of Jimmy's satchel carefully over my left shoulder and turned to leave.

Sal Lorenzo stood in the doorway.

My heart did a sick little jump in my chest before it landed in my stomach. Sweat trickled between my shoulder blades, following the line of my spine like a fingernail of dread. My knees knocked together, and it was all I could do to remain upright on feet that seemed too far away to be of any use.

He said nothing. He filled the doorway, not so resplendent now in an old pair of trousers and a grimy undershirt. His hair was dirty. He swept it back across his forehead, pinning me down with eyes gone black with menace. Judging by the look he was giving me he'd come here to finish what he'd started.

I took a step back before I could stop myself.

It took some doing, but I forced myself to look him square in the face. "Get out of the way, Sal."

"Why didn't you tell them the truth?"

His voice rumbled like thunder, low and threatening. *Always* threatening. He was angry at *me*, and he had no right to be.

He put his hands on either side of the doorframe, blocking the way out.

I renewed my shaky grip on the strap of Jimmy's satchel. "I'm *trying* to keep you out of jail."

"Why? Because you think you're better than me?" His mean eyes threw daggers into mine. "All my life I've competed with you. All I ever hear is, Vandy this, and Vandy that. Vandy's such a great rider. Did you see Vandy's act tonight? Poor Vandy ... his father walked out on him. Be nice to Vandy, Sal, he just lost his mother. Vandy's got a broken leg now. He's so *brave*. Why can't you be more like Vandy?" A froth of spit collected in the corner of his mouth, but he never paused long enough to wipe it away. "I'm so *sick of it*."

My own mouth was as parched as the Arizona desert. "I never thought I was better than you, Sal. You just never believed you were good enough. There's a difference."

His expression was grim. Unreadable. I searched for the *magie* and got nothing ...

He picked at a loose bit of paint on the doorframe. "Sylvia won't talk to me. She left ... and I don't know where she went. My father is sending me away. He's contacted some people in Las Vegas who will give me a job at The Golden Nugget waiting tables. He says it's either that or take my chances with the police."

"There's nothing wrong with waiting tables," I said.

His eyes grew meaner. "Why didn't you rat me out, Petruska?"

My heart was hammering against my ribs so hard they could probably hear it out in the hallway. "Circus honor."

He snorted out a short, unpleasant laugh. "Circus honor? *That's* why you're protecting me?"

I watched him pick more paint off the doorframe and tried not to faint.

"I always knew you were a *freak*." He glared at me through half-slitted eyes. "This just confirms it."

I scraped my courage up off the floor and put it back where it belonged, in my somewhat battered soul. "I'm not protecting *you*. I'm doing it for Jimmy. You can go to hell for all I care. Jimmy's always been like a father to me. He shouldn't have to visit you in prison. Not after losing the circus too. It would kill him. He can visit you in Vegas. You can wait on his table. You can smile, and you can get him a drink, and you can be damned grateful while you're doing it."

"*Grateful?*" The word was uttered with venom. His tanned face turned a bright shade of red and his hands balled into fists.

Jimmy's Golden Boy.

Underneath the gilded exterior was just a cheap hood with a penchant for violence.

"I should kill you," he said.

He almost had.

"You won't kill me," I retorted. "I've left a sealed letter with Detective Gordon. Call it insurance. If anything happens to me, I've left instructions with the police department that he's to open it."

I hadn't, of course, but Sal would never risk asking the police department about a letter involving his own participation in an attempted murder investigation.

I gripped the strap on the satchel for support. "I've written it all down, Sal. All of it. How you raped Grace. How you sawed through the guywire and dropped a tent on a hundred people. How you roped Matthew Lee and Jake into ambushing me outside the stable tent. You and your pals nearly beat me to death! Everyone knows it was you who put me in the box. Without my testimony though, the police don't have enough evidence to convict you. My letter will betray you. The whole world will know it was you who sabotaged the magic act. You could have *killed* Sylvia—*and* me. I wrote that you did it on purpose. Maybe you did, maybe you didn't, but Detective Gordon will never believe you were under the influence of something Otherworldly. They'll blame you for everything. You'll go to prison for a very long time, and Jimmy will know what you've done. He'll hate you. That's what you're really afraid of, isn't it? Your own father *hating you*."

He stabbed another banderilla into my chest. "Just like your father hated *you*?"

It seems he couldn't resist one last chance to hurt me.

I shifted the satchel so it wouldn't drag so much on my shoulder. "Go to Vegas, Sal. Mind your manners. Meet some girl. Have a bunch of kids. Bore everyone with your stories of how you used to have a magic show in the circus. If you come near me or my family again, I'll make sure you spend the rest of your life in jail. Those are your two choices."

Options. I was giving him options and he didn't like it.

Sal Lorenzo stepped aside and let me pass.

I heard the whisper of a voice inside my head say, *Well-played, Petruska. You've won this round, but I'm not done with you yet.*

I stopped dead in my tracks.

The ugliness residing in Sal's soul speared through my mind, cutting me worse than a Spanish blade.

My mouth sagged.

It was almost like … *magie.*

But … no. It *couldn't be.* I'd given it away. I'd used it to trick *Vigolii* back to the Underworld; to offer him a piece of myself after locking the door on him with Sal's sword.

I hadn't told anyone about my attempt to sacrifice myself on a matador's *estoque.* I would go to my grave keeping it a secret. Almost had. I hadn't *meant* to kill myself. I had put my faith in a family sworn to protect me, along with the tarot *magie* my mother had laid around my soul, and it had paid me back in kind. Throwing myself on the sword was the only thing I could think of at the time to keep *Vigolii* from taking control of me. Despite everything I'd put it through lately, I kinda liked my body, and I really didn't want him to have it.

But this voice in my head?

It *couldn't* be the *magie.* Could it?

Sal pushed himself away from the doorframe and gave me one last lick of hatred he'd beaten onto my back. "See you around, Petruska."

Chapter Twenty-Three

I went home to see my father. Even though I'd promised myself I would never go back, I joined Chuck and Ellen and Clarence in the Packard, and we made the trip to Scottsdale, with Karma and Copper settled in nicely in the horse transport trundling along behind us.

Karma's burns had been no worse than a few blisters and some missing hair. He healed in a week. He had a box stall in the truck, with Copper for company, and a window he could stick his head out of. We rode back to Vandemere Ranch in *style*. No mucky boxcars for us this time.

The air was warm. The top was down on the Packard. I had my arm around Ellen's shoulders and turned my pale face towards the Arizona sunshine.

Ellen wore a white dress with dainty pink flowers printed all over it. She leaned against my side. She'd worn her hair up for me, sweeping the golden lengths into a loose knot at the back of her head and pinning it there with a rhinestone brooch. She gave me a knowing grin while the desert wind whipped up my hair and blew it across my weary eyes. Even though I was grateful to the team of doctors and nurses for saving my life, I was glad to be outside again. Free of hospital walls and stuffy conversations concerning my miraculous recovery.

Chuck and Clarence sat up front, chatting amicably, already bored with our adoring glances.

Ellen teased me with a smile before leaning over to nuzzle the crook of my neck. I blushed to the roots of my hair. When it came to sex, I was a complete novice, but I had an idea of what I liked.

She had an even better idea.

When she slid her hand along the inside of my thigh, a bolt of electricity surged through my groin.

I grabbed her hand and gasped. We were in the car, for God's sake! With her father sitting less than two feet away!

She laughed at my embarrassment.

She whispered. "I'm going to destroy you, Petruska."

I grinned back. "I can't wait."

***

Lenora opened the door for me. She would have seen the truck coming up the dusty stretch of lane, with the Packard out in front, and she was already waiting for us in the hallway.

I left the business of getting Karma and Copper settled to Chuck. I asked Ellen to give me a few minutes before following me up to the house.

Lenora's mouth was strained at the corners.

As I moved into the shadowed hall, my own exhaustion mirrored hers.

"Thank you, Lenora," I murmured, "for staying with him."

"I stayed ... *for you*," she explained. Her hair was still as beautiful as I remembered, brushed to a dark shine, and it tumbled to her waist. Her eyes held a quiet strength I could only long for. "I stayed, but not for him. I hoped you would come back. They told me what you did. How you stood up to Dr. Franklin in town." Her lashes were starred with the many tears she'd cried, and her eyes were red and swollen. "Well ... I'm just so glad you're home."

"Where is he?"

"In the study. Sitting in the dark," she added. "He's been like that since the day you left. He knows you're coming."

I passed her my satchel. I kept something back though. Something that could save us both, if only he would listen.

My limp was barely noticeable now. I walked down the hall, past the sunken sitting room, through the tidy kitchen, making my way along another short hallway to the door at the end. A door that was firmly, unequivocally, shut against the world.

I knocked quietly. "Del?"

He didn't answer.

I found the door unlocked and went in.

My eyes took a moment to adjust to the gloom.

This room had a large window and a lovely view to the grounds outside, but its shutters were closed now, blocking out the daylight. The walls were composed of wood paneling; a study in manliness, with a large, heavy desk, and bookshelves behind it. There were oil sconces too, though nothing was lit.

A familiar twinge of claustrophobia clamped iron bars around my chest. I forced short breaths through bloodless lips. I was able to talk myself out of the rabbit hole again. I think I was over the worst of it, but I still didn't like airless spaces. Sometimes being brave meant facing the little things as well as the big. I gave myself permission to acknowledge its presence and closed the door behind me, locking us both inside.

"I'm home, Del," I said into the stillness.

He was sitting, not behind the desk, but in a separate chair in the corner. He sat with his back to the bookshelves. He'd dressed himself—ever the gentleman—in immaculate trousers and a clean shirt. He'd obviously kept up with his personal grooming. He was clean-shaven, with his hair brushed neatly, and his shoelaces were tied in proper bows.

The only thing that didn't belong in the picture was the revolver in his hand.

His voice had aged. "Oh, hi, Vandy. Lenora said you were coming back."

I crossed the study and knelt down in front of him. My thigh complained, but I had already resigned myself to a future of boring aches and pains, so I pushed it away.

I took the gun away from him and set it on the desk.

I pressed the tarot card into his palm instead and closed his trembling fingers around it.

"What's this?" he asked.

"One of Ma's tarot cards."

He peered at it. His eyes were tired and bloodshot. Baggy, and bruised. His voice was weary too, but steady. To hear him speak, I wouldn't have thought anything was wrong with him.

Something lurking beneath the surface of his calm exterior told me *everything* was wrong.

"It's *The Chariot.*" I found a better way to sit on the floor, arranging myself on my hip, and I tucked myself against his knee.

I pointed out the two horses in the image, ignoring the cut between them where the sword had gone through. There was a stain of blood soaked into the paper that wouldn't come out no matter what I did. "Look, Dad. The white horse is Dolly."

He stared. He saw the same thing I was seeing; a beautiful mare, with dapples on her back, and a mane that flew as she galloped out of the sun.

I slid my fingertip across the card to the other horse. "The black horse is Karma."

A tear collected in the corner of my father's eye. He remained still, letting it trickle down his weathered cheek.

"And this is me."

I ran my finger over the dark-haired Gypsy standing in the golden chariot, holding a silver sword aloft. A young man around my age. He was brave where I was not. His challenge welcomed all foes, and the speed with which the horses carried him forward was exhilarating. He drove them on with his mind, a tangible symbol of the Petruska *magie* that I had lost. His focus was inspiring. He trusted himself to the power of the horses. I had done that too, and I had won.

"I did it, Dad." I touched his knee. "I sent it back. I had to use a grifter's trick to get it to go home. It was a *Shade*, after all, and they don't play fair, so I gave it right back to him."

He was listening.

"All those things you wanted to do to me?" I told him. "They weren't *your* thoughts. It was *Vigolii*. It was a thing from the Underworld. Domenico trapped a demon here in our world. He bound it to Vandemere so he could protect the family on their way to America. It wasn't your fault. It was *never* your fault, Dad. It's gone now. So is the *magie*. I had to give it away. Except ..."

I paused.

He waited.

Something in his eyes cleared.

"I think the *magie* still here. I think Clarence—" God, what in the hell was I even *saying*? "Clarence gave me his blood, Dad. I was sick. They said I needed a transfusion. Clarence is a Petruska ..."

My father squeezed my fingers until his knuckles whitened.

I took the tarot card away from him before he could crush it.

"Clarence... he always had the *magie*. He used it all the time, he just never wanted to admit it. He's a cop, see. He's a logical thinker. He called it a hunch. He never saw it for what it was. He's as stubborn as a mule. You'd like him."

I was getting off track. Babbling. I tended to do that when my thoughts veered towards crazy.

"Clarence and I are related." I rested my temple against my father's knee. I felt his hand stroke my hair. Felt him shaken to the core. "It seemed the logical choice. He donated his blood to me, which is disgusting, when you think about it. I think he gave me the *magie* back, Dad. It's there. It's faint. Only a whisper, but it's there; I can tell. I'll need time—"

Never mind, I told myself. You're getting off track again.

We sat in silence. He rested his hand on my head; the hand that had wanted to hurt me, break my bones, kill me even. And the man behind it? Suffering a remorse no father should ever have to bear. Willing to put a gun to his temple and rid me of his presence.

All my fault.

"I forgive you, Dad." I whispered this, more to myself than anything. "And I forgive myself too. I have to. It's only through forgiveness that we can truly heal. Hate only fuels more hate and that's how wars get started. Chuck told me that once. I had so much hate in my heart …"

I cleared my throat with a violent hack. Caught my breath and went on hoarsely. "Anger fed a thing so loathsome, it nearly destroyed all of us. I had to shatter my leg, lose Ma and Dolly, and come to Arizona to finally realize *I* was the one to blame for all of it. People called me a freak … and I believed them. They called me a dirty Gypsy. But you know what, Dad? I'm proud of who I am. I'm a Petruska through and through, with a bit of Davidson thrown in for good measure. I don't want to be anything else except your son. If you can find it in your heart to forgive me too, I'd like to stay here awhile and get to know you a little better. If that's too much to ask, just say so. I'll understand. If we can't be father and son, maybe we could at least be friends?"

He had to work up the courage to speak a truth that cut him deeply. His voice shook with a timber that rose from the depths of his pain. "I never meant to hurt you, Vandy. I love you … *so much* I can't hardly stand it."

It was an apology that had been a long time coming, and it was good enough for me.

I exhaled the tightness out of my chest with a heartfelt sigh. "So, you see, Dad, it all worked out for the best. We're free of it. You don't ever have to worry about hurting me again. We can finally be a family. You, me, Chuck, and Lenora. And now I've got Clarence and Ellen too. Will you come out of the darkness, Dad? Come out, so you can meet them. I'll help you. I'll be your safety net. Come out of the darkness and stand in the light with me. Okay, Dad?"

The old Vandy Petruska would have run from so much pain. He would have cast up defensive walls just to keep from feeling anything. I *had* to forgive Del. I had to put aside all the anger and the hurt and the hostility I'd used to hoard my love away from the people who only wanted to love me back. So, I forgave him. I forgave him to save *myself*, and it was the hardest thing I'd ever had to do in my life.

He came out of the room with me. He came out of the darkness, and the despair. He needed time too, same as me. He was as wounded as I was and needed time to heal. I helped him as best as I could, and I forgave him because it was never his fault.

Lenora still had misgivings, but eventually her smile came back, and she often came down to the barn to watch me practice tricks on Karma.

It was embarrassing.

I worked up to some of the easier jumps on the ground first, with Chuck and Del spotting me.

"There's no shame in using the mechanical," my father insisted, watching me bungle yet another vault.

I picked myself up out of the dirt for the third time in a row and wiped my palms across my shirt. "It's okay," I said, laughing. "I have a hard head."

"I'll catch you," Del said. He cupped my cheek and I leaned into it, smiling. "For real this time."

One day in early February, I asked him if we could go into the desert to find Dolly's bones and bury them. I needed a sense of closure with her. As painful as it would be, I needed to find her and put her to rest.

We drove along the narrow road, neither one of us speaking. Del would have known what this was doing to me, and he gave me space to grieve without having to expose myself to any judgements, real or imagined.

I stared out at the liquid horizon and contemplated how the loss of a horse could hurt so much worse than a steel blade through my guts.

I closed my eyes and reeled out fragile threads of consciousness into the ether, homing in on Dolly's energetic footprint in the mists inside my mind.

She wasn't hard to find.

I asked Del to stop the car. We were in a place of solitude and silence. I recognized a few cacti here and there, and the land had a familiar feel to it.

The air shifted around me as I put both feet on the ground and got out.

I remembered the slight incline up over the sand dunes ahead of me. Somehow, it just felt *right*.

"Are you sure you want to do this?" Del asked. He was starting to get the hang of being a dad again and there was concern in his voice. He pulled a couple of shovels from the back seat of the Packard. "Maybe you should let me go first?"

I settled myself into Dolly's *magie* and smiled bravely against the sting in my throat. "Leave the shovels. I don't think we're going to need them after all."

He wouldn't have known.

Couldn't have known.

How do you explain the unexplainable?

I led the way up over the rise of the hill to the place where Dolly had lain and showed him what I'd seen in my mind.

She wasn't there. The shifting sand had covered her over and taken her down. There were no bones to bury. No remains bleached white by the sun. There was only a bed of desert flowers blooming on the ground where Dolly had lain, and the memory of a little girl's promise to protect her from harm.

My vision was so blurry I couldn't see a thing anymore.

I'd lost *so much*. Lost *everything*. It's true what they say—that you need to take something apart if you want to rebuild it into a better version of itself. I'd been taken apart piece by piece. Had my bones broken; my soul beaten down. I'd seen my blood spilled on the sawdust I'd been born into, and I'd sacrificed myself to a merciless demon. I had put my trust in a tarot magic. I'd ridden through fire on the back of a horse, and that horse had saved me.

Standing at Dolly's gravesite, I finally realized that horses had been the one true constant in my life. Horses had seen me through the loneliness, through the despair, the pain, and the joys. Horses had carried me *home* ... back to everything I'd ever wanted.

Dolly had been a huge part of my journey toward greatness, and I hoped, wherever she was, she understood how much she meant to me.

I turned away, stumbling, and fell into my father's arms.

He didn't seem to mind when I broke down and cried.

Chapter Twenty-Four

Clarence stayed with us for the month of February. He left in March, citing business back in Oklahoma. Plus, his wife and kids were missing him. He packed up right after breakfast and drove off in his dusty old Ford, with his long-lost *Liber Mortuorum* safely stowed on the seat beside him.

Considering what Ellen and I did out in the desert that evening, I was glad to see the backend of Clarence Dawson.

She took my hand and led me out past the stables. We strolled down the pathway between the fields, and she pulled me down onto a blanket she had spread out over the sand. A few stars were just beginning to poke through the gentle twilight and the sky was aglow with the retreating sun. The air stilled, and the sand was warm beneath me.

Ellen took some time unbuttoning the front of her dress. She knelt beside me and loosened her hair from the rhinestone clip.

I lay back, watching her, every nerve electrified.

"Ellen—" I said.

She leaned over me and stopped my voice with a press of her fingertips. "Don't talk."

I pulled her to me. Melted into her embrace. I ran my hands over her breasts, marveling at the swell of flesh filling my palms. Her nipples were hard when I brushed my thumb over them. Pink as rosebuds.

Beautiful.

I couldn't get enough of her. I kissed her ... everywhere. Her neck. Behind her ear. The inside of her wrist. There was an urgency in my ragged breaths that had nothing to do with all the smoke I'd inhaled.

Her lips were frantic. Hungry.

When she slid her tongue past my teeth, I almost died.

She abandoned my mouth and unzipped the front of my pants, freeing me from that prison.

I moaned.

Her eyes were fixed on mine. I wanted her *so bad*.

"Are you ready to fly, horse boy?" She grinned slyly.

I cupped my hand around the back of her neck. "Kiss me."

"I thought you'd never ask."

I rolled her over and pinned her to the blanket.

Clothes were shed. Undergarments got tossed. She laughed, and I groaned deep in my throat.

I settled myself over top of her, positioning myself between her thighs.

She guided me in with her hand.

I was so hard now it was almost painful.

I choked on a quick intake of breath. I tried to think of something profound to say and came up empty.

I thrust into her.

Her forehead creased as she held her breath.

I brushed the hair back from her temples. "Have you done this before?"

"Shut up, Petruska," she panted.

"Am I hurting you?" I stammered. "I don't want to hurt you—"

"You're *not* hurting me, Petruska." She clamped her arms around my neck and pulled me down, her mouth demanding.

I was all too happy to oblige.

She arched into me. Her breath crested and her muscles tightened their grip on me.

I had no idea women could do that!

Her eyes caught the stars and glittered. This time, I would have gladly burned for *her*.

"Oh ... *God* ..." I wailed.

She grabbed my backside and pulled me in deeper.

I writhed in delightful agony.

I don't know if she was enjoying herself half as much as I was. She would have told me if she wasn't having any fun ...

Shut up, Petruska, I reminded myself.

Her hair fell around her face like a golden cloud as she shuddered under me.

I held nothing back. I lost all sense of being bound to the earth for a moment. I shut my eyes and forgot how to breathe.

One last thrust released a spasming explosion, surging on and on ...

I threw my head back and yelled, "Oh ... my *God!*"

Ellen looked up at me and chuckled. "My handsome Gypsy." She reached up and caressed my damp brow. "Pretty good for a first timer." Her eyes smiled and her cheeks glowed with a satisfaction I'd never seen there before.

I collapsed beside her and lay still. My shirt was drenched from all that exertion and my heart galloped like a runaway horse.

"My lungs ..." I sputtered, coughing. I gripped my chest, but there was a lightness in my soul that could have flown me to the moon.

Ellen wasn't nearly as tired as I was. "Your lungs are *fine*, Petruska."

I rolled onto my side. I propped myself on a bent arm so I could gaze into her fathomless blue eyes.

She grinned up at me.

I slid my hand through the gap in her dress and feathered my fingertips over her nipples.

I felt so ... *different*. Older. Maybe a little wiser now too.

I shouted at the sky. "I'm not a virgin anymore!"

A flock of quail shot out from under a bush and fluttered off.

We laughed until I started hacking again, very unbefitting of a grown man.

I slipped the silver and turquoise ring I'd been hiding in my shirt pocket onto her finger and twined my hand into hers. "Marry me?"

She reached up and slid her hand around the back of my neck, pulling me back down to earth again. "Just try and stop me, horse boy."

***

In early June, my father drove us all out to the Grand Canyon. Ellen and I had both turned eighteen by then. We were planning to get married sometime before Christmas, but when she told me she was expecting our first child, we bumped up the ceremony to August.

I didn't spoil the surprise by letting on I already knew about the baby. You know ... the *magie* and all that ...

Jimmy had written from California, saying he had secured a new big top tent and some carnival rides from a now defunct operation based out of Detroit and would I like to come back as his star billing.

I wrote back to tell him I still wasn't up to the backflip, but I was working on it. Realistically, I might never be the same, fearless rider I'd been before the accident. My bad leg was still giving me trouble. No matter what Chuck put me through on his torture table, he couldn't entirely iron the limp out of my stride. But I was determined to perfect the new act Del and I were creating together, and I knew it would thrill the crowds.

I wrote, *I would love to come back, as long as you don't mind a little one tagging along.*

Always room for one more Petruska, was Jimmy's reply.

We brought Bonnie's ashes with us to the Grand Canyon.

Ellen kept her hands over my eyes as Chuck and Lenora walked me from the car to the south rim of the canyon. "No peeking. I want it to be a surprise."

The thing that struck me first was the *air.* There was a sweetness to the wind ruffling through my hair. A freshness that put an unbearable joy in my heart. I had a sense of immense space around me. I used the *magie* to connect to the land, and this time, I didn't need my eyes to see it.

The sun warmed this ancient place. An old heartbeat drummed through the ground, and I felt a sense of coming home.

"Can I look now?" I asked.

"Not yet," Chuck said, in a voice brimming with excitement.

I carried the Mason jar with my mother's ashes close to my chest. There was an ache in my soul that burned brightly, but I couldn't be sad for long. There was another Petruska on the way. He would come into a safer world, thanks to the *magie*, and my mother's courage.

Del put his hands on my shoulders. He guided me over the uneven ground while Ellen kept my eyes covered. We were all tripping over each other by now, laughing like a bunch of circus brats. There must have been other tourists nearby, watching these crazy people stumbling up to the edge of what was probably a very dangerous cliff.

Ellen turned me into the wind. "Okay. You can look now."

She took her hands away.

I believe I gasped.

I *know* I stopped breathing.

I looked across a gaping chasm of immeasurable distance and space, and my mind simply couldn't comprehend what I was seeing.

A deep scar in the earth stood before me, mined by time and wind and water, painted in a rainbow of greens and rust, and everything in between. There were jagged cliffs, and striations of color, and a haze that gave a sense of proportion I would otherwise have dismissed as a fantastical dream.

This *place*, this realm of majesty, *couldn't* be real.

Far below, miles down, a river of silver glinted. A sparkling jewel chiseled deep into the land. The Colorado River. A relic of this land's history. Borne out of the ages, and a symbol of America's tenacity and triumph.

There were tumbled rocks the size of houses all along the cliff face. Time had carved deep scars in the opposite rim, giving the canyon an ebb and flow kind of rhythm that defied the senses.

My heart swelled. Emotions got the better of me, and my chest burned as I fought back tears.

Shit, I thought. I'm going to cry.

"Is it everything you hoped it would be?" Del asked.

I scrubbed the dampness off my face and sniffed. "It's beautiful, Dad."

He brushed my hair back off my forehead and used his thumb to catch a tear that made it all the way to my chin.

The old me would have pushed him away.

The new me begged him to stay.

"Are you ready to let your mother go?"

I nodded, not trusting myself to speak.

I unscrewed the lid off the Mason jar, said a little prayer, and cast my mother into the Grand Canyon.

The wind sort of took the ashes and blew them every which way. I *know* some of them got caught in the bushes nearby. It wasn't the most graceful of exits for the woman who had loved me, but I could see her standing off to my left, holding Annie's little hand in her own, and she laughed right along with us so I know she didn't mind.

When I told Clarence he was going to be a grandfather, he sputtered and coughed and feigned shock. Then he looked pleased. "My Ellen's a feisty girl. Think you can handle her?"

I smiled back. "Care to make a wager, *Sir*?"

The End.

About the Author

Kimberley D. Tait was born and raised in Port Dalhousie, Ontario, Canada. Ever since she can remember, horses have been a huge part of her life's journey. As a child growing up on the banks of Lake Ontario, Kimberley dreamed of owning her own horse someday. She spent many hours at Silver Acres Riding Academy, where she acquired her first horse—an American Saddlebred mare named Duchess. Duchess came with two speeds: fast, and faster! Kimberley's subsequent horses were much more sedate, and hardly ever ran away at all.

Kimberley's working career spans many decades, working on racetracks, grooming for various racing stables, and obtaining a wealth of knowledge from medical practitioners in the veterinary field. From there, Kimberley went on to manage several dressage stables, and has worked with Olympic caliber coaches, both from Canada, and Europe. Currently, she resides near Orangeville, Ontario.

If you enjoyed this book, please consider leaving a rating and an honest review on Amazon, and Goodreads. Your words go a long way to help an independent author stand out from the crowd.

If you would like to hear more about Kimberley's writing journey, please check out her website at, https://kimberleydtait.com/

Manufactured by Amazon.ca
Bolton, ON